PRAISE FOR

MINOR DRAMAS & OTHER CATASTROPHES

"For those who like their privileged high schools dysfunctional, corrupt, and hilariously human."
—*Entertainment Weekly*

"A wry, engaging debut."
—*People*

"Just as good as Liane Moriarty's *Big Little Lies*."
—*Kirkus Reviews* (starred review)

"A progressive pressure cooker of a school and the explosive nature of social media combine in this thrillingly modern debut." —*Newsweek*

"A page-turning romp about competitive parenting." —*Real Simple*

"Fans of *Where'd You Go, Bernadette* will flip for this clever, drama-filled debut novel."
—*Woman's World*

"Welcome to Liston Heights High, where the drama is in no short supply. Whether it's a popular teacher suddenly facing criticism for her progressive curriculum or a helicopter mom who's finally gone one step too far in her involvement, this sharply observed high school novel is hilarious."
—*New York Post*

"West successfully unpacks the problems of shaming and cancel culture with tight plotting and clean prose. [She] demonstrates a worthy talent for tragicomedy."
—*Publishers Weekly*

MINOR
DRAMAS & OTHER
CATASTROPHES

KATHLEEN WEST

BERKLEY
An imprint of Penguin Random House LLC
penguinrandomhouse.com

Copyright © 2020 by Kathleen West
Readers Guide copyright © 2020 by Kathleen West
Penguin Random House supports copyright. Copyright fuels creativity, encourages diverse voices,
promotes free speech, and creates a vibrant culture. Thank you for buying an authorized edition
of this book and for complying with copyright laws by not reproducing, scanning, or distributing
any part of it in any form without permission. You are supporting writers and allowing
Penguin Random House to continue to publish books for every reader.

BERKLEY and the BERKLEY & B colophon are registered trademarks
of Penguin Random House LLC.

ISBN: 9780593098417

The Library of Congress has catalogued the Berkley hardcover edition of this book as follows:

Names: West, Kathleen, 1978- author.
Title: Minor dramas & other catastrophes / Kathleen West.
Other titles: Minor dramas and other catastrophes
Description: New York: Berkley, 2020.
Identifiers: LCCN 2019024647 (print) | LCCN 2019024648 (ebook) |
ISBN 9780593098400 (hardcover) | ISBN 9780593098424 (ebook)
Classification: LCC PS3623.E8448 M56 2020 (print) | LCC PS3623.E8448 (ebook) |
DDC 813/.6—dc23
LC record available at https://lccn.loc.gov/2019024647
LC ebook record available at https://lccn.loc.gov/2019024648

Berkley hardcover edition / February 2020
Berkley trade paperback edition / December 2020

Printed in the United States of America
3   5   7   9   10   8   6   4   2

Cover art by Brian Hagiwara/Getty Images
Cover design by Anthony Ramondo and Emily Osborne
Book design by Laura K. Corless

FOR DAN AND SHEF AND MAC,
ALL MY FAVORITES.
TIED FOR FIRST.

MINOR DRAMAS & OTHER CATASTROPHES

ISOBEL JOHNSON

Isobel Johnson spent most of each class period, and half of that afternoon's department meeting, obsessing over the message. She'd tried to place the strident voice and had ruled out suspects based on their holiday teacher gifts. How could someone give her a twenty-dollar Starbucks card, she reasoned, and then six weeks later threaten her via voice mail?

Isobel took a deep breath as she headed for the door closest to the teacher parking lot and felt her belly strain against the waistband of her wool pencil skirt. She sucked her stomach back in and recalled the language in the message. "Flagrantly Marxist" was there, as was "anti-American," and, she thought, "retaliation." She'd have to play the message for Mark when she got home. That would make for more interesting dinner conversation than the usual rundown of soccer practice and school-day antics. Thinking about it, Isobel let out a rueful little laugh as she walked into the dull February chill.

"What's so funny?" Isobel looked back at Jamie, whom she hadn't noticed was walking behind her. She'd first met her young colleague at the mentor luncheon during the woman's first week of work the year before. Now Jamie's scuffed Liston Heights name badge clattered against a button on her fitted gray cardigan as she shifted her backpack and threw her arm through the second strap. Isobel credited herself with Jamie's successful start at Liston Heights High, which had just that month been once again named the top public high school in the state of Minnesota. The school's high-powered parents usually devoured new teachers, but Jamie had made it through her first year and a half with relatively few tears and only three or four parent complaints. Of course, it also helped that Jamie herself had graduated from Liston Heights just six years before. She knew how to present herself as an insider.

"Oh, hi!" Isobel said. "I was just thinking over some of the kids' responses to chapter six. Would you believe that Justin Williams suggested the 'chain of drugstores' referred to Gatsby's secret cocaine ring?" Isobel rolled her eyes. "After that, I didn't even ask for their interpretations of Daisy's 'little gold pencil.'"

"What do you think of Eleanor's idea to move *Gatsby* to the fall?" Jamie asked, zipping her coat. They'd just spent fifteen minutes on that asinine proposal in the department meeting, Isobel staring resolutely at her notebook as their senior faculty member blathered on.

"Why not tell me quickly about the OkCupid guy instead?" They had a hundred yards or so before they reached Isobel's minivan. She could see Jamie's Prius parked a couple of spots beyond it.

"Oh, my gosh, yes!" Jamie gushed. "So, we've been messaging for, like, three days, and we finally made a plan to meet near my apartment for a drink after work tomorrow. Of course, everything is complicated by the proximity of Valentine's Day, but we already joked about that."

"Drinks on a school night?" Isobel couldn't help herself. She smiled, feeling old.

"I know," Jamie said, her dark eyes shining, "but remember the photo I showed you? He's super cute. I'm just marginally concerned about the fact that he's a chemical engineer. If we get married, it's possible my dad will love him more than he loves me."

Isobel flinched at "concerned," which had been the lead in the message from that morning. "This is a concerned parent," the woman had said, her voice piercing and angry. Isobel had frozen where she stood as it started, her tote bag weighing down her forearm, right foot halfway into her L.L.Bean boot. The kids had already tromped out to the van, and they were three minutes behind the ideal departure time when the phone rang. Isobel hadn't bothered to race to it—no one they knew used that number anymore now that even twelve-year-old Callie had a cell phone. Besides, who called at seven thirty-three a.m.?

"CrossFit," Jamie was saying now. "I mean, I suppose I could give it a try." The two stopped even with Isobel's minivan, a grimy "Live Simply So Others Can Simply Live" sticker affixed to the lower-right-hand corner of the back window.

Isobel reached into her pocket for the key fob and watched the hatch rise. "You know how I feel about lifelong learning," she said. "Why not master weight lifting?"

"Maybe tomorrow we can talk about what I might wear on this date?"

Isobel threw her tote into the minivan next to the bulk pack of Veggie Straws from Costco and a flattened baseball mitt. She hit the close button. "We can talk about it," she said as the hatch came down, "but we both know you have much better instincts than I do."

"But that skirt." Jamie pointed at the pink herringbone poking out beneath Isobel's coat.

"Caroline." Isobel smiled, referring to her high-fashion sister, her go-to answer whenever anyone complimented an outfit. "Hey, have a great night." With a wave, she got in the minivan and headed home.

Tuesdays were Mark's one day for kid pickup and meal prep, and Isobel knew Callie and Riley would likely be engrossed in the Disney Channel, homework ignored while Mark assembled something in the kitchen.

Things were just as she'd predicted when she opened the back door at five thirty-four.

"Hi, Mom," said Callie as she preemptively relinquished the remote to her eight-year-old brother and smiled widely. Isobel leaned over the couch and kissed both of their heads, her glasses slipping down her nose as she dipped.

"Mmm, Riley, maybe a shower tonight."

He screwed his face into a frown. "Bath," he countered.

"Fine."

Mark smiled over the kitchen counter, where a pile of green onion slices expanded under his knife. "How was your day?" she asked him, dropping her tote and jacket on a chair. She headed toward the landline console at the end of the counter.

"Good." He shrugged. "Busy."

"Wait," Isobel interrupted, reaching for the machine. "I meant to text you. You have to hear this."

"What is it?" Mark looked up.

"It's weird," Isobel said. "Just listen." She hit PLAY.

"First message," the machine's stilted voice said. As soon as the recording began, Isobel could hear the caller's breathing.

"Ms. Johnson." A tremor underlay her authoritative tone. "This is a concerned parent. I'm calling because *many* community members are alarmed about the flagrantly Marxist and anti-American content you're preaching in your so-called literature class."

"What?" Mark exclaimed, stepping toward her, knife still in hand.

The woman's voice continued. "I speak for a majority of Liston Heights families when I say we've chosen this community for the traditional excellence of the schools." The speaker took a breath. "I know *you* don't live here, and I'm not sure what you're aiming at, but we're asking you—*urging* you, really, for the sake of our children and, frankly, for the sake of your career—to stick to the board-approved curriculum." The speaker delivered the final line of what had to be a prewritten statement. "I'm choosing not to reveal my identity for fear that you'll retaliate against my child, but do know that I speak for a large constituency of parents, not just for myself."

"What the hell?" Mark said as the machine beeped.

"Dad!" admonished Riley from the couch. "Language!"

"Sorry," Mark said, not looking at him. "Who was that?"

"I don't know." Isobel squinted at the water streaks on the outside of the stainless steel dishwasher. "There's that one mom who said that thing to me at the Sadie's dance a couple of weeks ago. Julia Abbott?"

"Oh, right," Mark said. "That thing about, like, not being worthy of Liston Heights? What did she mean by that?"

"I guess it means I don't belong." Isobel pointed at the machine.

"Bizarre." Mark put the knife down. "Of course you belong. And how did that person get our number?"

"There's a directory," Isobel said. "You have to opt out, and I never do." She thought for a moment. "Let me listen again. Hey, Cal," she called to the couch, "can you turn that down?" She hit the play button without waiting for her daughter to comply and leaned toward the speaker. It didn't quite sound like Julia Abbott, with whom she'd talked several times. She wrapped her arms around her waist and hunched her shoulders, making herself smaller. The message represented a new level of aggression, for sure. Liston Heights parents had a widely known reputation for overstepping, but the most she'd experienced in previous years had been the occasional nasty e-mail. And now there was this, plus that Sadie's dance conversation.

"I don't know," Isobel said finally, turning back to Mark. She walked around to his side of the counter, grabbed a wineglass, and turned the spigot on the box of Cabernet they kept next to the fridge.

When she turned back to her husband, concern wrinkled his forehead in a way she found endearing. Isobel smiled in spite of her building anxiety.

"What did Lyle say about it?" Mark asked.

She hadn't told her closest colleague about the call. She and Lyle Greenwood had started at LHHS in the same year and generally chatted each day. The news of the voice mail had been stuck in her throat at lunchtime, but the truth was, she knew what Lyle would say, and she didn't want to hear it. "I didn't get a chance to tell him."

"Do you think you should tell Wayne?"

"Wayne?" Isobel blew a breath out of the corner of her mouth, picturing her bumbling principal. "I mean, I guess so."

"Have you had a Grow and Glow lately?"

Isobel thought of her most recent performance review—they were stupidly named "Grow and Glow"—with her department chair, about a month ago. The "Glow" had been about using Chimamanda Ngozi Adichie's TED talk about stereotypes and assumptions. The "Grow" had been to solicit comments from a wider cross section of her classes. It was a friendly meeting, but Isobel knew how quickly public opinion on teacher quality could change. She had only to think back to the firing of Peter Harrington during the previous school year for an example. He'd been a shining star one moment, and then he'd pissed off the wrong parent.

"It was pretty positive," she said to Mark. "It seemed before this morning like I was having a good year." She stared blankly at the television and took a several-second swallow from her wineglass.

JULIA ABBOTT

~

Just a mile from the high school in Liston Heights, Julia Abbott set her cell phone on the counter next to the Viking range and poured a second glass of prosecco into a stemless flute. She peered toward the back door. She could hear her daughter, Tracy, knocking snow from her boots in the mudroom. Andrew, her older child, refused to wear boots at all.

"Trace?" Julia called.

"Hey, Mom!" Tracy hollered.

"Was practice super cold?" The ninth grader had insisted on cross-country skiing as her winter sport, a choice that astounded Julia, who preferred Fair Isle sweaters and watching snow fall from the warmth of her living room. The prosecco's carbonation tickled her nose, and her eyes watered as she took a sip.

"Just a sec!" Tracy yelled. Julia heard the back door open a second time and knew Andrew must have made it inside. He appeared before his sister did, sliding in stocking feet into the kitchen.

"Well?" Julia said to him, her eyebrows raised.

"It was good." Andrew shrugged. He walked past his mother to grab a glass from the cabinet by the kitchen sink.

"Good?" Julia repeated, staring at his back. "Any surprises at the audition?"

"I mean—" Andrew ran the tap.

"Use the filter," Julia interrupted.

"It's fine." Andrew filled the glass with city water. "It was my first callback. I'm not sure what it's supposed to be like. Relax."

She bristled, but decided to ignore the condescending directive. "Did Mr. Dittmer seem pleased?"

"Mom." His voice took on a familiar edge. "I just don't know."

"Hi, Mom." Tracy came in, and Andrew slipped out of the kitchen, his glass rattling on the counter where he'd left it. "What's for dinner?" Tracy asked.

"Quinoa salad with roasted beets." Julia's smile was coy.

"I mean for us," Tracy deadpanned. She shook her hat hair, stretching a ponytail holder between her thumb and forefinger.

"Spaghetti," Julia offered, lips pursed. "With meatballs."

"Awesome." Tracy turned away, her thick mismatched socks pulled up over black workout tights that looked a little thin over her backside. "I'm gonna shower," she said.

Julia reached for her cell phone as Tracy padded upstairs. She'd order some new Smartwool knee-highs and decent leggings for her daughter that evening. Now she tapped out a text to Robin Bergstrom, another theater mom. Any buzz from callbacks? she asked. Andrew is useless. She watched her phone to see if the three blinking dots would appear, the indicator that Robin was texting back. When they didn't pop up, Julia put her phone on the counter and turned to the oven. Her beets smelled done.

The next morning, Andrew thundered down the stairs ten minutes before the tardy bell and refused the muffin Julia shoved at him.

"I've got a bar in the car," Andrew said. Julia couldn't look to Henry, her husband, for support about the importance of breakfast because he'd left at five thirty a.m. for his squash game.

"You need to eat!" she called toward the mudroom, thinking of Andrew famished and reaching for something even more sugary after second period. "The cast list will be posted today!"

"What does that have to do with anything?" Andrew said. Tracy breezed by and pecked her cheek.

"I'll take that." She grabbed the muffin from Julia's outstretched hand. "Love you, Mom."

Sweet, Julia thought. A twang of gratitude softened the nerves that suppressed her own appetite. She was so jittery, in fact, that she forgot to register Tracy's outfit as she headed toward the garage. Maybe she'd remembered pink? That Topshop button-down? Had she paired it with the midwash jeans that flattered her nonexistent waist?

"Have a good day!" Julia yelled, though they'd already gone. She grabbed her phone from the gray granite countertop and typed to Andrew, Text me as soon as it's up!

Julia's trainer, Ron, would be ringing the bell in five minutes. With only three weeks to go until the annual Theater Booster Club 5K, she desperately needed the cardio. She drained her can of Diet Mountain Dew and flipped on the electric kettle, which sat next to the Vitamix blender. She'd steep a cup of green tea and take a few sips as Ron lined up the weights in her basement. The trainer had lectured her so many times about the neurotoxins in artificial sweeteners that she'd started hiding her Diet Dew habit from him. "I did it!" she'd exclaimed a month ago after he'd asked how the quitting was going. She opened the recycling cabinet now and dropped the most recent can among six others just like it.

As she waited on her tea, Julia paged through a pile of graded work Tracy had left on the dining room table the previous night. She'd earned eighteen out of twenty on a recent math quiz, proving that Julia had been right to argue a space for her daughter in Honors Geometry after the dolt registrar had placed her in regular Algebra 2.

"Check your files," Julia had beseeched her, leaning across the counter in the school counseling office, her face inches from the clerk's. "Tracy Abbott has been a member of the Cirrus Program—which you must know is the gifted-and-talented pullout—since second grade."

"I'll verify with her counselor and get back to you," the flushed fiftysomething had mumbled.

And now Tracy was getting an A. Sometimes all anyone had to do was advocate for her child.

Julia paged past Mandarin character practice and a half-finished study guide on geology. And then she came across the posting schedule for Humans of LHHS, the Instagram account of the Liston Lights, a leadership team that Tracy had been tapped for that fall. Their posts mimicked the famous blog out of New York, portraits of community members and first-person stories pulled from interviews. Julia scanned it and found that Tracy wouldn't be set to post for several weeks. Maybe she'd be able to convince her to highlight Andrew, who'd certainly be deep in rehearsals for *Ellis Island* by then. She paused next on an assignment from English 9, a paper comparing Shirley Jackson's "The Lottery" to *The Hunger Games*.

Tracy's English teacher was a mostly attractive woman. Her hair, though, seemed to frizz over her ears in an unfortunate, slightly canine way. Julia placed the teacher in her mid-thirties and noticed she'd pulled distractingly at the waistband of a too-tight skirt during her parent-night presentation. That skirt, though. Julia thought she recognized it from last season's Michael Kors collection. "Good start, Tracy!" Ms. Johnson had written on the Shirley Jackson paper. "Now go deeper. What about 'unfairness' is important here? And, be sure to check for run-ons!" She'd scrawled the grade in pencil: B.

B? When Julia was in ninth grade she'd been summarizing the plot of *The Odyssey* via CliffsNotes, and here was her fourteen-year-old, comparing themes of texts written sixty years apart.

And for a B?

Julia put down the paper and grabbed her cell. She'd already complained to Isobel Johnson about her methods at the Sadie's dance. Maybe it was time to mobilize some other mothers. What do you think of this Johnson woman? she texted to Robin. Probably, she mused, everyone was having problems with the English teacher.

The kettle beeped and the doorbell rang simultaneously. Oh, well, Julia thought, leaving the mug empty on the counter as she went to the door. Ron could see her drinking green tea next week.

ISOBEL JOHNSON

Okay, everyone," Isobel Johnson called to her class as the bell rang. She put her Nalgene bottle down on the desk corner and pushed her black pencil into her falling-out bun. "Books open! Let's talk about Gatsby's drive into the city. Big stuff!" Fifth-period American Lit was usually a highlight, the second of three sections she taught in addition to her two ninth-grade classes. Today, though, a weight had settled in Isobel's stomach. Every time she caught herself enjoying her students, she began to wonder which of their parents might have left that voice mail. The words replayed in her head: "Marxist" and "anti-American" and "for the sake of your career."

Certainly, Isobel thought, it wasn't Sarah Smith's mother. Isobel watched Sarah walk to her seat, lean toward Erin Warner, and whisper something, her curly brown hair skimming Erin's desktop. They giggled, and Sarah glanced across the room at Andrew Abbott. The two of them had arrived together at the Sadie's dance just as Julia Abbott had said that mean-spirited thing to Isobel. She'd been getting along with the Abbott kids, but clearly that wasn't enough for their mother.

The bell rang then, three beeps from the intercom. Isobel licked her teeth behind her lips and cleared her throat, resisting a sidelong glance at Andrew. "Did anyone have a hankering to start our discussion today?" she asked, quieting the students. Maeve's arm popped up, bent at the elbow.

"Ms. Hollister," she prompted. It couldn't have been Maeve's mother, Isobel thought as the girl began to speak. Maeve was invariably enthusiastic, and she'd given Isobel a box of Godiva as she'd left for winter break. Perhaps Mrs. Hollister wasn't friends with Julia Abbott.

"Did anyone notice those eyes on the billboard?" Maeve asked. "Right over Wilson's garage?"

"What a marvelous place to start." Isobel tapped a pencil eraser on Allen Song's desk, and Allen promptly dropped his cell phone into the front of his backpack. Isobel gave him an exasperated stare and looked back at Maeve. "Maeve, tell us," she continued, "what struck you about those eyes?"

"Um, the color, for starters? The blue seemed to create such a . . ." She paused, looking at the ceiling. Isobel followed her gaze up to the speckled foam tiles wedged in their aluminum grid. "It created such a stark contrast to the brown of Myrtle's dress."

Isobel could always count on Maeve. She took a step away from her desk toward the first row of students, her low heels skimming the thin carpet. "I'm so glad you brought up color," she said. "And why would Fitzgerald want us to notice a contrast at this particular moment?" The front of Allen Song's backpack buzzed. "Allen!" Isobel said theatrically. "How hard is it just to turn it off?"

"Sorry, Ms. Johnson. It's my mom. She's relentless."

"Your mother is texting you?" Isobel put her hands on her hips. This was typical, actually. Liston Heights parents didn't like to wait until dinner to hear the news of the day. "Doesn't your mom know you're in the most important class?"

"The cast list for *Ellis Island* is getting posted at two thirty," Allen apologized. "My mom's a little nervous."

"Of course." Isobel's sarcasm elicited a few generous giggles. "Well, to keep her busy for the next forty-five minutes, why don't you ask your mom to construct a theory about the significance of the color of Jay Gatsby's car?"

"Really?" Allen asked, reaching for his bag.

"No! Just switch it off, would you? Now, everyone"—she scanned the room, lingering just a half second longer on Andrew, who looked placid—"what can we say about the colors?"

JULIA ABBOTT

At lunchtime Julia picked at a blueberry and goat cheese salad. Her phone pinged the arrival of a text from Robin Bergstrom. Anika says cast list will be posted at 2:30. Julia inhaled sharply and rotated her sterling silver Tiffany bangle, an ages-old gift from her mother, around her wrist.

While Tracy had been busy doing pullout enrichment projects, Andrew had tried out for every theater production since seventh grade. He'd finally, as a ninth grader, been cast as Ticket Seller #2 in some incomprehensible show about a shipwreck. Still, Julia and Henry had built sets on a Saturday and hosted the end-of-run cast and crew party. The next year, Julia had had her heart set on a speaking role for her son.

Andrew, alas, had won the part of prop master. She'd been livid. Nonetheless, she'd gritted her teeth and smiled when John Dittmer, famed Liston Heights theater director, complimented Andrew's impeccable organization on opening night. "He found all the props and costumes we needed!" he gushed. "Even the emerald green size eleven pumps!" Of course, it had been Julia herself who had scoured every secondhand store in the greater Liston Heights area to get her hands on those hideous shoes for Melissa Young. Who'd ever heard of a high school girl—and a thin one at that!—with size eleven feet? And with an untrained alto? In a lead role?

At the Percys' holiday party that year, she'd put a bug in the ear of the Theater Boosters' chair about Melissa Young's faults as a romantic heroine. "She's four inches taller than Allen Song," she'd whisper-shouted. *Not to mention,* she thought, *her enormous feet.* "Of course," she clarified, "I'm a hundred percent in favor of a multiracial lead couple."

This year's musical, *Ellis Island,* had a perfect midsized role for Andrew, who had dutifully taken voice and dance lessons every week throughout the summer between his sophomore and junior years. Meanwhile, Julia had ingratiated herself with Allen Song's mother at the juice bar after hot yoga. Vivian Song, the new board chair, had breezily offered her the communications position on the Theater Boosters. So this—Andrew's junior year and just in time for college applications—had to be his moment. The part of Inspector Adams had a short vocal solo and several humorous lines. As a senior, then, he'd be primed to headline.

Two thirty couldn't come soon enough.

WAYNE WALLACE

At twelve thirty-seven, just as second lunch dispersed, Principal Wayne Wallace meandered across the main entrance foyer, a gigantic Liston Heights Lion scowling down on the crowd from a banner mounted near the thirty-foot-high ceiling. He nodded at Jeanette, who sat smiling behind the welcome desk. "Chin up!" he said. The receptionist nodded, the phone to her ear.

"Everything okay at the district office?" she asked as she hung up.

"You know it, Jen," Wayne said. He stood next to the desk and high-fived a few students as they walked by. "Go get 'em this afternoon," he called to the room. "Go get 'em!"

"Wally!" shouted Per Skordahl, the starting center on the hockey team.

"Per shape!" Wayne shouted back his nickname for the boy as he thumped his chest. The kids had taught him this—the chest thumping—one afternoon when he'd swung through the weight room after school. Per raised two fingers in a peace sign and clumped toward the math hallway in his Timberlands.

Wayne turned back to Jeanette and leaned over the desk. "Hey," he whispered, "what time is Dittmer posting the cast list?"

"Word is two thirty." Jeanette smiled. "End of sixth period."

"Can you do me a favor and ask Johnny to meet me in my office in ten?"

"John Dittmer?" Jeanette's finger scanned the master schedule she'd tacked to the fabric behind her iMac. "I think he teaches fifth period."

"He can have Alice cover." Wayne turned toward his office as Jeanette dialed.

The principal had just enough time to crack open a bottle of green juice and scan the Instagram feed before John walked in. John had been featured on Humans of LHHS a year ago during the auditions for *Witches over Willow Street*. Wayne's leadership team ran the account, and the principal took pride in its fifteen hundred followers.

"John!" Wayne greeted him. "Come in! Shut the door, would you?"

John sighed. "I need to run scenes with the drama kids. Can we do this quickly?"

"Absolutely," Wayne said, gesturing to a chair at the black metal conference table. "I just wanted to check in on the spring musical. You all set for the cast announcement this afternoon?"

"I think we've got it."

"Who's getting the leads?" Wayne asked. "I'm assuming you've got Allen Song in there?"

"Allen"—John nodded—"and Maeve Hollister, of course. Justin Williams, Melissa Young. And I've got Tryg Ogilvie in the role of the inspector. Missy Porteus in the Russian ballet section . . ."

Wayne raised a hand. "Whoa," he said. "What about Andrew Abbott?" He took a slug of Odwalla and peered at John. The poster hanging behind the director's head was one of Wayne's favorites: "Good things come to those who hustle" in blocky black lettering over a gold background.

"Ensemble," said John. "He's a luggage handler."

Wayne nodded. "Listen, Johnny," he began, "I wonder if we might bump Andrew up a little bit."

John stiffened. "Wayne," he said too loudly.

"Johnny, I'm not talking about the *lead* lead, but what about that inspector part?" Wayne glanced through the rectangular window to the hallway, where Assistant Principal Sue Montague walked by with a slump-shouldered kid in a gray hoodie.

John sighed again. "Tryg is perfect for that role."

"Maybe," conceded Wayne, "but Andrew has paid his dues. Kid's a junior."

"And," muttered John, "his mother donated the new costume shop?"

"I think it'd be a nice gesture." Wayne bobbed his head. "Thanks for considering it, John. Sometimes, when kids are equal in talent, we've got to think of the growth of the program."

"Gotcha, Wayne." John stood.

"Okay, buddy. Hey, have a great class. Get those scenes in shape." As John left the office he drained his juice, and then slam-dunked the bottle in the small green recycling container next to his feet.

JULIA ABBOTT

⁓

Julia wrote to Andrew, 2:30?!?!? Text me back as soon as you hear. She sat in front of her computer, trying to read, but unable to stop watching the clock in the upper-right corner of her screen. Every seven to ten seconds, she glanced at her iPhone, her bracelet clacking against it as she picked it up.

She messaged Robin next. Does our assistant stage manager have the inside scoop on the CAST?! Robin's daughter, Anika, had fallen in love with behind-the-scenes work as a seventh grader when she'd run the light booth for the middle school production of *Suessical*. Now poor Robin had to attend every single show and pay her Booster dues, all so her daughter could wear black and hide in the wings. "It's the technical side that really fascinates her," Robin explained.

Julia had smiled supportively, but that evening over dinner, she surmised with her husband that if Anika were just a tiny bit more attractive or coordinated, she might have made a different "choice."

Julia's phone dinged. I wish she DID have the inside scoop, Robin responded, punctuating her short message with a string of eight or nine emojis. Hang in there! came the second text.

Definitely patronizing, Julia decided. Robin couldn't possibly understand the agony of waiting for news of an actual lead role.

"Do something," Julia told herself. She scanned *Women's Wear Daily* headlines on her laptop for a few seconds. Nothing, not even the Escada brand revamp, held her interest, and after a quick trip to People.com to survey the latest white-and-denim Kardashian family photo, she found herself holding her phone again. Maybe a message to her husband.

Nothing yet! Send.

Henry would be in a series of meetings all afternoon, she knew, and unlikely to speculate about the cast even if he weren't. "Is that Song kid trying out again?" he'd said last week when Andrew mentioned auditions at dinner.

"Of course," said Andrew. "You think Allen would skip a Liston Heights production? He'll almost certainly be cast as Evgeny."

Henry frowned. "Allen Song is going to play a Russian guy? Aren't there any Korean dudes at Ellis Island?"

"Dad, that's culturally insensitive," Andrew said. Ever since both kids had been assigned to Isobel Johnson's English classes, phrases like "culturally insensitive" and "multiple perspectives" had infiltrated their dinner conversations, the kids' eyes twinkling as they quoted their teacher. Andrew continued. "Mr. Dittmer is totally serious about color-blind casting."

"I'm totally serious about it, too." Henry winked at Julia as he took a bite of steamed kale.

This was the trouble with Henry—always making jokes. Everyone found him hilarious, but he refused to focus. The phone buzzed in Julia's hand. Try to chill, the text from Henry said.

"Chill?" she said aloud to herself. Her sudden anger propelled her to standing, her stool rocking on the hardwood floor. Couldn't anyone—Robin, Henry, Andrew himself—understand the significance of the *Ellis Island* cast list?

She scanned the room, indignant, and landed for a moment on a framed black-and-white photograph of the Empire State Building against the New York City skyline, a memento from her Manhattan days.

"Enough," she said, finally, remembering the bustling city, the marquees on Broadway. She'd take off her yoga pants and take a shower. There'd be more news when she got out.

JOHN DITTMER

John Dittmer, in his twenty-first year as the Liston Heights theater director, mentally reviewed the cast for a final time as he smoothed his khakis on the walk from the drama office to the teacher workroom. He'd print the list on pink paper, as was his tradition. He'd mark "FINAL" across the top in black Sharpie and post it on the Drama bulletin board at precisely two twenty-seven p.m. There was a certain ritual to these things, John knew, a solace in breaking teenage hearts in a routinized manner, tissues at the ready in his office for the ninth graders who'd been tapped for backstage crews instead of acting roles.

"Next year," he'd tell these criers as he herded them toward his assistant director, who'd convince them of the importance of props and set changes.

After John's meeting with the principal, the director had dutifully, if bitterly, switched the roles of Tryg Ogilvie—an unusually poised ninth grader with the height of a full-grown adult—and Andrew Abbott. Tryg would now be the most skillful luggage handler the school had ever seen, and with extensive coaching, Andrew could be a passable immigration inspector.

John punched his code into the copier in the teacher workroom. A pile of handouts sat in the output tray—something about "Apostrophe Appreciation Day." Had to be Isobel Johnson, he thought, as he removed the stack and put it neatly on the workstation, a high counter covered with faux-wood laminate.

"Oh, John!" Isobel breezed in from the hallway, her calf-length black skirt swirling.

"Hi, Isobel." John reached for the apostrophe handouts and held them out to her. They'd become friends in Isobel's first year when they'd been assigned Wednesday afternoon bus duty together. She'd always been a minute or two late, half running to their spot on the yellow curb, students streaming onto the buses all around her.

"Thanks." She smiled. "In a rush, as usual." Pieces of her chin-length hair fell from the bun she'd fastened at the back of her head. "The kids' phones are blowing up," Isobel said. "You'd better post the cast list. Put the parents out of their misery."

John wiped his brow as the copier hummed. He could hear it grab a single sheet of eleven-by-seventeen paper, the rollers pulling it through the machinery. "On my way," John said wryly. "Bets on which parent is the first to call?"

Isobel shook her head. Suddenly, her green eyes darkened, and her smile fell away.

"What is it?" John asked, as he grabbed the warm pink sheet—he loved that feeling, paper hot from the copier. He put it on the laminate and uncapped his Sharpie.

"Sorry." Isobel blinked twice. "I was just thinking of my latest parent problem. Unrelated."

John waited. She swallowed hard and looked up at him. "Have you ever gotten a voice mail from a parent on your home phone?"

"I'm sure I have," John said. "Liston Heights parents aren't exactly skilled at adhering to boundaries."

"But, like, a threat? If you don't do such and such, you'll lose your job?"

John put the marker down on the counter and frowned. "Who was it?" he asked.

"An anonymous concerned parent." Isobel gripped her stack of papers. Her thumbnail looked white against the blue paper.

"I haven't gotten a message like that," John said, carefully, "but it sounds like a very Liston Heights tactic. You gonna tell Wayne?"

"I suppose I should." The bell rang then, signaling the end of passing time, and Isobel jumped. "Oh, goodness." She turned away. "I've got thirty-six kids who will be staging a riot before I get back." She pulled the door open and smiled back at him. "Break a leg, friend!" She began to run, her skirt flaring behind her as the door closed.

John sighed, picked up his Sharpie again, and wrote each capital letter deliberately across the top of his pink list. F-I-N-A-L. He shoved the cap on the marker with more force than was necessary and put it in his pocket. The paper in both hands, he walked back to the performing arts wing. Once he'd looked left and right, checking for empty hallways, he took two pushpins from the side of the drama bulletin board and tacked them to the top of the list. He smoothed the paper and secured the bottom with two additional pins. Then, as was his tradition, John rubbed his palms together, washing away the audition process before tomorrow's first rehearsal.

JULIA ABBOTT

As soon as her hands were dry from the shower, Julia held her breath and grabbed her iPhone, clicking it awake. Nothing.

?!?!?!?!?! she tapped to Andrew. She knew for an absolute fact that fifth period had ended. Why not take a second to respond to his mother? Julia carried her phone with her into her bedroom. She placed it on her dresser and pulled on her clothes—black ponte leggings and an over-sized Equipment blouse. She tilted her phone up for another look. Still nothing. She opened Instagram and searched the Humans of LHHS feed. Maeve Hollister, another member of the Liston Lights, was running it this week, and Julia thought there might be a hint about casting since Maeve would certainly land a lead role herself. Sure enough, the latest photo was of Melissa Young in profile, her head tilted slightly back as she laughed. The folds of the theater's red curtain served as backdrop. **I never set out to be a leading lady or anything**, the caption began. Julia scoffed. Melissa was nothing if not ambitious, and Julia knew for a fact that her parents, Annabelle and Martin, had sent her to that prestigious arts camp in Michigan last summer. She scanned the rest of the post. It ended, **In order to do your best, you have to ignore** the haters, right? Like, people who think you're too tall, too raw, or even that your feet are too big.

Her feet are *too big.* Julia set her phone down and watched it as she blasted her shoulder-length blond hair with a dryer, tapping the screen every few seconds to keep it from falling asleep. When her hair had gone from dripping to damp, she scooped it into a low ponytail.

"I'm going over to the school," she whispered to herself as she dabbed on eye cream and reached for lip gloss. She texted Robin. Starbucks by school in 30? she asked. Cast list rehash?

She waited. Within a few seconds, the three dots appeared. Sure! and a smiley face with rosy cheeks.

Julia pulled her black Mercedes GLE into the high school parking lot at two twenty-eight. She cut the engine in a visitor spot in front of the performing arts entrance. As a member of the Theater Booster Board, surely she was justified in her desire to review the cast list. She'd then be able to contact the parents of the first-time actors, welcoming them to the LHHS theater family and, more important, coordinating their donations to the Theater Booster Fund.

Julia double-checked the pocket of her down jacket for her cell phone. Her idea was to snap a quick photo of the cast list, leave before Andrew or Tracy saw her, and zip over to Starbucks to speculate with Robin about Dittmer's choices.

She hurried toward the entrance and waved the key card she hadn't returned after last fall's set build in front of the lockbox. On a beeline for the bulletin board, Julia stopped short when Alice Thompson, the twentysomething assistant director, stepped out of the drama office ahead of her.

Damn it! Julia twisted her mouth into a smile. Alice looked back and paused, surprised. Julia caught an acrid whiff of industrial floor cleaner.

"Julia!" Alice cocked her head. "What brings you to school today?"

"Oh, I just wanted to check in on, um, Andrew."

"Is he sick?" Alice asked.

"He had the beginnings of a migraine this morning," Julia lied.

"That's too bad," Alice said. "I'm just on my way to post the crew list. We have a few new assistant stage managers for the musical. Their parents will probably want to be included on the e-mail blasts, especially information on the annual fun run."

"For sure," Julia said. "I'll walk with you."

They fell into step as they neared the drama board. "You don't have to go out of your way," Alice said.

"It's no problem." Julia pointed at the board. "Maybe I'll just take a quick peek at the cast list now that I'm here. Is it posted, do you know?"

"It is!" Alice smiled. "And I think I saw Andrew on it someplace."

"Oh," said Julia dismissively, "he just loves being part of the productions." The two were no more than fifty feet from the eleven-by-seventeen piece of pink paper. Julia could see "FINAL" printed across the top in large letters.

Right then the bell reverberated in the hallway. Students rushed from the classrooms that lined it on either side. Backpacks, backward caps, and swinging ponytails surrounded the two women.

"I have to get this posted," Alice apologized, weaving ahead through the throng. Julia followed uncertainly, hands in her pockets. A circle of nervous-looking students had already formed around the list. A girl Julia didn't recognize ran her finger down the paper until she found her name. She turned, beaming, and rejoined a friend who hovered on the fringes. The two high-fived. Julia could smell the watermelon gum in the mouth of the girl standing next to her.

Alice sidestepped her way out of the growing crowd and waved as she headed back toward the theater office. "Hope Andrew feels better," she called. Julia nodded, her mouth increasingly dry. She watched for a moment as others searched the list. The circle grew. She knew she was running out of time, and yet she was so close. She set her lips in a line, took her cell phone from her pocket, and opened the camera app. Her eyes trained on the cast list, she marched forward, lightly shoving the oblivious teens who stepped into her path.

"Excuse *you*," said one before turning and realizing she was an adult.

Julia reached the circle around the board, now two deep, and cleared her throat. Could she take a photo by lifting her camera above her head? A quick calculation revealed that she couldn't—the very tall Tryg Ogilvie, the ninth grader who had played the Scarecrow in last year's (marginal, Julia thought) middle school production of *The Wizard of Oz*, ruined the shot. She exhaled and turned to her right, scanning for options. She caught sight of Tracy exiting a classroom at the end of the hall, walking with Isobel Johnson, even though her English class was in the morning. *Why were they together?* If Tracy saw her here, she would be mortified. It was now or never.

Julia's arms shook with adrenaline as she moved. Her left hand gripping the phone, she bladed her right arm into the crowd and hooked some students roughly to the side. Her vision blurred slightly; blood whooshed in her ears. "Pardon me," she grunted. "Theater Booster Board coming through!" She caught a few frowns in her peripheral vision, and as if across miles, she heard Anika Bergstrom say, "Mrs. Abbott?"

"Hi, honey," Julia answered without making eye contact. "Booster Board business!" Now standing in front of the cast list, incredulous students all around her, Julia quickly snapped a photo of the paper. "Got it!" she whispered, and then, involuntarily, her feet rooted to the floor. She began scanning the names for the telltale double As of "Andrew Abbott." She started at the bottom of the list with the ensemble— groups of immigrants from different European countries—and with Andrew absent from that section, she began to hope, salivating lightly and color rising to her cheeks. The students, recovered from the initial surprise of her entrance, started to move again, to crowd back toward her, some reaching over her shoulders to point at names. Julia barely registered someone's finger slide into her line of vision and run down the list.

Finally, she found Andrew. And near the top! She raised her own index finger, as the students around her had, and traced back from his name to his role.

"Inspector Adams," she whispered, and inhaled deeply. "Inspector," she said more loudly. She closed her eyes and smiled, glee rising from her gut. The failed auditions, the board meetings, the lessons, the coaching, the emerald fucking shoes, the goddamn costume shop. And now! Finally! Andrew had the chance he deserved.

Without thinking or opening her eyes, she raised her right arm over her head and closed her fist, her bangle falling to her forearm. Energy coursed through her hand, radiating to her knuckles. She breathed into her belly. *Yes,* she thought to herself. *Yes!* Anxiety that she didn't even realize she'd been carrying bubbled up and out of her. "Yes!" she hissed aloud, holding the "s." She found herself jumping up a little, her eyes still closed. And then she felt her arm descending in a fist pump, a dance really. She swung her arm in front of her face and then back from her waist, fast and hard. Fast and hard, until her elbow encountered an obstacle, stopping its trajectory with a sickening thud.

Someone grunted behind her and then cried out. Julia heard the movement around her stop. She blinked her eyes open. The pink of the cast list swam before her, and she felt the plastic case of her iPhone weigh down her left hand.

"What the hell?" someone said, and Julia turned. Melissa Young— the lead actress with the size eleven feet—was doubled over in front of her. The girl moaned, rubbing the place where Julia's elbow had connected with her abdomen.

"Holy shit," one boy whispered. Others looked at their shoes. Maeve Hollister rubbed Melissa's back as the girl started to straighten up, her black hair hanging in front of her face.

"I'm so sorry," Julia whispered to her as she turned and began walking back toward the door. "I'm so sorry!" she called, louder. She kept her eyes trained forward although she could feel the kids' gazes. As she reached the outskirts of the crowd, focused only on the exit, she heard a distressingly familiar voice to her left.

"Mom?" Tracy said. Julia looked up to see her daughter's wide blue eyes, complexion paler than usual. Isobel Johnson stood beside her, her mouth pinched in a thin frown. Both stared. Tracy finally said, voice tremulous, "What are you doing here?"

ISOBEL JOHNSON

After helping Melissa to a chair in John Dittmer's office, Isobel patted Tracy Abbott's shoulder sympathetically.

"Have a good afternoon, kiddo," she said as Tracy turned toward the math hallway.

"God," Tracy mumbled, "my mom is so crazy."

"We're all a little crazy," Isobel said as the girl walked away. The scene at the drama board had been crazy, she agreed. Julia Abbott was clearly irrational. First the voice mail, and then the cast list?

Isobel planned to spend her free period telling Wayne Wallace about the message. She was rehearsing her recounting of it, her lips moving a bit, when Lyle Greenwood caught her. She and her "work spouse," as Mark referred to him, had bonded during the very first week they'd known each other. In the beginning, they'd gone for drinks after new-teacher orientation, already rolling their eyes at Eleanor Woodsley's overzealous tour of the building.

"How's it going?" Lyle asked.

"I just saw the weirdest thing." Isobel looked back at the thinning crowd near the drama board, just a few glum stragglers left checking the list.

"Tell!" Lyle clapped his hands over the manila folder he carried.

"You know the Abbott kids?" Isobel asked. "Tracy and Andrew?"

Lyle nodded. "Tracy was in my class first trimester," he said. "Nice girl. Mom was hyper, though. Must have called me once a week."

"Yeah, both of her kids are in my classes now," Isobel said. She swerved around a slow-moving student with headphones on his neck. "Anyway," she continued, "I just walked by the drama board. The cast list for *Ellis Island* was posted."

"Right," said Lyle. "My last class couldn't talk about anything else."

"Julia Abbott was there, standing in front of the bulletin board, taking photos of the list."

"The mom? Oh, God." Lyle shook his head. "That woman needs to get a life."

"It gets worse. She found Andrew's name and then, well"—Isobel hesitated, deciding how to characterize what happened next—"she somehow elbowed Melissa Young in the stomach."

"What?"

"I think she was sort of celebrating? Like she'd scored a touchdown or something?" Isobel slowed her pace to demonstrate the movement. "And she totally clocked Melissa."

"Figures." Lyle frowned.

"It was so odd. And"—she lowered her voice—"it's the first time I've seen Julia Abbott since the Sadie's dance."

"Right," Lyle said, knowingly. "*That* was unpleasant."

"Yes!" Isobel whispered. "Remember what she said?" She put a hand on the sleeve of Lyle's checked button-down, and they stopped walking. Isobel imitated Julia. "'I know *other* people say you're not quite good enough for Liston Heights, but *my* kids seem to enjoy you.'" Just repeating the words made Isobel feel sick. She tried to remember the quality of the voices—the one in her head from the dance and the one on the machine at home. She wasn't entirely certain they matched.

"She's the worst," Lyle said. The bell rang then, and the last few students in the hall jogged toward classrooms.

"Can you believe she actually said that? Like, out loud?" They started walking again. Lyle hesitated. "What?" Isobel demanded.

"Well, you know what I think," Lyle said, apologetic. "All of the parents would love you if you just read the books with the kids and let go of all of the political stuff. They love me"—he smiled—"and I'm even gay."

Isobel squared her shoulders and stared down the hall, avoiding eye contact with her friend. It was true he did "just read the books" with the kids—close reading and textual analysis, plus direct instruction on semicolons and Latin roots. Any ideas Isobel passed along to him about political contexts or any activity that involved multiple perspectives went right into his recycling bin. She'd argued with him before about his responsibilities as a white male educator, at which point he always asked her how risky she thought it was to be openly gay in the Liston Heights community.

That was a conversation stopper. She agreed on a fundamental level that Lyle was probably doing most of his part just by being visible. But still . . .

"Sorry," Lyle said. "It's just, you don't always have to be the *one*."

"The one?"

"The one person," he explained, "who takes the public stand."

"But if it's not me speaking out," Isobel protested, "who would it be? Jamie?"

"You know I don't understand what you see in her. Anyway . . ." Lyle closed the subject. The old argument between them would be there the next time one of them brought it up. "Where are you headed?"

"Oh." Isobel tried to sound casual. "I just need to chat with Wayne for a moment." She still hadn't mentioned the voice mail. She knew Lyle would more fervently repeat the same advice: to skip the edgy lessons and stick to the prescribed curriculum. And anyway, it embarrassed her to be the target of something so mean-spirited and also so noteworthy. Although she liked to push boundaries in her own classroom, she also liked being the type of person who had everything under control.

"What could Wayne possibly offer you today?" Lyle said dryly.

"I'm sure nothing. I'll catch you later." Isobel waved and headed past the copier to the adjoining administrative offices, procuring a Life Saver from the bowl on the school secretary's desk and peeling open the cellophane with her teeth. She peeked around the doorframe of Wayne's office, and there he was, hunched over his keyboard. She knocked tentatively and shoved the mint into a back corner of her mouth. "Wayne?" she ventured.

The principal turned his thick chest toward the door, his face lingering on the computer screen until it had to follow the rest of him. His usual smile took up half of his face, although Isobel thought she detected a shimmer of disappointment in his dark eyes when he registered who was there. "Isobel!" he boomed, recovering. "What's shakin'?" Wayne's expressions—"What's shakin'?," "Hey, pal," "Make it a great day!"—often made her feel that she was *in* high school rather than working in one.

She took a step into the office. "Do you have a minute?"

"Absolutely!" Wayne rose from his chair and took two steps toward the conference table near the door. "Have a seat! What's going on?"

"I'm not exactly sure," Isobel began. Wayne folded his hands on the table between them. She paused, timid and then irritated. Wasn't she the victim here? "I had an unusual voice mail at my home number yesterday." Isobel pushed the words out. Wayne knit his substantial eyebrows. "This is going to sound sort of dramatic, I guess," she said. She looked at the red-framed poster of Yoda. "Do or not do," it recommended. "There is no try."

"Okay," Wayne prompted.

"So," she said, "an anonymous parent left the message. It accused me of teaching an anti-American curriculum."

"Anti-American?" Wayne squinted at her, leaning forward.

"Yes," Isobel confirmed, feeling emboldened now that she'd begun, "and Marxist."

"Uh," he said, "have you been teaching something new?"

"Not really. I mean, I used a new TED talk recently about considering multiple perspectives."

"Multiple perspectives?" Wayne echoed.

He's trying, Isobel thought. She straightened her tortoiseshell glasses, which listed perpetually right. "As you probably read in my annual goals narrative," she said, "in AP Lit this year, I'd like to encourage kids to let go of tacit American exceptionalism. . . ."

Wayne looked over her shoulder at something in the hallway. She turned as John Dittmer knocked fervently. "So sorry, Isobel," he said when he saw her. "I just thought you should know right away," John continued to Wayne, "that there was an incident surrounding the cast list."

"What happened?" Wayne pressed his hands on the conference table.

"It appears that Julia Abbott may have punched Melissa Young," John reported, a bit breathless.

"Oh!" Isobel exclaimed. "I saw that!"

"What?" Wayne stood abruptly from his chair, sending it skittering backward a few inches along the industrial rug. "She punched her?"

"She didn't exactly punch her," Isobel said, but the men were talking over her head.

"Tryg Ogilvie's got it on video," John said. He looked feverish.

"Did you take it from the kid?" Wayne lunged toward the doorway. "I need to see that video right now." They nearly ran out of the office.

Isobel gathered her notebook and pencil. "Okay," she said to herself as she turned toward the "Good things come to those who hustle" poster. She'd have to check in with the principal another time.

JAMIE PRESTON

Jamie Preston wrapped her hands around the white ceramic mug containing her afternoon coffee, a treat she allowed herself during her free period. She'd peeked down the hallway toward Principal Wallace's office after she'd refilled her cup in the faculty workroom and could make out part of the back of Isobel's head, opposite Wayne's trademark smile. *What was that meeting about?* she wondered. She could probably get it out of Isobel later.

Now at her desk, Jamie resisted the pull to Facebook by scrolling through e-mail. A new message from English department chair Mary Delgado triggered a wave of nausea. The subject read, **Staffing: 2020-21.** Ever since last year when the school had decided to cut a member of the English department—not replacing her friend Peter Harrington after his unceremonious firing at the close of fall break—Jamie had felt the precariousness of her own situation.

"You have no job security," her father had pronounced over one of their twice-monthly dinners as Jamie recounted Peter's exit. She'd seen the disappointment in the set of her dad's jaw, the same flinch she'd registered when the final engineering school rejection had arrived in the spring of her senior year at Liston Heights High. None of them—not her mother, her father, or herself—had been particularly surprised or dismayed when the bad news had arrived from Michigan or Northwestern. But when CU–Boulder had rejected her, and then finally the University of Iowa, her dad stopped making eye contact. Two years later, when she declared an English major at the end of her sophomore year at the University of St. Stephen, a local liberal arts school with an 80 percent acceptance rate, she'd almost gotten used to his perpetual disappointment, limp arms in perfunctory hugs.

"I think I'll be okay," Jamie had said about her continued employment, although she wasn't sure. "I had a really good performance review last week."

"We'll see." Her dad had shrugged. Jamie's hand had drifted to the Prius keys she'd dropped in the pocket of her cardigan. Her parents had given her the car when she'd been offered a job at Liston Heights. *Will they take it back if I get laid off?* she wondered now.

Unfortunately, Mary's e-mail began, and Jamie groaned aloud, then forced herself to read on, **now that it's February, we know that enrollment is officially down for next year's ninth grade. We'll lose a class section or two. I'm anticipating a need to cut at least one contract to part-time.**

Part-time. Jamie was barely making rent, plus groceries and the mandatory retirement contribution set up by her father on her current full-time salary. She couldn't imagine a cut.

She flashed back, as she frequently did, to the session the career adviser in her education program had given on how to escape the dreaded pink slip, a common plague of new teachers with no seniority. "Ingratiate yourself to parents," the woman had said. "Parents can be allies, so get to know them." Jamie had scribbled that advice verbatim in a green college-ruled notebook. She wasn't sure the woman would have approved of the Facebook stalking she'd done to "get to know" the Liston Heights mothers, but she had to admit it had helped, as had the woman's next piece of advice: "Send good-news e-mails." Always an obedient, if not inspired, student, Jamie now kept a list of the compliments about students she'd sent via e-mail, complete with dates and topics.

"Give a great back-to-school-night presentation," the careers woman said. That had been easy, as it turned out. Isobel had pulled her into a half hug the week before the dreaded event in her first year and said, "Don't worry—I've got a killer PowerPoint for parent night. I'll send it to you, and you can replace my name and contact information with yours."

That had been the fourth or fifth time Isobel had come to her rescue in just the first couple of weeks of school. Initially, it was an ingenious way of organizing seating charts. Then a flash drive filled with complete unit plans for every book in the American Literature curriculum. Sure, Jamie had brought coffee for Isobel on the second day of the teacher workshops, but certainly a four-dollar latte didn't merit the level of caretaking Isobel embraced. Jamie had no idea why the older woman was being so nice to her. Although Isobel had been a teacher at LHHS when Jamie was a junior and senior, she'd never been in her class.

"I want you to be successful here," Isobel said when Jamie thanked her, relief flooding her chest. "We're all in this together. Plus," Isobel added, "Mary Delgado asked me to look out for you. She thinks you have a 'spark.'" Isobel put air quotes around the descriptor and smiled.

Jamie had held on to that compliment, often repeating it to herself after a difficult day. But would her supposed spark make any difference to Liston Heights' bottom line? Likely not. Jamie heard her father's dispassionate voice in her head: Budgets were budgets, and she was the one on the chopping block.

Unless, Jamie thought, someone left. Could Eleanor Woodsley retire? How old was she? Or someone could get pregnant? Maybe the parents would finally turn on Isobel, who regularly fueled political discussions when everyone else was dissecting metaphors?

Just then the classroom door banged open, and Jamie startled, bobbling her coffee. She slid her chair back and sucked her stomach in to avoid the splatter. "Shoot," she said aloud as several beads of liquid settled into her purple blouse near her belly button.

"Sorry, Ms. Preston." Jamie looked up to see a sad-faced Per Skordahl holding a paper.

"It's okay," Jamie said. "Coffee goes with purple." She clicked out of her e-mail and put her mug on the desk. "What can I do for you?"

Per stepped toward her and held out the paper. "I'm stuck on my Gatsby paragraph," he said, "and the study hall teacher said I could come and see if you were free."

Jamie motioned to the chair next to her desk, the one she kept there exactly for conversations like this. "Let's take a look." As she skimmed his topic sentence, she imagined the good-news e-mail she'd send his parents when they were finished. "Per took the initiative to see me during his free period," she'd report. With one hand, she brushed at the brown spots on her blouse and then tried to forget them.

ANDREW ABBOTT

Five minutes into seventh-period Pre-calc, Andrew Abbott raised his hand. "Could I use the restroom?" The teacher nodded, turning back to the equation he'd scribbled on the whiteboard.

In the hallway, Andrew rubbed his palms on the front of his jeans. He did plan to go to the men's room, but really, he needed to check the cast list. At the end of sixth period, when the other theater kids had rushed to the drama bulletin board, Andrew had walked toward the PE office. His story, if anyone had asked, was that he'd forgotten to register for spring fitness electives, required of students who wouldn't be on a Lions athletic team.

And, indeed, he had walked to the PE office and busied himself looking at the participants in "Lifetime Activities," which was Andrew's own choice. He scanned to the S's to check for Sarah Smith, his date to the Sadie Hawkins dance two weekends before, but her name wasn't there. In the last couple of minutes of passing time, Andrew had taken the long way to the math hallway and settled into his seat. He'd willed his right leg to stop twitching.

Now he made his belated turn into the performing arts wing, the yellow lettering above the bulletin board shining before him. He saw "FINAL" printed in Mr. Dittmer's precise all caps at the top of the list.

"Okay," he whispered, arriving in front of the bulletin board, heart pounding. He made himself start reading from the bottom with the members of the ensemble. He wasn't among the immigrants from Hungary or Russia. He passed by the Irish and Italian groups. As he read Tryg Ogilvie's name attached to the role of "Luggage Handler," he began to hope.

Finally, about five lines from the top, he found the twin peaks of "Andrew Abbott." "Here it is," he whispered. He put an index finder under his name and blinked hard. Then he traced back to the role: Inspector Adams. He'd hoped for this, a significant speaking part and a vocal solo. A definite supporting role.

Andrew felt his mouth widening into a grin and his shoulders relaxing. He'd done it. He was legit. Andrew tipped his head back and breathed in.

Behind him, the theater office door opened, and Andrew turned to see Melissa Young step into the hallway.

"It's you," she said. Eyes red, she held a crumpled tissue. Andrew glanced back at the list to confirm that Melissa's name was at the top in a lead role. It was.

"Are you okay?"

"Barely," she said, angry. "Are you just checking it now?"

Andrew nodded. "I got the inspector part."

His spirits sank as Melissa scowled. "Oh, I know." He didn't know what to make of her sarcasm, and then they both looked toward the academic wing, where they heard fast footfalls approaching. Mr. Dittmer and Principal Wallace bustled into view.

Andrew froze. He was supposed to be in class. He glanced at Melissa, who bent slightly at the waist, rubbing her stomach.

"Melissa," Principal Wallace said, half running. Andrew took two steps backward until his body made contact with the bulletin board. "Are you okay?"

"What are you doing here?" Mr. Dittmer turned to Andrew. Sweat beaded above the director's lip.

"I was just checking the list." Andrew looked down at his T-shirt, gray with the Deathly Hallows symbol from Harry Potter on the front. "I wanted some privacy," he mumbled. "I'm really excited—"

"You need to get back to class." Mr. Dittmer's tone was gruff.

Andrew glanced at Melissa, Wally's hand on her shoulder. Without saying anything, he headed back toward Pre-calc. His Converse squeaked on the linoleum, and he wondered what exactly had gone wrong.

JULIA ABBOTT

At the Liston Heights Starbucks, Robin Bergstrom, fixated on her cell phone screen, was waiting for Julia.

"Hey," Julia said, hanging her oversized handbag on the back of a chair. "Sorry I'm late—a little crowded at school." The bitter smell of coffee grounds enveloped her.

Robin looked up, concern in her eyes. "Julia," she said, "you were at school?"

Hadn't Julia told her the plan? Of course she'd been at school. "Yes, though a fat lot of good it did me." She pushed her iPhone at Robin. "The shot's blurry."

"Are you okay?" Robin asked, not looking at the photo.

"Yeah. Totally. Why?"

"I got a text from Anika."

"Robin, I'm so happy." Julia's words bubbled up. "He got it! He got the part! The inspector!"

Robin smiled for a second, and then it faded. "Julia." Her voice went low. "Anika says there was some kind of altercation at the school."

"Not at all," Julia said. "I just ran in there to take a photo of the cast list, and I ended up in the middle of a crowd. Actually"—she wrinkled her nose, remembering Alice Thompson, who'd waylaid her—"it never would have happened if not for that silly assistant director. Anyway"— she smiled— "people were bumping into each other all over the place."

"O-kay." Robin drew out the second syllable of the word. "But Anika said—"

"It was nothing," Julia insisted. "The important news is that Andrew got his part." She stared intently at Robin, enunciating carefully. "He's the inspector." She leaned back and threw both hands in the air, her eyes on the ceiling. "Finally!" One of the canister lights above her, she noticed, had burned out.

"That's great," Robin said, but a worry line materialized between her eyebrows.

"Let's talk business." Julia hoped to distract her friend. She couldn't let a minor misunderstanding get in the way of the most exciting day in Andrew's life. And all of her behind-the-scenes work—schedules, parties, and obviously the increased costume budget—would support his first lead role. "I'm thinking about the rehearsal-treat schedule," she said, "and I've decided I'll just let people sign up for as many slots as they want." Robin opened her mouth to respond, but Julia wasn't ready yet. "I mean, as long as they're committed to keeping things peanut-free. We all know there are those families that won't contribute anything. Ever." It was true that some people were happy to rely on the generosity of others.

That had never been her.

Robin shook her head. "Julia," she said.

"Oh!" Julia soldiered on, determined. "Right! The five-K! Do you want me to see if I can get you on the planning team this year?" She smiled puckishly. "The women on that committee can get a little wild."

"Um," Robin began, "I mean, I'm happy to help, Julia, but can we talk again about the cast list?"

"Mmm-hmm." Julia pursed her lips.

"It's just this thing with Melissa Young," Robin ventured. "Anika texted me again." She glanced at her phone. "It seems that Tryg Ogilvie has some kind of video?"

Julia's phone buzzed. She slid it off the table. The screen read, **LHHS Office**. She'd have to answer. "Hmm. Hang on a sec." She pressed the green button and raised the phone to her ear.

ANDREW ABBOTT

Students streamed quickly toward the exits after Wednesday's dismissal bell, but Andrew shuffled to his locker, staring at the seams between the floor tiles. His stomach felt unsettled, and he regretted the chicken patty he'd scarfed down for lunch—that and the seven-layer bar he'd gone back for at the last minute. Most especially, he lamented the tepid jalapeño poppers he'd sampled from a friend's tray. He shoved his hands in his pockets, picturing Melissa Young, her eyes red and cheeks flushed. He saw the way she'd bent at the waist when Wally had come into view in front of the drama board, heard again Dittmer's low command for him to get back to class.

What could have happened to Melissa? Andrew wondered. She couldn't have been disappointed in her lead role, which she'd basically predicted in that morning's Humans of LHHS Instagram profile. Was she ill? And how could Dittmer be angry with him just minutes after casting him in a big part?

Andrew felt a little better as he turned the corner into the English wing and noticed Sarah Smith standing next to his locker. She stared at her phone, but Andrew thought he'd caught a glimpse of her looking for him. He straightened a little, tugging his Deathly Hallows T-shirt, the one he'd been wearing when she'd asked him to the Sadie's a few weeks ago. Since then, he'd viewed the shirt as sort of a lucky charm. He'd picked it purposely for cast-list day.

"Hey," he said when he was close enough. He grabbed his combination lock with his free hand. "What's up?"

"Well?" She leaned against the adjacent locker and smiled up at him.

"Well, what?"

"The cast list, obviously." Sarah laughed.

Andrew grinned. "I'm in!" He popped the lock open and yanked the door.

"That's awesome," Sarah said. "What part?"

"Immigration Inspector Adams." He clicked his heels together as he imagined an Ellis Island official might, and then immediately wished he hadn't done that. It probably looked dumb.

Sarah's smile widened, though. "Inspector," she said. "Sounds fancy! Hey, what are you doing now? Do you want to—" Her phone buzzed. "It's Erin." She squinted, tilting her head to the side as she looked at the text. "Hang on." She turned away from him, her back against the lockers. After several seconds, she flinched and tapped at the screen. Andrew grabbed his copy of *Gatsby* and shoved it into his backpack, waiting. He watched her as he added his Spanish workbook and a torn green folder containing his readings for American History.

All the while, Sarah kept her eyes on the screen. "What is it?" he asked finally. He leaned toward her, trying to see.

Sarah pulled the phone away and stepped back. Her smile had disappeared, and her mouth hung open. A sourness rose in Andrew's throat, remnant of the jalapeño poppers.

"What?" he said again.

"Um," Sarah hedged. "It's just this thing from Erin. She got it in a group text from someone in her math class."

"What is it? Is it serious?"

"I don't really know," she said. "But . . ." She looked as sick as he suddenly felt.

"But what?"

"Maybe it's not that big of a deal. In any case, I'm not sure I should be the one to tell you." She took another step away.

"Please." He reached his hand out to her, feeling suddenly desperate, remembering Melissa's scorn at the drama board, the sweat on Mr. Dittmer's upper lip.

"It's just . . ." She placed her phone reluctantly into his palm. "You probably haven't seen this video?"

HENRY ABBOTT

Henry Abbott toggled the volume switch on his phone to silent as he sat opposite his business partner, Brenda Sutherland.

"How quickly can we vacate the current tenants at Tuolomee Square?" Brenda asked, scrolling over a spreadsheet and straightening her black-framed glasses. The two sat on high-backed leather chairs and leaned over an imposing table in the offices of Sutherland and Abbott, one of the premiere real estate development firms in Minneapolis.

"Within six months," Henry replied with confidence. "I've got Jean on the lease contracts, and we should be ready to demo the existing structures by October if all goes well."

"And which architect will draft the initial plans?" Brenda asked.

Several quick vibrations distracted Henry from his notes. He pulled his phone from his breast pocket and glanced down to see that Julia had fired off a spate of messages.

Andrew is the inspector!!!! ♥♥, read the first.

"Everything okay?" asked Brenda.

"Looks like Andrew got a meaty role in the Liston Heights High School musical."

"That's wonderful!" Brenda said. "You'll have to let me know the dates. I'd love to see him in action."

"That's nice of you." Henry smiled. "I'm sure Andrew would appreciate that." His phone vibrated again. "Julia," he explained, frowning. "She's excited."

Some silly call from Wayne Wallace, began the most recent text.

At the same time, Tracy, his daughter, buzzed in with Dad, SOS.

"I'm so sorry, Brenda." Henry shifted uncomfortably. "It seems there's more to this musical thing."

She nodded. "Go ahead. I've got e-mails to review."

Henry had just opened his texting app when William, his assistant, peeked in. "So sorry to interrupt, Mr. Abbott," William said. "It's just"—the young man looked nervous—"I have an urgent call for you from Martin Young."

"Martin Young?" Brenda looked up from her keyboard.

Henry's stomach dropped. Martin Young was the swing vote on the Liston Heights city council, which set zoning regulations for virtually all of Sutherland and Abbott's local projects.

"That's odd," Henry said. "I haven't even contacted the council about Tuolomee Square yet. But," he continued, "these school musical texts . . . I'm just wondering. Martin does have a daughter, Melissa, who's always a star in the shows."

"Take the call," Brenda said, signaling toward the door. Henry told William he'd pick it up in his office.

ISOBEL JOHNSON

Isobel had just unzipped the top of her backpack and slid in a bulging manila folder when Jamie Preston peeked around the doorframe.

"Hey," Jamie said. "How was your day?"

"It's over!" Isobel surveyed her cluttered desk. "How was yours?" She'd turned off half of the banks of fluorescent lights, and the room felt leaden, like the late-afternoon sky outside the windows.

"Nothing special except for that crazy video."

"Melissa Young and Julia Abbott?" Isobel asked.

"Yeah. My whole seventh period was watching the clip. Apparently Tryg Ogilvie has been texting it widely. Have you seen it?"

"Not yet." Isobel grabbed *Gatsby* from the chalk ledge and shoved it in her tote behind a half-empty bag of Chex Mix. "You did?"

"Yeah." Jamie wrinkled her nose. "I don't know. It's ugly." She perched on the edge of a student desk. "The mom stages a full-on attack."

Isobel shook her head. "No," she said, remembering. "Melissa just sort of got in the way of Julia's"—she paused—"victory dance?" She recalled Tracy's embarrassment, watching helplessly as her mom made such a public misstep.

"I guess, but it doesn't look good," Jamie continued. "If I were Melissa's parents, I might have a few questions for Mrs. Abbott. What was she even doing at school?" Isobel dropped into her desk chair, the well-worn upholstery smooth against the back of her skirt. "Have you met the Youngs?" Jamie asked.

Isobel frowned. She had, in fact, met the Youngs at last trimester's conferences, and then again at another meeting they'd requested. "I have," she allowed. She recalled Annabelle and Martin Young's itemized rundown of Melissa's grade report in AP Lit, how they'd asked pointedly about each deduction. Isobel had attempted to quash her resentment about their entitlement and their obvious lack of respect for her systems. "They're intense about grades," she said.

Both women looked suddenly toward the open door, beyond which they heard a girl's laughing shriek. "Anyway," Jamie said, turning back, "Mrs. Abbott needs to get a flipping grip. You should have heard the voice mails that woman left for me last trimester." She affected a nasal tone. "Have you considered, Ms. Preston, the implications of a B plus on a college application?" The imitation was spot-on, Isobel thought. Did the voice match the one on her machine? Isobel forced a laugh for Jamie's benefit.

"Did you stick with a B plus for Andrew?" she asked.

"No," Jamie said, "I rounded up. He had an eighty-nine. The fight wasn't worth it."

Isobel looked at her e-mail, annoyed. Was she the only one who ever held a line? Jamie relentlessly rounded up, and Lyle never challenged any of the kids' essentialist assumptions. "Hey," she said, pushing past her irritation, "have any parents ever tried to call you at home? Are you getting a lot of voice mails?"

"Some voice mails," said Jamie, "but no, never at home." Jamie picked a piece of lint off her ankle-length blue trousers, pale pink socks poking out beneath. "You told me to set limits with parents, remember? After Peter's thing?"

Isobel did remember the pep talk she'd delivered after Peter Harrington's sudden firing the previous school year. "You're not Peter," she'd said as Jamie, then only in her first months in the classroom, sat shaking in the very same desk on which she now lounged. "You're prepared, and you're careful. Don't let them see any weakness," she'd said. "You're the one with the teaching license. You know what you're doing. You know what? Rehearse every communication first. Write notes before you make calls. Never answer the phone—always call back when you're ready. And, for goodness' sake, don't friend any kids or parents on social media."

Jamie had walked out that day steady on her feet. She'd grown in confidence each month since, and Isobel felt proud of her transformation even though Lyle asked her over lunch one day why she was putting so much effort into the new teacher's success. "She's not even that smart," Lyle had whispered over the cafeteria's dried-out pot stickers.

"She is, too," Isobel had said. And in fact, shoring up a potential career teacher felt as important to her as molding teenagers directly. A good teacher could change the way kids interacted with the world going forward forever, could inspire them to take action for justice. And hopefully, in their second years of teaching, as Jamie was now, give students the grades they'd actually earned, rather than rounding up. She'd tackle that with her this spring.

"Julia might be the kind of stay-at-home mom who gets a little too involved," Isobel said now. "Maybe now that the kids are older, she needs a diversion. Maybe a nice full-time job?"

"Okay." Jamie rolled her eyes. "Or maybe she needs a nice new vial of Xanax." She kicked her legs out over a Jolly Rancher wrapper someone had dropped on the floor.

ANDREW ABBOTT

Back at his locker, Andrew stared at Sarah's phone in his outstretched hand. "What is it?" he asked. He tried to meet her eyes, but she looked at the floor between them.

"Um," Sarah mumbled, "was your mom at school when the cast list was posted?"

"Not that I saw," said Andrew.

"Maybe just watch it?"

When Andrew focused on the screen, he saw his mother's profile in the still frame, her upturned nose, the yellow "DRAMA" lettering at the top of the bulletin board looming above her head. Her outstretched finger touched the pink paper. Andrew frowned and hit the play button. The twenty-second video was jumpy, but there was no question of his mother's identity, her hair in its usual low ponytail, black leggings beneath her winter coat. She stood before the cast list, lots of kids crowded in behind her. Andrew could see Maeve Hollister, Allen Song, and Melissa Young. After a few seconds, he watched his mom take her finger from the cast list and raise her fist in the air. The silver bracelet she wore most days slid from her wrist to her forearm. She giggled a little—her whole body shook with it—and then she brought her fist down hard, past her waist. Her elbow crashed into Melissa Young. He could hear the person holding the phone half gasp and half laugh, and then Melissa—God, she was his *friend*—bent at the waist, her black hair swinging out in front of her chin to block her face. Next to her, Maeve Hollister crouched down and rubbed her back.

Andrew willed his mother to apologize to Melissa, to check on her. The seconds seemed to lengthen. An excruciating moment passed before she turned around to see what she'd hit. "Jesus," Andrew muttered.

He hit the replay button, hoping to see something different the second time through. What had she been doing at school, anyway? He knew she'd been counting the minutes to two thirty. He'd gotten her texts. But none of the other theater parents stalked the drama board. Sarah's phone grew heavier in his palm. Andrew handed it back to her after he'd watched the video a second time. Nothing had been different. Sarah winced as they finally made eye contact.

"Wait." Andrew shook his head, realizing something. "How'd you say you got that video?"

"From Erin Warner," Sarah said, apologetic. "She got it in a group text from someone in her math class."

Andrew held the door of his locker with one hand and looked up at the ceiling. "Can I come over to your house?" he blurted.

"Um, yeah," she said, surprised. "You mean today?" He nodded. He noticed when she dipped her head that a flush had appeared on her cheeks. She said, "I'll text my mom."

ISOBEL JOHNSON

sobel climbed behind the wheel of her minivan and brushed a stray hair off her cheek. She waved amiably at several kids and successfully avoided a student driver—the poor kid was stuck in the sedan with Mr. Glover, the stinkiest of the behind-the-wheel instructors.

She cruised out of Liston Heights toward home. Most houses in Mills Park, where Isobel lived, featured regular two-car garages, rather than the three-to-five-stall structures attached to her students' places. Mills Park was nice enough, a first-ring suburb just west of Minneapolis. She'd agreed to move out of the city when Mark got promoted to senior counsel, but drew the line at Liston Heights. "It doesn't reflect our values," Isobel told Mark. She'd already mentally allocated the remainder of Mark's pay raise to charitable contributions and to Riley's and Callie's college funds.

"But you work at the high school," Mark reminded her.

"That's different," Isobel said. "Someone has to make sure those kids are prepared for the difficult choices they'll face, having everything they've ever wanted. It's easy, as we well know, to become corrupted." She'd made this speech many times in the last eight years since she first applied for her LHHS teaching position the summer after Riley was born.

"It's actually not that easy," Mark said. "How many people do you know, besides your father, who've defrauded their friends and neighbors?" Isobel hadn't replied. The answer was none, obviously, but she'd resolutely refused to look at any homes over the Liston Heights city line. Somewhere near that line on this particular afternoon, she mentally ran through that evening's checklist. There was Callie's homework and Riley's travel soccer practice. After she picked Riley up in the carpool line, she'd have about forty minutes to get frozen pizza into both kids before she had to hustle them out the door again.

Isobel rubbed her neck with her free hand. Her cell phone rang. Mark, she saw, with a quick glance at the console. She punched the answer button on the steering wheel.

"Hi, hon."

"Just checking in," he said. "Remember tonight's that squash thing?"

"Yep." Isobel mustered enthusiasm for Mark's midlife friend-making endeavors.

"And Riley's got practice at six?"

"Yep, I'm on it."

"Great." And after a pause: "How was your day?"

"Oh . . ." She sighed, gauging how much detail to provide. "I mean, to be honest, you won't even believe the level of crazy we achieved today."

"What do you mean?"

"The cast list for the play was posted, and some of the helicopter moms went ballistic."

"Oh, no." She could picture him in his office, an outdated photo of Isobel and the kids in a frame before him, his pen poised above some document. Their jobs, she often thought—he in his law office and she in front of thirty-five teenagers at a time—couldn't really be more different.

"One of the moms actually stormed the drama board when the list was posted."

"Geez," Mark said. "Did she at least sign in at the security desk?"

"That's a good question." Isobel could tell he was only half listening. "Either way, when she was finished reading the cast list, she accidentally punched a kid."

"Oh," said Mark. And then: "Wait. What?"

"Yeah. This woman raced into a crowd of kids and accidentally clocked a girl in the gut."

"Whoa!" Mark exclaimed. "What's going to happen?"

"Don't know," Isobel said. "I guess we'll see." The two hung up, and Isobel thought again of Julia Abbott. What could she have been thinking? Probably she hadn't been, Isobel reasoned, just as she probably hadn't been thinking two weeks ago when they'd run into each other at the Sadie Hawkins dance. Isobel had been a chaperone, a necessary evil of a Liston Heights teaching contract, and Julia had been a parent volunteer.

Isobel had convinced Lyle Greenwood to dress up with her in the traditional faculty theme of scholars and ballers. If one went with "baller," as Isobel always did, it was an excuse to wear sweatpants and sneakers. Lyle naturally chose "scholar." He wore a button-down tucked into belted khakis, but he had also wrapped a little first aid tape around the bridge of his glasses.

At the chaperone table after assistant principal Sue Montague had expressed her thanks to the volunteers, parents started signing up for their jobs—coat check, concessions, and the like. Isobel recognized Julia Abbott among the group. She stifled a scoff at the woman's smoky eye makeup and sparkly shirt. Did she think the dance was for parents? Julia and Vivian Song took coat check, the job closest to the check-in table.

Isobel and Lyle's job would be check-in, as usual. She liked looking at the kids' costumes. "Now," Sue was saying as the parents walked toward their posts and out of earshot, "we all know that Sadie's is one of our more notorious events, and we don't want a repeat of last year."

Last year, twenty students had left early on a party bus and were promptly arrested for public urination and underage consumption in a local park. The Faculty-Parent/Guardian Alliance leaders had asked some pointed questions at the April meeting about how alcohol managed to make its way onto the dance floor in the first place. "Minors are becoming intoxicated at school events," proclaimed the attorney father of one of the urinators, "and that's on *you*."

"Here's how we're going to work it," Sue continued. "If a group walks in and you smell alcohol or notice erratic behavior, raise your red marker." She raised a Crayola to demonstrate. "That will prompt Officers Sullivan and Markert to Breathalyze."

Lyle whistled. "We actually got the Breathalyzer this year. I'm impressed."

Sue nodded. "If we can't get this dance under control, I'm ending it. So, Lyle, you and Isobel will work the table for the first forty-five minutes. The officers will turn away latecomers. The rest of you are roamers. Check in with the parents and monitor behavior. Let's make this happen."

Kids started streaming in through the doors at seven fifteen. Isobel stopped a group in revealing beach-themed costumes and matter-of-factly told them they could either put on the baggy gym shirts and shorts she would provide or go home and change. The kids tromped back to the parking lot, sunglasses perched on their heads. Others walked up to the table, smiled politely at Isobel, and provided their names and student IDs. Isobel had raised her red marker a couple of times, but so far, the cops hadn't denied anyone admittance to the gym.

"Good work, Johnson," Lyle said, during a lag. "Fifteen minutes to go."

Isobel noticed Julia Abbott lurking near the sign-in table, checking her phone. She'd felt the woman's gaze from across the foyer a few times during the evening. She hoped she wasn't planning one of those impromptu parent-teacher conferences that irritated her so much. There was nothing like trying on flats in DSW while answering questions from a Liston Heights mother about poor grammar.

"I'm just waiting for Andrew," Julia said when she looked up. "He should be here any moment. Andrew Abbott," she clarified.

"Yes," Isobel said. "I'm Isobel Johnson, his AP English teacher. I'm Tracy's teacher, as well."

"That's right." Julia stepped toward her. "I read Tracy's paper recently. The one on 'The Story of an Hour.'"

Here it comes, thought Isobel. She willed herself to maintain a neutral expression. "Tracy has a lot of potential." She glanced at the front door, hoping they'd both be distracted by more arrivals.

"I was curious," Julia said, "about the conclusions Tracy drew from the Chopin story. How are you mitigating the idea that marriage and children are nothing but traps?"

Isobel blinked. Beyond the door, she could make out a group dressed in Western garb descending the steps of a rented shuttle bus. "I don't mitigate their thoughts," she said. "My students draw their own conclusions about the themes of the literature we read. I just encourage them to support their ideas with evidence from the texts."

"I see," said Julia. Sarah Smith walked through the door wearing a cowboy hat with a red leather chin strap. Andrew Abbott followed in black jeans and boots. "But 'The Story of an Hour'?" Julia went on. "'The Yellow Wallpaper' *plus* an article about something called the motherhood penalty?"

Isobel flipped her spreadsheet to A and raised her eyebrows at Lyle. The new arrivals stopped twenty feet from the sign-in table for a selfie.

Julia said, "It's disconcerting to have my fourteen-year-old daughter claiming she never wants children. That's all. That motherhood is a trap."

Isobel turned toward her. "I'd never want her to feel that way," she said. "I love being a mom myself. I think my students know that."

Julia smiled, but there was an edge in her voice when she spoke again. "I know everyone says you're—I don't know"—Julia rotated her hand, a silver bangle shifting with each circle—"subversive and unpredictable?"

Isobel's smile froze.

"Anyway," Julia continued, her tone nonchalant, "people say you're not quite, well . . ." Isobel's mouth dropped open. "Not quite Liston Heights material? That you haven't really earned it?" Julia stared at Isobel's baggy wind pants and lingered for a second on the LHHS basketball jersey she'd layered over a long-sleeved T-shirt. "But I want you to know that despite all of that, *my* kids have actually seemed to enjoy your class."

Isobel fought the urge to turn to Lyle. She felt his hand land squarely on her right shoulder. "Isobel is one of our best," he said definitively. "Welcome to Sadie's!" he said to the teenagers before them. "Let's get you cowpokes checked in."

TRACY ABBOTT

Tracy clicked into her cross-country skis and headed straight for the wooded trail ahead of her teammates. She didn't want to talk to anyone or, more important, see anyone's Instagram feed for the next hour. "I want to get a few extra kilometers in," she'd explained to her coach, who was more than happy to let her go. On the trail, her cheeks cold on the February afternoon, she felt anger radiating from her tense shoulders even as she rhythmically stabbed the snow with her poles.

She'd texted her father from the locker room before practice. SOS, she'd written. He'd know what she meant. They'd all witnessed Julia's mania before, most recently after parent-teacher conferences when Julia had launched in on Tracy's near-perfect GPA. "You have a B plus in English! How could you like that teacher so much when she's ruining everything?"

Tracy didn't even want to think about her mother's reaction to the new Instagram video everyone had been talking about by the end of seventh period. Thank God, none of the kids in French II seemed to know the video's connection to her family. "I guess, according to the comments, it's Andrew Abbott's mom?" said someone who didn't even glance her way. "Lucky Tryg is so tall. You really get a nice view of the hit."

While Tracy didn't need to see the video to understand her class-mates' fascination—she remembered her glassy-eyed mother standing next to a crouched-over Melissa—she figured she should probably know what they were dealing with. While Madame Henderson appeared en-grossed in her e-mail, Tracy pulled out her phone. **So much drama at the drama board**, Tryg Ogilvie had captioned the video, and then Julia appeared in a twenty-second loop, thrusting her fist in the air like a crazed person and then slugging Melissa.

As she whizzed by snow-dusted pine boughs, Tracy remembered several of the comments people had posted on the video. She'd scrolled through them all, a pain forming over the bridge of her nose as she skimmed through the face-palm and laugh-cry emojis. **Loosen your Spanx, Mrs. A,** @ListonLioness had written. Of course, Tracy knew her mother would never actually wear Spanx. "If you need 'control top,'" Julia always said, "you've got bigger problems."

Well, here come some bigger problems, thought Tracy. She wasn't stupid—she could see the other moms' reactions to Julia's over-the-top behavior. She'd noted their meaningful glances at one another when Julia wasn't looking. Those moms, her friends' moms, would likely revel in this video, whispering to one another about it in the carpool line and at Starbucks. Tracy closed her eyes briefly against the winter wind and picked up her pace.

ANDREW ABBOTT

"Andrew!" exclaimed Sarah's mom as he walked into the Smiths' kitchen through the back door. "It's great to see you again." She sat back from her laptop. Mrs. Smith wore loose athletic pants and a Liston Heights volleyball sweatshirt. Sarah had been the captain setter on the team that fall, and Andrew had gone to a couple of games after Sarah and her friend Erin had joined his lunch table. It had taken him two weeks and some coaching from Maeve Hollister to figure out what they were doing there. Once Maeve clued him in, Andrew had suddenly noticed Sarah's thick curls and smooth brown skin. Her eyes twinkled when she smiled at him.

"Thanks," said Andrew politely. He pointed at Mrs. Smith's computer. "You, too. What are you working on?"

"I have homework for my grad school class," she said.

"Graduate school?"

"I decided to finish my master of social work now that George is in college," she said, "and Sarah's old enough to mostly fend for herself."

"Wow." Andrew was impressed. Graduate school? His own mother had the focus of a hamster, it seemed—only enough to urge him to practice singing or to stir up the Theater Boosters via group text. The most sustained effort he'd seen on her part was her campaign to convince his father that they should use some bonus money from a recent property sale to fund the costume shop at school.

"I think we're going to get some homework done." Sarah pulled Andrew toward the dining room table.

"Very responsible," Mrs. Smith said. "Help yourselves to a snack and a drink, if you want one."

"Thank you." Andrew glanced at the open Word doc on her computer screen as he walked by. She seemed to be writing a paper. Andrew had been worried that she'd have already seen the video of Julia punching Melissa, but clearly she was too busy to be trolling social media.

Andrew snuck a look at his phone as he grabbed his copy of *Gatsby* from his North Face backpack. He'd been avoiding the phone for the last thirty minutes since Sarah had shown him the video. As he expected, he had a string of messages waiting for him.

INSPECTOR! the text from his mom read. CONGRATULATIONS!! Let's celebrate at dinner! She'd followed this with a series of clapping-hands emojis. *Gross,* Andrew thought.

Where r u?!?!?! from Tracy.

Dad: Call me, ASAP.

And then, from Maeve Hollister, a smiley face and You're going to be great. Andrew didn't want to respond to any of them. Maeve, he knew, would have a separate text chain going with Melissa.

"Anything interesting?" asked Sarah from across the table where she'd spread her chemistry textbook and notes.

"A few texts from the family," he said flatly, "about the video."

"What are you going to do?" Sarah asked.

"I don't know." He stared at the giant blue eye on the cover of the tattered school-district copy of Fitzgerald's novel. "It's really embarrassing, you know?" He ventured a glance at her, catching sight of a dangly earring as she smoothed her hair.

"It wasn't you who elbowed Melissa."

"It might as well have been," said Andrew.

"But it wasn't."

"I'm waiting a while to talk to her," Andrew said, anger slipping into his tone. "My mom, I mean." He pulled his bookmark out of *Gatsby* as he opened the novel. "Do you like this book?" He held it up.

"It's fine." She smiled. "I mean, I don't love it as much as Ms. Johnson does."

Andrew laughed. "You mean more than life? That's a tall order for a hundred forty measly pages." Andrew's phone buzzed, and he looked over at it to see an all-caps text from his mom: WHERE ARE YOU? COME HOME! He clicked the off button on the side of the iPhone and watched the screen go blank. *No,* he thought. He wouldn't respond, and he'd go home as late as possible. The best-case scenario was never going home again.

"I'm not answering," he said to Sarah.

The two settled into silence, Andrew pretending to read as he alternately fantasized about moving out of his house and touching Sarah's smooth cheek, maybe letting his fingers slide into her hair. Their eyes met a few times as he thought about her, and when they did, he felt a zing from his shoulder all the way through to his fingertips.

HENRY ABBOTT

Henry opened his top drawer and popped a Rolaid from its package at the close of the call with Martin Young, breathing through his nose as he chewed. He was used to fallout from Julia—he'd made umpteen calls to various family members, friends, and acquaintances to smooth over her transgressions in the past twenty years, but doing this duty with a twenty-million-dollar project hanging in the balance? They'd moved past flippant comments about knockoff purses and store-bought Yule logs.

Henry's assistant peeked around the corner. "Sorry to bug you, Henry," William said, "but Brenda wants to know if you'd like to pick things up now or in the morning."

Henry blinked and sat up straight. "Could you tell her I'll be ready to go at eight tomorrow morning, please? I need to handle a bit of a family emergency."

"Everything okay?"

"I think I can fix it," Henry said, "but I have to get home."

William closed the door behind him. Henry grabbed his cell and scanned the list of texts, another from Tracy and two from Julia. Call me when you get this, his wife had typed.

He wrote a reply: Where are you right now?

Just home from picking up Tracy.

I'll be there ASAP. He stuffed the phone roughly in the front pocket of his briefcase, closed his laptop, and grabbed his coat from the hook on the door.

On his way home, he replayed Martin Young's call in his head. "Bruising to the abdomen," Martin had said. "Shock," "stress," and Melissa's "lingering feeling" after *Witches over Willow Street* that Julia didn't like her. Something about the wrong look for the part? Her feet were too big? It all seemed trivial. He glided his BMW into the three-car garage and sighed.

As he opened the back door, Henry recognized the familiar smell of warm butter and melted cheese, béchamel sauce for one of Julia's famous baked pastas. "It's me!" he called.

"Hi, honey," Julia said without turning around. "I'm doing mac and cheese for dinner. I know it's heavy, but it's Andrew's favorite. We have to celebrate!" Tracy raised her eyebrows at her father from the kitchen table. Her wet hair dripped on her gray sweatshirt.

"Dad," she whispered as he approached, "didn't you get my texts?"

"I did, sweetheart." He avoided her eyes. He wasn't entirely comfortable in his new complicity with their teenagers when it came to managing Julia. He could see their adoration of their mother waning each year, their eyes rolling harder when she offered advice. Their texts imploring him to forbid her from calling their teachers made him faintly queasy. Parenting had been more fun when he ran alongside their bikes and took them for ice cream.

"Julia"—he stood next to her at the stove—"we really need to talk."

"I know." She set her spoon down to the right of the burner. "I got the most insane call from Wayne Wallace. You know, the principal? He wants to meet with me tomorrow morning at seven thirty. There's been a crazy misunderstanding."

Henry glanced back at Tracy, who stared at them, leery, over the philodendron beside the breakfast bar. "Come upstairs with me while I change my clothes," Henry suggested to his wife.

"It's okay," Tracy said. "I'll do my biology in my room." She zipped an oversized textbook into her backpack and slid around Henry on the way to the stairs. He patted her back as she scooted past.

"Would you like a glass of wine?" Julia asked. "It's been quite a day." She sipped prosecco from a stemless flute.

"That might be good."

"Isn't it great about Andrew?" she asked airily. She pulled the Chardonnay that he liked from the fridge.

"It is," Henry agreed. "But, Julia, we have to talk about what happened with the cast list." He felt a familiar anxiety pulse from his chest down through his arms. He'd have to finesse this just right to get her to cooperate.

Julia shook her head. "It was a big misunderstanding. I got caught up in the hallway on my way to check the cast list, and there were all of these kids. . . ." She trailed off, her free hand making circles in the air, fingers extended.

"I got a call from Martin Young," Henry said, stopping her.

"Martin?" Julia frowned.

"Martin said that his daughter, Melissa, was badly hurt. He told me that—and this is hard for me to imagine—you assaulted her in the midst of a crowd of kids."

"Assault?" Julia blinked. She pushed Henry's wineglass toward him across the counter, her Tiffany bangle scraping the granite. He'd been there when her mother had given her that bracelet at a fancy dinner after their college graduation. She'd worn it nearly every day since even though he'd gifted her much nicer things.

"What happened, Julia?"

She shook her head. "No one would answer my texts, and I was so eager to see what part Andrew got. . . ."

"And?" he prodded.

Julia raised her glass to her lips and glanced at the ceiling as she sipped. "Assault?" she said again once she'd swallowed.

"Yes," said Henry, controlled, but barely. He'd been able to see her point when his sister brought that Target-quality Yule log to the first Christmas dinner after his mom had died, and he again acknowledged her concern at parent-teacher conferences when a single arbitrary B+ marred Tracy's report card. But punching a kid? In front of a crowd? This had crossed even Henry's generously thick line. "Martin Young said you elbowed Melissa hard in the gut." He reached a hand over to hers and held it. "Martin used the word 'assault.'"

She blinked again. "I just can't imagine anyone characterizing it that way."

"Well," said Henry, his patience fraying, "that's how Martin Young characterized it." A sheen formed over Julia's blue eyes then, her first sign of emotion. She pulled her hand away. More softly, he said, "Could you please tell me what happened?"

"No one was texting me back about the cast list, so I decided to just sneak into the school right at two thirty when it was posted and take a peek while the students were still in class. But the bell rang, and suddenly there were kids everywhere." She looked past him, thinking. "I just wanted to see . . ."

"You couldn't wait until Andrew came home?" Henry himself anticipated no problem waiting until dinnertime to hear the news about Andrew's part. It would have been fun, actually, to hear it straight from him, to watch his face light up as he made the announcement.

"No!" She slapped her hand against her yoga pants, her mood intensifying as it always did. "He's worked so hard, Henry!" She looked at him finally. "He really deserved that inspector part. I just wanted to see it. I wanted to see it for myself." She turned back toward the stove.

Henry exhaled, not realizing he'd been holding his breath. Heat escaped the oven as Julia cracked it to check on the mac and cheese. "And you ran into Melissa Young?" he prompted.

"There was a circle of kids. I just wanted to get a little glimpse of the list, so I excused my way through the crowd. I must have bumped into her right as I was leaving."

"Dad?" It was Tracy's voice from the stairwell.

Henry feared they'd lose momentum. "Can you give us a few minutes, Trace?"

"Dad." She came toward him with her phone outstretched in front of her. "You should probably see the video."

"There's a video?" As Henry took the iPhone, the back door crashed open.

A red-faced Andrew emerged from the mudroom, his untied shoe-laces clicking against the wood floor as he walked. He looked up at the family, all three staring at him, and zeroed in on Julia. "Mom," he said darkly, "I can't fucking believe you."

"Andrew!" Julia's glass clattered as she set it down hard on the counter.

"Andrew!" Henry shouted simultaneously. "Language!"

"But did you see it?" their son yelled, one hand migrating to his sweaty brow. "Did you see the video?"

"I just gave it to him." Tracy pointed at the phone in Henry's hand.

"Well, watch it!" Andrew fumed. "It has more than a thousand views."

Henry pressed the play arrow, dread spreading from his belly. After he saw it the first time, he blinked hard and hit PLAY again. The video was more damning than he'd imagined. When Martin Young had described the incident, Henry assumed it was a jostling, the kind of elbow one might catch while maneuvering through a crowded grocery store. But this was a full-on hit, Julia's elbow driving into the center of Melissa's stomach, the girl's mouth flying open in shock and pain as she doubled over. Julia stood in the center of the frame, the sole adult in a swarm of teenagers. *Nobody else's parents were even there,* he thought.

Without speaking, Henry walked toward Julia and placed the phone on the counter in front of her. He played the recording again, and her eyes widened. Her hand covered her mouth as it finished.

"Well?" prompted Andrew. Tears caught in his throat, and Henry's shoulders felt weak under the weight of pity and responsibility for his son. He looked alternately at each of them—Andrew and Julia. What was the right move here? Defend Julia's irrational behavior? Side with his son while his wife looked on? The moment required the negotiation skills he'd honed over years of working with city government. He turned to Andrew. "We understand why you're upset."

Fresh color flooded Andrew's face and spread to his neck. "I don't think you do! The entire school is watching a video of Mom having a fucking *fit* in front of the cast list!" Henry saw Julia wince at this, but neither of them said anything. "And I have to go to rehearsal tomorrow"—Andrew pointed at his mother—"with Melissa Young!"

"Take a deep breath," Henry said, stepping toward him.

"Dad! I know you understand this." Andrew staggered back. "I know you do!" His body appeared to spasm in rage.

"You're right." Henry reached a hand out to touch Andrew's arm. Standing face-to-face with him, he realized his boy had finally equaled him in height. A flash of pride broke through the tension. "Let's go for a drive," he said, thinking fast.

"A drive isn't going to fix anything," Andrew said, glaring at Julia.

"Andrew," she began as she raised a hand to her clavicle.

"Don't even say anything!" Andrew shouted, blasting Henry's ears with his ferocity. "Just *shut up!*"

"Andrew," said Henry firmly, sure that distance from his mother would help, "let's go." He steered him toward the door.

JULIA ABBOTT

Julia lay on her back, a cool washcloth over her eyes, when Henry opened their bedroom door. As he entered she pushed the compress up, inhaling the lavender essential oil in the cool-air diffuser by her bed. The idea was to calm herself, although it wasn't working well. Over dinner with Tracy, she'd cycled between fury and humiliation. What kind of child swore at his mother like that? What kind of mother allowed it? And how could she explain to Andrew what had actually happened at the drama board, despite what it looked like in that damn video?

"I can't believe Andrew," Julia had said out loud to Tracy over her leftover beet salad.

Tracy picked the golden crust from the mac and cheese with her fingers. "The Instagram video has over thirteen hundred views now," she said quietly.

Julia had poured a third glass of prosecco when Tracy excused herself to finish homework in her room. After she'd drained it, she closed her own bedroom door and tried the lavender.

"Well?" she asked Henry eagerly as he placed his keys and money clip on the dresser.

"Well." He exhaled slowly through his nose. "I think things are going to be okay."

Julia's head felt immediately clearer. She swung her legs over the bed, the washcloth limp in her hand, and said, "Oh, good. I'll go—"

"No." Henry kicked off his loafers and lay down beside her. "Give him some space." He opened his arms and gestured for her to rest her head on his chest. Julia hesitated. She wanted to talk to Andrew, both to allow him to apologize for using the f-word and also to assure him that she'd solve this problem, just as she had all the others.

"Trust me," Henry said. She felt irritated by his authority, and yet she remembered Tracy's forlorn recitation of the Instagram video stats. Was thirteen hundred viral? Surely not, and yet she placed the damp washcloth on the floor beside the bed and lowered her body to rest against her husband's. He held her loosely.

"What did Andrew say?" Julia asked.

Henry's chest rose and fell. Several seconds passed before he answered. "He's not happy you went to school, and he's especially upset about the video."

Julia felt a familiar panic, the flutter at the back of her esophagus that accompanied the helpless feeling of not being understood. She'd simply tried to make sure Andrew got the part he deserved, the recognition they'd all worked for. "But I was just seeing that everything turned out the way we planned." Her voice rose, and she tried to sit.

Henry tightened his grip, and she gave up. "We both know that," he said, his voice low and his eyes closed. "But Andrew doesn't see it that way."

She waited through several more of his breaths. "That's why I need to go talk to him," she said. "To explain what actually happened." Her voice caught on her final word, and she felt tears rising. "I just don't know how everything got so mixed up."

Henry's grip remained firm over her biceps. "Julia," he said, "neither do I."

They were both quiet for a moment, and Julia felt tears crest her eyelids and soak into Henry's blue Oxford button-down beneath her. "God," she said finally, "I just wanted Andrew to have this lead role. Now he has it, and he's not even speaking to me. And that video!"

Henry nodded his chin into the top of her head.

"Is thirteen hundred views considered viral, do you think?"

"Andrew said seventeen hundred at dinner," Henry said. "Try not to think about it."

Try not to think about it? Henry could be so inane sometimes. "Can we delete it?" she asked, her tears drying. "And also, did I tell you? Wayne Wallace scheduled a meeting at seven thirty tomorrow morning to talk about"—she paused—"to talk about the incident?"

"You mentioned that before Andrew came in." Henry reached for the phone in his back pocket. He tapped it several times and then said, "I'll go with you." She nodded into his chest. As much as she resented it, the principal always seemed to take her more seriously when Henry accompanied her.

"Do you have to reschedule something?" she asked, guilty.

"A meeting with Brenda about the Tuolomee project. We can do it at nine."

"Will she be mad?" Julia didn't want to add to the list of things for which she'd have to apologize. "I'm sure we can work this out. Wayne was so pleased when we gave the gift for the costume shop."

"It'll be fine." Henry put his phone on his bedside table. "Before we fall asleep, let's talk about how to play it tomorrow. We've got a good shot to repair things, but we have to get the tone right." Julia felt both relieved and annoyed that Henry was immersed in the situation. He generally left everything related to the children to her, ignoring sports registrations and academic blips. The kids' problems were hers to solve, Henry happily detached until now suddenly he wasn't.

WAYNE WALLACE

⁓

Wayne Wallace waited for the Abbotts at his office door. The meeting would be tricky, he knew—chastising significant donors to the Liston Heights Education Fund. He burped quietly, his stomach upset. Julia and Henry appeared in the administrative hallway, dressed up and looking grim.

Calm and matter-of-fact, Wayne told himself. *Let's get this over with.*

"Ah," he said as the couple drew close. "Come in." He shook hands first with Henry and then with Julia, his fingers grazing the white silk cuff of her blouse, and gestured toward the conference table.

"Wayne," Julia began as the principal sat down, "I'm so sorry about this misunderstanding."

Henry nodded at her approvingly. "We both are," Henry said. "I talked with Martin Young last evening, and Julia and I understand the severity of the situation."

"That's good." Wayne felt relieved that he wouldn't have to recount Martin's take on it. "As you know, safety is our first concern at Liston Heights High."

"Obviously," Julia agreed. "And"—she glanced at Henry before continuing her prepared speech—"I clearly let my emotions get the best of me. It was a mistake to come to school. I should have waited to hear the news from Andrew." The lines were stilted, but on the mark. Julia smiled. "It's just that I was so excited!" Her voice rose, and her hands came together before she remembered herself. "I was excited to see the result of his hard work, of course," she said, staid once again.

Wayne pursed his lips and looked away. "I'm sure you were excited, Julia. And I appreciate your candor. It's indeed possible for parents to become, ah"—he hesitated—"overly invested in the student experience."

Julia squinted and sat up taller. Wayne could tell that "overly invested" had rankled her, but he pressed on. "I've talked with Martin Young, and unfortunately Melissa feels—"

"Wayne," interrupted Henry. "Martin, to his credit, called me directly yesterday. He told me himself how Melissa feels, and we both—Julia and I—are committed to making this right."

"I'm relieved to hear you say that." Wayne took in Henry's gelled hair and his paisley tie as he prepared to impart the consequences for Julia's impulsivity. This guy, he figured, wasn't used to being told no. "I'm afraid, though, we're going to have to make some adjustments to the Theater Booster Board to accommodate Martin's wishes. He's assured me that he, his wife, Annabelle, and Melissa are opposed to pressing charges as long as the school can assure Melissa's safety and comfort."

"Charges?" Julia blurted. "I mean, that's insane! I—" Henry reached over and took her hand. Wayne bit down on his molars and steeled himself.

"Just listen," Henry said to his wife. "Wayne is saying they're *not*—"

"Henry, please." Julia shook him off. "The very idea of pressing charges for what was clearly an unfortunate accident is ridiculous. As you well know, Wayne, I have been fully dedicated to this program for two years." Here came the litany he'd been waiting for. "I've donated my time, my talent, and, of course, my—our—actual money"—she gestured toward Henry—"to ensure the success of the Liston Heights Thespians. As well as their safety and comfort! I'm surprised that given my track record you'd accuse—"

"Julia," Wayne broke in, "no one doubts your commitment to the program, and I'm sure, as you say, that this incident was an accident. However, certain compromises have become necessary." He kept his deep voice level.

"But I don't understand. Is Melissa Young even hurt?" Spittle appeared on Julia's lips as she asked.

"Since you spoke with Martin," Wayne said to Henry, "you probably know that Melissa is reporting soreness and bruising to the abdomen." Henry nodded, solemn. "And I'm not sure if you're aware of this"—Wayne's eyes flicked in Julia's direction—"but Melissa seems to know about some comments you may have made about *Witches over Willow Street* last spring. Comments regarding her performance and her appearance. She even alluded to them in her profile yesterday on the LHHS Instagram."

Julia pressed her lips together and squared her shoulders. "What do you have in mind regarding the Booster Board?" Henry asked.

"Ah," said Wayne. Here it came. He leaned in and made eye contact with Julia. "I'm afraid this much is nonnegotiable. I've decided that you will not serve on the Theater Booster Board for the next twelve months."

"What?" She shook off her husband's hand. "Wayne, I understand your impulse here, but I don't think you've really thought this through. For instance," she continued, "who do you imagine will take over communications for the cast and crew on such short notice? Who will plan and execute the annual five-K? This important community event doesn't just happen! I've been coordinating it for years."

"I appreciate your concern," Wayne broke in, "but it's already been handled."

"Handled?" Julia said, startled.

"Robin Bergstrom has agreed to step in," Wayne said. "She'd be glad to serve on the board, given the difficult circumstances." Julia's eyes went wide, and then she fell back against her chair as if she herself had been punched in the stomach. Robin Bergstrom, Wayne knew, was something of a friend to Julia.

Or at least until today she had been.

ROBIN BERGSTROM

Robin Bergstrom didn't have time to serve on the Theater Booster Board. She had three new freelancing clients and deadlines littering her calendar. But when Wayne Wallace had called her, she couldn't resist. Julia had been so smug about Andrew's potential for a lead role and at the same time so secretive about the workings of the board. "I can't tell you everything," she'd said when Robin asked about fundraising and 5K plans. "We'll ask for feedback from the masses at a specific time."

Robin was "the masses"? After fielding all those texts about casting and costuming and a barrage in the fall about Tracy's course placement? It hadn't escaped Robin that her own daughter, Anika, had earned a spot in Honors Geometry from the start. There was no need for Robin to threaten the registrar, even if she'd been so inclined. Plus, there'd been the myriad backhanders Julia had let slip about technical theater even when Andrew himself had been on the props crew.

"I hate to ask this, Robin," Wayne had said on the phone, "but Annabelle Young mentioned that Julia has made disparaging comments about Melissa before. Have you heard her talk about Melissa's skills or—I know this is unusual—her foot size?" Robin smiled, imagining Wayne, hulking frame hunched over the phone, forcing himself to ask her about theater mom gossip.

"It happened at the Percys' holiday party," Robin offered. "Julia said that Melissa's talent is overrated and that she has an untrained alto. Also, and I can't remember her exact words, but something about how she imagines it is difficult for Melissa to dance when she has size eleven feet." Wayne coughed. "Unfortunately," Robin continued, surprised and feeling rather liberated by her candor, "I wasn't the only one to overhear."

It irked Robin that Julia acted like she was the sole woman in Liston Heights who knew how to take advantage of an opportunity. She'd so carefully stalked Vivian Song's Instagram feed to discern which hot yoga studio she frequented and "coincidentally" ran into her there enough times to score a board invitation. Well, this call from Wayne was Robin's chance.

"I know it's a lot to ask," Wayne said, "but I'll need your answer immediately if possible."

"Wayne," Robin said, "it is a lot to ask, but I'll do it. I'll do it because the kids' experience is the most important thing—more important than a lapse in judgment by one overzealous parent."

"Thank you," Wayne had said before hanging up.

Now Robin looked at the time. Eight o'clock. Certainly Julia and Henry were finished with their meeting, and her friend had heard the news of her banishment. Robin held her phone in her hand, waiting for the inevitable text.

ISOBEL JOHNSON

Isobel was standing between her minivan and an Infiniti four-door when she overheard a couple in the Liston Heights High parking lot.

"Good news?" a woman half shouted. "It's good news that I've been kicked off the board? I mean, besides the whole meeting being a preposterous overreaction to a silly misunderstanding . . ." Her voice trailed off.

"Honey," said the man firmly—and condescendingly, Isobel thought—"we're lucky the Youngs aren't pressing charges." With that, Isobel realized who it was. She stepped into the lane and, as the Abbotts approached, tilted her chin down, surprised to see that they were still several cars in front of her. She hoped she wouldn't have to talk to Julia Abbott, especially after the voice mail. Even if Julia hadn't been the caller, Isobel knew she shared the sentiment.

"That's insane," Julia spit then, swinging her bag violently over her shoulder. "Don't you even care what really happened?" Her husband didn't respond. He walked briskly ahead, leading Julia now by several steps. Isobel grimaced, embarrassed for her. "To think that the board would be better served by the mother of a stage manager!" Julia hissed.

"The mother of someone who doesn't even have the talent to appear in front of the audience!" Her husband kept moving, and Julia had to take a hop-step to stay within a body's length of him. They were just ten feet in front of Isobel now, oblivious to her presence. She moved left, hugging the bumpers of the parked cars and hoping to slip past them.

But just then, the heel of Julia's navy pump caught a plane of ice on the asphalt. She pitched forward. Her arms shot out from her body. Her right hand grazed the salty ground, her handbag thumping behind it. She breathed hard as she hurried to right herself and stood too suddenly. She had to take two quick steps backward to avoid falling over the other way. Her husband marched toward their car and didn't notice her stumble.

Just as Julia had finally steadied herself, cursed under her breath, and looked up, Isobel was right in front of her, mouth gaping. She wouldn't be slipping by. Despite her desire to avoid this woman, she fought an urge to laugh at the slapstick choreography of her stumble. "Goodness," she said after a second when she was sure she wasn't smiling. She reached a hand out to Julia's elbow. "Are you all right?"

"Of course," Julia said without making eye contact. "Thank you." She smoothed her coat. The teacher withdrew her hand, and then Julia looked at her. "Oh," she said, "Ms. Johnson."

"Mrs. Abbott," Isobel said, tentative. She considered the timbre of Julia's voice, trying to match it to the one on her machine. The two were quiet for a beat, and then Isobel continued. "Congratulations to Andrew. I heard he got a significant role in the musical." *And,* she thought, unable to stop the creep of schadenfreude, *bummer about your altercation in the hallway.* She smiled, pleased that she'd taken the second to apply new lipstick in the car.

"Thank you. He's worked very hard." Isobel followed Julia's gaze. Behind them, Mr. Abbott stood at the bumper of a BMW, eyebrows raised.

"Julia?" he called, too loudly. Isobel looked back at her. She held up an index finger, her expression sour.

"Andrew is certainly diligent," Isobel said, letting her eyes fall to her own feet, sensibly safe in her L.L.Bean boots. Julia looked down at them, too, no doubt comparing them to her own fashionable—and obviously impractical—heels. Isobel would change into her wedges at her desk. They weren't stilettos, but they weren't her old Dansko clogs, either.

"Well," Julia said crisply, "have a nice day." Her handbag slapped Isobel's biceps as she walked toward her husband.

"Bye." Isobel peeked once more at the two of them. Mr. Abbott, exasperated, was scowling at his wife, and Isobel felt slightly sorry for her amid the satisfaction that she seemed to be getting what she deserved.

JULIA ABBOTT

Henry and Julia barely spoke on the five-minute drive back to their house. As he pulled into the driveway, she felt his eyes on her as she stared at the garage. The car smelled like coffee grounds, heat hitting Henry's crusty mug in the front console. "It's going to be okay," he said to her. She pulled her bracelet off and put it back on again, running her fingers over the engraved surface. "Next, you'll call the Youngs and apologize, and this can all fade into the background, where it belongs."

Julia felt anger rising again. "It's just so ridiculous." She squeezed the handle of her quilted tote. "I obviously didn't mean to elbow Melissa."

"There's video, babe," Henry said. "We're accepting Wayne's compromise."

"But Robin taking the board position?" Julia sucked in a breath. "She didn't even have the decency to tell me in advance." Henry didn't answer. Julia continued. "Anika isn't an actor, is all I'm saying." She unbuckled her seat belt.

"Listen," Henry said firmly. "Don't tell people about this. Don't text

Robin. Just let it be. Take a break from the Liston Heights drama." He smiled to himself before adding, "So to speak."

Julia's indignation boiled over again. She couldn't bear his condescension. He acted as if the theater stuff, the school stuff—all of the kids' stuff—were easy and inconsequential. He didn't realize it wasn't just about the winter musical, but rather about opportunities for the rest of Andrew's life, beginning with college. "I'm not an idiot, Henry," Julia said.

"Obviously not," said Henry. "But . . ." He trailed off.

"But what?" Julia sputtered.

"But, in this case, hon, you pretty much acted like one."

Julia grabbed her purse and opened the door. "I'll see you later," she said roughly, barely producing the words through her anger.

"Don't text Robin!" Henry shouted, his voice ringing out just before the slam of the door cut it off.

Julia stamped inside and kicked off her shoes in the entryway. Her handbag landed on the couch, and she padded barefoot into the kitchen and then automatically opened the refrigerator and extracted a Diet Mountain Dew. She popped the top and sat at the counter, flattening her hand against the cool granite, the veins of brown in its gradient snaking around her fingers.

The room smelled of cinnamon and vanilla, the reeds of a new diffuser peeking from behind the philodendron on the cookbook shelf. Julia gulped the soda and considered her day. Without the Theater Booster Board business—the e-mail list, the welcoming of new families, the treat rotation, the 5K, which actually was quite a lot of work—her schedule was suddenly clear.

Of course she'd still participate in the 5K, right? That was open to the public. No one could stop her. She walked back to the couch and extracted her iPhone from her tote. No messages. She opened the text app and composed a new message to her personal trainer. Let's shift focus, she wrote. I want to run my fastest 5K ever in three weeks. Possible? She collapsed into the micro-suede cushions and scrolled to her last exchange with Robin. Cast list rehash? she'd asked. The response had been a rosy-cheeked smiley and Sure!

And now? And now Robin was installed on the Booster Board, and Julia was banished for a whole year. Henry's voice echoed in her head: "Don't text Robin!"

"Screw that," Julia whispered to herself. She typed, Congratulations on your new post! Who knew backstabbing came so naturally to you! SEND. And then a second text: I hope it was worth it. She turned her phone facedown beside her, not waiting to see if Robin would reply.

HENRY ABBOTT

Henry checked the clock on the car console. Eight thirty-five. He should be just in time for his rescheduled meeting with Brenda. How much would he have to tell his business partner about the "unfortunate incident," as he and Julia had been referring to it? Henry squeezed the steering wheel, its heated leather soft beneath his palms. He'd probably have to share enough to explain why Martin Young was calling him at the office before Henry had even floated the Tuolomee Square plan.

Damn it, Julia, he thought. The remnants of her perfume—Shalimar, he knew because he bought her a replacement bottle each Christmas—stuck to the passenger seat beside him. These things—the "unfortunate incidents," the results of her "overinvestment"—had dogged them over the years. There had been the rec soccer T-shirt debacle, for one. Julia insisted that Tracy's team have orange shirts, their daughter's favorite color at the time. Several players cried when Julia's rush custom order arrived, and she'd tried to take the kids' original green jerseys away.

Five years after that, when Andrew had decided to try out for the seventh-grade play, Julia had immediately become the volunteer head of the running crew and disappeared for two straight weeks into tech rehearsals.

And so, over time, Henry had excused himself from the kids' activities—Julia had it covered. He dutifully showed up when she put games and performances on his calendar. He asked the kids light-hearted questions at family dinners.

And he'd been called in to smooth things over. ("I'm calling *you*, Mr. Abbott," the nervous math teacher had said, "because Mrs. Abbott seems especially invested in Tracy's understanding of quadrilaterals.") In the case of Melissa Young, Henry's role had expanded to keeping lawyers at bay with magnanimous apologies.

Of course, it was no surprise that Julia took charge. Her bluster, in fact, was what attracted Henry. The first time he'd seen her, she'd been eviscerating a TA in English 101 at the University of Minnesota, the lecture hall packed with two hundred students.

Julia's arm had seemed hyperextended from her shoulder as she waited to be acknowledged. Her slim body leaned over her desk; her nose rose in a point. She sat in the row in front of him, dead center. From his place on the right, Henry couldn't keep his eyes off of her. It was as if a spotlight illuminated her alone in the brown and musty classroom. The TA, though, had avoided making eye contact with her as long as he could.

"I have a question," she said to the nervous grad student, voice firm. She didn't wait for a reply. "What specific passages in Emerson's 'Over-Soul' led you to the conclusion that the dissolution of the human ego is inevitable? Because I feel that sentiment is more thoroughly asserted in 'Self-Reliance.'"

Henry's mouth had fallen open.

"Uh," said the TA.

"I read in the *Norton Anthology*," the girl continued, "and in the *Journal of Literary Theory* that the transcendentalists were essentially concerned with the relationship of the self to the environment. And how can we divorce ego from that?"

After class, Henry double-timed it across the quad to keep up with her. She was alone and clipping along, perhaps toward the student union. Could he luck into a lunch date?

"Hi," he'd called when he'd managed to catch up. She looked at him, her nostrils flaring. She didn't say anything and, after a brief pause, kept walking. "Uh, hi?" he tried again, hurrying along beside her. "I'm Henry Abbott. I'm in your English class."

She gave him a barely perceptible nod.

"It seems like maybe you should be teaching the class," Henry blazed on. "You certainly did your homework on Emerson."

Henry thought he noticed a tiny smile then. "I just think that if you're going to teach a course at a university, even if you're just a grad student, you ought to be prepared," she said.

"Obviously," said Henry. "You seemed to know quite a lot more than that guy." She smiled for real. He saw teeth, straight and gleaming. "Are you going to lunch?" he offered.

"No," she said. "I'm checking my mail, and then I have to study for my Calc quiz. Are you good at math?"

"Not particularly," said Henry honestly.

"Hmm," she said.

"Well," he continued, sensing the end of their conversation, "maybe I'll see you in class on Thursday?"

Julia smiled again. "I like to sit in the middle," she said.

Was that an invitation?

She tugged her backpack straps and kept talking. "What did you say your name was? Henry?"

He nodded at her. "Yes," he said, sticking out his right hand. "What's yours?"

She put her cool palm against his and shook firmly. "I'm Julia," she said. "I go by Julia. Not Jules or Julie or anything else."

"Okay," he said, turning toward the union. "I'll see you in class on Thursday, Julia. In the middle."

ISOBEL JOHNSON

Isobel's handouts were halfway printed when Mary Delgado, the English department chair, sidled up to her at the copy machine in the teacher workroom. "Another apostrophe-appreciation day?" Mary said.

Isobel smiled. "Not this time. We're working on introductory adverbial clauses." Mary nodded, but Isobel sensed hesitation. "What's up?" she prompted. She grabbed the copies from the output tray and tapped them on the top of the machine to align the edges.

"Can I walk with you?" Mary's smile faltered a bit.

"Of course," said Isobel.

"So, I've fielded a couple of phone calls about your American Lit curriculum." The two headed for the stairs.

"Really?" Isobel's eyes focused on the ground in front of her. Her black wedges flashed beneath her wide-leg trousers.

"You're sticking to the assigned texts, aren't you?" Mary asked.

"What do you mean?" Isobel asked quizzically. "Of course I'm sticking to the assigned texts. We're in the middle of *Gatsby*."

Mary tugged at her floral scarf. "Have the discussions gone okay?" They stopped in front of Isobel's classroom. Isobel hoped their conversation would end quickly, but Mary followed her inside and sat at a student desk.

"Mary," said Isobel, taking an adjacent one, "what's this about?"

Mary sighed. "You know how this community can be."

The department chair looked defeated, Isobel thought, her dark eyes tired, a smudge of mascara above her right cheekbone. "What are they saying this time?" She thought back to last year's debacle: a hullaballoo over a sex scene in a book she'd assigned for summer reading. Lyle had strongly objected to the choice, but Isobel forced it and, for once, Eleanor agreed. When the complaints rolled in, Lyle forwarded them to Isobel without comment.

Mary continued. "They're saying that you're making kids feel bad about where they're from."

"What?" Isobel squinted. How in the world had she managed that?

"Did you compare Liston Heights to East Egg? Did you tell the juniors that their lives are"—Mary looked down at her notepad and flipped back a page—"frivolous?" Isobel frowned and shook her head. "Did you compare the Sadie Hawkins dance to Gatsby's lawn party?"

Isobel sat for a moment, gazing at the "Read Every Day" poster above her whiteboard. She blinked. *Shit,* she thought. It had been last week during fifth period. She had been suddenly struck by the indulgences she'd witnessed at the dance—the rented shuttle buses with chauffeurs, the brand-new and never-to-be-worn-again costumes and accessories, the over-the-top dinners at Liston Heights' fanciest restaurants beforehand. When she'd read aloud the passage from chapter three about the heap of decimated lemons and oranges in Gatsby's weekly garbage, she couldn't help drawing the comparison. The waste of it all—couldn't the kids see it? Didn't they want a little more authenticity in their lives and less of the veneer that would crumble at its first test? Isobel knew the danger of false appearances too well. She wanted her students to slough theirs before they moved beyond her classroom.

"We talked about the frivolity of life," Isobel admitted, her neck suddenly itchy. "I encouraged them to think about what really matters." She met Mary's eyes. "I let them draw whatever conclusions they wanted to draw about what's really important. Isn't that the heart of *Gatsby*, anyway? Authenticity?"

Mary smiled sadly. "Your aims are admirable, but the parents are concerned about ideas that they consider to be radical."

"Radical?" Isobel bristled. "Connecting literature we read in class to their own lives is radical?" A puff of air escaped her lips as she registered the absurdity of the charge. She looked at the ceiling for a beat and then back at Mary. Even though she resented the accusation, she knew she needed to get a little radical to shake the kids out of their self-centeredness. That was the whole point of teaching in Liston Heights, the whole reason she'd allowed herself to leave her inner-city job. Her intention was to influence the kids who had the power to make big changes in society. Otherwise, what was she doing here?

"How many parents are we talking about?" she asked.

"It's not really about how many," Mary said gently, reaching a hand to Isobel's desk and placing it over hers. "It's about which ones." Mary patted her knuckles, her fingers limp like cooked spaghetti. "Stick to the curriculum." She stood up and walked to the door.

Mary left, and Isobel felt a coldness in her chest. *Stick to the curriculum for whose benefit?* Isobel thought. So they could all maintain the status quo? So the children of Liston Heights could move back to their suburb as adults and continue their lives in a bubble, never reaching beyond themselves?

And who, Isobel wondered, was behind these complaints? Her teaching hadn't changed significantly in several years, and yet suddenly she had a nasty voice mail on her home phone and a flood of parents bypassing her and complaining to her boss. She knew what Lyle would say when she recounted Mary's warning. He'd tell her to back off. But

Isobel knew she couldn't do that. What if the one kid who needed jarring didn't hear her message because she'd bowed to anonymous threats?

Noise started filtering in from the hallway. Isobel stood and walked to her desk. Her first-period juniors—who apparently felt bad about where they were from—would be here in seven minutes.

JAMIE PRESTON

That afternoon, when the bell had rung in American Lit and most kids were seated, Jamie watched Isobel reposition her Liston Heights lanyard over her turquoise belt. Jamie sometimes observed Isobel teaching during fifth period, the first of her back-to-back preps, always sitting in the empty desk in the back-right corner, the one with "FUCK" carved in all caps just left of center. She ran her fingers over the letters.

The fifth-period observations had turned out to be a solid strategy—she could watch Isobel and then re-create the lessons the next day herself. It relieved a lot of pressure and saved her from having to invent hundreds of new plans. "Let's talk about our perspectives of whiteness in *Gatsby*," Isobel was saying now. She smiled at her students, her wavy hair falling out of the barrette at the crown of her head.

Isobel never shied away from discussions about race. "We have to go there," she'd told Jamie when she'd asked about it the previous September. "I mean," she qualified, "I feel *I* have to as a white teacher in a majority-white school."

Nevertheless, Jamie avoided the conversations. Although she had some credibility with Liston Heights kids, having been a Lion herself just six years before, she was still only twenty-three, not exactly seasoned enough to tangle with hot-button topics.

"Whiteness? Seriously, Ms. Johnson?" Allen Song asked now from the second row. "You don't want to start with Myrtle Wilson splayed on the table?" Those who were paying attention tittered a bit.

"We'll get there," said Isobel, "but let's start here. We've talked before about identifying missing voices." She gestured over her shoulder to the bulletin board, where she'd hung a hand-lettered sign that read, INTERROGATE MULTIPLE PERSPECTIVES. "So, what are the missing voices in Fitzgerald's work?"

Jamie watched Isobel utilize "wait time," that horrible stretch of silence when teachers prayed someone, anyone, would raise a hand. Finally after what seemed like a minute, but was probably only ten seconds, Maeve Hollister's white, freckled forearm rose from her desktop as it often did.

"Maeve?" Jamie could hear the hope in the teacher's voice.

"All of the characters are white," Maeve said.

"Is that explicit in the text?" Isobel thumbed through her own worn copy of the novel. Several students—the usual suspects in the first two rows—followed suit. *Was it explicit?* Jamie wondered. She thought back over the chapters, Jordan and Daisy's white powdery fingers and Tom's startling brutality.

Hands popped up in the front of the room, and Isobel surveyed them. "I'd love to hear from someone who hasn't spoken much this week," she said, scanning. Jamie watched several kids, including her former student Andrew Abbott, duck their heads. Cold-calling—choosing a student who hadn't raised his or her hand—was a practice Mary Delgado encouraged her to try, but Jamie resisted. It was the worst feeling in the world to be on the spot. Isobel used the strategy regularly.

"Erin?" Isobel said. "What do you think?" Erin Warner, who barely spoke except to whisper to her friend Sarah Smith, looked up, panicked. Isobel smiled at her.

"Um?" Erin stalled, flipping pages with desperate concentration.

Jamie cringed as Erin's shoulders tensed. She pulled the handout Isobel had given her from the back cover of her notebook to avoid watching. She'd slid it in without looking at it at the beginning of the hour. Now she saw that the light green paper had the words **Queer Theory and Sexual Binaries** emblazoned across the top in bold font. The subtitle of this new handout read, **Reading Against Heteronormativity.**

Queer theory? They'd introduced feminist theory, of course, and also Marxist, which Jamie regretted. She could see students drooping in their seats as she explained power and privilege and asked them to do a close reading of the scene with the lemons. Isobel seemed obsessed with those lemons.

"It actually seemed to me that chapter seven is more about money?" Erin was saying. "I mean, more about money than race." *Nice dodge,* Jamie thought. She'd noticed that Liston Heights kids were masters at avoidance during Isobel's discussions.

In this case, Isobel went with it. "Okay!" she said cheerfully. "Excellent. Let's talk about who has money and who doesn't."

Jamie read further down on the queer theory handout, perusing questions about Nick's admiration for Gatsby. The worksheet prompted students to reread several scenes, including one in chapter two where Nick wakes up with Mr. McKee after a party in the city. Jamie's stomach dropped as she realized Isobel's aim. **Given your answers above,** she'd typed at the bottom, **what is Nick's motivation for helping Gatsby?**

Clearly, Jamie realized, Isobel planned for students to posit that Nick is gay. A gay infatuation at the heart of the Great American Novel?

Too much, Jamie thought. Parents would flip. The conversation pinged around up front, kids citing passages and building on one another's thoughts much more effectively than they did in Jamie's own classroom. "It's experience," Isobel explained whenever Jamie mentioned her insecurity.

Experience would also be the reason Jamie's teaching position would be cut to part-time. Unless the right people—the mothers Jamie had spent so much time courting—understood how a left-wing litera-ture teacher tried to brainwash their children.

Jamie stared down at the queer theory handout and allowed herself to consider a new idea. Perhaps she wouldn't have to break the news to her own parents that her contract was cut. Maybe getting the right eyes on this handout could outweigh the influence of seniority when Wayne Wallace made his staffing decisions.

ISOBEL JOHNSON

~

At that afternoon's faculty meeting, Isobel scanned the snack table, searching for Chex Mix among the spread of processed comfort foods. Jamie pointed at it over the bowl of Hershey's Kisses. "Bingo," Isobel said. She reached for a plastic cup and scooped some. "Let's get back to the table before Wally starts chanting," she whispered.

Just then Wayne Wallace called, "Hey, gang!" from the front of the library, where he always conducted meetings.

"Too late," Jamie whispered. Wayne clapped twice.

"Oh, crap," muttered Isobel.

"I say 'Liston'; you say 'Lions'!" The women scuttled to a table framed by the fiction collection as the principal began his ritual.

"Make it stop," Isobel said, looking down at her Chex Mix and the single Oreo cookie she'd placed on top at the last minute.

"Lions!" yelled Jamie obediently after the first round of the cheer. Isobel frowned at her. Jamie leaned over and whispered, "I don't have tenure."

Isobel acknowledged this argument with a smile and clapped along.

The sooner everyone engaged, the more swiftly Wayne would stop embarrassing himself. Sure enough, after a good 75 percent of the teachers pumped their fists in rhythm, their principal gestured toward the agenda, written in bullet points on an easel next to the snacks. The first bullet read, *What's going well?*

So very little, Isobel thought, looking up at her boss through a smudge on her right lens. His face was split into an exaggerated grin. She pulled off her tortoiseshells and rubbed them on the edge of the T-shirt she'd layered under her sweater.

Wayne introduced his activity in an overloud voice for the size of the room. "Gang," he boomed over the hundred or so teachers seated before him, "today we're talking about positive communication. What we're going to do is, we're going to start in teams. And we're going to give ourselves a little credit for what we're doing well in the communication department. I've been thinking about it," he said, suddenly philosophical, "and we're world-class professionals here in this room. I know we have a lot to celebrate." Isobel didn't dare look at Jamie, lest she laugh aloud in anticipation of the spot-on impression of this speech Jamie would later give. "So, I want you to get into a triad. Three people"—Wayne thrust three raised fingers toward them for emphasis—"and just really pat yourself on the back for an interaction with a parent or guardian that went just great. What did you do? How can you replicate it?" He scanned the crowd. "Are you with me?"

Isobel turned from Wayne toward the table, immediately uncomfortable. How could she participate in this activity when Mary Delgado had just that morning issued a cryptic warning about several prominent families' complaints? And, in addition, she had the voice mail. It was Isobel's bad luck, then, that Eleanor Woodsley had chosen the seat nearest Jamie and her. Isobel smiled forlornly at her friend Lyle at the other end of the table, who was forced into a partnership with two members of the social studies department. Faculty meetings were always more pleasant when Isobel could whisper her sarcastic comments to Lyle.

Eleanor, on the other hand, would have umpteen pristine parent interactions to share. Better to get this over with. "Anyone have anything to
start with?" Isobel prompted.

"I'll start," Eleanor said. *Of course she would,* Isobel thought. "I had
a lovely conversation with a parent just the other week," Eleanor continued.

"Oh yeah?" Isobel said. "What was the concern?" She dragged her
eyes up.

Eleanor looked unsurprisingly smug. "The mother expressed her
perception that our junior curriculum doesn't adequately cover college-
essay writing, especially as the early-decision applications have to be
completed right away in the fall of the senior year."

"And how did you handle it, Eleanor?" Jamie asked kindly. Of
course, Isobel already knew that Eleanor Woodsley with her white
cardigan and jeweled reading glasses would have handled it impec-
cably.

"I validated the mother's concern, obviously. We all know that
the parents in our community are preoccupied, and justifiably so, with
college acceptance. And I assured her that the skills we do cover—
organization, word choice, proofreading—all support college-essay
writing." She made eye contact—condescendingly, Isobel thought—
with Jamie, the youngest among them by more than ten years. "Finally,
I assured her that the teachers of seniors assign, read, and edit college
essays right away in the fall. And that was it! The mother ended the call
by telling me she's planning to request me as the student's senior teacher."
Eleanor shrugged and smiled.

Oh, barf, Isobel thought. "Well done, Eleanor," she said aloud, and
then she giggled at the incongruity of her impulse and reaction.

Eleanor stared at her, smile fading.

"I'm sorry," Isobel covered. "It's just that I was imagining my own
blunders with parents. In fact, I'm always a bit afraid to make parent
phone calls."

"Phone is always best," said Eleanor, fervent. "When I get an e-mail, I immediately ask for a time to talk on the phone. We need to reclaim human interaction if we want to actually get anything done."

"Yeah." Isobel stuffed a handful of Chex Mix in her mouth and chewed.

"Jamie," said Eleanor, "let's hear your perspective as a newer teacher. What strategies are working for you with Liston Heights families?"

Jamie shook her head. "Honestly, I just try to say yes to whatever the parents want." Isobel stifled another giggle, coughing as a hunk of rye crisp caught in her throat.

Eleanor stared. "What do you mean by that?"

"Usually parents want a pretty innocuous accommodation—a test retake, a deadline extension. It's easier to just say yes."

"I'm sorry," said Eleanor, her pointy chin pitched down, "but don't you think that attitude undermines your authority? What about your professionalism?"

"Eleanor," said Jamie, her voice matter-of-fact, "how much authority do you think I have at age twenty-three in this school?" Isobel felt a rush of pride in her young colleague. She'd come so far, speaking assertively to Eleanor like that! Jamie continued. "I certainly don't want to end up like Peter."

Isobel nodded. Peter Harrington had been a twenty-four-year-old graduate of the University of Michigan's prestigious teaching program, but that hadn't mattered to the gaggle of mothers who complained about his slow grading and questionable social media posts. The poor guy was replaced by Judith Youngstead, a battle-ax of a long-term sub, after a mere six weeks during the previous school year.

"But," Eleanor said, flipping to a clean page in her legal pad and beginning to write a note, probably a reminder to inform on Jamie's grading practices to Mary Delgado.

Isobel felt compelled to interrupt. "Fair enough," she interjected, saving Jamie from further interrogation. The others stared at her, waiting for her to continue. "Speaking of phone calls," Isobel ventured, "have either of you gotten any weird voice mails from parents on your home phone?"

"Home phone?" said Eleanor. "When I call at home, I almost always do that star-six-seven blocking thing so they can't see my number."

"Me, too," Isobel said. "But I got an odd message the other day anyway."

"What did it say?" asked Jamie.

"It was about curriculum." Isobel clung to nonchalance, wishing she hadn't brought it up. She knew Eleanor would be alarmed by the call. Alarmed and also judgmental.

"What about it?" Eleanor pressed.

Isobel inwardly chastised herself for not thinking of a better way to protect Jamie than to open herself to criticism. "Something about sticking to what Liston Heights families expect," Isobel said, twisting the top of her Oreo.

"As opposed to . . . ?" Jamie probed. *Let it go,* Isobel thought.

She popped the top half of the cookie into her mouth, stalling. "Um," she said when she'd swallowed. "Marxism?" Eleanor scowled, and Isobel felt even more desperate to change the subject. "I'm sure the message was an anomaly," she said, chewing. "It seems like most parents are satisfied with their kids' experiences in my class."

"I'm not so sure about that." Eleanor peered at Isobel. "That message just might reflect something bigger."

"What do you mean?" asked Jamie. *Let it go,* Isobel willed again, resisting the urge to kick her under the table.

"I wasn't going to say anything in this setting." Eleanor glanced at Wayne, who appeared poised to signal the end of the activity with another call-and-response cheer. "But I have to admit that some of my senior families said that your American Lit course was"—she paused— "unconventional."

"Unconventional?" Isobel echoed. The Oreo pieces stuck to the roof of her mouth.

"I'll just be frank," Eleanor whispered. "A few people have mentioned, and I'm quoting here, a 'blatant liberal agenda.'"

Isobel felt a bit light-headed. She met Eleanor's gaze and forced the cookie down her throat. Wayne began a rhythmic clapping routine up front. "I guess I'm just unwilling to sacrifice my commitment to social justice to appease Liston Heights parents."

Eleanor looked at her paper and pulled a face. Jamie clapped the same pattern Wayne had demonstrated.

Isobel lingered on Eleanor, who had begun writing the next agenda item on her legal pad, her blond pixie light against the backdrop of paranormal romances on the bookshelf behind her. "It's one thing to have ideals," Eleanor said calmly. "It's another to disregard our established curriculum. That disregard is what families are complaining about, Isobel." Eleanor kept her eyes on her notes, her pen skimming the paper. "And everyone knows you need to pay attention."

JULIA ABBOTT

By three thirty, in the eight hours since her meeting with Wayne Wallace, Julia had the house thoroughly cleaned, including Andrew's repulsive third-floor bathroom and even Tracy's closet. While she was in there, she noticed the dress she'd chosen for her daughter's piano recital last month with the tags still on. Tracy had worn a blue sweater and slacks, despite Julia's surprise gift. "It's great, Mom," Tracy had said, "but I'm more comfortable in pants." Julia hadn't wanted to return the dress, its Empire waist accented with sophisticated cording. She'd worked so hard to find a fantastic winter knee-length. Maybe she could at least get Tracy to wear it to the opening of *Ellis Island*. She considered which color tights would match it as she recycled the three Diet Dew cans she'd lined up on the counter during her cleaning effort.

At school, Andrew would be heading to his first rehearsal. She'd texted him twice that afternoon: How's it going? and Excited for the first day?? She'd punctuated that second text with the jazz hand emoji all the theater moms loved so much.

There'd been no response, not that she'd really been expecting a reply after last night's debacle. She'd nearly spit her prosecco when Andrew had sworn at her. Never had either of her children accosted her like that. And then he'd faced no consequences. Henry had taken Andrew out for dinner, like a celebration for disparaging his mother.

The cans recycled, Julia looked at her to-do list, the neat column of checkboxes and accompanying items recorded in black flair pen in her customized planner. Of course, most of the tasks had become moot the moment Wayne Wallace removed her from the Booster Board.

Should she send the list on to Robin Bergstrom? Julia opened her messaging app and read once again the response Robin had sent to her text. I'm really sorry about how this happened. When Wayne asked me, I felt I had to do my part.

That was all.

Julia resented her diplomacy, and a melancholy had overtaken her after she'd rinsed the sponge for the final time. She remembered Henry's admonishments, his "Don't text Robin" directive. As if Henry or Robin knew what it took to stage a high school production, to raise the funds needed for a first-class program. No, she'd been the one to learn the ropes and target the department's needs over the past two years. She'd gotten up at four a.m. to mark the course of the annual 5K. She'd ordered the shirts and drafted the budget. She'd been the one to suggest the costume shop as the perfect use for the remainder of Henry's unexpected distribution payment last spring. And she'd been the one to place the call to Wayne to remind him that it was Andrew's turn, really, to appear on the Liston Heights stage in a significant role.

She looked from the to-do list to a photo on the front of the stainless steel refrigerator door, of Andrew, Maeve Hollister, and Allen Song at last fall's one-act festival, their arms around one another, Andrew's smile the broadest she'd seen it.

Julia looked back at her list. The one item she couldn't pass on, regardless of what she decided about contacting Robin again, pulsed at her from the page. *Call the Youngs,* her handwriting read, the box next to it conspicuously void of a checkmark. Just the thought of picking up the phone made Julia feel nauseated. Despite her involvement in the theater department, she and Annabelle Young weren't particularly close. And Wayne mentioned that someone—who? Certainly not Robin?—had repeated Julia's assessment of Melissa's performance in *Witches over Willow Street*. She recalled that night at the Percys' holiday party when she'd made the comments about Melissa's untrained alto. She'd also said something about the size of the girl's feet, she knew, but had she pointed out the wooden quality of her delivery? She could picture an empty second glass of wine. Probably she had.

Oh, God, Julia thought, dread overtaking her.

During her cleaning blitz, Julia had rehearsed the call a few times. Now she ducked into the powder room off the kitchen. She ran her own dialogue once more while watching herself in the mirror. "Annabelle?" she intoned. "It's Julia Abbott calling. Yes, hello. Listen, I need to tell you, I'm so terribly sorry for the misunderstanding at school yesterday." Julia gave herself a tiny nod. Her voice sounded steady and sincere. *Okay,* she thought, breathing in through her nose. "It's time."

Julia marched back into the kitchen and picked up her cell phone from the counter where she'd left it. A text from Henry lit the screen: How'd the call go? *Hold your horses,* Julia thought. She referenced the notes section of her planner, where she'd written Annabelle Young's number, retrieved from the Booster database, which Julia herself maintained. She dialed.

Four rings, and then a woman's "Hello?"

Julia cleared her throat and began just as she'd practiced, only maybe a little bit faster. She uttered "misunderstanding," and then allowed herself a breath. Meanwhile, Annabelle paused, making a nondescript "ah" sound. Julia's mouth felt sticky as she waited for the other woman to speak.

"I appreciate the call," Annabelle said finally.

"Absolutely," Julia said.

"Both Martin and I"—Annabelle's voice grew louder in her ear—"well, we both really wish this had never happened."

"I completely agree." If Annabelle understood that the whole thing was an accident, perhaps she could steer the woman toward encouraging Wayne to reverse the board suspension?

"I have to say, I haven't stopped thinking about what happened since Melissa called me crying from John Dittmer's office after the incident."

"She was crying?" Julia sank onto a kitchen stool. She noticed a damp smell and realized she'd forgotten to take out the compost.

"Yes. Melissa was embarrassed and in pain. And all of this on what should have been a very happy afternoon for her." There was no mistaking Annabelle's anger now.

The conversation probably wouldn't be headed toward a board reinstatement. "I'm so sorry." Julia felt helpless. It occurred to her to congratulate Annabelle on Melissa's behalf, but as she opened her mouth to do it, she found that she hadn't even registered her assigned role. Her elation over finding Andrew's name overshadowed every other memory of the scene. "She's really a terrific actress," Julia offered.

"Look." Annabelle's voice became a shout. "Things have gotten completely out of hand. First, you publicly criticized Melissa's work in *Witches over Willow Street*—"

Julia sat up straight, her cheeks warm. "I didn't."

Annabelle's voice went cold. "We both know you certainly did."

Julia tried again. "I'm not sure where you heard that, Annabelle, but I assure you that I respect Melissa's talent very, very much." Julia thought she heard a *humph* from the other end of the line, but Annabelle didn't say anything further.

"Annabelle," Julia ventured, "what else can I say except that the whole thing was a terrible accident? I obviously didn't mean to hurt Melissa. I only meant to zip into the theater wing, check to see which role Andrew was given, and sneak back out. I got—" She paused. "Well, the bell rang, and there were so many students crowded around."

Annabelle laughed then. "Checking to see which role Andrew was given, Julia? Do you mean which role you bought for him?"

"What?" Julia felt her own anger heightening. How could Annabelle suggest that Andrew hadn't earned the part? That he hadn't paid his dues?

"Anyone can see through the costume shop," Annabelle said. "Andrew's inspector will probably be the most expensive minor speaking role anyone's ever performed on the Liston Heights stage."

"I have no idea what you're talking about." Julia heard herself going shrill. "And can we get back to the heart of the matter?" She didn't wait for a response. "I'm calling to apologize for an unfortunate accident. I would never purposely hurt a child. I'm wishing Melissa well in the play, and I'm looking forward to her performance." *The end,* Julia thought.

"Okay." Annabelle sounded snide. "Thanks for the call."

"You're welcome," she said.

"I'd say I'll see you at the Booster Board meeting," Annabelle added, "but I hear you're taking some time off." Julia's eyes bulged, and her chin dropped. She was trying to be gracious! Only the most ungenerous person would gloat over her suspension. "I think that's an excellent idea." The anger had vanished from Annabelle's voice, replaced by faux sweetness. "You could really use a big, long break."

Julia pulled the phone from her ear and gave the red end button a decisive push. She felt a buzzing in her forehead and stood still, staring into the backyard through the sliding-glass door in the kitchen. Snow crusted over her favorite hydrangea, last year's blooms brown and dry beneath the drift.

When her heartbeat had slowed, she walked back to the powder room and splashed cold water on her face. She stared at herself again in the mirror. This time she noticed the gray patch beneath each blue eye. She reached an index finger up to touch one, papery with a little give. Julia flicked off the lights. She grabbed her phone from the counter. *It's done,* she tapped to Henry.

Back to business, she thought. Julia sank onto her stool and flipped open the cover of her MacBook Air to begin an e-mail to Robin. She'd send the documents for tomorrow's board meeting after all, let them see all of the work she'd done. If they didn't start publicizing the 5K, it wouldn't raise money, and she didn't want Andrew's big chance attached to a subpar production. Julia's fingers hovered over the keyboard for a beat before she started typing. **Dear Robin,** she began, **I'm attaching a folder of crucial Booster files, as well as to-dos for the fundraising subcommittee. I'm assuming, as my replacement on the board, you'll also be taking care of the annual fun run.** She paused. Just the thought of Robin planning a fund-raiser seemed laughable, and she felt a smile forming despite the stress of the phone call. **As you may not be aware,** she continued, **we're facing a budget shortfall due to the overages on the sets from the one-act festival. Who would have thought the giant apple tree could have required so many materials? Anyway—**Julia built to her closing—**I'm sure you'll come up with something, and the 5K will go off without a hitch. Break a leg!**

She clicked SEND. *Done,* she thought. *And good luck managing all of that without me.* She scanned her in-box before closing her laptop and paused on a notification from Facebook. **Lisa Lions has tagged you in a video,** the message title read.

Oh, shit, Julia thought. It had been bad enough that the video at the drama board had been circulating via Instagram and group text, but at least most of the parents lacked direct access to those things. If it was on Facebook, her entire circle would see it. And it was posted by Lisa Lions? Julia didn't actually know who that person was—the username was obviously not a real one, the last name the mascot of Liston Heights High School. But she'd friended the "woman" that fall to gain access to a secret Facebook group that many of the other mothers had joined. "A Behind-the-Scenes Look for Parents Who Need to Know," "Lisa" had called it. And it was true she'd enjoyed some of the posts there— little tidbits about faculty skirmishes and gossip about who took the longest to grade geometry finals. She and the other theater moms, Annabelle Young included, had laughed about it at many Booster meetings.

Hands shaking now, Julia clicked the link from her e-mail. She lowered her head to the kitchen counter as she saw the footage there at the top of the Inside Liston group page. Lisa Lions, her avatar the athletic department's logo, had written, **Your kids have all seen it, but have you? It's Moms (or rather just one mom in particular) Gone Wild at the drama board.** And then the bitch had tagged her, Julia's name highlighted in blue. Julia looked to the upper-right-hand corner of her screen, her notifications accumulating as other users had added their comments on the video. She had nine so far.

The very definition of "going too far," someone named Sheila Warner had written.

Was that poor girl hurt? someone else asked, to which Lisa Lions responded, **Bruising to the abdomen and of course the shock and embarrassment of getting wrecked by your costar's mother.**

Julia stopped reading right there.

ANDREW ABBOTT

Andrew pushed through the vestibule into the theater, and the door whooshed closed behind him. The front rows overflowed with cast and crew members talking loudly and laughing, everyone waiting for the start of *Ellis Island*'s first rehearsal. Andrew recognized Melissa Young's chin-length black hair immediately. She leaned forward in her seat, chatting with Anika Bergstrom. Andrew willed himself down the aisle, placing one Converse deliberately in front of the other. Behind Melissa and Anika, Allen Song dipped his head toward Maeve Hollister, pointing out something in the script. Andrew touched his back pocket, making sure his copy was still there.

When he was close enough to the front, he ducked into a row by himself. His leg immediately started to jiggle, and his palms felt damp. He looked at the concrete floor. The residue of a wad of gum, stained brown around the edges, poked out from the seat in front of him. A minute later, the directors walked onstage. "Gang!" Mr. Dittmer shouted.

The noise from the group diminished. "We've arrived at one of my favorite moments. You've all worked hard to be here, and I know you're as committed as I am to making *Ellis Island* a powerful theatrical experience." He paused, surveying the students. Tryg Ogilvie sat in the center of the second row, his head six inches above everyone else's. Andrew felt a wave of anger, and his eyes narrowed at the back of Tryg's head. *Thanks for the Instagram post, asshole,* he thought. As if things hadn't been bad enough. And then, that morning, Andrew had seen Tryg's photo on the Humans of LHHS Instagram account, a hand in his light brown hair, head cocked toward the drama bulletin board with the pink cast list out of focus behind him. "Of course I'm thrilled to be one of the only ninth graders in the cast," the blurb began. Tryg already had 412 likes, and at the same time, the video posted on his own account was everywhere.

"We're going to start," said the director, "with a time-honored tradition in the theater. The read through." He paused, lifting his copy of the script in the air and smiling. "When I'm finished talking here, the crew will meet Ms. Thompson in the lobby. The rest of you cast members will join me onstage with your scripts."

Andrew lifted his hip and pulled his copy from his pocket. He flipped to his first line on page four. "'Good day, sir,'" he repeated to himself. That was it. Easy enough.

"The goal is to get oriented," Mr. Dittmer said. "Just to hear the words in our mouths and see each other's faces. Ms. Thompson?" He smiled, glancing at her. "Do you have anything to add?"

"Nope," she said cheerfully. "Let's do it!"

"Okay, then!" Mr. Dittmer waved the actors onstage with his clipboard. Andrew waited until most of the kids had moved in their assigned directions. Then he stood, his mouth uncomfortably dry. Melissa took Allen Song's outstretched hand to help her up from the orchestra pit while Andrew chose the stairs, grabbed a chair from stage right, and dragged it toward the circle that was forming in the center. He aimed for a spot next to Maeve, at whom he smiled nervously.

Maeve smiled back. "Hey," she said to him. "Yeah, sit next to me."

A momentary relief relaxed Andrew's shoulders. "Thanks," he said, and then when he was close enough, he whispered, "I'm kind of nervous."

"It's gonna be okay." Maeve leaned back toward him. "No one thinks it's your fault."

"Are you sure? I mean, I've been worried."

"I talked to Melissa about it." Maeve patted Andrew's knee with her book. "You weren't even there."

"But—" Andrew's chair scuffed the stage.

"Look," Maeve said, "I know it sucks, but everyone knows your mom is a total psycho." She offered a sympathetic smile. "That's not on you."

ISOBEL JOHNSON

In the parking lot the next morning, Isobel dug in her tote for mascara. She flipped open the mirror on the driver's-side sunshade and swiped a coat on each eye, pushing her glasses back into place once she'd finished. She inspected her hair—only slightly poofy today—and exited the van, bag over her shoulder. There were copies to make for first period, but with twenty-nine minutes to spare, she couldn't help thinking she was golden. She smiled to herself. Surely, she'd picked up that "golden" expression from the kids, either her own or her students.

When she reached the door, she paused to check her outfit in its reflection. Her green A-line skirt was unwrinkled, her blouse trendy beneath her hip-length down jacket. Her sister, Caroline, had even sent a note with this top—*Try it with last season's green skirt*. Isobel wondered what she'd do without Caroline's seasonal hand-me-downs. Both times she'd needed maternity sizes rather than the usual sixes or eights, she'd caught Mark frowning at her outfits over their morning coffee.

"You could spend a little money on your own clothes," he'd said just once, but she shook her head. The maternity items were from Savers, and she'd already told him any extra cash was going in equal amounts to a new account for their children and to the Rochester Area Charitable Foundation, to which she made a monthly contribution. Mark knew enough to drop it. Isobel had been happy to lose the pregnancy weight from Riley rather quickly, though, because in her first Grow and Glow at LHHS when the baby was six months old, she'd been wearing some oversized pilled-acrylic trousers with an elastic waistband. Mary Delgado had told her that Liston Heights parents really expected more professional attire. *That* had been humiliating, but she'd gotten the message.

She pulled open the door. As Isobel's eyes adjusted to the light, she made out Eleanor Woodsley and Mary Delgado huddled in conversation just beyond the door to her classroom. A twinge of trepidation zinged from her collarbone, and a reflexive broad smile overtook the lower half of her face.

Would Eleanor be recounting Isobel's story about the voice mail? She watched Mary catch sight of her. "Good morning!" sang Isobel as she rummaged in her tote for her lanyard. The bag's straps slipped from her shoulder, and she braced against the weight of it as it fell to her elbow.

"Do you need help?" Mary said, squinting at her.

"Oh, no." Isobel shook her head. "I've got it." She felt the key turn in the lock, blew stray hairs from her left cheek, and pushed inside. The fluorescent lights, set on a sensor installed the previous spring by members of the Environmental Club, began their familiar flicker, and Isobel lurched toward her desk.

No sooner had she kicked off her right boot than Mary peered through the tempered glass rectangle on the door.

"Knock, knock!" she called.

Isobel waved her boss in. "Hey," she said, dipping her head down below the lip of her desk and flicking off her second boot. A ring of road salt, tracked in from the parking lot, outlined the spot where she always left them. "How's it going?" She straightened, smoothing her hair again as Mary walked toward her.

"I was really wondering how things were going with you." She slid into a student desk.

Isobel raised an eyebrow. "Fine," she said. "Why do you ask?"

"Eleanor was just mentioning your discussion at the faculty meeting yesterday."

Isobel reached down again, this time pulling her laptop from its sleeve. "It's nothing," she said. She flipped the MacBook open and impatiently typed her credentials. Isobel hoped that if she avoided eye contact, Mary would just leave.

"I'm actually wondering . . ." Mary trailed off. Isobel peeked over the silver frame of her computer screen. "I'm wondering, Isobel, if that voice mail that you mentioned to Eleanor is actually part of a larger pattern."

Isobel sucked in an openmouthed breath. "A pattern?" she echoed. Mary had mentioned parent complaints just twenty-four hours ago, and then Isobel had been stupid enough to confess the voice mail at the faculty meeting.

"The rumblings I've been hearing," Mary said, "some concerns shared by your colleagues, *and* a voice mail at home from a parent . . ."

Isobel bristled; a spark of fear and anger ignited her lungs. She'd seen what happened when parents homed in on a teacher with their complaints. They snowballed. Peter Harrington was just the most recent example. "Concerns shared by my colleagues?" Isobel repeated. "You mean, Eleanor's concerns?"

"Eleanor is concerned," Mary confirmed. "She shared with me this morning that you received a disturbing message on your home phone." Isobel opened her mouth to explain, but Mary carried on. "And Eleanor and I have both noticed the discrepancies between your syllabus and hers when you're supposedly teaching the same course."

"Since when does Eleanor Woodsley have sole ownership and decision-making power over the Liston Heights American Literature curriculum?" She forced herself to take a deep breath. *Calm down*, she thought. Yelling at Mary would only set her back—provide another example of perceived instability.

"Of course she doesn't," Mary said. "But, as you know, at Liston Heights, we say that kids are taking a *course* with *standards—*"

"I address all of the standards!" Isobel felt panicky; her rigid fingers hovered over her keyboard. She looked to her right, where she actually had the curricular standards for eleventh-grade American Literature taped to the cinder block, checkmarks in various colors of ink indicating that she'd assessed them.

"I'm here to support you," Mary said, raising both hands, a finger on her left catching the filmy end of her scarf.

It didn't feel supportive, this drop-in conversation. It felt more like an ambush. Isobel looked down and clicked the attachment for the queer theory activity she needed to copy. "Mary," she said, "I really have to get something copied before the bell."

"Here's what I'm going to do," Mary said, standing. "I'm going to spend a few hours in here today during your American Lit classes. That way, I'll have context for addressing the inquiries I've received."

Isobel's chest felt hot. Inquiries? Plural? She'd been holding out hope that it was just one. And now this impromptu meeting followed immediately by an hours-long observation with no warning? Usually, Mary scheduled her visits at least a week in advance. Drop-ins were for teachers who struggled. Everyone knew that. Peter Harrington had endured several in the weeks before he went on fall break and never came back. "You're going to spend *hours* in here?" Isobel asked.

"It's for your benefit. And," Mary added, facing away, "it's my job."

Isobel ducked her head behind her computer again and clicked PRINT. "I have to print something," she said. She felt tears threatening and clicked on her e-mail to buy herself another few moments. After pretending to read something, she looked up, more composed.

"Where would you like me to sit?" Mary surveyed the room. A trio of spider plants sat atop the bookshelves near the windows, Isobel's lame attempt at something green.

"Why don't you sit right here?" Isobel indicated her own chair as she stood. "First hour is crowded."

"Oh, no," Mary began. She glanced toward a spot in the back corner, beneath the healthiest of the plants.

"No," said Isobel. "If I have perfect attendance, there won't be space." She paused, tears catching again. She reached under the frames of her glasses to wipe her lower eyelid. "You'll be comfortable in my chair. I'll be right back," she mumbled.

While she was on her way to the office, Lyle stuck his head into the hallway as Isobel passed. "What did Mary want?" he whispered, conspiratorial.

Isobel slowed for a second. "Can you walk with me?"

"Sure." His oxfords slapped the linoleum as he caught up to her.

"Mary plans to spend several hours in my room today," Isobel blurted. "She didn't schedule in advance. She says it's for my own good." She glanced up at her friend. He took a deep breath and kept his eyes on the floor, his silence stretching uncomfortably. "What?" she demanded. "Isn't that ridiculous?"

Lyle took several more steps before answering. "Are you still doing those lessons about Marxism and feminism? The multiple-perspectives stuff with *Gatsby*?"

Isobel swallowed. Of course she was doing the "multiple-perspectives stuff," as he called it. That was her primary purpose—to get kids to see literature and the world in new ways. "Of course I am," she said.

"That's your problem," Lyle said. "Give it a rest for a while. This community isn't ready for it. You've got to dole out your liberalism in small increments."

"Lyle!" Isobel exclaimed. "It's not liberalism; it's the truth! The kids need to know!"

He put a hand on her shoulder, and she resisted the urge to shrug it off. "I'm on your team," Lyle said. "Always! But you don't need to go wholesale." Isobel looked at the floor. "Incremental is good, too. Follow Eleanor's or my syllabus for a couple of weeks, and this will all calm down."

"Okay," Isobel said, walking away from Lyle as he slowed.

"Hey, I've got to return a couple of e-mails before the bell."

She waved over her shoulder. "See you later."

In front of the Xerox machine, she considered tossing the queer theory follow-up discussion questions in the recycling bin. She could take Lyle's advice and improvise a lesson on subject-verb agreement for the department chair's benefit instead.

But she shook her head. *Courage,* she told herself. She wasn't at Liston Heights to teach about grammar. She came here to make a tangible difference in the trajectories of these kids' lives. She came here to show students that when people think only of themselves, they make terrible and dangerous decisions.

She put her handout on the glass of the copy machine and hit the start button.

Back in her classroom with ninety seconds to spare and kids arriving, Isobel watched as each of the students noticed Mary Delgado at the teacher desk. She herself stood near the door, greeting the teenagers. Despite the awkwardness of Mary's presence, Isobel valiantly peppered her hellos with questions about the kids' activities, hoping her boss would notice the personal connections she'd forged with them. "How was hockey last night?" she asked one girl. "How was the first crew meeting for the musical?" she queried another.

The bell rang, and she called for attention. A sourness rose in the back of her throat. She could still change her mind—give kids time for journaling and use the seven minutes of their silence to dream up an alternative plan. *Cowardly,* she thought to herself. "Let me tell you what we're up to today," she began, chatter still rising from the crowd.

"Shhhhhhh," the rule follower in the first row blasted. The girl whipped her hair around to target her loudest classmates in the back.

"Thank you, Susan." Isobel smiled. "Okay." She tugged her skirt down with her free hand, as she gripped her fresh copies. "Last night I asked you to read and annotate a handout." She smiled playfully at the class. After all these years, she had been an expert at faking a cheerful teaching persona even when things went sideways in her own life. "Today," Isobel continued, "I want to go back a little ways in the novel and look at some events through that new lens. Do you remember when we talked last week about chapter two?" She stepped toward the whiteboard and could see Mary in her peripheral vision, her boss typing madly.

The trusty front-row pet's arm shot up. "Susan." Isobel called on her.

"You mean, when we talked about feminism?"

"Exactly. What about feminism did we discuss?" She waited. Students flipped through their notebooks, and within seven or eight seconds, a few tentative arms cleared their desktops. She pointed at Charles.

"Uh," he began, "we talked about how the men, especially Tom, have the power in the scene. And, uh . . ." Isobel willed him to continue. She sensed he'd have an answer that Mary would appreciate, despite her criticisms. "And it especially showed when Tom actually broke Myrtle's nose," he finished.

"Yes," Isobel said, noting with pleasure that Mary nodded at her computer screen. "Okay," she continued, "and this next part may require you to take a look in your books or take out that primer I gave you in class yesterday."

"You mean the queer theory thing?" blurted Clayton, a stocky kid with hat hair, his emphasis on the "queer." At this, she detected a twitch from Mary.

"That's right." Isobel glanced at the three spider plants behind Clayton and felt suddenly calmer. Why shouldn't she ask kids to think about Nick's sexuality? The whole book hinged on sexual attraction. She'd just had a positive Grow and Glow with Mary. Even if her boss questioned this particular tactic, no one could claim she wasn't in good standing. "So," she continued, "do you have your books turned to chapter two? What's Nick doing at the end of that scene? What motivates Nick to be there at all?"

She waited. She could see a realization forming behind Clayton's eyes. "Wait a second," he said, staring at his book and then back at the definition of "queer." "Wait a second, Ms. Johnson." Other kids in his row turned toward him, and Isobel held still. She could feel his idea congealing. "Ms. Johnson," he said, "are you saying that Nick is *gay*?"

Isobel smiled and began distributing the set of analysis questions. "I'm saying"—she punctuated her sentence by putting a sheet firmly on Clayton's desk—"let's talk about it."

Mary's eyebrows shot up. Isobel gave her an unreciprocated half smile, and the boss adamantly resumed typing.

When the bell rang to signal the end of first period and the kids walked out the door, some thanking Isobel for the lesson, Mary finally closed her laptop.

"Well?" Isobel said.

"How do you think that went?" quizzed Mary.

Isobel looked at the bright white snow on the track beyond the window, its icy surface reflecting the sunlight. The anger and frustration she'd experienced that morning had dissipated during the discussion, during which every child had participated. Isobel knew for sure, with the benefit of experience behind her—eight years in this very classroom at Liston Heights High—that the lesson had been solid.

"Mary," Isobel said with a smile, "it went great."

"How so?" she said, stony.

The first of next period's ninth graders, Tracy Abbott, appeared at the door. Isobel smiled at her through the window and raised a finger. *One minute,* she mouthed. She turned back to Mary. "You saw it," Isobel insisted. "Every kid, Mary—all thirty-four in this class—spoke! Everyone was engaged! Their books were open. They read passages with care and for deeper meaning." Isobel gestured, rather too passionately, at the empty student desks before her.

Mary sighed. "So you're going to teach that lesson all day, then?"

"Why wouldn't I?"

Mary glanced at the growing gaggle of first years—Isobel herself had led the charge at Liston Heights to formally discontinue use of the sexist term "freshmen"—and then back at Isobel. "I'll be back for your fifth-period class," she said.

Isobel headed for the door; her students would be blocking the flow of traffic in the hall.

"If I were you," Mary said, zipping her laptop sleeve and sliding out from behind the teacher desk, "I'd consider toning it down this afternoon. For your own sake."

TRACY ABBOTT

Tracy raced to English 9 that morning, anxious to see Ms. Johnson, and she ended up having to wait for a moment in the hallway. There wasn't anything in particular she wanted to discuss with her. Rather, she just liked being in her room. Unlike her mother, Ms. Johnson never scanned her outfits, assessing fit or flattery, and she never reached out to fix her hair. Not that teachers generally did that sort of thing, but still . . . Tracy felt accepted.

During discussions, Tracy found herself gazing at the "Interrogate Multiple Perspectives" sign that Ms. Johnson had taped above the bulletin board, the one to which her teacher so frequently referred. "What's missing?" she'd ask the class as they talked through a short story or poem. Tracy thought extra hard in these moments, yearning to be the one to raise her hand, to provide the answer that provoked Ms. Johnson's obvious pride.

What is *missing?* She'd repeat to herself as she reread the texts. At first, she hadn't been able to identify anything, but as the trimester went on, as they discussed "The Yellow Wallpaper" and "The Story of an Hour," she'd seen it.

"It's women," she'd said in response to Ms. Johnson's familiar query one morning. Women's voices! The realization came like a firework behind Tracy's eyes. Women were missing everywhere, and when they weren't missing, they were focused only on children and family. She kept seeing it in television shows and hearing it on the news her parents watched while they washed dishes. And now, for her "mini-research paper," as Ms. Johnson called their current project, Tracy had chosen the topic of the motherhood penalty.

"What's the motherhood penalty?" Tracy's own mother had asked defensively when she'd leaned over her shoulder and seen the all-caps heading in her notebook.

Tracy had bit her lip and paused. She didn't think Julia would like hearing about the wage gap. She might once again describe her prestigious summer internship in New York City after her junior year in college and recap her short-lived job at that local magazine that still arrived in the Abbott family mailbox each month. She'd say for the zillionth time, "When I looked into your beautiful little eyes, I knew I couldn't let someone else—a stranger in a day care center—raise my children. I had to quit. And I was happy to do it."

Tracy had looked down at her notes. "The motherhood penalty means that women's wages don't recover after taking maternity leaves," she had said quickly. "I'm reading about it for English."

Julia had turned away, and Tracy could tell she was doing that thing where she tried not to say what she was thinking. Tracy could hear the words building up in her throat, little grunts and puffs from her nostrils.

"I'm finished with English now, anyway," Tracy had blurted before Julia could speak. "I'm going to work on geometry for a bit before dinner." She could smell the enchiladas in the oven, her favorite. "It smells awesome."

"Thanks," Julia had said tightly. Tracy had kept her eyes down, hoping the moment had passed, and switched the books in front of her.

Keeping her eyes down was something she didn't bother with in

Ms. Johnson's room. Ms. Johnson stood at the board, her green skirt shifting as she pointed at the question she'd written there: *What is your essential understanding?*

"It's the boiled-down one-sentence version of what you really want to tell your readers," she said. "It's clear, reasonable, and arguable." Tracy scribbled those words in her notebook. "Can we say it together?"

"Clear, reasonable, and arguable," Tracy said along with about half the class.

"Oh, no." Ms. Johnson smiled. "Everybody's going to say it." And the next time, they did.

As Ms. Johnson circulated, checking on students' thesis attempts, Tracy watched her reactions as she tweaked her own, crossing out and adding words. Occasionally, the teacher laughed or smiled. Tracy longed to be one of those students with the perfect thesis statement that thrilled Ms. Johnson. By the time she arrived at Tracy's desk, she'd written, *Women who forsake careers in favor of taking care of children close the door on a lifetime of professional opportunities.*

"Forsake" had taken her several tries, and she'd crossed out "leave," "sacrifice," and "abandon" before landing on it. Tracy held her breath while Ms. Johnson reviewed it, her glasses slipping on her nose as she leaned over. After a moment, she stood and beamed at Tracy. "It's clear, reasonable, and arguable," she said happily. "Let's go with it."

JAMIE PRESTON

Jamie sat at her desk until five o'clock that Friday afternoon, recording grades for a sophomore vocabulary quiz before her eyelids grew irrevocably droopy and her stomach simultaneously hollow with hunger. *It's time to go,* she told herself, and blearily stuffed the ungraded papers into her backpack.

Her down coat zipped, she turned back to grab her copy of *Gatsby*. She'd have to reread the ending over the weekend to prep for next week's lessons. She pushed out into the dim hallway where the garbage can smelled of spoiled milk. Next door, Eleanor Woodsley's room was typically dark. Somehow, Eleanor managed to leave by four each day and still be the most respected member of the department. Jamie plodded past Isobel Johnson's empty room, as well. Isobel's departure was timed to her kids' soccer schedules and her husband's squash matches. She always exuded a harried quality and yet maintained peak productivity. Jamie, on the other hand, struggled with the basics of grading and lesson prep despite an uncluttered calendar.

Earlier that afternoon, Jamie had made up an excuse rather than telling Isobel the truth about why she wouldn't be observing her fifth-period class: There was no way she'd be teaching that queer theory lesson. When Isobel, her head buried in her tote, had asked Jamie whether she'd had any recent flak over the curriculum, Jamie had said no.

"But you have?" she asked.

Isobel had retrieved her *Gatsby* paperback from her bag and turned toward the board. "Rumblings." She uncapped a whiteboard marker. "I was just wondering if it was widespread, but then again, I guess I'm really the only one that teaches the more controversial lessons?"

Jamie hadn't answered for a beat. She let Isobel turn around and begin writing that night's assignment. "I'm still new," she said finally, her voice thin and on the whiny side.

"Have a great day," Isobel had said then, dismissing her.

Before Jamie backed out of her spot in the nearly empty parking lot, she checked her phone. Happy hour? a friend had texted. I'm downtown! Omg, did you see The Bachelor last week? another asked, followed by Coffee this weekend?

Jamie shook her head. Of course she couldn't go to happy hour or watch reality television or meet up for coffee. There were assignments to grade and lessons to plan, always. Even on Friday night. *Were engineers living like this?* she wondered fleetingly, even though she'd tried to be one and failed.

And now, according to Mary Delgado's recent e-mail, even if she did her second-choice job really well, there was still no guarantee that LHHS would keep her for another year. I have to work, she texted back to both friends, with the crying emoji to elicit some extra sympathy.

On Friday night? came one's immediate reply. On Valentine's Day?

Yes, thought Jamie. Or, more likely, early on Saturday morning. She'd be in bed by eight.

ISOBEL JOHNSON

After dinner and the kids' bedtime stories, Isobel padded down the stairs in her Smartwool socks. Mark sat on the couch in front of an episode of *Game of Thrones*, sipping a Jameson on ice. Isobel slid in next to him and rested her head on his chest. At least she had Mark after a day from hell. He wouldn't judge her or suggest she stick to a more vanilla curriculum.

He grabbed the remote and hit PAUSE. "Want to watch something else?" he asked. She appreciated it. He knew she hated the gory violence of his favorite show.

"*West Wing*?" It was an old favorite, a comforting panorama of people who always tried to do the right thing.

"Sure," he said, navigating to Netflix.

Isobel took a deep breath as Apple TV loaded on the screen. "So, something really weird happened at work today."

"Oh yeah?" Mark clicked through to "Recently Watched."

"Yeah." Isobel stared at the pattern on a couch cushion and reached her arm around Mark's chest. "You know my boss, Mary Delgado?"

"The department chair?" Mark confirmed. "Which episode?"

"I don't care. Something from season two?" Mark scrolled through the titles, and Isobel kept talking. "So, Mary came in this morning and, like, demanded to sit in on my American Lit classes all day."

"Why?" Mark asked. "This one?" He stopped on a midseason offering.

"Sure, but wait a second." She sat up and turned toward her husband. "She sat in my room for three class periods, and she kind of warned me." Her arms felt weak, a light headache spreading across her forehead. In all her years at LHHS—and she'd pushed plenty of boundaries—Isobel had never been explicitly warned off a line of inquiry or a teaching practice.

"Warned you about what?"

"First, she told me she was trying to protect me," Isobel said. She absently tugged at the fraying left cuff of her UW–Madison sweatshirt. "And then later she told me to tone the lesson down."

"Tone what down?" Mark asked.

"I was talking about queer theory. It's this idea that literature can perpetuate heteronormativity," she explained. Mark started to smile, as he did anytime she riffed on curricular concepts. "Anyway," Isobel continued, swatting at him, "it doesn't matter. She told me to tone it down. Like, not to talk about homosexuality. She said it was for my benefit."

"Sounds like it's related to the voice mail," Mark said. "Did you tell Mary about the message?"

"No," Isobel said, miserable, "but Eleanor did." She pressed her cheek against Mark. "I mentioned it in a small-group discussion at the faculty meeting." She regretted it all over again. Lyle was always telling her to think things through before she did them. He'd have been especially irritated that she'd spilled the story about the voice mail to protect Jamie.

"Figures." Mark nodded now. He'd heard enough about Eleanor to know she'd be the type to report something to the boss. "Did you get any sense of who in particular might be making the anti-American complaint?"

Isobel glanced at the television, the synopsis of the *West Wing* episode on the screen, an earnest Rob Lowe in the thumbnail. "Mary mentioned that more than one parent complained. Julia Abbott has to be one of them."

"The Sadie's mom," he confirmed. "Well, did Mary say anything at the end of the day?"

"Not really." Isobel blinked. "She just kind of walked out with the kids when the bell rang."

"Well"—Mark pulled her back toward him, and she rested her head once again on his cotton T-shirt—"maybe it's just a wait and see?" He rubbed her arm.

"I guess it is," she said. She pushed her hair away from her face and looked back at the television. "Press play."

ROBIN BERGSTROM

think I'm ready to get started." Robin smiled around the table at Starbucks on Saturday morning. It was her first Theater Booster Board meeting, and Annabelle Young had just pulled up the last chair. She felt a rush of satisfaction, sitting at this table with all of the most influential theater moms. And she was here on her own, rather than as Julia Abbott's sidekick.

"Can I just say," Annabelle began, her voice warm, "that I'm just thrilled you've agreed to take over communications for us this spring, Robin?"

Robin beamed. "It's my pleasure. Anika so enjoyed the fall play and the one-act festival." She looked down at Julia's materials in front of her, any guilt about her friend's displacement quelled by the memory of that "backstabbing" text. Julia, she realized, never really thought about anyone but herself. On the morning after the cast list was posted, Anika had shown Robin the Instagram video of Julia and Melissa Young, and she'd read all of the accompanying comments. **Loosen your Spanx, Mrs. A.** Robin had winced at that one, and then couldn't help giggling.

"Mom!" Anika had scolded.

"Sorry," she'd said, trying to recover. "It's just so unbelievable."

Robin had gotten text messages from several other ninth-grade the-ater moms, too, after the video appeared on the Inside Liston Facebook page. They collectively shook their heads over Julia's behavior and as-sumed that Robin, as her friend, would have the scoop. "I'm sure it was an accident," Robin had responded to each of them. And she was sure it was. This was Julia, after all—overinvolved and unable to mind her own business, yes. Malicious and violent? Rarely, and then only toward school personnel.

Julia fumed about Robin's new role, but could she really expect unquestioning loyalty? After all, she had unceremoniously ditched Robin in last year's theater department 5K, Robin's first, mentioning several times on their way home that she'd finished five whole minutes ahead of her. What kind of adult rubbed in a fun-run victory?

And now Robin sat at the table with Vivian Song, Annabelle Young, and Sally Hollister. There would be opportunities for both her and Anika if she could shape board policy. Maybe increased resources for technical theater, in addition to acting? Stage-managing seminars for Anika over the summer? Sitting here with these women? She felt great about it, regardless of Julia's ire.

Robin smiled at the group. "Should we start with the carpool list?" she asked, tentative.

"I think we should start with the real issue." Vivian leaned toward Annabelle. "How is Melissa?"

Annabelle crossed her arms. "What a disaster."

"I can only imagine the trauma," Sally offered. "And all of this after those unfortunate comments Julia made about Melissa's brilliant per-formance in *Witches over Willow Street*."

"It's inexcusable," Vivian piled on. "I'm assuming we've all seen the video?"

"I think the entire city has seen the video," Annabelle said. "It's on Facebook now. Did you see?" The women nodded. "Martin down-loaded it and sent it to our attorney." Robin's eyes widened. Would the Youngs sue? She supposed she shouldn't have been surprised. "Of course, Martin thought it best to assure Wayne Wallace that we wouldn't be pressing criminal charges. We haven't ruled out a civil suit." Robin raised a finger to her bottom lip, trying to suppress rising glee, and Annabelle noticed her. "I'm sorry, Robin," she said. "Is this making you feel uncomfortable? I know you're friendly with Julia."

Robin shook her head. "You're certainly entitled to your feelings," she said, and then she changed the subject. "Did you also see that handout from the English teacher on the Inside Liston Facebook page? The one about *The Great Gatsby* being gay?"

"Yes!" Sally Hollister laughed a little as she clacked her latte against the laminate table. "I'm a lit major, and I've never heard of such a thing. It's outlandish! Does everything have to be about liberal politics?"

"Allen loves that teacher," said Vivian quickly, her tone defensive.

Annabelle broke in. "Melissa doesn't have Ms. Johnson this trimester, and I'm glad. She has Eleanor Woodsley, who was actually my own teacher at LHHS. Lisa Lions mentioned that Ms. Woodsley's requests for senior English are up because of college essays, which makes sense. I credit her for my own acceptance to Dartmouth."

The table fell quiet then, and Robin figured it was really time to get started. "So," she said, "should we tackle the carpools or the five-K?"

"Let's do both," Vivian said, magnanimous. "Knock out the carpool, and then hammer out the run."

"Fabulous," Robin said. She picked up her sharpened pencil and spread the pages of Julia's materials in front of her.

WAYNE WALLACE

~

Wayne swiped a stack of papers from his mailbox on Monday morning, including a letter-sized envelope emblazoned with the return address and seal of US Senator William McGuire, perhaps the most famous resident of Liston Heights. Just the previous fall, Senator McGuire had presided over a town hall meeting in the high school auditorium. Wayne had sat in the front row and been acknowledged in the "special thanks" section of the program.

The principal thrilled a bit as he pushed a finger under the flap of the envelope and ripped it open. Perhaps the senator wanted to plan another event? Would he then agree to an office tour for the AP Government students that spring? Inside, he found a single sheet on official letterhead. Wayne scanned to the bottom of the page and saw that it was signed not by Senator McGuire himself, but rather by his state director, a woman named Sheila Warner, whom Wayne knew to be an LHHS parent.

This was less exciting than he'd imagined, but still, they'd embossed the letterhead with the official seal. He walked toward his office. When he'd sat down in his black padded chair and retrieved his second green juice of the day from his mini fridge, he began reading.

Dear Principal Wallace,

As you know, I have been an engaged and supportive Liston Heights parent for eleven years. During the past decade, I have had the distinct pleasure of collaborating with a number of top-notch Liston Heights educators. On many occasions, I've connected classrooms—some of which have included my own daughter, Erin Warner, as a student—with various elected officials. Last fall, you and I executed a town hall event held at Liston Heights High School with Senator William McGuire, for whom I serve as state director. As you'll remember, Senator McGuire and his wife, Rita, sent their own children through the Liston Heights school system. I know firsthand that the senator counts our schools as one of the treasures of the state.

It pains me, then, because of my long and happy affiliation with the district, to bring an unfortunate matter to your attention. For many months now, I've been concerned about the pedagogy and professionalism of Isobel J. Johnson, a member of your English department. I checked with the State Licensing Board, and while Ms. Johnson does appear to be properly credentialed, I'm quite certain that her teaching is far below the standard I've come to expect of the faculty. I will outline my specific concerns below, but before I do, I want to point out that this is only my third formal complaint against a Liston Heights teacher. That is to say, I don't take this action lightly. I think, if you'll review the files of Mrs. Margaret Hall and Mr. Peter Harrington, you'll see my complaints mirrored the eventual findings of the administration, and neither teacher continued to be employed by the district following my intervention.

Principal Wallace, you may not be aware that right in your own building, Ms. Johnson is infecting your students—bright and open-hearted young people—with a dangerous, insidious feeling of anti-Americanism. With each classic Ms. Johnson hands to our children, she encourages them, under the guise of "seeing multiple perspectives," to undermine these timeless works of literature. Imagine my surprise, for instance, when my daughter reported to me that Atticus Finch represents white supremacy, rather than being the beacon of justice generations of Americans have known him to be. And now, while reading what is truly a Great American Novel, Ms. Johnson is not only asking what The Great Gatsby *has to say about the American dream, but requiring teenagers to question the sexuality and sexual preferences of the characters. I saw a handout of her suggestive questions posted online.*

Principal Wallace, I'm asking you to investigate Ms. Johnson's methods and sources. I can't be the only Liston Heights parent to object to a teacher of American literature flaunting her own anti-Americanism. Once you've concluded your review of Ms. Johnson's practices, I'd like to meet with you to discuss your findings.

You have my very best wishes,
Sheila Warner
State Director
The Office of Senator William McGuire

ANDREW ABBOTT

~

On Monday afternoon in the theater, Andrew dropped his back-pack on the seat next to Maeve Hollister just before rehearsal. She smiled up at him. "Hey," she said, pencil poised over her *Ellis Island* script.

"Ready for act one, scene one?" Andrew asked.

"I think so!" Maeve said cheerfully. "Looks like you have a couple of big moments."

Andrew straightened an imaginary bow tie and recited his favorite line, " 'If it's all right with you, sir, I'd prefer a group that doesn't speak English.' "

"Someone's been practicing." Maeve smiled. Andrew sat and pulled his copy of the script from the front of his backpack. He set it in his lap and rubbed his bare arms. Heat never seemed to make its way to the auditorium. As his goose bumps relaxed, Andrew peeked at Melissa Young, who sat three rows up, mouthing her lines. "Have you talked to her yet?" Maeve asked. Andrew startled; he hadn't realized she'd been watching. He shook his head and flipped the pages of the script nervously. "She's not mad," Maeve continued. "Just go over there and break the ice."

Andrew tried to ignore the nausea rising in his throat.

"Go!" Maeve urged, looking back at scene one. Andrew watched her write *exaggerated* in the margin next to her opening line. She was probably right—tension between him and Melissa might distract everyone from their performances, and Andrew desperately wanted to fit in with this "lead role" crowd.

"Save my seat," he mumbled. He wandered up the aisle and paused at Melissa's row. "Um, Melissa?" he said. She put a finger on her page, marking her spot, and turned toward him. When their eyes met, hers narrowed slightly.

"Uh," he started. "Hi?"

"Hi," Melissa said, her face softening a bit. They stared at each other for a second, and Andrew tried to smile. Melissa did, too, just at the corners of her mouth. Andrew felt his forearms relax. He realized he'd been holding his hands in fists.

"Melissa," he began again, "I just wanted to say—"

"It's fine," Melissa interrupted, shaking her head. "I know it wasn't your fault."

Andrew breathed. "Thank you."

"I mean," she continued, "some people's mothers have no lives." She looked down at her script again. "They just completely, like, lose themselves in their children." She underlined something and took a breath. Andrew felt his goose bumps return.

Had his mother completely lost herself? Maybe it did seem that way, he thought. She repeated the same stories about her one claim to fame—that internship in New York she'd had in college. And now he couldn't think of any of her interests beyond yoga and him and Tracy. "My mom tried to explain it to me," Melissa said. "I mean, this is why she runs a business from home. Not having your own life, it's sad. And makes you sort of psychotic. So, I know your mom's attack has nothing to do with me, even though she did say those terrible things about my performance in *Witches over Willow Street*."

Andrew felt his mouth drop open. What terrible things had his mother said? Had she said them to Melissa herself? More likely, she'd made some gossipy comment—Andrew had overheard enough of them while she was on the phone—to the wrong person. Melissa kept talking. "And, like, I know her attack didn't have anything to do with you, either. So we're cool." Without waiting for him to reply, she went back to reading.

Andrew's nausea intensified at the word "attack," which he repeated in his head. Would it be fair to call it that? Wouldn't Julia have needed a weapon or something to take it to that level? "Okay." He stepped backward, ready for the conversation to close.

"But like I said," Melissa blurted, "I know it's not your fault."

"Thanks." He turned away and shrugged at Maeve, who was watching.

HENRY ABBOTT

Henry sat with Martin Young at the conference table the next morning and hoped he only imagined the tension building between them. He pushed a dark green pocket folder containing the specs for the Tuolomee Square project toward Martin, who grunted as he flipped it open. As they waited for Henry's partner to arrive, the silence became arduous.

Henry looked at his watch and regretted not more strenuously advocating to postpone this meeting until the cast-list hubbub had died down. But Brenda insisted they begin the process of lobbying the city council, specifically the swing vote.

"If we can't get Martin to green-light the zoning changes, the project's on hold indefinitely. Let's see if he's at least amenable," she'd said, and Henry felt he had no option but to agree. Now it seemed that Martin's recent memory of Julia's bad behavior might sabotage the whole thing before it began.

"How are you?" Henry ventured, testing the mood. Martin began thumbing through the folder, glancing at each page quickly. He didn't look up. *Not a great sign,* Henry thought. He wished he'd invented a reason to sit this one out, even though he and Brenda usually worked the zoning board in tandem.

"I'm just fine." Martin's tone was bland.

"Cold outside?" Henry nodded toward the window, where snow-flakes drifted lazily.

"It's not too bad. Roads are clear."

"Good." Henry steepled his fingers in front of him, and when Martin didn't answer, he repeated himself. "Good." His relief was tremendous when Brenda arrived, her laptop beneath her arm. Her professionalism might lift them out of this.

"Don't get up." She smiled and reached her hand across the table to the city councilman. "Martin," she said, "what's jumping out at you about the proposal so far?"

"I'm wondering about the price range for the rentals," Martin said, not looking at Brenda as she sat, "as well as the concentration of low-income properties near the proposed construction site."

"Great questions." Brenda launched in. "If you'll refer to page six, you'll see we're looking at nineteen hundred per month for the two-bedrooms. Tuolomee Square is not a low-income space. Rather, we're targeting young professionals who will contribute to the Liston Heights economy, as well as the surrounding suburbs." Martin peeled back the pages.

Henry cleared his throat and jumped in. "We're planning a host of amenities aimed at attracting millennials," he said. "Everything from a high-end workout space to events on a social calendar—mix and mingles around the indoor pool."

Martin peered up at him. "What kind of liquor license will you require for those?"

Liquor license? Henry swallowed. He'd never heard of one for a residential space. "I don't think we'll need a commercial license for events limited to residents and their guests." He shifted in his seat. "Do you?"

"I don't know." Martin raised an eyebrow. "Alcohol weakens inhibitions, right? Allows people to say what they mean, even when it's not the politically correct thing?"

"I guess so." *Shit,* Henry thought. They were off the rails already. He avoided eye contact with Brenda, who'd be understandably concerned. He'd try to steer Martin back to Toulomee Square and away from Julia's insufficient inhibitions, which he had almost certainly referenced. "But I'm not sure what kind of liability we'd accept in that case," Henry tried. "Millennial residents will certainly have their own parties on-site."

"The bottom line here is that the Tuolomee Square project will open Liston Heights to a new demographic," Brenda interrupted, more insistent than she had been before. "Provide an affordable way for second- and third-generation residents to follow in their parents' footsteps ten years earlier than they might otherwise be able to."

Henry picked up the ball. "The retail spaces could be filled with coffee shops, maybe a high-end grocery store, a wine bar," he added.

"You an expert on wine, Henry?" Martin's voice had gone even colder. *Damn it,* Henry thought. Something was hanging Martin up on alcohol. But Julia hadn't been drinking when she'd gone to school to look at the cast list. What was he missing?

"Not at all," Henry said, trying to keep it light, and then he realized that it was the comments Julia had made at the Percys' holiday party. The thing about Melissa's large feet. To think a teenager's shoe size could torpedo an entire deal. Well, to be fair, he guessed, it would be Julia who torpedoed it, not Melissa Young's feet.

"Really?" Martin asked. Brenda looked at Henry, perplexed. He'd have to apologize later. Grovel, in fact, to make up for this potential debacle. "Not an expert on wine even with your wife's"—Martin paused—"proclivity?"

Henry put both feet on the floor and sat up straight. He'd give it one last effort before bagging it for today and moving on to the other council members, who might see the value of a younger generation spending their disposable income in Liston Heights. "Martin, can we keep this to Tuolomee Square? If there's something else you'd like to discuss about the"—he rubbed his nose—"the unfortunate incident—"

"Incidents." Martin drew out the "s." "Plural."

Brenda gave Henry a Mayday look. "Okay," she said. "It seems as if—"

"You're right." Martin slammed the folder shut. "It's not the right time. I'm distracted by the situation at home. I'm sure both of you will understand if we reschedule this meeting for another week or so?" He stood, jostling the table. Coffee threatened at the rims of their mugs.

Henry stood as well. "Let me know whether there's anything I can do to ease your mind." He could smell the vanilla creamer Brenda always used, sickeningly sweet.

Martin laughed dryly. "Muzzle your wife?" he said, and Henry blanched. Martin turned to go.

JAMIE PRESTON

All Jamie could think about at her winter performance review that afternoon was whether this was her last one before learning her contract would be cut. "Shall we begin the 'Grow' section?" Mary smiled, seemingly oblivious to Jamie's discomfort. They'd already whipped through "Glow" at lightning speed. Mary's compliments included preparedness for class, punctuality, and appropriate professional attire. "Liston Heights families expect a level of formality," Mary had said once again, as if dressing appropriately were the trickiest and most critical aspect of teaching teenagers. Jamie had looked down at her cashmere sweater, a gift from her parents, and khaki pants. She'd ironed the pants for the occasion of this meeting, rather than fluffing them in the dryer as she usually did. Apparently, that had paid off.

Even though she felt Mary's comments about clothing were endlessly shallow, so much of working at LHHS did seem to be about appearances. Jamie's mother knew this, too, expertly selecting the pencil skirts and blouses she'd purchased for her on their second annual back-to-school trip to Banana Republic. Jamie felt that faking it, at least in the wardrobe department, had kept her insulated from Peter Harrington's fate. Peter had resolutely stuck to untucked flannels and jeans with rolled cuffs. Perhaps Mary hadn't made such a big deal about "appropriate professional attire" with him.

Now, more than a year after the day Peter had been canned, Jamie's mouth tasted stale. The remnants of her lunch, a Thai-curry frozen thing that had taken six minutes of her twenty-minute reprieve just to heat, emanated from the trash bin. Mary's "Glows" were based on such small things—no-brainers. Hadn't she noticed anything else— anything substantive—about Jamie's teaching? Jamie thought she'd be reaping the benefits by now of ingratiating herself to parents. She'd been doing the good-news e-mail messages religiously and she kept the parents up-to-date on curriculum. "Uh"—Jamie looked down at the list of Evaluation Criteria for Probationary Teachers on the dingy desktop in front of her—"could I make an addendum, actually?" Isobel had advised her to do this—to point out the positive steps she'd taken that Mary might not recognize. It made her nervous, but it seemed worth it, especially if Mary thought her best quality was her ability to dress herself.

"Absolutely." Mary held her pen poised above her own copy of the criteria.

"I think—" Jamie paused, gathering her courage. "I think I'm pretty skilled at technology integration." She watched Mary circle the corresponding bullet point.

"Okay," Mary said, "I agree that you've made an effort to use the course management system and to provide appealing visuals. Good point. Anything else?"

"I volunteered for the Sunshine Committee," Jamie blurted, and then regretted it. Who cared that she sometimes ordered flowers for teachers "experiencing life cycle events," as the committee described their charge?

"That's a good way to get to know your colleagues," Mary said kindly. "Okay." She looked at her pile of paperwork. "I think we're ready now for 'Grow,' yes?"

"Yes. I'm ready for 'Grow.'" Jamie gripped her red felt-tip, preparing to transcribe Mary's advice.

"Let's start with turnaround time for essays. I've noticed that you typically take three weeks to post grades for student papers."

Jamie wrote *Grading* on her list. "Is that too long?" She hoped not.

"Now that you've been with us for a year and a half, I'd like you to focus on getting that down to about two weeks." Mary pulled at the scarf she'd looped around her neck. "How does that sound?"

Jamie shifted at the desk, her knee bumping the underside of the attached tabletop. She took a breath, embarrassed by the curry smell. The only possible answer was that the two-week turnaround sounded great, but in fact, Jamie wasn't sure how she could possibly work any faster. She already spent every evening and at least one weekend day on grading and planning.

"Okay." She nodded. Maybe she could write fewer comments on the papers? She scraped her boot along the blue-gray carpeting and bit her lip.

"I think speeding things up will go a long way in building your reputation in the department," Mary said. "Parents like real-time feedback, especially with the online grade portal."

Got it, Jamie thought. *And now, please God, let this meeting be over with just one "Grow."*

"And the second 'Grow' I have for you," said Mary, as Jamie's stomach twisted, "is to begin making positive calls home."

"Positive calls?" *What the hell?* Jamie thought.

"It's a great practice," Mary continued. "Pick a couple of students in each class, and call home with a compliment. Leave a voice mail if you have to."

"Okay," Jamie said, again, writing *positive calls* on her notepad. When would she accomplish these? In between speed-grading assignments and incorporating the newest educational technology? Jamie underlined the word "positive." "I do already send good-news e-mails to families," she ventured. "Will those suffice?"

"Liston Heights parents love a voice-to-voice connection. It makes them feel like teachers really appreciate their children, that we notice the small things they're doing to make our community great." Mary gave her a meaningful look. "If you really want to become indispensable here," she said, "I'd start making the calls. Get the parents totally on your side."

"I'll get right on it." Jamie would just have to make time. "Indispensable" meant that her contract couldn't be cut, right? "I'll do my best," she told her boss. She could hear voices in the halls, as the students made their way from the cafeteria to classes.

Mary tucked her notes into a folder and swung her legs out from under the desk. "Okay," she said with finality. "I think that's it."

"Thanks," Jamie said. "Great advice, as usual." She hoped the comment about "indispensable" meant she was on the cusp of that. If faster grading and a few phone calls could put her over the edge, surely she could acquiesce. As Mary disappeared into the hallway and Jamie's students started straggling in she thought about how she'd perhaps make a few calls during her prep period.

JULIA ABBOTT

On Tuesday afternoon, Julia had been tempted to go to her usual hot yoga class, but there was the possibility that she would run into Vivian Song at the studio, as she had many times before. She couldn't see Vivian now that the board had met once without her. Who knew what she, Annabelle, and Sally had gotten out of Robin, who'd turned out to be such a backstabber? Julia's criticisms of Melissa's acting were hardly the only observations she'd made to Robin over the years. What else would her "friend" repeat?

Still, Julia felt claustrophobic in the house. She'd been doggedly avoiding Facebook since she'd discovered the video on the Inside Liston page. And then the same day, the Liston Lights had profiled Tryg Ogilvie on Instagram, as if humiliating Julia was worthy of public praise. "I love sharing my point of view on my YouTube channel and my Insta," Tryg had said in his interview. *I bet,* thought Julia ruefully. But certainly, she reasoned, other posts would rise to the top of her feeds while she stayed away, and her humiliation would blow over.

She felt twitchy without a full to-do list or access to social media and finally decided on a quick trip to the grocery store. At the Whole

Foods, she picked up a superfood salad and some Broccolini for dinner and then detoured past Bloom, her favorite Liston Heights boutique, on the way back to her car. The front window of the shop was filled with winter white—sheer blouses with raised polka dots, high-necked sweaters, a sleek-yet-playful bomber jacket shown over distressed white jeans with artful holes in each leg. Was she too old for the ripped-denim trend? She cocked her head to the side as she stared at the pants. She'd pair them with ankle boots and a chunky knit sweater. *Not too old,* she decided. After all, she'd seen women in their sixties with frayed patches on their jeans who looked chic—as long as the holes were far from the inner thigh.

Wanting just a peek at the jeans up close, Julia opened the door to the shop, a bell tinkling her arrival. Once she was inside, the cerulean accent wall where they kept dresses distracted her. She'd been browsing just like this when she'd found that dress for Tracy, the one she'd almost convinced her daughter to wear to her piano recital. Julia thought back to the event, Tracy playing the Rachmaninoff beautifully, her hair in a high ponytail, Italian merino sweater slim over tapered slacks. Her girl looked cute. *Sporty,* Julia thought. But she'd hoped Tracy could try for elegant just one time.

Julia saw another dress that would flatter her size-zero daughter—a spring style, bright pink with a fitted bodice and slightly flared skirt. She picked it off the rack and spun it. It'd look great with a contrasting belt and some neutral lip gloss. If only she could get Tracy to wear makeup regularly. "A little mascara would really pull that outfit together," she'd say some mornings over breakfast.

But since Tracy had started in Ms. Johnson's class, that seemed even less likely. "I'm concerned about the artifice society insists women keep up," Tracy had said one recent morning. "Is that the right word, Mom? 'Artifice'?" It went right along with her comments about not having children and the motherhood penalty. Julia had never heard of such a thing before English 9 had become a liberal think tank. In any case, if she couldn't get Tracy to wear a muted long-sleeved dress, the chances of getting her into this pink one were nil. She felt wistful as she put it back on the rack. Tracy's narrow calves would have looked divine in the right heels below that skirt. Maybe if Ms. Johnson mentioned that pink dresses were a universal sign of feminism, Tracy would take three of this one.

Julia could smell the olive oil in her salad dressing through her grocery bag, and her stomach groaned. She'd had only Diet Mountain Dew so far today, which she'd sipped while researching the theater programs Andrew would visit this summer on a college trip. She'd also reluctantly called her mother. She unfolded a pair of the white jeans as she recalled their stilted conversation about the family's lake place and her father's recent physical. The Bloom clerk approached. "Anything I can help you with today?"

"I'm just browsing." Julia scanned the store, her ponytail sliding over her shoulder as she turned her head to survey the displays. "You always have the cutest things."

"Thanks," the woman said. And then: "You look familiar. Have we met?" Julia looked back at her. They'd probably interacted here in the store before, she thought, and was about to tell her so when the clerk began blinking rapidly and took a step back. "No," she said. "I know." And suddenly she was giggling.

"Excuse me?" Julia half smiled, confused.

"I'm sorry." The woman covered her mouth. "It's just," she whispered and leaned in, "I saw the video."

"The video?" Julia turned her head again, this time toward the exit. How could this woman have recognized her from that grainy footage? Julia's arm fell, the jeans dusting the floor.

"You're the theater mom, right?" the saleswoman said. "In that video? The girl?" She laughed again. "Oh my goodness." She covered her mouth as Julia stepped back.

"Could you take this?" Julia held the pants out. "I have to go."

ISOBEL JOHNSON

Isobel had just slipped off one of her flats and stretched her toes under her desk when Wayne Wallace rapped on her door after school and blustered in. She scrambled to slide her foot back into its shoe even though her feet were concealed.

"Ms. Johnson," Wayne said, crossing the room in large strides, "have you got a minute?" Isobel felt panic rising. She couldn't remember the last time the principal had appeared in her classroom. Something bad must have happened. Had Mary talked to him about the queer theory lesson? Had he decided to circle back about the voice mail she hadn't finished recounting?

"I've got a minute." Isobel tried to smile, but faltered. She closed her laptop and folded her hands over it, the metal top cool against her skin. She wondered briefly if she should stand, but Wayne quickly maneuvered his large frame into a student desk near her. She stayed put.

"The other day," Wayne began, looking over her head, "you mentioned something about a voice mail? I'm afraid we didn't have time to finish that conversation. I'm sorry about that."

Isobel silently cursed her decision to go to Wayne with the voice mail, especially now that Mary had criticized her curriculum. "That's okay," she said.

"You said something about the caller accusing you of—" He paused, frowning. Clearly he couldn't remember exactly. Could she revise her comments? Soften things? "What did the caller accuse you of again?"

"Actually, as I reflected on it, it seemed like less of a big deal," she tried.

"But what did the caller say?" Wayne pressed. "I was thinking of it again because I got a letter from Sheila Warner. Her daughter, Erin, is in your class?" Isobel nodded. Erin, as far as she could tell, tried as hard to avoid speaking aloud in American Lit as she did on anything Isobel assigned. "Sheila works for Senator McGuire," Wayne said.

"Okay." Isobel wasn't sure how this fact connected to the voice mail. She glanced down at that morning's coffee, an iridescent sheen on the top. She quickly considered whether to mention that the message had accused her of "anti-Americanism," "Marxism," or a "blatant liberal agenda." Marxism, she decided, was the least sweeping. "The caller mentioned Marxism," she said.

"Did you tell your American Lit class that Atticus Finch was a white supremacist?" Wayne blurted.

"What?"

"Sheila said something about Atticus Finch and white . . ." He stared at her. "Maybe it wasn't supremacy. Did you talk about Atticus Finch being white?"

The helpless feeling she'd had when Mary delivered the news that she'd planned to observe her classroom rushed back to her chest. Isobel swallowed against it.

"I've always made it a point to notice the prevailing voices in the books I read with students," Isobel said. She'd used the line many times at faculty meetings and in conversations with parents. "We ask, 'Whose voices are we hearing? Whose voices are we missing?' In *To Kill a Mockingbird*, we hear all the white voices—Scout, Atticus, Miss Maudie. And the black voices—"

Wayne shook his head. "Look," he said, more urgently now, "this parent, Sheila Warner—she works for Senator McGuire, who sent his own children here when they were young. The senator's office would prefer that American classics remain classic."

Isobel wasn't sure how to respond. Of course *To Kill a Mockingbird* was iconic. It wasn't as if she could single-handedly remove texts from the canon. "It's definitely a classic," Isobel said.

"I'm not getting letters from parents in Lyle Greenwood's class or Eleanor Woodsley's class or even Jamie Preston's class about Atticus Finch's white supremacy." Wayne looked tired and not a little peeved.

Isobel glanced at her desk calendar, where she'd written *Pick Riley up at carpool* in pencil on today's date. "I don't think I called Atticus a white supremacist," she said. "We did talk about the white-savior complex." She kept her voice above a whisper. "It's the idea that white characters defend and protect—," she started to explain, but Wayne cut her off.

"I know what you're trying to do, Isobel, and it's not that I don't agree with you. But the community isn't ready for conversations like that. Have you seen the Humans of LHHS feed today? The theme this week is marginalized voices, and today we've got the head of the Young Republicans claiming the school is discriminatory toward conservative-leaning students. You've got to tone it down." Isobel could hear the echoes of Lyle's warnings in his words. And Mary's cautions, and Eleanor's snide suggestions. Much to Isobel's horror, tears threatened. She had the adolescent feeling of being utterly misunderstood, of trying to do her best and yet somehow not measuring up. Still, she was an adult, and crying in front of the boss was something she'd advised Jamie never to do. She repeated her own advice to herself now: *Keep it together at all costs. Then cry in the car when the meeting is over.*

She cleared her throat and tried to speak. "I always aim to give the students what they need to become critical thinkers." Her voice was hoarse, but steady. Wayne hoisted himself from the desk.

"Just give them the books," he said without looking at her again.

"There's buzz in the parent community, and you've got to shut it down." He opened the door to the quiet hallway. "Give them punctuation and vocabulary. Sentence structure." He waved a hand at her and didn't look back. "Have a good evening."

When he was gone, Isobel felt tempted to turn off the lights and put her head on her desk. She had a wild thought that she never should have left East High School in downtown Minneapolis, her first job. No parent there had ever written the principal about her teaching practices or decisions. But there was no time to wallow over her scolding or to regret the last eight years at Liston Heights. She had to leave now in order to be on time to pick up her son.

Isobel robotically packed her tote bag, including her plan book and a copy of *The Crucible*, the next classic for her American Lit students. She willed herself through the empty hallway, relieved not to see any member of her department as she headed out into the parking lot and shuffled toward her van. Once she was safely in the driver's seat, her seat belt pressing on her chest, Isobel leaned back against the headrest and closed her eyes.

What had just happened?

As soon as she'd asked herself the question, she knew the answer. She'd been officially censored. This went beyond a friendly warning from Lyle or a self-important "reminder" from Eleanor. It was even more serious than Mary's furious note-taking as she observed Isobel's classes. This was the big boss—the guy who would either renew her contract or dismiss her. And he was telling her to stop doing what she loved to do—getting to the moment when students realized something important, when they started seeing their world through a different lens.

Isobel opened her eyes and turned the key in the ignition. Cold air blasted from the vents, and she turned down the fan. The clock on the dusty console read three forty-five. If she hurried, she'd make it to the carpool circle.

Automatically, she drove toward Mills Park Elementary. She pulled into the carpool line just in time to be officially not late and stared blankly at the blue Accord in front of her. As she inched forward, she lowered the passenger-side sunshade, which held her pickup sign: JOHNSON RILEY (3RD GRADE). It was the first year Callie had been omitted. Isobel couldn't believe her daughter was old enough for middle school.

As Isobel moved forward in line, her mind wandered back to her own middle school experience. It had been during eighth grade that her family—well, she, Caroline, and her mother—had moved from their five-thousand-square-foot home in a Rochester subdivision to that tiny two-bedroom rental ninety minutes away in a smaller town. She remembered the first night in the mildewed apartment when she'd left her own twin bed and crossed the small room to crawl in with her sister. Caroline had thrown an arm around her and breathed into her neck, mostly asleep. "Everything changes," Isobel had said to her.

"Just for right now." Caroline's words slurred together as she squeezed Isobel's middle. Isobel shook her head against the pillow, tangling her hair.

"It's forever," she'd said. "We'll be paying for Dad's mistakes forever."

Isobel had been slightly embarrassed that she needed her sister when Caroline was younger by eighteen months. But she couldn't help it. She'd been staring at the dingy popcorn ceiling above her stiff bed, picturing her friend Meera standing in front of the for-sale sign at her family's nearly identical five-thousand-square-foot home across the cul-de-sac from theirs. Anxiety flooded her body, feet to chest, and she had to sit up in bed in order to breathe.

It was after Meera had stopped speaking to her on the school bus—had shoved her into their usual seat before walking toward the back—that she'd learned that her father hadn't stolen money just from the Rochester Area Charitable Foundation, but also from other investors, investors including Meera's parents. Isobel still, even as an adult, repeated to herself the lines from the indictment she'd read one evening after sneaking into her father's study. She saw his name in bolded all-caps and skimmed down: "ROBERT JOHN MILLER did knowingly devise and participate in a scheme to defraud and obtain money by materially false and fraudulent pretenses."

She shook her head, thinking of it again now. That indictment hadn't just changed her father's life. It had prescribed her own as well. Just as she'd donated all of her nicest clothes, including the new-that-Christmas Girbaud jeans, and replaced her wardrobe with secondhand and inexpensive pieces, she'd later eschewed plans for study abroad, finishing at the University of Wisconsin ahead of schedule and with an extremely practical teaching license.

In front of her in the carpool line, two kids climbed into the Accord, their backpacks weighing them down. Isobel watched their mom turn around and say something toward the backseat.

Her own mother's voice veered into Isobel's consciousness then. "You don't personally have to atone for Dad's mistakes," she'd said over the Chinese takeout Isobel had lobbied against in favor of less expensive ramen doctored with rotisserie chicken. Anger surged into Isobel's cheeks as she remembered.

"Mom," she'd said then, and still believed now, "of course we do." The Accord she'd followed to the front of the carpool line moved forward, and she inched along, as mindlessly as she had during the entire ten-minute wait. She drove around the circle and headed back down toward the street.

Eight years after she'd read that indictment, when Isobel had just been hired at East High School, her father had called. "I'm out. Can I see you?" *No,* she'd thought then.

Suddenly, the car behind her started honking. Isobel's head jerked, and in her passenger-side mirror she caught sight of Riley, running toward the van. Mrs. Khatri, the art teacher, hurried along beside him, the pom-pom on her hat flopping. Riley's mouth was moving. The teacher's arm waved as she held the loop on the top of Riley's backpack with one hand.

"Oh, my God," Isobel said aloud, realizing that she'd moved through the whole line without stopping to pick up her son. She braked and slammed into PARK, just as Riley pulled the handle on the automatic sliding door. Isobel couldn't form words as she looked back at Mrs. Khatri, who stared at her from the sidewalk.

"You forgot to stop!" Mrs. Khatri said.

"I'm so sorry," Isobel managed. "I don't know what I was thinking."

"Mom!" Riley scolded as he pulled the seat belt over. "You forgot me!"

Isobel pressed the close button for the back door and waved sheepishly at the incredulous teacher. "I need to get it together."

"Geez, Mom," said Riley, sitting back. "Having to chase you in the carpool circle? That feels like a new low."

"Yeah," Isobel agreed. She glanced at the playground on her right, icicles hanging from the monkey bars at one end. "I bet."

JULIA ABBOTT

After avoiding it all for days, Julia finally clicked open Facebook to find 124 notifications in the upper-right-hand corner of her screen. *One hundred twenty-four?* She'd never had that many hits on anything, not even the adorable photo she'd posted of Tracy at her eighth-grade graduation with the braided hairstyle they'd accomplished by watching and rewatching YouTube tutorials.

Shaking, she clicked the bell icon. Her eyes popped as her fears materialized. **Annabelle Young has shared the video you were tagged in,** read one notification. **Sheila Warner, Vivian Song, and six others reacted to the video you were tagged in. Marilyn Ogilvie has shared the video you were tagged in.** The list went on and on.

Julia skimmed the rest. By a quick estimation, she figured the video posted on the Inside Liston page by "Lisa Lions" had been shared by at least twenty-seven people so far. She had direct messages from two acquaintances and one of her cousins. They'd written, **Are you okay?** as if she had been diagnosed with cancer rather than simply bumping into someone at the high school.

Although it occurred to her to respond to the messages, Julia's fingers felt numb. She put her fists in her lap and stared at her screen. Two more notifications pinged as she sat there. *Close the browser,* she thought to herself, but she found she couldn't move her arms.

"This, too, shall pass." Julia tried whispering her frequent mantra to herself. Her mother had often repeated it when she obsessed over a low test score or panicked that she'd said the wrong thing at a get-together with friends.

"You're much harder on yourself than you need to be," her mother had whispered as Julia nearly hyperventilated.

After her college graduation—there'd been weekly calls during her university years when Julia perseverated on grades, the Greek system, and, of course, Henry Abbott—Julia's mother had presented her with a blue Tiffany's box. It had contained the silver bangle she now wore most days. "Check the inscription," urged her mother. Before she looked, Julia knew it would be that old comforting phrase, the one her mom repeated while she ran her palm over Julia's back. *This, too, shall pass.*

Though she now moved her fingers over the engraving, Julia felt her breath coming quickly, inhalations too close together. Her thoughts raced. How could she remove that video from Facebook? Could she e-mail the company? Mark Zuckerberg himself? Her vision began to blur around the edges as it did when she felt on the verge of losing control. "I can't," she whimpered, and it occurred to her that now that Robin was on the Booster Board, aligned with Annabelle and all the others, she actually didn't have anyone she could call for reassurance. Could she rely on her mother once again? In order to do that, she'd have to explain the video, and there was no way her mother would understand the context.

Just then she heard the mudroom door open. "Hi, Mom!" Tracy called. "We got out of practice early, and I got a ride." Julia swallowed hard and tried to speak. She couldn't force the words past her sticky throat or slow her breathing. The kids didn't know about her panic attacks, and the prospect of losing control in front of her daughter only compounded her anxiety.

When Tracy appeared several seconds later in her stocking feet, as usual, Julia forced a smile, but Tracy wasn't fooled. Rather, she walked quickly toward her as though on a rescue mission. "What are you doing? What's wrong?" Tracy asked. Facebook updated the number of notifications as Tracy looked over Julia's shoulder. There were four new ones. "What's going on?" Tracy pressed.

"The video." Julia cleared her throat, hoping to erase the thickness she could hear in her voice. "It's all over Facebook."

Tracy turned the computer and hovered her fingers over the keyboard. "Have you untagged yourself?" she asked, businesslike. *She has so much of her father in her,* Julia thought, at once proud and slightly disappointed.

"No." She hadn't thought of untagging. She wasn't sure she knew how.

In a few clicks, Tracy said, "Okay. I made it so no one can tag you in anything without your permission. So, no one can retag you in that video, for instance." She glanced at Julia, whose breathing had slowed slightly.

"Thanks," Julia muttered, unsure of how to feel about being the recipient of her daughter's help.

Tracy clicked again, on notifications. "But probably we should ask the person who posted the video to delete it? That way there won't be any more shares. Hey," said Tracy, "it was first posted on a page called 'Inside Liston.' What is that?" She clicked the notification and opened it.

"Don't click on that." Julia's reaction was slow as her panic waned, and she realized too late that Tracy would see the secret group. Her daughter wouldn't like it. She'd always seemed as indifferent to gossip and girl drama as she was to mascara and heels.

"Wait. Is this something from Ms. Johnson's class?" Tracy leaned toward the screen and read the caption of the image at the top. "'Ms. Johnson claims Jay Gatsby is gay'? What the heck?" She clicked the image of the handout and immediately scrolled down to the comments. Julia could see that the first of them said, This is malpractice. Is no one supervising this teacher? The second read, I'm a Yale English major, and I've never heard anything so outlandish. Where did this teacher go to college? Does she even have a degree?

"Ms. Johnson went to Madison," Tracy blurted.

Julia found her voice. "This is just a place parents complain about things," she said, trying to minimize it.

Tracy studied other posts, including pictures of teachers' cars and even the assistant principal's shoes with the caption, Don't they pay Sue Montague enough to buy new kicks? "Mom," Tracy said, her voice thick with emotion, as Julia's had so recently been, "this is just mean." She scrolled further. "It's bullying. Why are you a member of this group?"

"I'm not really in it," said Julia lamely. "I just like to know what's happening at school."

"Who is Lisa Lions?" Tracy asked. Julia tried to turn the computer away, but Tracy grabbed the edge of the screen. She clicked on Lisa Lions's profile. "This is a fake account," she said, announcing the obvious truth. "Mom, this person posted the video of you. She's making you miserable. She has to take it down." Before Julia could protest, Tracy had clicked on Messenger and begun to type.

ISOBEL JOHNSON

When Isobel walked in to school the next morning, she saw Jamie standing outside her classroom, flipping through a stack of papers.

"Hi, kiddo," Isobel called from the entryway, her tote bag in the crook of her arm as she stomped her boots on the mat. "What's up?"

She unlocked and opened her door and led Jamie in. As the sun was still rising, Isobel could see the two of them reflected in the windows overlooking the track. She unwrapped the scarf from her neck. Jamie held a paper in her outstretched hand. "Can you look at this?" she asked. "I'm not sure if I should score it 'exceptional' or 'proficient,' and Lyle and Eleanor always seem kind of annoyed when I double-check with them."

Isobel shrugged out of her coat and reached for the paper, sliding it onto her desk as she got situated. "Sure." *Lyle and Eleanor could take their turns,* she thought, *rather than leaving all of the mentoring to me.* Still, she grabbed a black Dixon Ticonderoga from the top desk drawer and had started to skim the paper when a knock on the door startled them both. Isobel glanced up at the window and made eye contact with a grim-looking Mary Delgado. *Enough already,* she thought. Between the voice mail, the impromptu observations, and Wayne's unprecedented visit to her classroom, she already felt she was under attack. And now here was Mary hovering first thing in the morning again.

With no choice, however, Isobel waved her in. "Good morning." Isobel kept her voice even.

"I'm sorry to bother you so early."

Mary's weak smile stoked Isobel's anger. "What can I do for you?" Isobel asked.

"Do you have a moment to talk?" Mary looked pointedly at Jamie.

"Oh," Jamie said, "sure." She took the paper back from Isobel's desk.

Isobel smiled at her. "I'll come and see you in a few minutes, okay?"

"Sure," Jamie said again. "No hurry." She looked sidelong at the department chair as she rushed into the hall, and Isobel stared at Mary expectantly.

"I'm here," Mary said, her weight shifting from foot to foot, "to tell you that Wayne and I need to meet with you right after school today in his office."

Isobel looked down at her blouse, sure she'd be able to see her heart beating through the material. Another meeting in the wake of Wayne's warning? "Why?" Isobel asked.

Mary squared her shoulders. "We're going to address some curricular complaints," she said, turning back toward the door before "complaints" was fully uttered.

"Wait," Isobel said, standing. "This is serious?"

"It is," Mary said. "I'm sorry." She paused and half turned back around. "I probably shouldn't tell you this, seeing as I'm an administrator." Her eyes landed on the F. Scott Fitzgerald poster at the back of the room. "But you and I have known each other for a long time." Isobel swallowed. "You might want to bring a union rep," Mary said, looking back at her. "Ask Lyle Greenwood to come with you to this meeting."

Isobel's sharp inhale made an "ah" sound. "Mary!" she said when she was able. "A union rep?" Union reps were for criminal accusations and termination papers. "What is going on? Wayne was in here yesterday telling me to stick to the books. I'll do it, but I haven't even had time to adjust yet."

"Things have gotten more complicated." She grabbed the doorknob. "I'm sorry." She disappeared into the hall.

Isobel wilted into her chair, her chest pounding. She looked down at the ring of road salt beneath her desk and tried to breathe deeply. "Things have gotten more complicated," Mary had said. That could mean only that they'd gotten more complaints about Isobel's teaching. Was there some kind of campaign? She thought back to the voice mail, her first sign all year that something was different and wrong. "Anti-American" and "blatant liberal agenda," the caller had said.

She still wasn't certain that Julia Abbott had left that message. She'd been comfortable enough to tell her in person at the dance that everyone disapproved of her, so why would she need to leave an anonymous message? And Sheila Warner, the parent Wayne had mentioned the other day—the one who worked for Senator McGuire—had sidestepped Isobel entirely and gone straight to the big boss. Certainly she wouldn't also leave a message? It occurred to her to call Mark, but the classroom clock read eight ten. She had to get to Jamie's room to deal with that paper and then to Lyle, all before the bell at eight thirty. She could skip Jamie's, but she didn't want her to think anything was amiss. Not only did Jamie rely on Isobel for advice and stability, but she also seemed to be among the few who still admired her.

Isobel quickly swapped her boots for her wedges. She stood and checked for hat hair in the little square mirror she'd pasted inside her cabinet—not too bad—and then walked down to Jamie's room. "Hey," she said, swinging the door open. She aimed for nonchalance. "Want me to take a look at that paper?"

"That would be great," Jamie said, holding it out. Jamie's classroom had a spare look. It lacked the piles of clutter Isobel knew to be standard in most veterans' spaces. Instead, Jamie's bulletin boards all had fresh backings, unsullied borders, and shiny posters with inspirational quotes. *Go confidently in the direction of your dreams! Live the life you have imagined*, read one, memorializing American Lit standby Henry David Thoreau.

"What did Mary want?" Jamie asked eagerly as Isobel scanned the essay.

"Based on the intro," Isobel said, ignoring her, "I'd go with proficient, but I can see how you'd get tripped up." She stepped back toward the door.

"Even if the conclusion is great?" Jamie asked.

"For exceptional, it's got to check all the boxes."

Jamie nodded. "Wait, but what did Mary want?" she asked again.

Isobel bit her lip, annoyed. She'd have to say something. "She scheduled a meeting for this afternoon."

"About what?" Jamie's eyebrows knit. "Is it about the voice mail?"

"Curriculum," Isobel said. "Hey, I've got to go. I need to catch Lyle before the bell." She tried to keep her voice light. "See you at lunch?"

TRACY ABBOTT

Tracy had been looking forward to going over her concluding paragraph with Ms. Johnson that morning in English 9, but the teacher seemed distracted. She sat at her desk, flipping through a thick file of papers. Tracy had wanted to share her realization that if women decided to have children (and Tracy didn't think everyone should—the cost to the planet in greenhouse gases per capita was enough reason to abstain), they owed it to their kids to ensure their financial stability by working steadily.

Of course, she also wanted to warn her favorite teacher about the Facebook group she'd seen, the handout from American Lit and all those mean comments from her mother's friends, but she wasn't sure how to bring that up. Lisa Lions was probably some mother, Tracy thought, who'd given up her job and her responsibilities. For all Tracy knew, her own mother had written bitchy comments in that group, along with all the others.

She wanted to tell Ms. Johnson all of this, but the teacher hardly looked up from her file all period. In fact, at one point, she put her head into her hand and wiped at the lower lids of her eyes. Could Ms. Johnson be crying? Maybe she already knew about the Facebook page?

Tracy scribbled a note to Anika Bergstrom in her notebook and flashed it across the aisle. *Have you seen the Inside Liston FB group?* Anika shook her head subtly and glanced up at Ms. Johnson, verifying that they wouldn't be caught.

"What is it?" Anika mouthed.

Tracy went back to writing. *A gossip page for our moms. Stuff about teachers. Very* Fahrenheit 451. Tracy wasn't sure if that comparison was particularly apt, but she felt pleased that the title had occurred to her. They'd read the novel in middle school, and she'd mentioned it once before this trimester when the class had discussed an article on biased policing, eliciting Ms. Johnson's particular proud smile.

An idea occurred to Tracy then, as she tilted her paper again toward Anika. Maybe she could also join the Facebook group? Lisa Lions wasn't the only one who knew how to make a fake account. Tracy wasn't sure what she'd post, but something to push Ms. Johnson's Gatsby handout—and her mother's video, to be fair—down the page?

Just before the bell rang, Ms. Johnson stood and gave reminders about due dates. Tracy considered staying after class, but the teacher looked so distracted and her face so pale that she left with all the others.

ISOBEL JOHNSON

~

When Isobel walked into the principal's office that afternoon, her legs felt weak. She worried she wouldn't make it to a chair. Wayne sat at the conference table, next to a small-featured woman Isobel vaguely remembered as Amanda from human resources. The last time Isobel had seen her, she'd been running seminars during new-teacher orientation eight years before. Mary Delgado hunkered behind her laptop next to Amanda. She brought her eyes up to Isobel's forehead when she walked in, but wouldn't meet her gaze.

Lyle Greenwood put a brotherly hand on Isobel's shoulder and pulled out a chair for her. She sank into it as he flipped his legal pad to a fresh page and dropped his ballpoint on top. "What's this about, Wayne?" Lyle asked. His voice had weight to it. In his soft-sided briefcase, Isobel knew he had a copy of her personnel file.

When she'd walked to Lyle's classroom before first period that morning, her hands shaking, he'd pointed at the nearest desk, handed her a peppermint Life Saver from the bulk bag he kept next to his computer, and given her a to-do list. The first item was to walk over to the district office, request her file from the superintendent's assistant, and make two copies. She'd wondered if he'd also tell her "I told you so," but he hadn't. Instead, he'd hugged her and promised to try to help.

When she got the copies, she'd turned to the last page of her most recent performance review first. *An innovative and effective teacher*, it read, and Wayne's scrawling signature monopolized the bottom two inches of the page.

She'd always taught her values, and while she knew not everyone approved of her methods, she'd still been a respected and successful member of the faculty. How could the parents have turned on her so completely between last spring and now?

Wayne looked at Lyle, whom Isobel knew he respected, and then at Isobel herself. The "Good things come to those who hustle" poster glittered on the wall behind him, level with his head. "I'm going to be frank with you," Wayne began. He cleared his throat lightly. "We're dealing with some pretty serious concerns about misconduct."

"On Isobel's part?" Lyle asked. She felt grateful for the incredulity in his tone. She willed herself to match Lyle's impeccable posture, shoulders back, neck straight.

"Indeed," Wayne said. He opened a folder on his desk and took out copies of what Isobel could see were a series of bullet points.

Isobel's tongue felt oddly thick, and she was glad that she and Lyle had decided before the meeting that he would do as much of the talking as possible. "What's the nature of the complaint?" he asked.

"Isobel," Wayne said gravely, looking at his paper, "when you were hired at Liston Heights High School, you completed the new-faculty orientation, correct?"

"Of course," she said, pleased that her voice sounded normal. "I did the orientation in twenty twelve."

"And at that training and at several department meetings since, you've been made aware of the Liston Heights curriculum requirements?" Wayne looked at Mary to confirm, and the department chair bobbed her chin in assent.

Isobel stiffened. "Wayne," she said, "I follow curricular guidelines. I've never deviated from the list of approved texts."

Wayne exchanged a glance with Mary. "The nature of the complaint against you, Isobel, is not about following the letter of the curricular requirements, but rather the spirit of them." Isobel folded her hands and squeezed her knuckles together. Wayne's cologne, thick and woody, wafted across the table. The principal held the bullet points out to her. "This is a list of curricular aberrations we've cataloged from students, parents, and some of your supervisors." Isobel reached for the page. In the top-left corner, she saw her name, last name first, and Liston Heights employee number.

Lyle reached confidently for a copy that Wayne held out for him, as well. It occurred to Isobel that Lyle must have been at meetings like this before, and yet even though they were close friends, he hadn't divulged any details of other people's professional problems. When she looked down at the bullet points, she could hardly make sense of the words before her. *Insinuation that Atticus Finch represents white supremacy,* read a bullet near the top.

"I didn't say this," she blurted. She didn't look up. The next bullet said, *Introduction of queer theory as a critical lens although it's not approved by the district office.* "Wait a second!" Her eyes found Mary. "I'm not allowed to offer perspectives on the texts?"

Mary looked at Amanda and Wayne before she answered. Anger washed over Isobel, seizing her arms and hands. She stared at an athletic trophy sitting behind Mary on Wayne's desk. *Boys' State Swimming and Diving,* the inscription read. Of course she was allowed to offer additional perspectives, Isobel thought. Every teacher in the department did it, even Lyle.

Mary said, "All of our materials need to be developmentally appropriate and sufficiently contextualized for students."

"But you watched me teach about queer theory." Isobel leaned toward Mary. "You saw how engaged the students were."

Mary sat up straight. "Not all of them were engaged," she said pointedly. "Not all of them felt safe."

Isobel turned to Lyle, whose face remained remarkably placid. "Isobel," Lyle said, "it's customary in cases like this to offer a written rebuttal to the complaint." He looked at Amanda for confirmation, and she nodded. "You'll be able to submit your response to the allegations in writing as soon as tomorrow."

"That's correct," said Wayne. "And as you begin working on that document, we will begin a full investigation of your compliance with school policy."

"Investigation?" Isobel heard a faint buzzing in her ears.

Lyle broke in. "Isobel told me you asked her just yesterday to adhere more closely to the assigned texts. What's happened since then?"

Amanda spoke slowly. "A formal complaint has been brought against you," she said. "And we've had six additional calls from concerned parents in the last twenty-four hours. Members of the community feel you're applying undue influence on students and overpoliticizing classic works of literature." Six additional calls? Isobel's jaw dropped. That had to be some kind of coordinated effort. There was no way six parents randomly decided to complain on the same day.

Lyle scribbled *formal complaint; overpoliticized* on his legal pad. Isobel had no idea what to say. Although the queer theory arc was new, in general, she wasn't doing anything remarkably different from any other year.

Lyle looked at Wayne. "What course of action will you be taking in this matter?"

Wayne flicked his eyes toward his manila folder. "Ms. Johnson will be relieved of her duties for one week while we review her lesson plans and course materials, and interview students and families."

"What?" Isobel recoiled so violently that the front legs of her chair lifted from the floor. Lyle reached a hand over to steady her.

"Who will be conducting the investigation?" he asked, still calm.

"That'll be Mary and me," Wayne said. "We'll report our results to Amanda, and then to you." He pointed at Isobel.

Even in her shock, she had to quell the urge to correct his pronoun usage. *"I," Wayne,* she thought, *"Mary and I."*

Lyle made a note. How could he remain so unruffled? "And who will be teaching Isobel's classes?"

Mary piped up. "Judith Youngstead has agreed to step in for the week."

Judith Youngstead, of course, had stepped in last year when Peter Harrington hadn't made it to Thanksgiving. She was like the grim reaper of the Liston Heights English department. "Will I need to provide her with lesson plans?" Isobel asked weakly.

Mary shook her head. It didn't really make sense for Isobel to provide lesson plans, she guessed, as she'd been ousted for them. "The other members of the department and I will take care of that," she said. Isobel imagined Eleanor wandering into her classroom and cheerfully asking Judith if she needed help. Eleanor, she knew, would probably revel in her suspension. She blanched at the word "suspension" when it appeared in her consciousness, bending slightly at the waist.

"We'll be in touch tomorrow," Lyle said to the room. He reached a hand to the back of Isobel's chair. "Ready?" he prompted.

Isobel wasn't sure if she'd be able to stand. If she left this meeting, she felt she would essentially be leaving her job. She'd prized teaching above everything else, rejected a study-abroad program in college to finish her student teaching within the course of a regular four years. She'd toiled at East High for six years, spending her own money on supplies and food for the kids' weekends and holiday breaks. She applied for the Liston Heights job because these kids reminded her of herself and her father. And she thought if she could trigger their social awakenings at a young age, they'd be better citizens—they'd make change—going forward.

And now she'd failed.

Lyle looked so confident, though, and nodded at her so expectantly that she managed to push her chair back and apply weight to her feet. He reached for her elbow. She let him steer her out of the office, and he closed the door behind them.

They said nothing until they reached the top of the stairs, where they'd part, Lyle heading to the parking lot and Isobel to her classroom. "Take this," he said when they stopped. It was her copy of the official complaint. She took it and let her arm drop by her side. Lyle continued. "You need to go home and write rebuttals for each point." Isobel blinked at him. "Okay?" he said. "Stop by your room and grab any paper files if you don't have digital copies of everything."

"I do have digital copies," Isobel said.

"Good." Lyle clapped her on the shoulder. "Then go home, sit down, and refute every damn bullet." Lyle meant to pump her up, she knew, but misery welled up from a pain near her navel, tears threatening. "It's going to be okay," Lyle said. "Text me while you work." He smiled at her as he turned toward the door. "I've done these before."

"Here?" Isobel asked, calling after him. She couldn't remember a single teacher who had been put on administrative leave while being investigated. Even Peter had just been summarily fired without much rigmarole.

"It's more common than you think."

"But I know you think they're right," she blurted, hopeless.

"I don't think that," he said seriously. "I think you have strong convictions, and you're a risk taker. And I think the kids are lucky to have you." Isobel sniffled as he grasped her shoulder again. "I'm heading out," Lyle said. "I'm expecting a text from you before seven."

Isobel lifted her right hand to wave, forgetting she still clutched the complaint. It flopped over, grazing her wrist, and she dropped her arm. She turned from the main entrance and shuffled to the second-floor faculty restroom, the only single-stall bathroom in the building. Once inside, she faced the door, locked it, and turned back into the room. She slid to the tiled floor and let her laptop bag slip from her shoulder and the complaint fall from her hand. She folded both knees to her chest, the cool of the tile seeping in through her skirt and tights.

It occurred to her to call her husband. Would she need Mark to come and pick her up? But her arm felt too heavy to move, even to grab the phone from her bag. Actually, her entire body felt heavy. It seemed a lot to ask to hold her head up, so she lowered it to her knees and closed her eyes against her cable-knit tights. "Oh my God," she whispered. Isobel expected to cry, but nothing happened. Her breath felt hot against her thighs. Her friend Meera popped into her head then, standing in front of the sold sign, glaring at Isobel as her mother drove their U-Haul out of their once-comfortable neighborhood. Isobel hadn't thought she'd deserved comfort ever again after that, which was the reason she was always pushing back here at Liston Heights. Otherwise, the three-car garages and the Ivy League acceptances—they just became the default, the things that everyone deserved. That was the trap that her father had fallen into, the entitlement that had ruined all of their lives.

In three minutes or ten—she couldn't be sure—she unfolded herself and leaned back against the bathroom door. "Okay," she said aloud. "Okay." She put her right hand down next to the folder and pushed herself to standing. She walked to the sink and washed her hands, cool water running over her fingers. She took a long look in the mirror. Her usual winter paleness had given way to a sickly pallor, but her green eyes were still clear. She held her own gaze for a moment. "I didn't do anything wrong," she said in a whisper. In fact, she was probably working closer to her mission than ever if she'd triggered this kind of response, right? Still, she wondered what had prompted the six calls just in the last day.

But before she lost time ruminating about how she'd wound up suspended, she'd have to fight the complaint. Her students needed her, especially now, when she'd somehow touched a nerve.

JULIA ABBOTT

Julia reclined in the driver's seat, her knee lightly brushing the steering wheel. She stared straight ahead at the snow-covered tennis courts opposite the Liston Heights parking lot, forlorn metal poles jutting up from the ground, awaiting the nets that would hang there in just six weeks or so. Tracy said she'd be done in the Nordic ski waxing room at four fifteen. According to the clock in her dashboard, Julia had eight more minutes to wait. She hadn't quite been able to make eye contact with her daughter that morning after she'd helped her with the Facebook problem the day before. Julia was the one who should be solving problems, after all, not her fourteen-year-old.

"Did that Lisa Lions write back?" Tracy had asked after Julia handed her a muffin. Julia could only shake her head. "Unfriend her, Mom. That woman, whoever she is, is only making everything worse." There was no arguing that the child sounded like the parent, which made Julia feel like even more of a failure.

She knew she'd have given Tracy the same advice if their roles were rightfully reversed, but if Julia unfriended Lisa Lions, she'd no longer be able to see the Inside Liston page at all. She wouldn't be able to track her own crisis or any of the others.

She closed her eyes and leaned back against the smooth leather headrest. She wished she could talk the dilemma over with a friend, but in the week since the cast list was posted, she hadn't heard one word from Robin Bergstrom. She also hadn't heard from the other handful of moms with whom she normally texted or chatted. She'd received not a single text from Vivian Song, not that she expected to after how the conversation with Annabelle Young had gone. She'd also heard nothing from Andrew himself, who moved around the house without acknowledging her. The previous night Andrew had tried to take a dinner plate up to his bedroom rather than sitting at the table with the family. When Henry said, "No," in response to Julia's arched eyebrow, Andrew had shoveled his green beans and pan-roasted salmon into his mouth at lightning speed. Julia could see the pink bits of fish he was still chewing as he perfunctorily answered Henry's questions about rehearsal.

That interaction and all the others—the call to Annabelle, Tracy intervening on Facebook, Henry managing the meeting with Wayne— exhausted her. Julia yearned for normalcy.

She turned up the teen pop radio station that both of her kids had pretty much outgrown. The music, an upbeat ballad by the Jonas Brothers, sounded like the stuff she'd listened to between her junior and senior years at the University of Minnesota.

That summer she'd scored an internship at *YM* magazine, a dream job, and slept on a cot in the living room of her mother's cousin's one-bedroom apartment in Brooklyn. The accommodations didn't matter. She was thrilled—New York, fashion, journalism, shepherding the finalists in *YM*'s annual modeling contest around the city. "I'm going to move here," she'd tell herself as she left work at the end of each day, her scalp damp from the moment she exited the office's air-conditioning.

The first time she'd handed in two hundred fifty words of copy, a bio on one of the modeling finalists, she felt as if her chest would burst. Professional writing! It didn't matter that the features assistant didn't even look as she took the paper, each word selected painstakingly. Julia would have written a hundred bios of teenagers from small towns in Arkansas if it meant a shot in publishing. When the eight-week internship ended, Julia wrote thank-you notes to all of her superiors and started reworking her résumé. She'd apply widely at magazines that year, hoping for something permanent in this city she'd come to love.

And then, three months later at Christmas, after his parents' traditional Yule log had been sliced and enjoyed, Henry had held her coat and asked her to take a walk with him. The snowflakes drifted from the sky, coating the trees with a silvery sheen.

"How beautiful," she'd said, looking at the old-growth oaks in Henry's Minneapolis neighborhood, not fifteen minutes from where they lived now in Liston Heights.

"*You're* beautiful," he'd said, tugging her hand to stop her walking. She turned to him, and suddenly she knew exactly what was happening. She'd dreamed of it, of course—rings, bridesmaids, cake—but they'd talked about getting engaged in a year or two, after graduation and first jobs. Julia kept saying, "New York," and Henry teased her. Called her a go-getter.

"We'll settle here, though," he'd said each time she mentioned midtown Manhattan. "This is the best place to raise a family."

They had never really held that debate, as it turned out, or had come to a shared decision about where they'd live. And now here was Henry, pinching a diamond solitaire between his thumb and pointer finger before she'd even begun her last semester of courses or mailed her job applications.

Now, twenty years later, Julia looked down at her diamond in the traditional setting. It was true she'd never imagined spending so much of her time waiting for her children in a parked car. To be honest, in those early days, she hadn't thought of children at all. It had been a welcome surprise when she became pregnant with Andrew. It hadn't made sense, Henry said, to continue her work at *Twin Cities Monthly* magazine when the need for day care came up. It would have cost more than her salary, after all. And didn't Julia want to raise her children herself?

She caught a flash of movement in her rearview mirror as someone walked, head down, across the parking lot. She recognized the canvas tote first, and then placed the mousy brown hair stuffed beneath a black pom-pom hat. It was Isobel Johnson.

As she watched Isobel shuffle toward her car, she wondered again what Tracy saw in her. How had Isobel achieved such high status with her daughter? Tracy herself appeared in the rearview mirror then, too. One strap of a heavy backpack weighed down her left shoulder, and she had an LHHS athletic duffel slung across her chest, messenger style.

Tracy's face tilted up in happy surprise when she saw Isobel in front of her. Julia flinched.

The two of them talked. Certainly, Tracy wouldn't tell her about the Inside Liston Facebook page? Their exchange didn't look like a serious conversation. Isobel's pale cheeks shone in the fading light. *She looks young,* Julia thought. How old was she, anyway? She watched as Tracy pointed at the car. The teacher nodded, still smiling. She reached out a mittened hand and gave Tracy a friendly pat on the upper arm, and then they parted.

Julia clicked open the trunk and waited for Tracy to come around to the front seat. Meanwhile, Ms. Johnson looked back toward the Mercedes and waved, perhaps at Julia. The minivan she walked toward had a "Kindness Matters" decal on the back window above several other bumper stickers.

Figures, Julia thought. Although Julia had opinions, too, she didn't feel the need to broadcast them via her vehicle. She turned and smiled at Tracy. "Hi, honey," she said, pushing her irrational jealousy away. "Get those skis all waxed?"

"Yeah," Tracy said. They pulled out of their spot and drove toward the minivan. "Oh, wait," Tracy said as they pulled even with Isobel. She rolled down her window, cold air rushing in. "Ms. Johnson!" she called.

Julia tensed. "What is it?" she asked her daughter as Isobel turned toward them.

"I forgot to ask you whether you'd heard about the new PBS adaptation of *Inherit the Wind*."

Isobel leaned down toward the window. She looked blank. "No," she said. "I'll check it out. Thanks!" And then, looking at Julia: "Hello, Mrs. Abbott." Julia recalled the last time she'd spoken with the teacher, also in the parking lot, just after Julia had been excised from the Theater Booster Board. Her jaw twitched as she thought of it. It had been so embarrassing to fall like that, and right in front of the woman Tracy so admired. She forced herself to make eye contact and noticed that Isobel's eyes looked red.

"Is everything all right?" Julia asked, squinting at her.

Isobel blinked. "Of course," she said, rubbing her nose with a green woolen mitten. "Everything's fine." It wasn't a very convincing "fine," but before Julia could follow up, the teacher straightened and walked away.

JOHN DITTMER

At four forty-five, John Dittmer dropped his head into his palm and rubbed his right temple and cheekbone. He checked his watch. Fifteen minutes left in today's rehearsal. "Okay," the director sighed, leaning against the piano. "Let's take it from the top of the scene. From the intro, Alice?" he said.

Assistant Director Alice Thompson, her face hidden from the students by the upright piano, raised her eyebrows. John took a step away from the piano and breathed in the faint smell of sawdust, the beginnings of the set build. "Andrew," he said, on a long exhale, "let's make it a little less blustery in the arm movements"—the director pantomimed jerky pointing—"and go more subtle. You're friendly in this scene. Try leaning down toward your paper, study it, and then turn your whole body toward Anna." He demonstrated from the pit.

Maeve Hollister, as Anna, nodded supportively. "I think that would work well." She had pulled a tulle crinoline over her jeans to simulate the dress she'd be wearing in performance and tucked in an LHHS Drama Club T-shirt. John gave her a thumbs-up. If Maeve would continually coach Andrew, they might actually be able to make this work.

Melissa Young, the director noted, seemed especially unwilling to do any coaching. She stood, hands on her hips, next to Maeve. "This is an important entrance for my character," she said, scowling at Andrew. "It seems like the body movements should be almost nil, except for Fiona's." She raised a script at Mr. Dittmer. "I mean, am I right?"

Something clattered backstage where the prop crew was working. "Sorry!" a voice called.

John ignored it. "Yes," he said to Melissa. "We'll go subtle for the inspector and Anna, and Fiona, you go bigger. Tryg," he continued, indicating the lanky ninth grader who held a weathered hard-backed suitcase loosely in his hand, "you echo Fiona, following about ten steps behind her, moving backward and forward when she does." The director tapped his fingers on the upright. "We'll get this," he muttered.

"Well, some of us will," Melissa snorted.

John glanced at Andrew, who stood at the inspector's podium center stage, studying the script and whispering something to himself. Fortunately, he hadn't seemed to have heard.

John knocked on the top of the piano, the raps ringing in the empty auditorium. "Let's keep it positive," he said, and then he called for action.

JAMIE PRESTON

⁓

Jamie expected an empty apartment when she clattered through the door that night, but her roommate was home, standing in the kitchen.

Leslie looked at the clock. "You're early," she said. It was five forty-five, more than two hours since the final bell had rung, and still this counted as early. Jamie once again lamented her teacher's salary, which was not nearly enough considering she'd basically take a dinner break and then speed-grade papers until she fell asleep.

"I guess." She dropped her backpack and her Prius fob next to the boots she kicked off.

"How much grading do you have to do tonight?" Leslie asked.

"Some." Jamie's mouth started to water, and she stood on her tiptoes to see over Leslie's shoulder as she stirred pasta on the stove. Would there be enough for two?

"I think I'm going to have more than enough of this," Leslie said, reading her mind, "if you're hungry."

"Yes," Jamie said, with more fervor than she'd meant to. "I just realized I'm starving." She walked toward the kitchen counter, where she saw a neat stack of mail. "Is there anything I can do to help?" she asked. Her student loan statement sat on top of the pile. She'd had to pay for a quarter of her tuition, her dad's plan for teaching her the value of her education. She pushed the statement aside and flipped through the rest of the envelopes. A square one appeared to be a save-the-date for her college roommate's wedding. Jamie sighed. No one was supposed to get married before thirty these days. Rebecca was six years too young.

"No," Leslie said. "I'm just going to add cheese and then dump that into a bowl." She gestured toward a prewashed Caesar salad mix on the counter.

"I can do that," Jamie said. "Give me a sec to change into my sweats."

"When you get back, I have to show you this text from Todd."

Jamie rolled her eyes. "Text from Todd" was one of Leslie's most frequently uttered expressions.

All set with her elastic waistband and a heaping bowl of pasta, Jamie studied the text. Saturday night is the better one this weekend, it read.

"Do you think he wants to go out?" Leslie asked, breathless and hopeful.

Jamie shoveled penne into her mouth with her free hand. "Yeah. I think he wants to hang out on Saturday," she said, sarcastic. Leslie laughed and grabbed her phone back. As she chewed, Jamie pulled her laptop out of her backpack. While Leslie worked on a reply to Todd, Jamie logged on to Facebook. The profile pic in the upper-left-hand corner depicted the Liston Heights Lion, its mouth open, teeth gleaming. The name next to the thumbnail read, **Lisa Lions**.

"What are you doing?" Leslie lowered her iPhone. Jamie startled.

"Just checking Facebook," she said, nonchalant. Of course, she hadn't told Leslie about her second account, the fake one she'd made to keep tabs on the parents at LHHS. It had started innocently enough after Peter Harrington was fired. Although Peter had been a talented teacher—Jamie thought his lesson plan ideas were as good as Isobel's and certainly better than her own—he clearly didn't understand the Liston Heights culture. Maybe, Jamie had reasoned, if she *did* understand it—all of it, the parent side in addition to the student experience she'd lived—the mothers wouldn't complain about her to Wayne Wallace like they had about Peter.

"Did you see Rebecca's engagement photos?" Leslie asked, pulling Jamie out of her thoughts.

"Oh, not yet," she replied, stalling.

"There's a lot of gazing," Leslie continued, oblivious to Jamie's preoccupation. "And a ring shot. Gross."

"I'll check it out." Jamie looked down at her own empty ring finger. Her OkCupid endeavors hadn't been overly successful.

She navigated to the "Inside Liston" page she managed as Lisa Lions. She'd created the secret group using her second account when she'd first heard the words "declining enrollment" during the superintendent's back-to-school address that fall during teachers' workshops. In the beginning, she'd just friended the moms to see what they were like, and then she had the idea of giving them a forum to report on school quality. Although she felt weird about it, she'd started posting snapshots of controversial assignments and carefully worded personnel updates on the page. Sometimes between classes, she'd check for new comments, thrilling a little when something particularly nasty came up. Lately, parents had begun posting their own items—criticisms of hard graders and even a picture of Mr. Danforth's rusted-out car. **If this guy had any talent, he'd actually be making money doing something else,** the caption read. She'd laughed at that, although she felt guilty and, if she was being honest, just a little bit jealous. She'd rather be noted for something positive, but no one ever bothered to post anything about Jamie at all. She looked the Liston part with her stick-straight brown hair and freckled skin, but her trendy boots and borrowed lesson plans didn't generate any special interest.

Certainly, Jamie thought, the secret group was shady, but it did increase her job security, keeping everyone else in the department on their toes. And now Mary's recent e-mail made it clear that someone would actually have to leave in order for Jamie to keep her contract. She wasn't lying on Inside Liston, she rationalized, just amplifying other teachers' choices and statements. **Breaking,** she'd typed after last week's faculty meeting. **Eleanor Woodsley flooded with requests to teach seniors due to her superior college essay coaching.** This had prompted a comment thread about which teachers "ignored" the college process, which ones "half-assed" recommendations, and how to convince Sue Montague to honor teacher requests beyond the two the school currently permitted (because avoiding Mr. Limmer's AP Calc was critical for maintaining the senior fall GPA). It was all interesting to Jamie, and it did help her understand the parent mentality.

"Okay," said Leslie, interrupting again, "what do you think of this?" She shoved her phone into Jamie's face.

Saturday would be great for me, the text read. Dinner?

"Too forward?" Leslie frowned.

Jamie's eyes drifted back to her computer. "The tone is perfect. I'd say you have a date for Saturday night."

"Pressing send!" Leslie giggled. "I'll be right back." She jogged toward her bedroom.

As she left, Jamie dismissed a pathetic message from Julia Abbott asking her to delete the drama board video. She couldn't do that—the incident had massively increased her engagement on the page. She scrolled through the reactions to the queer theory handout she'd posted from Isobel's class. She had never done that before, posted something of Isobel's. To be fair, the parents had begun to discuss Ms. Johnson on their own. Several mentioned that their ninth graders had announced they never wanted to be mothers after Isobel's most recent unit, on nineteenth-century women's short stories. The yoga-pants moms hadn't been happy with the literature selections featuring mothers going crazy, and they hadn't needed any help from Lisa Lions to manifest those feelings.

And now, with the declining enrollment, Jamie didn't feel she could afford to risk losing her teaching position. She had to make rent. Isobel had been nice to her, but in the end, wasn't it every woman for herself? Wouldn't Isobel, given her curriculum, agree that women's ambitions were paramount?

Jamie had finished perusing the comments—one subset of parents was investigating whether Isobel actually had a college degree—and had her browser pointed to People.com for a quick break before grading when Leslie walked back into the kitchen. She brushed crouton crumbs from her sweatpants as she stood.

"Vodka soda?" she asked Leslie.

ISOBEL JOHNSON

When Isobel had made it through dinner and bedtime, she and Mark huddled together over their laptops. An open bottle of Pinot stood between them on the kitchen table, an upgrade from their usual boxed wine, given the circumstances. Mark crafted sentences while Isobel found and attached lesson plans and scholarly articles supporting her pedagogy. She and Lyle exchanged texts intermittently, and though Isobel searched for it, there wasn't a bit of an "I told you so" tone to his messages. Instead, he offered his own suggestions and agreed to edit the first draft. Just after midnight, when Isobel and Mark had finished documenting her philosophy on teaching the works of Mark Twain and scanning her college transcripts (all A's and a Phi Beta Kappa distinction), Mark leaned over and kissed the hair above her ear. "Let's head to bed," he said.

"I don't think I'll be able to sleep." Isobel felt tears welling again. She'd sniffled through dinner, telling Riley and Callie that she was allergic to something in her classroom.

"Let's just try." Mark stood up, arched his back to stretch, and held a hand out to Isobel. She took it.

"I just can't believe this," she said again. She'd been saying it over and over as they worked.

"I know," Mark said. She collapsed into him, feeling the soft terry cloth of his sweatshirt against her face, her glasses askew. "But it's going to be okay."

"The thing is," she said. Her lips brushed his shirt as she spoke, and her chest felt tight. "If I lose my job, this whole thing will have been a colossal waste of time."

"What do you mean?"

"I came to Liston Heights to impact privileged kids, remember? That's why I told myself I could even apply for this job. I was going to try to disrupt their thinking. I was going to prevent them . . ." She trailed off. She'd said this before to Mark. She'd said it to Lyle; she'd even told Eleanor some of these ideas. Maybe it was time to face the fact that she'd been wrong to come to Liston Heights all those years ago.

Mark squeezed her harder. "You've taught hundreds of kids there," he said. "Thousands even, in the last eight years. I think your message has come through."

"If what happens is that I get escorted out and Judith Youngstead takes my place, everything I've worked for is just gone. The school tells the kids that I was wrong or bad, even. The kids accept the status quo, which in the case of Liston Heights is incredibly unfair." She imagined the horror and shame of emptying her desk and closing her classroom door forever. She imagined Lyle's sad smile. He'd warned her, after all, and he'd been a good friend.

Mark didn't respond right away. Then finally, he said, "You don't have to be fighting all the time. You can do what Lyle and Eleanor and all the others do."

Isobel pulled back from her husband, leaving his embrace. "What?" She felt a familiar indignation rise.

"Couldn't you just tone it down, like Wayne and Mary said?" He sat back down in his chair.

"I can't believe you're saying that," Isobel said, her voice rising. "You know that when I took this job, the goal was to make the kids think, to stop them from treating other people like nothing. If there's anything I learned from my father—"

Mark's voice was level, but firm. "Your whole life can't be about atoning for your dad's sins. It's been almost twenty-five years. You can let it go now. Back off just a little bit and keep your job."

Isobel took two steps away from him. "Keep my job?" she repeated.

"Don't you want to?" Mark asked. "The money's good, and we're saving for college. I have to imagine it's harder to get a teaching job after you've been fired. You'd probably have to go to some place like East High. That was stressful in its own way, and it was expensive. You spent a quarter of your salary on classroom supplies and extra snacks for the kids."

Isobel gritted her teeth. She looked away from Mark, at the family room; one of Riley's sweatshirts was crumpled at one end of the couch. She thought back to the many times her mother and sister had similarly told her she could forget her father's indictment and subsequent imprisonment. But Isobel knew that wasn't true—it was the easy way out. Something in Robert Miller had allowed him to steal from the Rochester Area Charitable Foundation. He'd taken money from people in need. And he'd also stolen from her friend Meera and from other families just like hers. It was Isobel's duty to foster empathy, to make her high school students see issues from others' perspectives. She had to keep them from making Robert Miller's mistakes.

"I don't think you understand." The fact that he didn't made her desperate.

Mark stood again and looked past her toward the stairs. "I do understand," he said, "but you've done it already. You've been paying for your dad's mistakes since you were a kid. Now you can do something for yourself and for your own children. You can keep your job." He walked past her toward their bedroom. After a few minutes of standing in the kitchen replaying his words, she followed him. There wasn't anything left to do, and she was tired.

WAYNE WALLACE

After Wayne had dispatched Judith Youngstead to Isobel's classroom, he grabbed a fresh Odwalla and turned his attention to the spreadsheet Amanda from HR had handed him that morning. It listed every kid in Isobel Johnson's classes. He'd put it on a clipboard with the preapproved questions Amanda had provided.

"I have to call all of these?" Wayne had asked.

"Do a random sample of thirty-five," Amanda said. "Sue will handle the student interviews, provided you want to do this one the way we've done the others."

Wayne sighed. "It's important to follow the protocol here," he said, "especially . . ." He stared at his diplomas on the wall behind Amanda.

Amanda nodded. "Especially if we're thinking termination."

Now Wayne dialed the first number on the spreadsheet, the parents of a kid named Addie Anderson. Mother's name, Rachel.

A breathless woman answered on the second ring. "Hello?" she blurted.

"Rachel Anderson?" Wayne asked in his usual genial tone.

"Yes." Rachel's voice sounded clipped. "Is this the school? Is there an emergency?"

"Oh," Wayne said, realizing he'd forgotten to lead with the information that everyone was safe, "no. I'm so sorry to worry you. This is Wayne Wallace, principal at Liston Heights High School, but there's no emergency. Everything's fine."

He could hear the woman breathing. "Whenever I see the school on the caller ID, I imagine there's been a shooting," the woman said.

Wayne stared up at his Yoda poster and sighed. The woman's panic seemed a bit of an overreaction, but he wasn't surprised. He got four or five e-mails per week about active-shooter preparedness. It was on the kids' minds, too. That fall, one of the Liston Lights had profiled each of the school's security guards on Humans of LHHS. "I'm happy to say that's not why I'm calling today," Wayne said. "There's no emergency and"—he glanced at his paper to double-check the name—"Addie isn't in any trouble."

"What about Drew?"

"Drew?" Wayne repeated.

"I have a son in the ninth grade," Rachel said. "You're not calling about him?"

Let's get to it, Wayne thought. "I'm calling to see if I might ask you a few questions about Addie's experience in AP American Literature."

"Oh." Rachel's voice slowed. "I mean, sure."

Wayne flipped the spreadsheet up and looked at Amanda's list of questions. "Do you have the sense that Addie feels safe in Ms. Johnson's American Literature class?" He grabbed a blue ballpoint from the Liston Lions mug next to his computer screen.

"Safe?" Rachel sounded panicked again. "Are you telling me there are violent kids in the class? What are you saying?"

Wayne glanced at the little screen above the touch pad on his phone. It showed he'd been on this call for only ninety seconds, and yet it seemed far too long. "Mrs. Anderson," he said calmly, "I'm trying to get a feel for the student experience in Ms. Johnson's English class. What are Addie's impressions of the course?"

"Hmm," she said. "To be honest, I wish Addie liked Ms. Johnson more. I got a good vibe from her on back-to-school night, but Addie's totally blasé about her."

"Can you say more?" Wayne wrote *blasé* in the line for notes after Addie's name, the blue letters jagged and cramped.

"The teacher seems smart, right? Nice? I mean, I remember her talking about her credentials, and I was impressed. But now"—she held the vowel—"based on Addie's experience, I'd say she's marginal." Wayne wrote *marginal*. "And," Rachel added, "uninspiring." *Harsh*, thought Wayne as he transcribed the woman's final adjective and moved on to the next question.

ROBIN BERGSTROM

Later that morning, Robin sipped her five-dollar latte and opened her new Theater Booster Board notebook, ready for the last-minute meeting. It had been Vivian Song's idea. Brainstorm! The text had read. 11 am at Starbucks? The other board members had immediately agreed, so Robin moved her client call back an hour. It seemed worth it to connect with the group. While the Booster Board was never something to which she particularly aspired, now that she had a seat, she realized its appeal. She felt powerful—a little bit special—making these decisions for the theater department.

Vivian's lightning bolt that morning had turned out to be Statue of Liberty finishers' medals for the annual 5K, fitting with the Ellis Island theme. "I was also thinking we could decorate the course with flags," Vivian said, "like from countries the immigrants represent in the show?" Robin had just written these ideas on her clean page when she spotted Julia Abbott in line for a coffee.

For a second, Robin thought it couldn't be, but Julia was unmistakable: the shiny blond hair, signature black leggings, and long down coat. Julia's quilted tote hung on her forearm.

Sally Hollister had pulled up the awards company's website, and Vivian and Annabelle crowded in toward her iPad. Only Robin had noticed Julia, who at that moment turned toward the table where the women sat. Robin gasped as they made eye contact.

"Robin?" said Annabelle. "What is it?"

"Oh," she said, shaking her head. Annabelle followed Robin's gaze.

"Oh, indeed," Annabelle said coldly. "I should have known she couldn't stay away."

Although the meeting hadn't been planned in advance, Robin admitted it was odd that Julia was here midmorning, just as they had gotten started. "Maybe she's stalking me?" Robin said, not really believing it. The women laughed.

Julia raised a hand to the group and smiled. Robin waved back. The rest of them did not. Julia placed her order. Robin knew it would be a decaf almond milk latte with a pump of sugar-free vanilla. The espresso machine hissed, and Robin felt her ears getting hot.

"Let's just get back to it," Vivian said, determined. Her straight black bob curved perfectly under her jaw as she leaned toward Sally's screen.

Julia tossed her ponytail, stuffed her phone in her pocket, and marched toward their table. Robin's eyes widened. Before she could decide what she'd do, Julia was standing at Vivian's shoulder. "Hi, Boosters!" she said brightly.

"Hi." Robin offered a cool smile. Everyone else was quiet. The women's silence buzzed in Robin's ears, broken by the repeated slam of the espresso portafilter at the barista station. "We're just working on the five-K," Robin said finally. She picked up her pen. *Why should I feel uncomfortable?* she asked herself. *I'm on the board.* Julia, on the other hand, was clearly unwelcome.

"Yeah?" Julia looked right at her, and Robin held her gaze with new confidence. "Have my notes been helpful?"

"Very helpful." If Julia expected her to fall all over herself with gratitude, she'd be disappointed. After all, it wasn't Robin's fault that Julia's poor choices had finally had consequences.

"You're not supposed to be here," Annabelle interjected. She turned to face Julia, her long dark hair swirling around her shoulders.

Julia froze for just a second and then broke into a smile again. Robin could smell her usual perfume even over the richness of the coffee beans. It seemed old-fashioned to her, less fresh than the scents the other women at the table wore. "Don't worry," Julia said. "I'm not staying. I just wanted to say hello." She paused. "You know, since I saw you." No one responded, and Vivian crossed her arms. "It looks like everything is in order. The show, as they say, must go on!" Julia caught Robin's eye again. "When you have a moment, Robin," she said as she turned back toward the pickup counter, where her latte lay ready, "text me, would you?" She walked away.

A blender sparked to life behind the counter as Julia's ponytail swung toward the door. "Well," Robin said, looking around at the women, who seemed to anticipate her reaction, "she might be waiting for that text for a long time." The group tittered, and Annabelle reached over and patted Robin's arm. It was hard to imagine that Julia, with her brashness and impulsivity, had ever fit in with this group. "Back to the medals?" Robin asked. "What's the cost per?"

"Looks like three dollars?" Vivian squinted at the iPad.

"That's a little steep," Sally said, "but maybe doable. Can we save on the T-shirts?"

And they were off again. Robin watched Julia push the door open and slide her sunglasses over the bridge of her nose. She didn't look back.

TRACY ABBOTT

⁓

Tracy frowned as she turned the corner into Ms. Johnson's classroom only to see a grandmotherly substitute licking her pointer finger and paging through a stack of paper. Tracy looked at the board before turning down the aisle toward her assigned seat. *Mrs. Youngstead,* the cursive read, the "t" perfectly crossed with a slanted edge. The leaves of the spider plants near the windows, she noticed, drooped in front of their pots.

"Sub," Tracy whispered to the girl who sat across from her, frowning.

"Yeah," said her classmate. "Bummer. I was hoping to ask Ms. Johnson for help finishing up the revisions on my research project. Is she sick, do you know?"

Tracy shrugged. "Maybe one of her kids?" The bell rang then, and the class fell reasonably quiet. Tracy thought Ms. Johnson would have been pleased with their behavior for the "guest teacher," as she liked to call them.

Mrs. Youngstead's gray cardigan swished over her dark blue skirt as she walked to the center of the room. "I'm Judith Youngstead," she said.

"I've subbed in many Liston Heights High School English classes since I retired in twenty fifteen." She smiled at the students over the rims of her reading glasses. "I may have taught your older brothers or sisters, or even your parents!" Mrs. Youngstead laughed then even though she hadn't been particularly funny. "In this case," she continued, "it looks like I'll be here for at least a week while Ms. Johnson focuses on some curriculum development."

Tracy turned back toward her neighbor. *What?* she mouthed. Ms. Johnson hadn't mentioned anything about being out for an extended period. What about their research projects?

The teacher turned to write *Research* in red marker on the whiteboard. "Lucky for all of you," she said, "I'm very familiar with the process of writing papers." She smiled tightly. "My notes say you should be working on revisions." She pointed at the laptop cart against the front wall. "Why don't you grab a computer if you need one and get to it? I'll be around to offer some final suggestions."

As Tracy opened Google Drive, she clicked her e-mail for a moment. After looking up to make sure Mrs. Youngstead was occupied with another first year—sure enough, she'd been waylaid by Jake Tremaine, who never understood what to do—she clicked COMPOSE. She typed her mother's address in the TO section and quickly wrote, **Mom. I'm in English, and there's a sub here who says Ms. Johnson is out for at least a week working "on curriculum." Don't you think this has something to do with that post on the Inside Liston Facebook page?? I told you that group was evil!** SEND. Tracy scanned the class then, looking for other kids who'd also be dismayed by Ms. Johnson's absence. Jake wouldn't, obviously, but she thought ten or twelve others would, especially if they knew parents—maybe their own mothers—were badmouthing the teacher online.

Before Mrs. Youngstead could catch her with the extra browser tab open, Tracy clicked on her research doc, ready to toggle over to it if the substitute ever finished with Jake. Back to her new tab, she signed out of her official e-mail and hastily created a new account on the Gmail home page. She decided impulsively on the handle kate.awakened23@gmail.com, twenty-three for her graduation year, and smiled to herself after she entered the password, FreeIsobel2020.

Certainly, Ms. Johnson would recognize the allusion—a word Tracy had learned in her class—in the username. She'd told her teacher last month that she'd so loved "The Story of an Hour" that she'd borrowed Kate Chopin's novella *The Awakening* from the school library.

"Intense, right?" her teacher had said, a proud smile spreading across her face. They'd walked halfway to Tracy's math class together, debating Adèle's influence on Edna.

Tracy popped her head up to verify the substitute's whereabouts. Mrs. Youngstead had left Jake and now stood hunched next to Lauren Virgil, still a full row away. Slow progress. Tracy loaded Facebook and clicked SIGN UP. Kate Awakened needed a profile picture. For that, Tracy considered a sepia-toned Google image of the real Chopin, but rejected the idea for something that would blend in with all the other mothers' thumbnails on Inside Liston. She searched "stock photo mom and teenager," and screenshotted the second option, a woman with long brown hair and unusually white teeth, dipping her head toward a blond kid, their temples touching. Perfect.

Now "Kate" just needed an invite to the secret group. Tracy logged on to Facebook with her mother's credentials, the same password they used for their family Netflix account. She navigated to the group and quickly typed her new e-mail address into the INVITE bar. As a member, Julia had access. Then Tracy hastily closed the Web browser and glanced up to track Mrs. Youngstead's progress. She was behind her now, just three students away. A more astute supervisor—someone like Ms. Johnson—might have caught her on Facebook, but not this sub.

Still, Tracy felt shaky and took some deep breaths. She'd never so deliberately used class time for something other than an assigned task, and her heart pounded with the risk of it. She forced herself to read through her conclusion as Mrs. Youngstead approached.

Given all of the evidence of the motherhood penalty and its far-reaching consequences, women should think hard about leaving the workforce when their children are small, she'd written. *Good,* she thought. *Even though they may plan to get back into the swing of things by the time their little ones are toddlers, they may never recover their earning potential. Of course, another option is to skip having children altogether.* She'd have to change that last sentence, she knew, and highlighted it. Ms. Johnson had said no new ideas in the closing paragraphs.

HENRY ABBOTT

∽

When Henry arrived home after his squash match that evening, he found his daughter uncharacteristically involved in an argument with his wife. "It has to be related," Tracy was saying.

"It's a coincidence." Julia raised her voice. Andrew was nowhere to be seen.

Tracy walked from the kitchen to the family room couch and sat down hard. "Mom, it's obviously not a coincidence." She looked at Henry, aiming to recruit him to her side. He felt the now-familiar discomfort of toggling his alliance between his wife and one of his children.

He dropped his racquet and his duffel and walked past Tracy into the kitchen. "What's not a coincidence?" He waded into the conflict as he filled a glass from the tap.

"Use the filter," Julia said automatically. Henry dumped the water and turned to the small spigot at the left of the faucet.

Tracy spoke toward the television in the family room, staring resolutely at the black screen. "Mom is a member of this gossip group on Facebook. Someone posted a handout from Ms. Johnson's class, there were tons of mean comments, and now I have a sub in English who says Ms. Johnson won't be back for a week or more."

Henry's head felt light, and he guzzled the water, not wanting to move from behind the counter in the kitchen. It was true he'd imagined scenes like this when Tracy turned thirteen. He'd had friends with teenage girls at home, guys who rolled their eyes on the squash courts and mentioned hormones. But Tracy had always been so levelheaded. And he hadn't expected the prime instigator of girl drama to be Julia. "You're a member of a Liston Heights gossip group?" he asked her, his voice low.

"It's not like that," she said. "It's a page for parents of kids at the high school."

"It's evil!" Tracy shouted. "The person who runs it has a fake account. She posted the video of mom and the cast list and, like, fifty people shared it."

Julia sank into her usual stool at the breakfast bar and clicked something on her iPhone. Henry stared over her head and Tracy's at the blank TV. The video had been shared on Facebook? It was one of the many times Henry felt grateful he didn't have an account. "Did you delete the video?" he asked the room.

"I untagged her," Tracy said, "which is how I saw the Inside Liston page and all the mean comments about Ms. Johnson. Don't you even care about her?" Tracy whipped her head toward Julia.

Henry looked at his silent wife. He held out an open palm, signaling for her to speak. Certainly she could just apologize to Tracy, sign off of whatever Facebook page was causing the problem, and let things blow over. Daughters weren't so opaque, were they?

"It wasn't shared fifty times, and of course I care about Ms. Johnson," said Julia, her voice sharp. "It's just that I don't believe that site has anything to do with her missing class today. There are a million reasons why she might have been absent." Henry frowned at his wife. She hadn't struck the conciliatory tone he'd been hoping for. He thought back to Martin Young's remark about a muzzle and then felt immediately guilty. He put a hand on her shoulder.

"Well, if she's gone because of some discipline thing, you'd better believe I'll be starting a protest. Dad, don't you think I should, like, write a petition?" asked Tracy. Henry winced. For the second time in a week, he'd have to choose a side—his wife or his child.

"Wait a second," he said suddenly. "Who saw the video on Facebook? Anyone in the family?"

Tracy gave her dad an imperious look. "Oh, it's out there." Her tone was so unlike her—so much like the Disney Channel teenagers they used to watch when Tracy was younger—that he almost laughed. "I saw that Gloria Olson shared it, for instance. Isn't that Mom's cousin?"

"Second cousin," Julia said, still sulky. "On my mother's side." Certainly she could have been doing more to help herself in this situation.

"Okay, so what does untagging do?" Henry asked. "Does that delete the video?"

"No," Tracy said. "Only Lisa Lions, whoever that is, can delete the video, because she's the one who originally posted it." She stood up from the couch and took a few steps toward her parents in the kitchen. "And that's what you get," she said to Julia, "for friending people you don't know on Facebook. You're the one who's supposed to teach *me* that lesson. That's irony," she added. "*Ms. Johnson* taught me that."

Henry knew Tracy had crossed a line. Julia's face flushed, and she opened her mouth to speak. Henry could no longer hover between them. He'd have to side with his wife. "Why don't you go upstairs for a while?" he said to his daughter. It was the closest he ever got to "grounding," the punishment his own parents had so frequently relied on when he was a child.

"Fine." Tracy stomped past them to the stairs, ski socks making soft thuds on the wood floor.

"Do you know what else that teacher taught Tracy this trimester?" Julia said when she was probably still within earshot. "She taught her that motherhood is a depressing dead end. Tracy told me that not only did she not want to be a stay-at-home mom, but that she didn't even want to have children."

Henry could see the pain beneath the anger in Julia's face. Even with all of her missteps and unpredictability, he knew there was nothing she cared about more than being a good parent. Still, engaging in this particular hurt would only distract from the problem of the video on Facebook. "Tracy's fourteen," Henry said. "She has no idea what she wants."

"Still," Julia persisted, "do you think that's an appropriate message? That motherhood is a penalty?"

"No," Henry said honestly.

"And now both of the children are furious with me."

Henry bent over Julia, putting his arms around her. She kept her hands in her lap. After a minute, Henry spoke again. "But can we get the video off of Facebook?"

She shook her head. "I can try messaging Lisa Lions again and asking her to remove it," she said. "That's the best we can do."

JULIA ABBOTT

～

Julia jogged down the stairs the next morning in Lululemon pants and a long-sleeved performance top. She planned to pour coffee into a thermos and catch a six a.m. yoga class. She'd be back before the kids left for school. When she looked up, she saw her son seated at the kitchen counter.

"Oh," Julia said, startled. Andrew stared at her, his face bland. Not hostile, she noted, hope fluttering somewhere around her wide waistband. She checked her inclination to rush to Andrew and throw her arms around his broad shoulders. "Good morning," she said instead, half smiling.

"Hi." This was the first time Andrew had voluntarily spoken to her in ten days. Julia drew a shaky breath. She passed him at the counter and reached out to touch his arm. He didn't flinch, and she patted him lightly. She smiled to herself as she switched on the coffeemaker, set, as usual, to brew the dark roast she preferred.

"Why are you up so early?" Julia ventured. She faced him and leaned a hand on the cool granite.

Andrew shifted in his seat. His hair stuck up near his left temple, just as it had every morning when he was little. "I need to study some lines," he said finally. He looked down at the glass of water he held between both hands.

"Okay." Julia tried to sound encouraging.

"I don't think I'm ready for rehearsal." Andrew glanced up at her then, his eyelids heavy.

"I bet you're more ready than you think."

"I don't know." Andrew kicked his feet away from the stool, toes thudding against the cabinets beneath the counter. "It hasn't been going well."

"What do you mean?" The coffee's aroma floated between them.

"I can tell I'm not doing what Dittmer wants. He seems— I don't know. . . ." Julia willed herself to wait, not wanting to wreck the moment. "He seems irritated," Andrew said finally. "He seems mad at me."

Julia considered. What should she say? She didn't want to disregard his feelings by insisting she was sure he was doing well, and she also didn't want to confirm his fears by overvalidating. She looked at the philodendron behind him and finally asked, "What is Mr. Dittmer's criticism?"

"Something about my blustery body language." Andrew shrugged. "I worked on toning it down, but"—he sighed—"I don't know. After that, it was something about the tonality of my voice."

Julia watched the coffee collect in the carafe and kept her voice mild. "Want me to review lines for today's scene?"

He looked dejected. She'd always hated seeing Andrew upset. When he was a little boy, she'd been able to scoop him into her lap and distract him, but once he'd turned eight or nine, she'd felt more and more helpless, just as the disappointments became more and more real.

"I think I'll just read it over." He hopped off the stool, unfurling to his full height—over six feet—and walked toward the stairs. "Thanks, though, Mom." He glanced back at her, and she felt something spark in her chest.

TRACY ABBOTT

Tracy had just finished her geometry homework in afternoon study hall and was about to tweak the language of the petition she'd drafted to reinstate Ms. Johnson when a text popped up from Anika. Of course, she wasn't supposed to have her phone, but like every other first year, she had gotten into the habit of hiding it on her lap during her free period. The study hall monitor always seemed too engrossed in his own paper grading to notice.

911, the text read. Tracy furrowed her brow.

Are you okay? she typed back.

Can you talk? Anika asked.

In study hall, Tracy typed. Aren't you?

I got out to work in the set room. Ask to use the bathroom and call from there? Tracy felt nervous. Whatever it was had to be serious if Anika was asking her to break out of study hall. She slid her phone into her back pocket as she stood up from her desk. The teacher grunted affirmatively, not looking up from his work, when she asked to leave.

In the bathroom, Tracy checked for feet (none, thank goodness) and locked herself into a stall that stank of urine and Clorox. "What is it?" she asked as Anika picked up.

Her friend emitted a low moan.

"God," Tracy said. "Are you okay?"

"No," Anika said, the "o" elongated for a second or two. "It's just"—Tracy could hear Anika breathing—"have you seen Tryg Ogilvie's Instagram?"

"No." Her voice rose. She scanned the graffiti on the salmon pink stall divider. Someone had etched *Your dad is hot* right below the toilet paper roll, along with a detailed drawing of a pair of lips. "What?" Tracy said. "Did Tryg repost the video?"

"No, but it got picked up."

"Picked up?" Tracy echoed.

"Yeah," Anika said. "You know that site called Watch This!?"

"I mean, I've seen their stuff in my feed."

"Well, they—that site," Anika went on, "they reposted the video."

"Oh my God." Tracy realized what she meant. "It's on their site? The Watch This! site?" The video had been fading from their lives a bit. Even Andrew had stopped calling their mother "that horrible bitch" on their rides to school together. Tracy had begun to relax again, with no notifications to manage on her mother's Facebook page. But now, if the video had gained an audience beyond Liston Heights, it would start again.

"I'm so sorry, Trace." Anika sounded like she was about to cry, confirming the gravity of the situation. "It's on their site and their Insta and their Facebook."

Tracy leaned her forehead against the locked stall. The bathroom door opened and shoes squeaked on the tile. She closed her eyes. "I'm going to hang up," she whispered.

"Okay," Anika said. "Text if you need me."

Tracy looked down at her shoelaces, trying to decide what to do. Would her mom already know about the video when Tracy got home from practice that evening? She worried that her mother might cry. Or vomit. And no amount of untagging on this version could stop it from being widely shared on social media. The point of Watch This! was to go viral—and not just two thousand views, but millions. Their accounts had tons of followers all over the country, and her mother's repeated exposure suddenly seemed just as big and dark a problem as Ms. Johnson's absence. Both messes, Tracy realized, stemmed from that Facebook group she'd just joined. Tracy let the phone dangle in her fingertips for a moment and felt the cool plastic of the door against her hairline.

Then she lifted her phone and logged in as Kate Awakened. She jabbed an index finger at Lisa Lions's name, opening her public profile. It was time to convince this person, whoever she was, to shut the group down. It wouldn't stop the gossip entirely, Tracy knew, but it would definitely slow the spread of it.

HENRY ABBOTT

Henry sipped unsweetened iced tea from a straw on his way back from lunch on Friday afternoon. He and Brenda had met another member of the Liston Heights city council at her favorite taco place. They'd had a pleasant conversation about Tuolomee Square in the very neighborhood in which it was set to be built. The council member would vote to approve, and perhaps they could push the project through zoning even without Martin Young's endorsement.

When he opened the outer door of his office, Henry's assistant startled and scrambled to close something on his computer. Henry appreciated the impulse, but wasn't concerned about a little web browsing over lunch as long as William still answered the phone. "It's okay," he said. "You get a lunch break, too." It wasn't until he took a few steps toward William that he noticed the strange look on the kid's face, furrowed eyebrows and a clenched jaw. "Everything all right?" Henry asked.

William paused, clearly nervous. "What?" Henry prompted.

"Um," William began. "I'm not sure how to ask this, but do you know about a video—" As soon as he said the word, Henry had over-taken the reception desk.

"Where?" he asked, bent over William's shoulder.

"So you've seen it?" William cowered under Henry's torso as he maximized the browser he'd rushed to hide, the blue frames of Face-book filling the screen. He pointed at a post that read, *Wild times at my alma mater.* "I went to LHHS with that guy," William explained. Henry blanched as he recognized Julia in the still. A watermark on the video read **Watch This!**

"What's Watch This!?" Henry asked, hurriedly, as he grabbed the mouse and scrolled into the comments. He grimaced as he saw there were already two hundred eighty-two. **Crazy bitch** stood out. **Get a life**, read another.

"It's an aggregator," William said. "They usually have stupid things like people falling off their skateboards or getting chased by animals. It's like *America's Funniest Home Videos*, kind of." Henry kept scrolling, not caring that he had to reach awkwardly in front of William's body. He recoiled as he read, **How embarrassed would you be if this were YOUR mom? #AndrewAbbott.**

"How do we get this off of here?" he asked.

"We could try calling the company, I guess?" William said. "Or do you know who took that video in the first place?"

Henry clicked the window closed and took a step back. He brought his fists to his hips and stared at the carpeting. Of course this had hap-pened just as the initial buzz about the video seemed to have died down. He and Brenda had started lobbying the rest of the council. Henry didn't need the additional scrutiny just as prospects for Tuolomee Square were looking up. "Yeah," he said. "Can you try to find the con-tact information for someone at the video place? And then can you get me Larson Ogilvie's office phone?"

"Ogilvie?" William repeated, scribbling the name on a notepad.

"That's the father of the kid who took the video," Henry explained. "There can't be too many of those in town. Guy's a lawyer, I'm pretty sure." As he turned toward his office, the phone on William's desk began to ring.

William winced as Henry looked at him questioningly. "It's Martin Young," he said.

Henry threw his arms up and kept walking. "I'll take it at my desk."

WAYNE WALLACE

The phone rang in Wayne's office, and he turned away from the list of next fall's teaching assignments. There was no way around it, he was coming to realize. They'd be down at least three full-time staff in the fall. There'd be layoffs.

The little screen above the phone's touch pad didn't improve his mood. It was one of the parents in Isobel Johnson's American Lit class calling him back. He'd been filling his phone-call quota, making himself do one or two per hour between meetings. This time, it was Sally Hollister.

"Good afternoon," Wayne said, his voice warm despite his mood. "This is Wayne Wallace."

"This is Sally Hollister returning your call."

"Yes, Mrs. Hollister. Thanks for calling back." Wayne grabbed the roster of Isobel's students and lifted his blue ballpoint from the desk.

"I've heard from a couple of friends," Sally said before Wayne could continue, "that you've been calling the parents of kids who have Isobel Johnson for English. Is that what this is about? Maeve said she's had a substitute for English this week."

"Indeed," replied Wayne as he made a decisive check next to *Hollister, Maeve* on his list. "Could I ask you a few questions about Maeve's experience in Ms. Johnson's class?" At this point, most of the parents started to sound nervous, as if Isobel were potentially dangerous. "Our interest," he added, "is limited to Ms. Johnson's pedagogy."

"Certainly," said Sally, "but can I just say before you start that Maeve seems to adore Ms. Johnson? She tells me that American Literature is her favorite class. Outside of Theater, of course."

"That's great to hear. You seem to have the sense, then," Wayne continued, "that your daughter feels safe in the class?"

"Safe? Oh yes," Sally said. "As I mentioned, she loves it. I do wonder, however, whether Ms. Johnson always has to push the envelope."

Wayne looked at his list of questions, wanting to classify this feedback in the right column of his spreadsheet. "Are you saying that you or Maeve perceive a bias in Ms. Johnson's teaching?"

"Yes," Sally said. "They never seem to just"—Wayne could hear her intake of breath—"read the book in that class. The teacher is always asking them to find some kind of alternative meaning."

Wayne wrote, *Pushing ideas.* "Can you give an example?"

"Sure!" Sally was warmed up now. "Just last week, Maeve came home all excited about Nick Carraway. You know, the narrator in *Gatsby*?"

"I do." Though he hadn't remembered Nick before Mary Delgado had reminded him during last week's discussions, he was now familiar and knew what Sally would say next.

"Apparently Ms. Johnson claims that Nick is gay," Sally blurted. "She asked the kids to consider his motivations in terms of his"—she lowered her voice—"his erotic love for Gatsby. Now, I haven't read the book since high school, but I don't remember anything like *that*. And Maeve said 'erotic'! Did you even know that word when you were seventeen?"

Wayne wrote *GAY* in all-caps, his shorthand for the recurring Nick Carraway complaint. "I'm not sure," Wayne said, moving on. "Would you say that you think Ms. Johnson prefers certain types of ideas?"

"She seems quite leftist." Wayne jotted *leftist* on his list. "It's not that she shouldn't have political beliefs, but really, are they all relevant to American Literature? Could she just spend some time talking about metaphors?"

"Okay," Wayne said as he reached the last of his four prescribed queries. "Finally, is there anything else you'd like to add?" He dreaded this open-ended opportunity, having learned long ago that given the chance, Liston Heights parents would provide endless feedback on any number of school-related policies and issues.

"I don't think so," Sally said. "As I mentioned before, Maeve loves Isobel Johnson. Then again, Maeve is an excellent student and adores many of her teachers. You may have heard from the counseling department that Maeve scored thirty-five on her most recent ACT? I mean"—she laughed—"this is not a student who struggles to get along."

"Gotcha." Wayne pulled the phone slightly from his ear and rolled his eyes. "Congratulations to Maeve, and, Sally," he said, "I really appreciate your time. Have a wonderful afternoon."

"Oh," Sally said, sounding surprised that the conversation was over, "you're welcome. Anytime!"

ANDREW ABBOTT

Mr. Dittmer's frustration was obvious at that afternoon's rehearsal. As the minutes ticked by, Andrew felt more and more out of control, as if his arms and legs had lives of their own, flailing without any direction from his brain.

After the third missed cue—"Mr. Abbott!" Mr. Dittmer had yelled from the orchestra pit—Andrew caught Melissa raising her eyebrows at Maeve. Dittmer called for a five-minute break and asked Andrew to join him in the wind section. Andrew had clutched his script as he sat on the edge of the stage and hopped down. The familiar sawdust smell mixed with that of drying paint.

"I'm sorry, Mr. Dittmer," Andrew began. "I don't know what's happening to me today." Andrew stared at his too-small Converse, where his toes bumped uncomfortably against the ends. "I got up early to run these lines and everything."

"It seems like you're having a hard time remembering the blocking from yesterday," Mr. Dittmer said, not unkindly.

Andrew nodded miserably. "It definitely seems like that."

"Let me see what kinds of notes you took while we were going through it." The director reached a hand out for the thin paperback Andrew gripped so tightly.

He meekly handed it over. "Clearly, I'm not doing something right," he said, aiming for humor. Dittmer ignored him and flipped through act one. He turned the script sideways to read the marginalia.

"Okay," he said finally. He returned the book to Andrew, who attempted a half smile. Dittmer held his stare for a beat, and then said, "This is your first stage role, isn't it? Did you act in middle school?"

"I was in the chorus in seventh grade. *Anything Goes.*"

Dittmer nodded. "You need extra coaching." Andrew's stomach flipped. He knew it—he was the worst. Even after all of the work over the summer, and even though he'd somehow been cast in this show, he couldn't keep up. "Can you meet me in my office next week during study hall? Would Wednesday work?"

"Yes," Andrew said, as if he had a choice.

The director took a deep breath. "Good. We'll run act one, scene two, first. I'd like you to be off book."

"I can do that." Memorizing the lines, at least, didn't seem to be Andrew's major hurdle.

"I imagine you can." Mr. Dittmer looked upstage, where most of the cast sat sprawled on the floor, chatting with one another and underlining text in their scripts. "Now, go get a drink of water, and then we'll rustle the troops for another go." He turned toward the piano.

Andrew walked to the back of the auditorium and felt a heaviness settle in his chest. Rehearsals were harder than he'd imagined, harder than his classes at the local theater. The rest of the cast, they just seemed to understand what to do, even before Dittmer gave direction. How had they gotten so good? They all—even Tryg Ogilvie, whose entire part seemed to be shadowing Melissa wherever she went onstage—seemed to be naturals.

As he reached the top of the ramp at the back of the theater, he pushed the double doors and stepped into the vestibule. In the dark there, Andrew stopped and raised his head toward the ceiling. He stretched his arms behind his back, joined his palms, and thrust his chest forward. The little room smelled like paper, and Andrew envisioned the stacks of programs that sat there during each show's run.

And then, as he stretched, he heard Maeve's voice just on the other side of the doors to the theater.

"It's not his fault that Dittmer cast him," Maeve said insistently. Andrew backed up against the wall, next to the empty program stand.

"But if it were you," said another voice—Melissa's, Andrew thought—"wouldn't you at least want to know?"

"But how do *you* know?" Maeve pushed. "How do you know for sure?" Andrew felt a lump grow in his throat. What did they know? And was there any chance they weren't talking about him? Andrew raised his hand to his mouth, and bent his head into it, fingers cradling his jaw.

"Are you kidding?" Melissa said. "My mom has been on Boosters with her for years." *Her?* Andrew wondered. Could they mean his mom?

"So?" Andrew felt a rush of gratitude for Maeve's skepticism.

"So," replied Melissa, meaningfully, "I'm saying a costume shop isn't free. Did you notice the plaque on the wall above the light switch?"

"No."

"It says 'Abbott,'" Melissa replied. Andrew closed his eyes, blocking out the red of the exit signs and the white light seeping in from the hallway where the girls stood.

"But Andrew's not bad." Maeve's voice wavered.

Melissa's laugh was strident. "He belongs in the chorus," she said. "You know that's true."

Just then, Alice Thompson played some dramatic chords on the upright, the cast's signal to convene on the stage. Andrew pushed back into the theater, walking quickly to put space between himself and the girls. He was halfway down the aisle before he heard the door open again behind him.

JULIA ABBOTT

Julia got the text from Tracy just as her daughter would have been boarding the bus for ski practice. Mom, she'd written, you should probably check Facebook. Anika told me the stupid video's been spreading again. Julia dropped a basket of whites she'd just pulled from the dryer and ran for the basement stairs. *What about the untagging?* she thought desperately. Tracy had said that would keep it from reappearing.

Once upstairs, she crossed to the kitchen counter in three steps and woke her laptop. She quickly loaded Facebook and blinked at the number of notifications in the upper-right-hand corner. Another forty-eight? But how? Julia's eyes goggled as she clicked on her profile. **Is this you, Julia Murphy Abbott?** cousin Barb had written. Below the question, Julia saw the familiar still image at the start of the footage, her finger on the bulletin board. Fluorescent yellow lettering appeared in the lower-right-hand corner of the video this time. It read, **Watch This!**

What's Watch This!? She clicked the link, fingers shaking. The cinnamon-and-vanilla diffuser she usually enjoyed seemed sickeningly sweet. She hit PLAY, and the familiar scene at the drama board began.

Julia stabbed the pause icon before her elbow slammed into Melissa. If only she could go back to that moment and scoot by Alice Thompson faster on the way to the bulletin board. Then the bell would have rung after she'd seen the list as she'd intended, and none of this would ever have happened. She and Robin would have squealed over Andrew's role at Starbucks; she'd never have known her closest friend in Liston Heights was actually a conniving opportunist. Everything would have been fine. Better than fine, in fact, because they'd all have celebrated Andrew's role together.

Loosen the Spanx, Mom, the Watch This! headline read. Julia re-flexively ran her hand down her torso, feeling the definition in her ab-dominal muscles. *I don't even need Spanx,* she thought. She scanned the other videos on the home page of the site: **Hilarious Diving Board Fails**, one caption read. Another said, **Shopping Cart Disasters!** How had she ended up here with these pathetic people enduring public humiliation?

She clicked back to Facebook and deleted cousin Barb's post on her page. She clicked over to Inside Liston and saw that the watermarked version of the video had been posted there, too, by Marilyn Ogilvie. **Tryg's video's gone viral!** she wrote, as if she were proud. *Some parenting,* Julia thought, *teaching your child to benefit from someone else's embarrassment.*

She dialed Henry at work. They'd have to find some way to remove the video, and quickly, before Andrew had time to get mad all over again. Tracy's instinct had been right: Julia should have unfriended Lisa Lions the first time the video had been posted; or better yet, she should have found out who she really was and made her pay.

ISOBEL JOHNSON

⌒

Isobel worked late at her desk on Friday, her second day of suspension. She realized this seemed crazy, entering the school building when everyone else had left for the weekend. The first day of her banishment, she'd resolutely stayed on school grounds, sitting at a high top in the hidden back corner of the library, catching up on her professional reading and, by the fact of her presence, deterring would-be truants. Although Mary had told her she didn't need to report on these days—and it was indeed tempting to flee, given her anxiety and embarrassment—she worried leaving would be like admitting guilt. And she hadn't, in fact, done anything wrong.

On Thursday afternoon, though, Lyle had convinced her to take the next day off. "Think about how much you could get done on a workday when you don't have to be here," he'd said, appealing to her drive for productivity. And sure enough, on Friday after her own children were dropped off at school, she'd cleaned her kitchen, even weeding through their aging collection of spices. She'd then hit both Target and the grocery store before picking Riley and Callie up at carpool. She'd left Callie in charge in front of YouTube and promised deep-dish for dinner, which she'd pick up on her way home. Once the school parking lot was clear of the Friday rush, she used her key card to head back to her classroom.

It felt comforting to sit at her desk with no one else around. She cleared her top drawer of her favorite black Dixon Ticonderoga pencils (Judith could provide her own writing implements) and optimistically outlined her upcoming unit on Steinbeck for the ninth graders. This might be a waste of time, but Lyle said he thought she wouldn't be fired. And if the investigation went according to schedule and she was reinstated, she'd be back in the classroom as early as the end of next week. She might as well be prepared.

At the end of an hour of work, Isobel called ahead for the pizza. She sat back in her chair and surveyed the classroom. Had Judith wrecked anything in her brief tenure? *Not yet,* Isobel thought, though her spider plants suffered. She reached into her tote and grabbed her Nalgene water bottle, which she dumped evenly into the three pots.

She had a few minutes to kill before the pizza would be ready, so she opened Facebook and found a new post from her college roommate on her page. Immediately, she recognized the image of Julia Abbott, her blond ponytail and upturned nose. The Watch This! logo splashed at the bottom of the image. Her roommate had written, **This is your school, right? What the heck is happening over there?** Her sister had commented on the post as well: **Forget to tell me something?!** Isobel hadn't told Caroline about the video, in part because if she called, she'd also have to reveal the suspension, which she couldn't bear.

Although she knew Caroline would never admit to it, Isobel always felt she was disappointing her little sister. It had begun that first night in their small apartment, the first of many she'd crowded into Caroline's twin bed. And as an adult, Caroline still took care of lots of details in Isobel's life, down to choosing her clothing.

Caroline claimed she had to update her wardrobe constantly to keep up with the other women in her DC law firm, but Isobel knew she added a few extra things to keep her big sister from looking like a schlub. To admit her career was now in jeopardy due to the same moral imperative that kept her from J.Crew? Isobel wasn't sure she could keep Caroline in her corner.

Isobel clicked the video and found the Watch This! version already had more than two hundred thousand views. Seeing it again, Isobel realized how damning—and, yes, funny—the video was, even though poor Melissa took that hard hit. A mom's victory dance gone wrong in front of a crowd of kids? The scenario seemed made for a sitcom.

Isobel quickly typed a response to her roommate and her sister on the post. **There's no accounting for crazy,** she said, adding an eye-roll emoji. She hit ENTER, clicked the home button, and scrolled through photos of her friends' kids' sports victories and her neighbor's new baby.

JULIA ABBOTT

On Saturday morning, Julia opened a can of Diet Dew and put it on the counter as she stretched her quad muscle. She'd just finished her prescribed four-and-a-half-mile run in preparation for the annual 5K. Bracing against a subzero headwind that morning, she had thought once again about lobbying to move the fun run to the spring so no one would have to contend with winter's punishing conditions. But, as Vivian Song had pointed out at a board meeting last fall, the program consistently needed a cash infusion before the spring musical, Liston Heights' signature production. Julia asked whether they couldn't just refrain from overexpenditures on the fall play and the one-acts, but no one had spoken in support of that idea.

Andrew, sleeping now, had gone as icy as the weather after the Watch This! video had popped up in each of their social media feeds. Julia pounded out some of her frustration on her run, but dinner the previous night had been tense. She'd convinced the kids to eat together before heading to the high school's Friday night basketball game, and although she and Henry both detailed efforts they'd made to call Watch This! and, in Henry's case, Tryg Ogilvie's father, no one felt particularly optimistic about getting the clip off the Internet. They'd just have to wait it out. Julia hoped the children would keep speaking to her as they did.

Now she startled at her ringing cell phone. "I'm looking for Julia Abbott?" It was an unfamiliar male voice.

"This is she," Julia said.

"Mrs. Abbott," the man continued, "this is Randy Carlson. I'm a producer for *Local News Six at Six*. How are you doing today?"

"Fine." Julia sat a little straighter. Certainly the local news couldn't want a comment about the video? Would her humiliation be broadcast on TV, in addition to social media?

"Mrs. Abbott, I'm calling to see if you'd like to comment on a story we're producing for tonight's newscast."

No, Julia thought. *No comment, no story.* She sipped her soda and tried to ignore the pounding in her chest. "I can't imagine I have a comment," she said. "What's the story?" She bit her lip, hoping.

"It appears that you were"—the producer paused—"caught on video at Liston Heights High School? Are you aware that a video of you at the school has over two hundred thousand views on a popular social media aggregator?"

"Two *hundred* thousand?" she gasped.

"These things spread quickly, and there's a lot of public interest," the man explained, not even a little apologetic. "It's probably in your best interest to offer a comment. We can send a crew to your house this morning."

Julia pictured the potential news graphic—"Loosen the Spanx, Mrs. A" in a red, semitransparent font, splashed over a still of Julia's elbow making contact with Melissa Young's belly.

"I wish you wouldn't do it," Julia said, dropping her forehead to her palm, elbow propped on the granite. *No, no, no.* She pictured Tracy's beleaguered little face, her businesslike efforts to save Julia from the Facebook publicity. After a news story ran, there would be an additional media clip to hide—the story itself from Channel 6, not to mention

Andrew's simmering anger and Henry's barely contained exasperation. She didn't think she'd be able to withstand another round of publicity. "You see," she said, desperate, "the whole thing was an accident. There are a lot of hurt feelings. This story will cause harm for everyone involved—I'm not just thinking of myself. Wait," she said, realizing that she was speaking with a representative of the news media. "We're not on the record, right?" She'd suddenly remembered her journalism courses at the University of Minnesota.

"No, ma'am," said Randy, "we're not on the record, but in terms of doing the story, I'm afraid that ship has sailed." He sounded determined. "But you can have your say. You can comment on camera."

Julia raised her head, her fingers dragging over her eye and onto her cheek. "Is the school commenting?" she asked. She looked into the family room, gazing at the beige chenille blanket thrown over the brown micro-suede couch.

"We're in contact with the principal's office, and we have one comment from a teacher," the producer said.

From a teacher? "Which teacher commented?" Julia asked.

"We can discuss the details when we get there with the camera crew. Are you available this morning?"

No. Julia blinked at her snow-covered hydrangea through the sliding-glass door next to the kitchen table. "I don't want to comment," she said suddenly.

It was the right call. She tipped her soda can up again. Appearing on television would prolong the exposure. She'd learned about news cycles, first at *YM* and then at *Twin Cities Monthly*, a print magazine with a thirty-minute live weekend show on the local ABC affiliate.

"Are you certain?" Julia could hear the urgency behind the producer's question, and she smiled. Why should she make this guy's life easier while her own fractured?

"Indeed," Julia said, her voice back to its usual crispness, her can clinking against the countertop. "Thanks for calling."

WAYNE WALLACE

⁓

Wayne sat in his study on Saturday morning with a second cup of coffee. He'd told his wife he just wanted to catch up on a couple of e-mails, which was true, but which also took about ninety minutes longer than he'd planned. A particularly angry one had arrived the day before from Allen Song, who couldn't understand why Isobel Johnson had been taken out of *his*—he emphasized the possessive pronoun—classroom. "I'd rate her instructional skills as very good to excellent," Allen had written. "If you're going to suspend a teacher, why not go with Mr. Danforth? He shows two movies per week while he's supposed to be teaching me AP History. It's a travesty."

Wayne wrote *travesty* on a sticky note, a reminder to add this comment to his spreadsheet of feedback. He'd typed a neutral response to Allen, who wasn't the first person to express surprise and even anger about the investigation. Before they'd left on Friday Sue Montague had come to him with rumblings about a ninth-grade petition to reinstate Isobel.

"How many signatures?" Wayne had asked, exasperated.

"I think fewer than a hundred so far," Sue said, "but it's out there."

Wayne wasn't surprised that Isobel was polarizing. Still, he wasn't sure what he thought of her. Mostly, he preferred teachers who didn't make waves.

He was just about ready to close his laptop and leave his office when his cell phone rang. He frowned at the unfamiliar number and decided he'd better take a chance. One never knew when a custodian on weekend duty or an athletic team at a Saturday contest would need to reach a high school administrator.

"Wayne Wallace," he said.

"Wayne, it's Randy Carlson from *Local News Six at Six*. How are you?"

Wayne knew Randy. The station did frequent stories on LHHS, its sports teams, and its academic programs. A call from the local news channel usually meant good exposure for the school. "Good to hear from you, Randy," Wayne said. "What's news this time around?" Wayne thought it could be the undefeated boys' basketball team or perhaps the policy-debate squad. According to the coach's incessant tweeting, they'd recently achieved "unprecedented success."

"It's this video," Randy said. "The one with the theater mom taking out the girl."

The video? Still? It had been almost ten days since he'd suspended Julia Abbott from the Booster Board. Hadn't that clip faded into Internet oblivion yet? It had been four days since he'd even heard from the Youngs. Their attorney, it seemed, had talked them out of a civil suit.

"Wayne?" Randy prompted.

"Sorry, Randy. I'm just surprised this is news. It was one unfortunate interaction, and it happened almost two weeks ago." Wayne pinched the bridge of his nose. "I'm off the record, of course."

"Whatever you say. It's just that the video got picked up by Watch This! You know that site? Anyway, it's being widely shared. It's over two hundred thousand views already, and the local community recognizes it as LHHS. The station's gotten several tips, even."

"Jesus." Wayne tipped his head back and looked up at his bookshelf, where he kept the bottle of Johnnie Walker Blue that his dad had given him when he'd gotten the principal position. The two had clinked glasses and toasted to leadership.

"You on the record yet?" Randy asked.

"No." Wayne came back to himself. He'd have to call the communications people at the district office, which meant more time in his study. "I doubt we're going to comment, Randy, but when are you going to air?"

"We're slated for this evening's broadcast."

Wayne looked at the clock—ten already. "That doesn't give me a lot of time," he said.

"A few hours should be enough to get your ducks in a row," Randy said, unsympathetic.

Wayne frowned. "I'll call you back in fifteen."

Just then Wayne's daughter came to the door, a gangly eleven-year-old with enough height to be a pretty decent starting center on her traveling basketball team. Wayne smiled at her and held up his index finger, signaling her to wait. "Think about it," Randy said. "I'll tell you we do already have a comment from a teacher."

Wayne felt his chin drop in defeat. *What?* his daughter mouthed, and he held his finger up again. Which of his teachers could have been shortsighted enough to comment? "Who?" he pressed.

"Well," Randy hedged, "it's really a comment the teacher wrote on her Facebook page. We've got an intern who's a friend of a friend."

"What was the comment, and who was the teacher?" Wayne would need to know when he called the Liston Heights PR person, who'd be just as annoyed as he was to be dealing with this on a Saturday.

"The comment was 'There's no accounting for crazy.'" Wayne could hear the producer rustling through papers on his end. "And the teacher is someone named Isobel Johnson."

Wayne double-underlined "travesty" on his sticky note, the word having taken on new meaning.

ISOBEL JOHNSON

Isobel had been happy to escape into Riley and Callie's indoor soccer games that Saturday afternoon. She chatted easily with the Mills Park parents on the sidelines. None of their children were in her classes, and most didn't even remember she was a teacher. She hadn't put any makeup on that morning, not having to worry about running into the Liston Heights set. For the first time in days, no one would look at her sadly or accusatorily. Even an e-mail from Eleanor that morning about teaching act four of *The Crucible* had caused her only mild consternation.

"Put your phone away," Mark advised as she groused about the message. "Take a break from the drama."

He was right, she realized. She didn't need to respond immediately to e-mails from Eleanor on the weekend. She'd decisively stashed her iPhone in her tote for the duration of not one but two full youth soccer games.

When she finally checked in after the kids had finished victoriously, Isobel was shocked to see six missed calls and four new voice mails, all from unfamiliar numbers. "Something's happened," she said to Mark as he drove. Callie and Riley squabbled predictably in the backseat, flicking each other with the straps of their backpacks.

"Quit it," Mark said halfheartedly to the kids. "What going on?" He glanced at Isobel as she scrolled through Siri's imperfect transcripts.

"I have calls from work," Isobel said. "Hang on."

She clicked on the oldest of the messages and heard Wayne Wallace's voice, loud, as usual, in her ear. "Isobel, it's Wayne Wallace. Sorry to bother you on a Saturday, but it's pressing. Call me right away at this number." When the message had ended, she looked back at the list and chose Wayne's second call. "Isobel. Hoping to reach you. It'd be great if you could delete the Facebook post immediately, although I'm sure the station already has a screenshot. Kind of a mess and certainly bad press for the school. And to be honest, not great for you, given your current situation. Call me back ASAP." Dread swelled through her as she listened to Wayne's short sentences and gruff tone. *What Facebook post?*

Isobel felt light-headed as she heard the third voice mail, from someone named Randy Carlson at Channel 6, the local NBC affiliate. "You may have heard we're running a story on the Watch This! video featuring Liston Heights High School. The story will run at six. We'd love to have an expanded statement."

"But I didn't make a statement," Isobel said aloud, confused.

"What's going on?" Mark asked as he turned onto their street.

"It's bits and pieces." Isobel shook her head. "Hang on."

She clicked on the last of the four voice mails. This one was from a woman, someone named Grace from the Liston Heights School District communications office, her voice thin and nasal. "As you probably remember from new-teacher orientation, it's district policy that teachers not comment publicly on any student or parent matters. You apparently made a comment on your Facebook page? We'll need you to take that down. And please call me at your earliest convenience so we can walk this back as much as possible."

Isobel clicked out of the recording and looked at the time at the top of her phone screen: four thirty-seven p.m. Before she returned any of the calls, she opened her Facebook app.

"What's happening?" Mark asked again, concerned.

"Hang on." The post from her grad school roommate, the one that included Julia Abbott's video, sat at the top of her profile. It had garnered fifteen likes and a couple of those surprised-face "reactions." A few more people had liked Isobel's own comment on the video, **There's no accounting for crazy.**

That remark must have been what set off this emergency? She selected the post and deleted the whole thing, not just her comment. Still, Isobel couldn't think how it had made its way off of her own profile page. She wasn't friends with any students or their parents on Facebook. She'd been meticulous about that.

In any case, there wasn't time to puzzle it out now. The news segment was set to air in eighty minutes, and she decided she ought to make the call that could potentially stop that first. She dialed Randy, the news producer. Mark pulled the minivan into the garage. "You go in with the kids," she told him as the phone rang in her ear. "I've got to take care of something."

"You'll get cold," Mark said, wary.

"I'll be quick." The kids clattered out of the backseat with their soccer bags over their shoulders, still whipping the dangling straps at each other. As the doors slammed shut, Randy answered, sounding harried. Maybe if she denied permission to use her comment—if she somehow disavowed it?—it wouldn't appear in the story.

"Randy, it's Isobel Johnson," she said quickly.

Randy paused and then said, "The teacher! Thanks for calling back. Do you want to offer an expanded comment? I've got just enough time to amend the story."

"That's great news," said Isobel, "because I actually don't want to comment at all."

Randy fell silent, and Isobel waited, too. After a few uncomfortable seconds, Randy said, "You already have."

"I haven't," Isobel said firmly. She felt tempted to go on, to explain that she had no idea that a stupid, innocent comment on her seemingly private Facebook page could be used in a local news story, but it seemed best to give Randy as few details as possible. "I have no comment."

"Are you saying you didn't write 'There's no accounting for crazy' on your Facebook page?"

Isobel felt angry now, in addition to desperate. What right did this guy have to mine her profile, to encroach on her conversation with her roommate? "I'm saying," she said clearly and slowly, "I have no comment."

"Ms. Johnson, we've got your statement. If you don't want to add anything, I'm afraid—"

"I want to retract whatever you think is my statement!" Isobel felt surprised to be shouting.

"I'm afraid our story is locked. Have a good evening." Isobel pulled the phone away from her ear as it beeped at the conclusion of the call. She blinked, letting her eyelids close for an overlong moment. The heat faded in the front seat, and when she opened her eyes, she could see her breath. February, she knew, was too early for the Minneapolis public schools to post their job openings, but maybe she should reach out to her former principal at East High. Plant the seed that she'd love to return to her roots. Certainly she'd be fired from Liston Heights after this.

JULIA ABBOTT

The local news story was as demeaning, minimizing, and one-sided as Julia imagined it would be. She was right about everything in the piece down to the tacky graphics overlay, red font and all. And though she was horrified by the image, she couldn't help being pleased that she'd called it. Even as an intern at *YM*, she'd had a sense for design, in addition to copy writing.

The only thing she hadn't predicted was the extra jolt of rage she experienced when Isobel Johnson's comment appeared as a Facebook screenshot, her words circled in red. The serious-faced anchor said, "While the Liston Heights School District declined to make an on-the-record comment, one teacher perhaps reveals officials' true feelings. On her Facebook page, English teacher Isobel Johnson wrote in response to the clip, 'There's no accounting for crazy.' And, George, that's certainly one way to describe Julia Abbott's behavior as depicted in this viral video."

At that point, the camera panned out to include the torsos of both anchors, George, to the right of the woman who'd read the comment, barely containing his mirth at Julia's expense. "We've heard of parents removed from sports fields," George said. "Maybe we need time-outs for theater parents, too."

Julia covered her face with her hands and felt a rush of gratitude that Tracy was out babysitting and Andrew had made last-minute plans to see a movie with a group of friends. Henry watched the piece and then grabbed his duffel bag from the mudroom.

"I can't believe that teacher made that comment," Julia moaned.

"I'm going to the gym," Henry said. "Blow off some steam." His anger had simmered through the last day since the video resurfaced, but she couldn't bring herself to apologize one more time for the same ten-second incident. She didn't say anything as he shuffled around in the mudroom and eventually slammed the back door behind him.

When he'd left, Julia walked to the kitchen counter and opened her laptop. How could Isobel Johnson call *her* crazy? The teacher was clearly unhinged. She'd poisoned Tracy against motherhood (and her mother!) and was currently suspended from her job. Of course, the television station didn't mention any of that.

Though Julia dreaded finding another story about herself, she thought it better to know what people were saying. She clicked on the Inside Liston Facebook page. There was nothing new on Channel 6, thank goodness, but just above Marilyn Ogilvie's Watch This! post, Lisa Lions had added something. **Breaking: Isobel Johnson suspended from teaching pending investigation.** The usual comment storm exploded beneath the spare announcement. Julia skimmed the responses until one in particular stopped her. **Has anyone actually verified this woman's credentials?** someone asked.

There were no responses yet, and Julia had a Saturday night alone to do some digging. Perhaps she could help Wayne Wallace along to a favorable conclusion of his investigation.

TRACY ABBOTT

When Tracy had first read the Facebook page, she'd been certain that Lisa Lions was a mother, someone who'd lost herself like those missing-voices women from the stories in English class. But once she'd retreated to her room on Sunday night under the pretext of preparing for her vocabulary quiz (SAT words beginning with "s") and pored over posts by Lisa Lions, she realized she'd been wrong.

There was the breathless "Breaking" update on Ms. Johnson's suspension, the tidbit about requests for Ms. Woodsley, even periodic little dispatches from the lunchroom detailing which poor food choices were most popular among students. Lisa Lions had a particular disdain for the chicken patty, Andrew's favorite. She'd even photographed one once, the sandwich under the heat lamp in the ready-made section of the cafeteria.

This is not a mother, Tracy decided. There was no way a kid would stand for their parent hanging out at lunch and taking pictures of food.

Lisa must work at Liston Heights High School. Tracy imagined her skulking (a word from the SAT list) around the building, being friendly with everyone while always on the lookout for her next post, as salacious (another one) and stupid as one of those shows on the CW. Who would do that? She pictured the surreptitious (and again) photo of Ms. Montague's clog against the blue-gray carpet they had in every classroom. Had an adult in the building taken that picture during some faculty meeting? And there'd been a recent post about layoffs—something the teachers would know about first.

An older teacher, Tracy reasoned, wasn't likely to do something as shortsighted as moderating a forum for online gossip. A younger teacher would worry about layoffs and find Ms. Montague's clogs notable enough to publicly ridicule.

Meet me in the bathroom? Tracy texted to Anika Bergstrom on Monday during study hall.

"You couldn't have chosen the set room, where at least it doesn't smell?" Anika asked once they'd each arrived.

"This is closer. I didn't want to raise suspicion."

"Raise suspicion?" Anika rolled her eyes, and then her playful smile transformed into a look of sheepish concern. "I was actually wondering how you are. Like, at home."

"Did you see the news story on Saturday night?" Tracy imagined this was why Anika would be worried. "Now that's floating around social media, too, in addition to the Watch This! video. Even my dad's barely speaking to my mom at this point."

"Did you see Ms. Johnson's comment on the story?"

" 'There's no accounting for crazy'? Yeah, I saw it." Tracy shrugged. "Crazy" was exactly how Tracy herself had described her mother to Ms. Johnson after they witnessed the cast-list incident. Ms. Johnson's response that afternoon by the drama bulletin board had been "We're all a little crazy." The Facebook comment seemed harsher, but wasn't it a version of the same idea? "It's not important right now," Tracy said, leaning her hip against a sink. "I want to show you something." She shoved her phone at Anika, Inside Liston already loaded on the screen.

"This is that secret group on Facebook that our moms are in, the one I mentioned in English." Tracy had already checked Anika's mom's activity. Robin had liked a few things, but had never commented. "It's awful, and it has this anonymous moderator."

"Oh my God," Anika said, scrolling. "It's like *Gossip Girl* for adults."

"It's exactly like that," Tracy said. "And I want to find out who Lisa Lions is."

Anika handed the phone back. "Why?" she asked.

"Because this person is getting everyone in trouble. Well, getting my mom and Ms. Johnson in trouble. The video is ruining my life, and also, don't you hate the sub?"

Anika shrugged. "She's fine, right?"

"Okay," Tracy conceded, "I don't hate her, but Ms. Johnson is, like, getting fired and it's because someone's writing stuff—posting stuff— about her online without context. And I think it's another teacher." Tracy quickly summarized her reasoning, and Anika reacted strongly to the chicken-patty evidence.

"So, what do you want us to do?"

"I'm not totally sure, but I thought we'd start by making a list of every teacher hired within the last three years. The people with tenure wouldn't risk this, right? It's pretty dumb."

"Start a Google Doc," Anika said. "I'll get on it back in study hall. First"—she swirled her finger toward the ceiling—"I want to get out of here."

JAMIE PRESTON

On Monday afternoon, Mary skidded a desk along the carpet, moving it so she and Jamie sat facing each other, tabletops touching. Jamie felt oddly relaxed, a contrast with how she usually experienced a meeting with her boss. This wouldn't be a Grow and Glow, but rather a conversation about Isobel. Mary had been making the rounds, the other members of the department whispering about their meetings at lunch while Isobel was absent. She hid in the library, Jamie knew, or, as was the case on Friday, didn't even come to work. Everyone was careful about what they said in front of Jamie and Lyle, Isobel's friends, and changed the subject when they approached. Still, Jamie had heard that some people—Eleanor, especially—had unloaded when they'd had their chances with the department chair, using the occasion of Isobel's suspension to vent eight years of frustration with their self-righteous colleague.

Mary smiled at Jamie apologetically now. She cleared her throat and glanced at the teacher desk, where neat piles of paper sat in front of a potted jade.

The department chair looked nervous. It struck Jamie that their usual roles were reversed. Jamie typically fretted as Mary marched composedly through her agenda. This time, Jamie's impressions would set the tone. "I need to talk to you about Isobel," Mary began hesitantly.

"Okay." Jamie matched the slow pace of Mary's speech. While she'd known this meeting was approaching, she hadn't totally decided what to say. It was true Jamie needed some of Isobel's class sections to retain her full-time contract. How far should she go in her criticism? What would be impactful and yet not suspicious? She didn't want to seem as if she were angling for anything. At least, not yet.

"So," Mary began again, "I imagine you're aware of Isobel's situation."

"Her situation?" Jamie thought it best to force Mary to do most of the talking.

Mary raised her eyebrows, clearly surprised. "Well, we—Wayne and I—have fielded a number of complaints about Isobel's . . ." She looked over Jamie's shoulder. "Isobel's interpretation of the Liston Heights curriculum."

"Okay." Jamie pinched her lips together.

"And I'm trying to gather some more information." Mary scrolled through what seemed to be several pages of notes. "I'd like to know what types of mentoring you've received from Isobel in the last year." Mary tugged at her scarf, pulling it tighter against her neck.

"Isobel's been wonderful to me," Jamie said, "generous with her time and materials from the very beginning." She scanned the back wall as Mary made notes. Rows of novels lined the shelves behind the student desks, hundreds of copies of *The Scarlet Letter* stacked neatly in front of the cinder block.

"What kinds of things does Isobel share with you?"

"Everything." Jamie looked up, thinking. "Assessments, lesson plans, discussion questions . . ."

"For all of the novels?"

Jamie nodded. "Everything I need for American Lit. I don't teach ninth grade."

"Right. Okay." Mary's fingers clicked over the keyboard. "Do you notice any patterns in Isobel's teaching materials? Certain pet topics?"

"Like what?" Jamie pulled her black cardigan across her blouse, wrapping her arms around her middle. They were getting closer now. Two students laughed in the hallway outside the classroom, and they both glanced toward the closed door. "Do you feel Isobel has a political agenda?" Mary asked, eyes back on her laptop.

"Well, everyone knows Isobel is a social justice educator." She told Jamie at least monthly that "teaching for change" was every professional's responsibility.

"And within that identity," Mary continued, "do you think that Isobel maintains an openness to students who might disagree with her positions?"

Jamie considered. The honest answer was no, she knew. While Isobel enjoyed discussing controversial issues with students, she maintained an inflexible stance on many. "Isobel isn't one to compromise her ideals."

Mary typed, the glow of her screen accentuating the shadows beneath her cheekbones. Jamie's boss looked exhausted. "And what does that look like in class? I know you observe her teaching sometimes. Do you think students feel marginalized?"

Jamie thought about the angry mothers on the Inside Liston page, the ones whose daughters no longer wanted to have children. She also recalled those who, in response to the news that Isobel had been suspended, wrote that they hoped she'd never return. In fact, the number of people requesting to join Inside Liston had picked up after Isobel's suspension. She'd recently approved more than fifty new members, so many that she'd given up the minor vetting she used to do before accepting them. No matter how nice Isobel had been to Jamie, she was clearly a lightning rod. "Mary," she said, confident, channeling Lisa Lions, "it seems like you're asking me if Isobel has a liberal bias. Is that right? Are you asking me if she's using literature to impart a certain message to kids?"

Mary pulled at her scarf again. "Yes," she said, "I guess that's what I'm asking."

Jamie leaned back in the student desk, ready. "Isobel's teaching is steeped in liberalism. In fact, I'd call some of her work white liberal elitism." She folded her hands on the desktop as she delivered the phrase she'd read on CNN.com last weekend. A wave of relief spread over her. Although Isobel had always been nice to her, the current flood of complaints indicated the egregiousness of her agenda. Jamie had always walked her own lessons back from the leftist stance Isobel embodied. There should be consequences for political indoctrination. Though Jamie—Lisa—had given that most recent queer theory handout a wider audience on Inside Liston, Isobel had created it all on her own.

Mary's mouth dropped open. "You're sure?" she asked.

"Each book becomes a tool for advancing her agenda." Jamie looked up from her hands to meet Mary's eyes, feeling old and experienced for the first time since she'd begun teaching.

Mary coughed. "I have to say, Jamie, I'm surprised by your candor."

Jamie shrugged. "If Isobel's taught me anything," she said, "it's that teachers should tell the truth."

TRACY ABBOTT

Tracy grabbed her ski duffel from her locker after the final bell rang and she startled when someone tapped her shoulder. She turned to find Anika close behind her, her eyes darting.

"You scared me." Tracy smiled, recovering. "What's up? You look like you're here to deliver a coded message. Do you have a new theory?" The girls had typed the names of newish teachers by department during study hall, using the LHHS website to generate their list. They'd planned, via comments on the Google Doc, to narrow the field to an initial list of suspects that evening. Tracy had shared Kate Awakened's log-in credentials so they could both investigate.

"I think things have gotten worse," Anika said. "There's something new on the Facebook page."

"Since study hall?" Tracy glanced at her Apple Watch. It had been less than two hours since she'd introduced their task.

"Your mom posted something about Ms. Johnson's suspension."

"Shit," Tracy said, and then reflexively looked up and down the hallway, checking for adults who might have overheard her. None, thank goodness. She pulled her phone out and loaded the page. "It's long!" she exclaimed, scrolling through the multiple paragraphs Julia had written.

"It's going to take you a little bit of time," Anika said nervously. "You might want to sit down."

"Thanks." Tracy left Anika and hurried toward the library. Her friend was right: It was easier to assess her mother's embarrassing behavior without witnesses.

Walking through the fiction section, she clicked over to texts and, for the first time ever, lied to her ski coach. Feeling sick, she wrote. Heading home. Sorry. She felt slightly guilty for missing practice, but the Facebook thing seemed like an emergency. One practice, she reasoned, shouldn't change the outcome of next week's conference championship.

Tracy looked up from her phone and headed for an armchair near the periodicals, far from the librarian at the circulation desk. She navigated back to Facebook. As the page reloaded, Tracy felt her breath quicken.

Her mother's post began with a bolded headline.

Isobel Johnson's father was convicted of multiple felony charges.

What? Tracy started reading.

> In addition to the sentiments already posted here about Isobel Johnson's lack of regard for American history and literature, I want to mention that Ms. Johnson further scorns Liston Heights parents, particularly mothers. After just a month in her class, my daughter began to express a disdain for motherhood, the fact of it and the work of it.

Tracy winced. It wasn't disdain, exactly. She read on.

> Imagine my shock when Tracy told me I'd "wasted my life" by caring for my children. It seems the heroines in the stories Ms.

Johnson has chosen for our ninth graders share this sentiment. In fact, one of them killed herself rather than continue
to face the tedium and hopelessness of motherhood. It's no
surprise, then, that Tracy decided she no longer wishes to
become a mother herself.

I find Ms. Johnson's perception of high moral ground, especially her comments regarding respect and empathy, suspect
for a couple of reasons, which I'll detail here.

Tracy's cheeks burned. She glanced around the library. The room
was empty, save for the librarian, engrossed in her own screen, and one
romantic couple—juniors, Tracy thought—entangled beneath the 300s,
SOCIAL SCIENCES sign. Tracy quickly looked away from them and
blinked at her sneakers, thinking. Her mother's essay—that was what
it seemed like to Tracy, a persuasive essay in the format Ms. Johnson
had taught them—made Ms. Johnson seem sinister, like she had tried
to turn Tracy against her mother. But it wasn't like that. Why didn't her
mother ever understand? Tracy kept reading.

I began my research on Isobel Johnson with a desire to confirm her credentials—many members of this group have questioned in recent days her education and good standing—but
I discovered something even more critical. Isobel Miller Johnson is indeed a licensed teacher. She has fourteen years'
experience and a degree from the University of Wisconsin–
Madison. And she also has an interesting past.

Many lifelong Minnesotans will remember the case of Robert
John Miller, a financial adviser in Rochester, MN, who defrauded clients including the Rochester Area Charitable Foundation, which funds children's cancer treatments, in addition
to other lifesaving medical procedures at the Mayo Clinic.
Miller was convicted of several felony charges and served

eight years in a minimum-security prison in northern Minnesota.

I'm linking here an article detailing the specifics of his parole. In it, the reporter lists members of Robert Miller's family, including daughters Caroline and Isobel Miller—the same woman who now teaches so many of our kids at Liston Heights High School.

Tracy wiped her brow, which had dampened as she read about the cancer treatments. *Poor Ms. Johnson,* Tracy thought. *Her dad was a criminal? That might be worse than having a mom who punched Melissa Young.*

Now Tracy arrived at that bolded sentence her mother had cut and pasted to use as a title:

Isobel Johnson's father was convicted of multiple felony charges. Can she really maintain her holier-than-thou stance? Liston Heights parents, how comfortable are you now with this woman influencing your children?

Tracy clenched her jaw. Ms. Johnson would never have allowed a student to end an essay with a question like that, she thought, although on Facebook, she guessed it made more sense. People would answer it in the comments. Vivian Song had done so. **Stop being so petty,** she'd written. **This woman is not responsible for her father's mistakes.**

Go, Vivian, Tracy thought. She scrolled. Many of the other parents were less positive. Sheila Warner had written, **Makes sense that this vile woman would be the spawn of someone so morally bankrupt. Get her out.**

The librarian stood from her desk and headed toward the couple in nonfiction. She'd circle past the periodicals next. Tracy didn't want to explain her presence there. She had to decide quickly whether to comment on her mother's post. *She had to, right?* That had been the whole purpose of Kate Awakened—not just to bear witness, but to make a difference. Tracy smiled at the idea, at the phrase "bear witness." Ms. Johnson, she thought, might have chosen the same words about her moral responsibility. Tracy watched the juniors, chastised, slink toward the exit. The librarian turned, arms folded, and walked toward Tracy.

The small text beneath the Facebook post indicated that her mother's essay had already been seen by 456 people. She checked the total number of members of the group—there were almost seven hundred. She clicked the comment icon and began furiously typing, deterring the librarian, she hoped, with her concentration. **This exposé is written by someone whose most significant journalistic experience is a summer internship at *YM*.** She quickly posted and then clicked LOG OUT, standing to leave just as the librarian opened her mouth to ask her what she was doing.

WAYNE WALLACE

The principal reached for his Odwalla on Tuesday morning and looked down at the roster of Isobel Johnson's students. She'd certainly muddled things with the Channel 6 comment. Of the four parents he'd talked to yesterday, two had mentioned it. "Is it appropriate for a professional to be so judgmental?" one had said. He hadn't answered definitively, but scribbled *judgmental* on his spreadsheet. Another strike against Isobel.

As Wayne scanned the families he hadn't yet called, the Songs stood out. He'd received that e-mail from Allen about suspending Mr. Danforth instead of Ms. Johnson. Danforth was a dinosaur, Wayne admitted, but he wasn't polarizing. He kept his head down, and Wayne appreciated that.

Now he was curious to know whether the Song parents had the same feelings about Isobel as their son. He dialed.

"This is an atrocity," Vivian said as soon as Wayne had identified himself. "I can't believe you'd deprive my son of the educational experience he deserves to conduct this unwarranted investigation."

"I appreciate your opinion," Wayne said robotically, his curiosity satisfied. "We're trying to ensure that each student at Liston Heights High School is getting the experience they deserve." He took a breath. "Can I ask you a few questions?"

"Of course," Vivian snapped.

Wayne looked at his script. "Do you have the sense that Allen feels safe in Ms. Johnson's class?"

"Safe?" Wayne held the phone away from his ear to buffer Vivian's volume. "Ms. Johnson's English class is a highlight of Allen's day. She's been his teacher for three trimesters. She's been wonderful."

"Thank you," Wayne said. He marked a zero with a line through it in the notes section of his roster to indicate that Vivian Song had no complaints. He looked at the next question on his list. "Has Allen perceived any bias in Ms. Johnson's teaching?"

"In what sense?" Vivian asked.

"Are there particular ideas that Ms. Johnson prefers? Ideas that she validates more than others?"

Vivian laughed, a bitterness on the edges of it. "Is this about the white-savior thing? From *To Kill a Mockingbird*? Because I've got to be honest with you: It's such a relief to encounter a white teacher in this school district who will actually acknowledge race."

"Oh?"

"We are Korean, Mr. Wallace. Our culture is important to us." Vivian spoke quickly.

Dr. Wallace, Wayne thought to himself, glancing up at the framed diploma above his desk. "Of course," he said aloud. "Mrs. Song—"

"Dr. Song," the woman interrupted.

Wayne sighed and raised an exasperated arm. "Dr. Song." He wished he could skip his last question, but he knew the importance of uniformity. "Do you have anything else to add? Anything that might help us understand Allen's experiences in American Lit?"

"This whole thing is ludicrous." Wayne once again held the handset from his ear. "Allen finds Ms. Johnson to be supremely fair and completely qualified. In fact, if you want to conduct an investigation, may

I suggest you begin with that Danforth fellow? Allen tells me he shows a movie twice a week in Advanced Placement American History! I don't pay Liston Heights property taxes for *that*!"

Wayne looked at his watch. "Thanks for the feedback, Dr. Song," he said, his voice jovial again. "I've noted your concerns, and I'll take these into account as we proceed. I appreciate your time."

"And I hope you're not penalizing Ms. Johnson for her comment about Julia Abbott on last weekend's news," Vivian blurted. "Julia Abbott *is* crazy. You probably know that she's now retaliated against Ms. Johnson, dredging up that story from her past and posting it on that horrible Facebook page. The woman is disturbed."

"Facebook page?" Wayne asked. "You mean the Liston Heights High School Facebook page?"

"Of course not," Vivian said. "I'm talking about that gossip page."

"Gossip page?" Wayne repeated.

"You don't know about it? The parents involved do call it secret, but there are so many. Hang on. I'll give you the whole title." Vivian paused. He could hear that she'd put him on speaker.

"I appreciate that." Wayne's gaze settled on an open box in the corner of his office—custom water bottles for the Liston Lights—as he waited.

"Okay," Vivian said after a couple of seconds. "The group is called 'Inside Liston: A Behind-the-Scenes Look for Concerned Parents Who Need to Know.' Julia Abbott posted an article about Isobel Johnson's past, as if her father's criminal record is of any relevance to her current efficacy in the classroom."

"Inside Liston?" Wayne felt woozy as he wrote the phrase on his spreadsheet. "Isobel's father has a criminal record?"

"I'm surprised you haven't heard. Julia posted the story on Monday afternoon. She must have spent all day writing it, as if she's some kind of investigative journalist. Ironic, since her only journalistic experience consists of a summer internship at a teen magazine." Wayne could practically hear Dr. Song's sneer.

He leaned forward and pressed the space bar on his computer to wake it. "I'm sorry," Wayne said, hating to ask. "Can you tell me again how to get to the Facebook group?"

"You have to friend Lisa Lions," Vivian said, impatient. "She's who runs it. That's obviously not a real name. Her group is how I first heard about Ms. Johnson's suspension last week."

Wayne hurriedly typed **Facebook** into his Web browser. "Someone announced her suspension last week?" His own profile loaded in front of him.

"I'll find the post." Vivian was quiet for a moment. "Here it is," she said. "Last Thursday morning. 'Parent success: Targeted complaints about curricular overreach result in suspension and investigation of English teacher Isobel Johnson.'"

Wayne's mouth felt dry. Thursday morning? They'd informed Isobel of the investigation only on Wednesday afternoon. "Could you repeat that?" he asked. Vivian read it again. *How would parents have that level of information?* "Who posted that?" Wayne demanded. "And what's the group called again?"

"Inside Liston, Wayne." Vivian sounded smug now, and curt. "But you won't be able to see it unless you're friends with Lisa Lions. She moderates the group."

Wayne searched for Lisa Lions and perused the thumbnail of the athletics department's logo. Certainly tech support could do something about this.

"Mrs.—Dr.—Song, I want to thank you for your candor. You've been, uh, very helpful."

"Get Isobel Johnson back into the classroom," Vivian said. "My Allen plans to go to an Ivy, and a washed-up substitute isn't going to get him there."

"Okay," Wayne said, standing. It occurred to him to defend Judith Youngstead, but that would take time. "I do appreciate it. Have a great day." Without waiting for her reply, he put the phone back in its cradle and strode toward the door.

ISOBEL JOHNSON

Later that morning, Isobel killed her minivan's engine in the parking lot of the Mills Park Core Power Yoga studio for the first time since winter break. She'd found it easier in the last couple of days just to stay away from Liston Heights entirely, especially with the added humiliation of the Channel 6 story.

She desperately hoped Wayne and the district PR person could see that she hadn't actually offered a comment about the video to a reporter, but neither had responded to her messages or e-mails since the story aired. To atone, she'd done as Lyle Greenwood suggested: suspended her Facebook account and deactivated her Twitter. Best that Wayne et al. not see her retweets about Democratic politics as they carried on their investigation, Lyle said. She agreed.

Isobel's top priority since Sunday had been avoiding anyone who knew of her work situation or of her connection to the news story. A midmorning weekday class in a dimly lit yoga studio in Mills Park ought to be the perfect escape.

She signed in at the front desk. "Enjoy." The chipper spandex-clad receptionist smiled as she pointed toward the women's locker room.

Isobel marched into a changing stall and yanked the curtain shut. She breathed in the lemongrass and eucalyptus, replacing her black Loft pants with Old Navy yoga crops. She turned sideways in front of the mirror to check things out. *Not terrible,* she thought, hiking the Lycra high enough to smooth out the ripple beneath her belly button.

She was unhooking her well-worn bra, more grayish than white, when she heard a familiar voice outside the curtain.

"No, Henry," the woman was saying. "I just think the community has a right to know. It's a public service announcement."

Isobel froze. *No way,* she thought. What would Julia Abbott be doing in Mills Park? Liston Heights had at least six boutique yoga studios of its own. Isobel inched toward the gap between the curtain and the wall, her bra hanging loose on her shoulders, and peeked. The woman faced away, but her blond ponytail looked familiar.

"It's her history, and it was public knowledge! It proves she's a hypocrite." The woman emitted a grim laugh. That spiteful tone matched Julia's at the Sadie's dance and the shouting Isobel had overheard in the LHHS parking lot. It had to be her. Isobel fought the urge to sit down on the floor. *What are the fucking chances?*

"I found it in the *Star Tribune,* Henry. It's not as if one has to be KGB to unearth news of a major white-collar crime."

White-collar crime? It hadn't occurred to her to wonder what Julia was talking about, but now she had Isobel's attention. Of course, that phrase always conjured up her father. She envisioned his sad hazel eyes, their color nearly matching her own. The last time she'd seen them, he'd stood on the stoop of the apartment she shared with Mark, rumpled and deflated, recently released from prison.

Isobel looked down at her clothes now, puddled on the dark wood floor. The last thing she wanted to do was yoga with the most vicious of the Liston Heights mothers. Gone were her visions of escape and relaxation. And yet she'd made it here. She'd already used her punch card. Her bare skin prickled in the cool air. *Don't let stupid Julia Abbott run you out of here,* Isobel told herself. *Mills Park is your turf.* She stifled a chuckle at the thought, but it was true. This was her yoga studio. She grabbed a sports bra from her bag and wriggled it over her head.

"Of course I'm deflecting!" Julia was saying. "Do you think I want more attention? I want back on the Booster Board, and I want Tracy—" She stopped, her voice catching with emotion that surprised Isobel. "Henry, I have to go," she said then, sharply. "No, I'm at yoga." She paused. "Yeah, that's what I thought. And I drove all the way to Mills Park to be sure to avoid everyone."

So they were both hiding. Isobel pulled a loose tank top over her belly and secured her bangs with a bobby pin. She shoved her street clothes into her bag. "Okay," she whispered, and she pulled the curtain back.

Julia's ponytail flipped over the top of her head as she bent over her tote. Isobel paused for a moment, wondering if she should wait until she stood up. In a split second, she decided against it and stepped quickly past her into the hallway. Perhaps she could do the whole class and get out again without having to acknowledge Julia. Maybe she could just be extra Zen and do poses with her eyes closed?

Isobel walked into the warm studio. The eucalyptus intensified, tinged with the sweat of the previous students. She unrolled a borrowed mat in the back corner, as far as possible from the four other women who'd already arrived. She watched the door while resting in child's pose. In a few seconds, Julia breezed in, shoulders square in a form-fitting top with crisscross straps across the back. Once settled in the front near the door, she raised her arms over her head, then folded her torso against her legs in an impressive display of flexibility.

Jesus, Isobel thought.

It wasn't until the class had begun and moved into its second or third Warrior 2 that Julia finally caught Isobel's eye.

I belong here, Isobel told herself as Julia stared. She offered a closed-mouth smile and then looked over her fingertips as the instructor prompted.

As she lay back in corpse pose at the end of class, Isobel felt accomplished. Finally, the instructor rang a chime and wished the class "namaste," and Isobel moved to get the disinfectant from the cabinet near the door, where Julia was rolling her mat.

Julia looked up just as Isobel was grabbing a cloth rag from a wicker basket. Isobel had already decided she'd speak first. "Hello, Mrs. Abbott," she said.

"Ms. Johnson," Julia said flatly.

"I'm surprised to see you all the way out here in Mills Park." She dampened a cloth with the minty cleaning solution and handed the spray bottle to the next woman waiting.

"I was trying to get off the beaten path." Julia paused, and Isobel started back to her mat. "I'm surprised to see you here, too," Julia called after her, "as it's the middle of the school day."

Isobel turned back around and ran a hand over her hip, deciding what to say. "Yeah," she offered, her voice quieter than she meant it to be, "I have some time off."

Julia smirked. "Oh, that's right," she said. "I heard about the investigation." Isobel stepped backward, away from Julia's inappropriate volume, and bumped another woman's shoulder.

"Excuse me," she muttered to the person she'd jostled. "I'm sorry."

The woman waved her off, and Julia maintained her smug smile. "Wayne Wallace is calling all the parents," she continued, "though you probably know that. Had you heard people weren't sure you had a license?"

Isobel looked at the chalkboard on the wall over Julia's head, trying to tamp down her trepidation. *Tension is who you think you should be,* the quotation there read. *Relaxation is who you are.* A wave of dizziness passed over Isobel, her vision blurring in the heat. The letters on the chalkboard ran together. She couldn't remember the last time someone had been openly mean to her. Were other people in the studio noticing? How could they not, when everyone else spoke in the whispers that matched the instructor's good-bye? "I knew Wayne was making some calls," Isobel said, clinging to professionalism.

"It seems like you're having a difficult time," Julia said. "That's really too bad." She stood, her ponytail swinging, her rolled mat tucked under her arm.

"I love teaching," Isobel blurted. She lifted the rag in her hand, marking her point.

"Yeah," Julia said, "but maybe Liston Heights isn't the right venue for you?" Julia seemed so composed, while Isobel felt as if she were disintegrating. "People there have really high expectations," Julia continued. "I'm sure—and obviously I'm not telling you anything you haven't thought of yourself—people would rather not have the daughter of a notorious financial criminal lecturing their children on social justice." She laughed then, that same grim laugh from the locker room before class, though nothing was funny.

Isobel nearly dropped to her knees. A sharp pain presented above her right ear. The instructor approached suddenly and grabbed Isobel's elbow. "Are you all right?" she asked. "You look woozy."

"I need—" Isobel looked past Julia through the glass door beyond the studio.

"Let's get you out of the heat," the instructor said. She helped her to her feet and pushed her lower back as she opened the door. Isobel blinked in the bright light and let herself be hustled away.

HENRY ABBOTT

D ad," Andrew whispered in Henry's ear at eleven thirty that evening. Henry registered a hand on his biceps, gently shaking. In a blink, he sat up and reached for his glasses. "Sorry," Andrew said. Henry swung his legs onto the floor. The cuffs of his threadbare pajamas slid down over his ankles.

"What is it?" Henry asked, coming to himself.

"Kitchen?" The boy pointed at the hallway.

"Are you okay?" Next to Henry, Julia sighed heavily in her sleep. Andrew looked at her warily.

"I'm okay."

Henry hefted himself from the bed and creaked toward Andrew.

At the kitchen table, Henry could see his son's teeth grinding beneath the flesh of his cheek. When had his face become so thin and defined? Henry felt nervous suddenly. He couldn't remember seeing Andrew so agitated. "Do you want water?" he asked.

"No," said Andrew, his hands flat on the oak in front of him. "Is it true?" His upper lip twitched.

"Is what?" Henry asked.

"Dad," Andrew insisted, "you know what I'm saying." Henry rubbed the stubble on his jawline, feeling a slight looseness to his skin there. "Did you—" Andrew breathed. "Did you and mom buy my part in the musical?"

"What are you talking about?" Henry asked, still squinting under the bright kitchen lights.

"You know," Andrew said, more loudly. "You know exactly what I'm talking about." He stared at his dad. "Did the costume shop buy my part?" Henry blinked at him. "My part in the musical," Andrew clarified, looking down at his hands, now balled into fists.

"Of course not," Henry sighed. "That's not how these things work."

"What things?"

"Decisions like the cast of the Liston Heights High School musical." He stood. "I'm going to get some water." He needed a second to decide how to play this. Neither of them said anything as Henry turned on the tap and filled a glass that had been sitting on the edge of the sink.

When he got back to the table, his son looked slightly abashed. "What do you mean, 'that's not how these things work'? You and mom donated money for the costume shop, right?"

Henry looked at the clock, its spindly second hand ticking past twelve. He'd be as straight as he could, he decided. At seventeen, Andrew was old enough to understand the basics of negotiations. "Yes," he said. "We love Liston Heights, we support you and your activities, and we wanted to contribute to the program."

"But did you ask for anything in return?"

"Where is this coming from?"

Andrew's eyes widened. "It's coming from the cast! It's coming from my friends." Henry noticed the red rims around Andrew's eyes. He'd been crying. "It's all anyone's been saying since the video."

"How does the video factor into this?"

"Dad," said Andrew, "no one's been talking about anything but the video since the day it happened. I can't escape it. It's been on Watch This! and then the news, and now . . ." He drew in a shaky breath.

"And now what?" Henry shivered and wished for his and Julia's thick duvet.

"Last Friday Melissa Young said that Mr. Dittmer had to give me the part of the inspector because of the costume shop. She said that Mom . . ." He searched for the vocabulary of the deals and handshakes he didn't know existed.

"I'm sure that wasn't exactly how it went," Henry said, calm.

"But?" Andrew pressed, tears coming now, catching in his eyelashes.

"But," Henry surrendered, "that's a little bit of how the world works." Andrew stared at him. "You have to know that, right?" Andrew shook his head weakly, and Henry's heart broke a little. He recalled another evening eight years before, Andrew's big eyes aghast, when Henry finally confirmed that he himself was Santa Claus.

"So it is true," Andrew moaned. "I didn't earn it."

"Son?" Henry leaned across the table and put his big palm over Andrew's quivering fist. "No one really earns anything."

JULIA ABBOTT

On Wednesday morning after the kids had left for school—Andrew's eyes had looked bleary, Julia noticed—Henry lingered in the kitchen.

"No early meetings?" Julia glanced up from her laptop, where she'd been skimming headlines on *Women's Wear Daily*, trying to distract herself from the Inside Liston Facebook page. Henry's tie hung askew, the short end caught on the buttons of his shirt.

"Andrew woke me up last night," he said. The words sounded rehearsed, as if he'd been thinking about them for hours.

Julia blinked at him. Her hands migrated from her keyboard to her lap. "Why?"

"He wanted to know whether we bought his role in the musical for him."

"What?" She rubbed the pad of one thumb over the nail of the other and glanced out at the snow-covered hydrangea.

"Apparently, the other kids in the play have told him that we donated the costume shop in exchange for his part."

"That's ridiculous," Julia said, looking back at him. Henry grabbed his travel mug from beside the sink and crossed to the coffeemaker. "What did you tell him?"

"He's not an idiot," Henry said, his tone low. "He's seventeen years old."

"Wait." Julia stood from her stool, her stocking feet flat on the hardwood. "You confirmed that? You told Andrew that we bought him a role in the musical? What were you thinking?"

"I didn't say that we *bought* the part."

"Well, it sounds like you didn't *not* say that." She raised her voice. The last thing Andrew needed when he'd been struggling in rehearsal was the impression that he didn't belong, that he was inferior.

"Calm down," Henry said, maddeningly staid. He put a hand to his forehead. "Can you just listen to what I have to say for once?"

Julia clenched her teeth. *For once?* She listened to what Henry said all the time. He'd choreographed their meeting with Wayne Wallace, for starters. Then he'd "advised" her on the video. He'd been running interference between Julia and the kids for two weeks straight since the cast list had been posted.

"You know very well that we did, in fact, buy Andrew's role," Henry said tightly, "or at the very least, we strongly encouraged the school to cast him. Andrew knows that. The other kids know that. It's the way of the world. If we pull the strings—and I'm not saying we shouldn't—there will be consequences."

Behind them the coffeemaker hissed, spitting the last of the water from its reservoir. Julia's hands felt itchy. "You think I haven't had consequences?" she said. He didn't even know yet about Kate Awakened, the fourteen laughing responses to her *YM* comment on the Inside Liston page. "You think I need punishment? Is that what you're saying?"

Henry turned away from her and straightened his tie. He didn't like to argue, she knew. He'd always back off. She'd seen his reticence in their very first English class together, the one during which she'd so enjoyed hassling the TA, and Henry had so enjoyed watching her do it.

When he turned back to her, Henry's voice was tighter, more urgent. "Julia, you've been getting us into jams like this Melissa Young thing for years. When Wayne mentioned overinvestment? That's you. At some point we have to let the kids live their own lives." The floor felt slippery beneath her socks. It was easy for Henry to talk about overinvestment. She'd handled everything for the kids, from birth till now. "When do we all get to make our own decisions and our own mistakes?" Henry said more quietly. "Or will we always have to dodge yours?"

Julia sat back down on her stool, the perch from which she managed the entire household. She didn't speak.

"Did you know the Tuolomee Square project looks dead?" Henry continued. "I don't think I can get Martin Young to sign off on the zoning change, and there are a couple of other members he's blocked." He exhaled loudly. "My deal might be off because you punched Martin Young's daughter."

Julia's eyes filled, tears of helplessness more than of anger. She made everything happen in their family. Every team the kids had joined, every play, every academic program—it had gone well because she'd been paying attention. She'd given up on her own journalistic dreams as a twenty-year-old and poured every bit of her ambition into making their family work. And now Henry saw her only as a liability, and multiple fake accounts mocked her on social media. A pause extended between them. Steam rose from Julia's coffee. She reached a hand up to swipe the tears.

Finally, she looked at him. "Can you change?" he asked quietly. "Can you stop doing stuff like this?"

"Like what?" she asked weakly.

"I need you to be different," Henry said. Julia hooked her toes around the stool's rung and dipped her nose toward her coffee cup. *Could she change?* She had no idea. She had always just been herself.

ANDREW ABBOTT

Andrew knocked tentatively on John Dittmer's office door just as the bell rang for afternoon study hall.

"Come in," called Mr. Dittmer. Andrew pushed the door open, the handle warm against his hand. "Ah," said the director, standing up from his desk. "Andrew! Have a seat." He sounded friendly enough, not nearly as irritated as he'd been at last night's rehearsal.

"Hi." Andrew moved toward the table, then sat. The room smelled like corn. Andrew glanced at Dittmer's desk and saw an open bag of Fritos. "So," the director said, "*Ellis Island* is your first speaking role. That's a big transition from the chorus and the behind-the-scenes work you've done in previous productions."

Andrew nodded. He shifted in his seat, legs stiff.

"How's it felt so far?" Mr. Dittmer prompted.

"Um." Andrew stalled. What could he say? He almost laughed, thinking of what the truth might sound like. *The whole thing has been terrible? First, my mom humiliated our entire family. It's clear the entire cast knows she's psychotic. And now I'm not even capable of doing the basic things you ask in rehearsal. Besides all that, I know you never wanted to cast me in the first place?* "I guess," Andrew tried, "I guess it's been a little rough."

"The leads this time are extraordinarily experienced," Mr. Dittmer said. "You're jumping into a seasoned crowd." He waited again. Andrew heard footfalls in the outer office, an adjacent door closing.

"Melissa especially," Andrew said, drawing in a breath. "She seems, uh . . ." He searched for the word. "She seems disappointed in my performance."

Mr. Dittmer brought the tips of his fingers together and nodded slowly. "I can imagine your relationship with Melissa is a little strained." The director was quiet for a moment. Meanwhile, Andrew's mind was racing. He felt an overwhelming desire to get out of this situation, to feel comfortable in practice, to be able to face his friends.

"The thing is, Mr. Dittmer," Andrew said. He could hear his pitch rising. "The thing is," he started again, wanting to sound mature, "I don't belong up there with those kids." He forced himself to make eye contact. "I know I don't deserve my role." He spoke the words, and a heaviness lifted as if the truth of the situation had been holding him down.

"Why would you say that?" Mr. Dittmer asked.

Andrew felt suddenly calm and emboldened. "Can we be honest with each other?"

The director's mouth opened slightly, and he nodded. "Okay," he said.

"I know you felt like you had to give me the inspector role because my parents donated the costume shop. I know—" He swallowed, replaying Melissa's pronouncement in his mind. "I know I belong in the chorus."

Mr. Dittmer tilted his head. "There are lots of reasons casting decisions are made," he said finally.

Andrew felt a strange new energy in his legs. He had an urge to stand up. Instead, he leaned forward and put his elbows on the table. "I want to be a luggage handler. I want to be in the chorus."

Mr. Dittmer blinked a few times. "You want me to reassign the inspector role because you want to be in the chorus?"

Andrew slapped the table with an open palm. He felt happy, relieved. "That's what I want," he said. "Can we do that?"

Mr. Dittmer patted his thighs and looked at the Fritos. Andrew felt like taking a handful in celebration. "Well"—he considered—"we're in our second week; the blocking is just emerging." He looked back at Andrew and waited, thinking. "Yes," he said finally, "I can switch your role for Tryg Ogilvie's. You can be the luggage handler, and Tryg can take on the inspector."

Andrew blanched at the mention of Tryg—he still hadn't talked to him about the goddamn Instagram video that wouldn't die—but the idea of holding the suitcase seemed right. "Okay," Andrew said. "I'm game."

ISOBEL JOHNSON

When Isobel had arrived home after yoga the day before, her first call had been to Mark. After she'd told him through her hiccups and sniffles what had transpired in the studio, he advised her to call Mary Delgado. "It's harassment," Mark said. "First the voice mail, which had to be from Julia Abbott, and the calls to Wayne's office, then bullying about your father? Something's happening. There's, like, a conspiracy. Should I come home?"

"No," Isobel whimpered. There was nothing he could do.

"Mention 'hostile work environment.'" Mark had gone into lawyer mode, which Isobel appreciated, especially in her distress. "Text me once you talk to her."

She'd called Mary next, and her boss had immediately agreed to an in-person conversation. Now she walked to the table at the back of the library where the department chair sat waiting. Isobel looked terrible. It had seemed tasteless to wear expensive clothing when parents in the district knew about her history, her dad's treachery. So she'd pulled on her Merona brand jeans and an ages-old button-down with a rumpled collar. She hadn't bothered with makeup. Mary looked stunned when she saw her, and Isobel wondered if she'd overdone it.

"Are you okay?" Mary asked, her voice a whisper. Isobel surveyed the near-empty space. The students were in fifth period, lunches finished.

Isobel shook her head, her hair puffing around her ears. "Have you heard the latest?"

"I don't know any 'latest,'" Mary said. "I've finished meeting with your colleagues, though." Mary looked compassionate, apologetic even. "You have to know that almost everyone adores you," Mary said. "You're well respected in the department."

Isobel wanted to ask her why she hadn't provided this perspective at the meeting with Wayne a week ago when he'd declared her suspension, but she decided to stay focused on the crisis at hand. "I know I'm not going to survive this," Isobel said, thinking of the investigation. Mary opened her mouth to speak, but Isobel waved her off. "There was that stupid comment on the news story, and, Mary, now the parents know something else. I ran into Julia Abbott at yoga yesterday."

Mary leaned forward and knit her eyebrows. "Regardless of what happens with the investigation here," Mary said fervently, "*you* are going to be fine."

"I mean, I'm not *dying*," Isobel said, suddenly worried that she seemed suicidal, "but I realize my employment prospects are looking bleak." She held up a hand to stop Mary from arguing. "I don't want to talk about that right now. I want to tell you what else they know."

"What do you mean?" Mary asked.

"My dad," Isobel began. Her eyes closed, and she felt nausea rising in her throat. She hadn't eaten anything since lunch yesterday. "He committed felony fraud. He stole money from a charitable foundation and several families." Isobel rushed on, her eyes open now and focused on Mary's forehead. "This was back in the nineties. You might remember it."

"I'm from Indiana," Mary said, baffled. "So I wouldn't remember anything."

Isobel's impatience bubbled. "Felony fraud," she said again. "My dad went to prison. I don't broadcast this information, obviously, but Julia Abbott knows. She mentioned it yesterday when she was calling me a hypocrite for teaching about social justice."

Silence opened between them. Mary looked pathetic. Stupefied. Her paralysis stirred Isobel's action. "So, things seem to have moved beyond regular complaining. This seems more like harassment, right? Digging up stories from my past and somehow spreading them around the community?"

Mary blinked rapidly. "It's definitely disturbing," she said. "How are they spreading the information? E-mail?"

"I don't know. But that's not the point." Isobel's agitation intensified. "Regardless, you'd agree that my father's criminal record has nothing to do with my teaching?" As she said it, her jaw dropped.

My father's criminal record has nothing to do with my teaching.

The thought shifted her mood entirely, and Isobel stood up from the table. "I just thought you should know," she said, suddenly in a rush. "There's some kind of smear campaign. It started with that voice mail. Julia Abbott seems to be behind everything, and I don't think I should lose my job over it." She felt new confidence, the realization of her independence from her father overcoming her. "Especially now." She took a step back and then remembered her phone call with Mark. "It's a hostile work environment," she blurted. "I'm not the one who should be under investigation here. It's Julia. Make it stop, or I'm calling a lawyer." She almost laughed then, picturing herself in a TV drama rather than in the high school library. She didn't give Mary time to respond before walking away.

TRACY ABBOTT

The bell had just rung to signal the end of fifth period when Tracy caught sight of Ms. Johnson near the door to the parking lot. Without thinking, she jogged toward her. "Ms. Johnson!" she yelled.

Her teacher turned, and even from down the hall, Tracy could see that she looked ragged, her hair messier than usual and her eyes sunken. When Tracy stopped in front of her, she realized that though she felt certain she needed to talk to Ms. Johnson, she actually had no idea what to say. "I'm sorry," she began. And then, to her horror, tears didn't just threaten, but rather overcame her. She opened her mouth to breathe, and a sob came out.

"Honey!" Ms. Johnson said. She stepped forward and put an arm around her, pulling Tracy toward the wall, out of the sight lines of the kids streaming toward their next classes. "What's wrong?"

Tracy tried to slow her crying. It was humiliating, this reaction. She'd meant to offer support to Ms. Johnson, maybe to hint at her new investigation of Lisa Lions, and here she was, hysterical. "I know about the Facebook post," Tracy managed.

Ms. Johnson looked blank. "Facebook post?" she repeated, rubbing

Tracy's back. Tracy blinked a couple of times. It hadn't occurred to her that Ms. Johnson might not know about the Inside Liston page. She pressed on, not caring for the moment what her mother would think of her indiscretion, just as she hadn't considered what her mother would think of Kate Awakened's trolling comment on her exposé. "There's a Facebook group called Inside Liston," Tracy said. "Parents post all kinds of mean things about school. And my mom—" She wasn't sure how to continue. How could she confess that Julia had exploited Ms. Johnson's secret?

"I'm sorry," Ms. Johnson said, her eyebrow cocked. "Can you explain that again? There's a Facebook group for parents?"

"I saw it by accident," Tracy said. "My mom had all of these notifications when the video first got posted, and then it went viral, and I helped her untag herself." Tracy knew she was babbling, but thankfully, her sobs had been short-lived. Now more manageable tears leaked intermittently from the corners of her eyes. She wiped them every few seconds. Ms. Johnson stared at her, waiting. "But on Monday, Anika told me my mom had posted something about you, after you made that comment on Channel Six."

"Tracy"—Ms. Johnson reached a hand to her own chest, brushing the top button of her wrinkled shirt—"I'm so sorry about *that*. I had no idea that what I thought was a private comment on my own Facebook page could possibly make the local news. Of course, I've lectured my students so many times about social media not being private—"

"After the news story," Tracy interrupted, "my mom posted something else about you. Anika told me, and then I read it." Ms. Johnson's mouth was open, the words she'd planned to speak next already forming in her throat, but Tracy kept going. "She posted about your dad."

Ms. Johnson's eyes bulged, and she bit her lips between her front teeth. She took a step back, and Tracy thought the circles beneath her eyes grew even more pronounced in the seconds during which she processed what Tracy had told her.

The two were quiet for a moment, and Tracy wondered whether she should now confess how she had gained access to the page, the petition she'd drafted, and her new Google Doc of suspects. Would that be the right thing, chasing her teacher down and telling everything? Ms. Johnson already looked so overwhelmed. Tracy had decided she'd start easy, with the petition and the signatures she'd collected, when Ms. Johnson finally said, "How many people are in the Facebook group?"

Tracy shrugged, suddenly shy about her reinstatement efforts. Her hundred fifty signatures seemed insignificant compared with the roster of seven hundred Inside Liston members. "A few hundred?" she offered, not wanting to alarm Ms. Johnson. "It's weird. It's run by a fake account. Someone called 'Lisa Lions.' I'm trying to figure out who that is," she blurted. "I know my mom is causing problems for you. I feel like—" Tracy's tears came faster again, and she breathed deeply to fend them off. "I just feel like it's my fault."

She didn't tell her teacher about the paragraph in her mom's post about Tracy's changing views on motherhood, but she knew that her disloyalty—what her mom saw as a betrayal—played a big part in how much Julia must hate Ms. Johnson.

The bell rang then, and Tracy looked nervously over her shoulder. "I'm late for PE," she said, wiping at her face again. "Can you tell I've been crying?"

"Hardly," Ms. Johnson said. "It'll just look like you were in a hurry. Do you want me to write you a pass?" She dug into her tote, searching for a pen.

"It's okay." Tracy had already turned and started toward the locker rooms. "If I run, I can change fast and still make it."

"But, Tracy," Ms. Johnson said, and Tracy stopped for a second, eager to hear what her teacher might say. "You're not responsible for your mother's decisions." Ms. Johnson's hair fell over her ear, and her eyes looked far away, focused over Tracy's head. She worried for a moment that her teacher might cry, too. "You can only control yourself. Remember that."

ANDREW ABBOTT

Andrew parked his RAV4, crunching as he pulled in over the ridge of ice that built up every winter in front of the garage. He killed the lights, leaving the concrete wall in front of him dark. He felt calm and happy. The meeting with Mr. Dittmer and rehearsal had gone remarkably well.

"I want to commend Mr. Abbott on both his selflessness and self-awareness," Mr. Dittmer had said to the cast, smiling at him for the first time since they'd begun. Tryg Ogilvie and Melissa Young grinned at him, as well.

"Are you sure?" Maeve whispered.

"Totally."

And Andrew felt relaxed holding the suitcase. Melissa hadn't scowled at him once. After rehearsal was over, as he was packing his backpack in the front row of the auditorium, Tryg Ogilvie approached him. Andrew had avoided any direct interaction with Tryg since the day the cast list was posted, had come close to deleting Instagram from his phone when the Liston Lights featured Tryg on Humans of LHHS. The sight of the ninth grader still ignited a flash of fury, a memory of standing with Sarah Smith, watching the video Tryg had shot. Andrew tried to swallow the anger as Tryg sidled up. The rest of the cast mingled in the rows just behind them, their voices loud and laughing.

"I just wanted to say—" Tryg shrugged. "Thanks, man. The inspector role is, like, a great opportunity for me."

Andrew nodded and looked back down at his copy of the script, waiting for Tryg to move. He didn't. Andrew breathed in the smell of fresh-cut plywood, the flats for the upcoming set build stacked stage right.

"Also—" Tryg cleared his throat. "I wanted to tell you that I deleted the video from my Instagram account this afternoon. My dad told me that your dad called him at his office, and I can totally see how that video would cause problems for you." He waited. *Problems?* Andrew raised his eyebrows at the understatement. Tryg continued. "Anyway, I took the video down this afternoon. I can't get it off Watch This!, though. They control their own account, but I did take it off of my Instagram and my YouTube."

"Thanks." Andrew shoved the script into his backpack.

"Have a good night." Tryg turned toward the door and caught up with the rest of the cast members who had filtered into the theater lobby.

Andrew felt a loosening in his stomach then, a thread of hope that perhaps things could be okay. That feeling had lasted until he parked his car in the garage and imagined telling his mom about the switch in roles. He could see her face—a crevice between her eyebrows, and her mouth pinched in a frown. He looked at the clock on the dash—five forty. Dinner would be on the table. His father's BMW was already parked in the garage. There was no choice but to go in and face the family.

He paused in the mudroom, uncharacteristically stomping his Converse. "Andrew?" his mother called from the kitchen. "Oh, good! Spaghetti's just on the table!"

"Great," Andrew said, too quietly to be heard, and willed himself into the family room. He kept his eyes on his backpack as he dropped it to the floor.

"How was rehearsal?" Julia asked.

He smiled, still delighted by his new, comfortable role. "Mr. Dittmer seemed really excited about how the scene came together."

Julia beamed. "That's excellent!" she said. "See? I told you you'd get the hang of it."

"Yeah," Andrew said.

And things seemed so pleasant—his mother's congratulations, the smell of her marinara, his father coming down the stairs—that he decided to leave the role news for now. No need to spoil the mood.

JULIA ABBOTT

Julia laid breakfast out a few minutes before the kids were scheduled to leave for school on Thursday morning. She'd microwaved some nitrate-free sausage, a new brand her trainer had recommended, and decided to once again offer sprouted toast, the kids' prior unfavorable reactions to this healthier bread notwithstanding. Tracy had hardly eaten anything at dinner the night before, even though Julia knew she loved spaghetti.

Andrew came down first, slid past Julia, and grabbed a mug from the cabinet over the sink. Julia laughed as he poured himself a cup of coffee. "You're a coffee drinker now?"

Andrew lifted his chin, looking pleased with himself. "Maeve likes it. It's an actor thing." He took a small ceremonious sip, and Julia laughed again as he shuddered, nearly spitting it out. "How do people drink this?" He coughed.

Julia opened the refrigerator and grabbed a pint of organic half-and-half. "Try it with cream and sugar, like your dad." She took Andrew's mug and began doctoring it, using the proportions she knew so well from fixing Henry's coffee for twenty years.

When she was finished, Andrew added an additional teaspoon of sugar and took a sip. He frowned, but nodded. "Maybe I can do this."

"You could wait until college?" Julia patted his back, and then Tracy appeared, her hair in a messy ponytail and a large LHHS Nordic Skiing sweatshirt over leggings.

Julia squinted at her. The look was casual, even for Tracy. She glanced back at Andrew, who wore jeans and a T-shirt. "Is it pajama day?"

Tracy shook her head silently and grabbed a piece of breakfast sausage, which she ate with her fingers.

"I have plates," Julia offered.

"No," Tracy said. She wiped her hands on her pants and marched toward the mudroom.

Julia followed. "What's wrong?" She'd pushed away thoughts about Kate Awakened, the detail about *YM* included in her comment. Her so-called friends knew about that internship, of course, but all of them posted on Inside Liston with their real names. Could Robin Bergstrom have made an alter ego? Or, worse, could Tracy have? Her daughter's distance—the anger Julia could feel between them—had thickened in the last few days.

Tracy turned in the doorway now and glared at her. "I know what you did," she said. Julia almost laughed. It sounded like a threat in a movie.

"And what's that?"

Tracy ignored her. "Andrew, are you ready for school?" she asked her brother, her fury palpable and, unfortunately, amusing in the way a three-year-old's tantrum might be. He squeezed past Julia, his backpack brushing her shoulder. Andrew smiled at her, mildly apologetic. A week ago, he'd been so angry, and Tracy had been placated.

Why am I always on someone's shit list? Julia wondered.

"We can go," Andrew said.

Tracy shoved her feet into her sneakers. "Why don't you think really hard about Facebook?" Tracy said as she disappeared into the garage. "Think really hard about what you're doing to other people's lives."

Julia stood still as the door closed, her hand still resting on the molding between the family room and the mudroom. So Tracy had seen the Facebook post. She knew about Isobel's father, and she knew that Julia had shared it. Tracy's juvenile anger upset her, but she wasn't that surprised she'd found out. It was Facebook, after all. That was the point. And she wasn't sorry she'd written the post. But Kate Awakened, then. That was Tracy? Julia didn't want a public battle with her own daughter.

She turned toward the kitchen and fixed herself a plate of toast and sausage while she waited for Ron. Sometimes parents had to take over and make the right decisions, she reasoned. Kids, no matter how sophisticated and bright, didn't always know what was best for them. And what was best for Tracy, Julia was certain, was a teacher who'd respect her family—uplift all of them, not pit them against one another.

"You're allowed," Lyle said, "since you're not being investigated for inappropriate student contact."

"There's that, thank God." Isobel approached his desk. "But the Facebook group?"

"Wayne did mention a Facebook group yesterday when I checked in. It came up in a parent interview. What is it, do you know?"

"Tracy Abbott told me about it, crying, in the hallway yesterday after my meeting with Mary. It's some mother gossip group. Apparently, Julia Abbott posted some private information about me." She paused, hesitant for the first time since she'd donned her power dress. "I should probably tell you. . . ."

Lyle, sheepish, interrupted. "Is it that your dad was a financial criminal?"

"Word travels fast," Isobel said, staring at her shiny shoes. She was quiet for a beat and then said, "I'm sorry I never told you. You're my closest friend here. I just haven't talked about it for so long."

Lyle shook his head, his hair falling a bit over his brow. He swiped it easily back into place. "I can see how you might want to keep the family felonies private."

She laughed, appreciating his aim at humor. "Still," she said, "you're a good friend."

"It's all good," Lyle said. "But really, what are you doing here today?"

"I want my job back," she said. "I'm ready to do a little more of what you said. I'll put my head down—be more like you and Eleanor."

Lyle peered at her, skeptical. "And you'd feel okay about that?"

"Is it too late?" The fear of missing her chance made her short of breath. She could still impact students at Liston Heights—she could still watch them understand the power of empathy—without alienating everyone.

"Isobel!" Jamie poked her head into the room. "I thought I heard your voice." Lyle, Isobel noticed, went right back to the paper he'd been grading, ignoring their young colleague.

ISOBEL JOHNSON

⁓

On Thursday, eight days since she'd been suspended, Isobel dressed in one of her favorite work outfits—patent leather heels and a DVF wrap dress, a Christmas present from the early aughts. It was something she'd normally wear to parent conferences or back-to-school night, but today was just as important as one of those community-facing events. Today she planned to start campaigning in earnest to keep her job. No more cowering, hiding in the yoga studio during the school day. Going forward, she could both placate parents and lead students to new ideas. She just needed to convince Wayne, who still hadn't returned any of her messages since the Channel 6 story, to reinstate her.

Isobel made her first stop in Lyle's room. "Have you heard of the Inside Liston Facebook page?" she asked as she pulled the door open.

Lyle looked up from a student's paper. "You really don't know how to take advantage of a mandatory vacation." He smiled. "What are you doing here?"

"Am I not allowed?" No one had told her she couldn't come to school. In fact, on the days she'd stayed away, she felt like she was admitting some kind of guilt.

"Hi." Isobel smiled.

"Wow, you look great," Jamie said.

"Thanks. Hey, I was just asking Lyle, have you heard of a Facebook group called Inside Liston?"

Jamie recoiled, her smile disintegrating and her mouth forming a small shocked circle.

"That's a yes, then?" Isobel asked, amused.

Jamie shook her head. "I think Mary mentioned it to me," she said, and Isobel instantly doubted that this was the whole story. After years of working with teenagers, she had a pretty good radar for adolescent half-truths, and Jamie was only twenty-three.

"Are you sure?" Isobel pressed.

"I think she asked me about it during our meeting. . . ." She trailed off. She obviously didn't want to mention the interview she'd had with Mary, either.

Isobel studied Jamie's face. "I know Mary interviewed everyone."

Jamie took a step backward. "Anyway," she said, "it's really nice to see you."

"Do you want to have lunch?" Isobel asked. "I'll meet you in your classroom," she said smoothly, not giving her any time to back out. *Why would she want to back out?*

"Okay," Jamie said, her pale cheeks pink as she retreated into the hallway.

Isobel shrugged as she looked at Lyle. "What was that?" she asked.

Lyle opened his desk drawer and flipped through the legal pad he had stored there. "You know, Mary said that the interviews with your colleagues were almost universally positive."

"She told me that, too," Isobel said. "I'm assuming just Eleanor trashed me, per usual?"

"I don't have all the specifics." Lyle looked up at her. "But I heard Jamie said a couple of things. Mary was vague."

"Jamie?" Isobel blurted. What could Jamie Preston possibly have said against her?

"You know I've never seen that 'spark' or whatever you like about her."

Ordinarily, Isobel would have offered a defense of her protégé, but she'd just behaved so oddly.

"Go schedule a meeting with Wayne," Lyle said, waving her away. "Tell him you're willing to change a little. He'll be open to it, especially since there's that ninth-grade petition going around. No one wants angry, unvindicated freshmen."

"First years," Isobel corrected him. "And what petition?"

"You don't know?" Lyle smiled mischievously. "Something like a quarter of the ninth graders have signed a petition demanding your reinstatement."

Isobel smiled, gratified.

"Go," Lyle said again. "Get your meeting, and then see what you can find out from Jamie over lunch."

Isobel made it to the administrative wing as the intercom indicated the start of first period. Wayne wasn't at his desk when she popped her head in, so Isobel sent him an e-mail from the library asking for a few minutes that afternoon. In the meantime, she'd plan some lessons for American Lit, perhaps discover some new poets for the upcoming unit she desperately hoped she'd be teaching.

At lunchtime, Isobel still waited. She refreshed her e-mail every three or four minutes, but Wayne's reply never materialized. She'd stop back in his office later, she decided, but first, she'd get to Jamie.

Isobel buzzed through the cafeteria line for the Chinese chicken salad, skirting a gaggle of competition cheerleaders in uniform. Back in room 213, she settled into a student desk adjacent to Jamie. She put one paper napkin over the graphite smears on its surface and another on her dress.

"How are you?" Jamie said, a forkful of lasagna halfway to her mouth.

"I'm exhausted," Isobel said, deflated by the principal's silence.

"I can only imagine how hard it's been." Jamie's voice sounded far away in Isobel's head.

"It's excruciating, wondering who knows what. And now—you might have heard—there are all these rumors flying around about my past." Isobel stabbed a piece of cubed chicken with her plastic fork. She glanced up at Jamie, whose cheeks had begun to flush again. "I'm sorry," Isobel said. "I know it's a lot to burden you with the details."

"I just wish . . ." Jamie paused, her mouth open. "I wish it were all over," she said finally. "Did Wayne say when they'd be finished with the investigation?"

"A week?" Isobel shrugged. "Channel Six made things worse for me, obviously. And then that Facebook group. Earlier, it seemed like you knew something about it?" She aimed for casual, but scrutinized Jamie's agitated response.

Jamie grabbed her water bottle and took a long swig, her neck craned back unnaturally far. "No," she said finally, not making eye contact. "What is it?"

Isobel looked out the window at the flat February sky. "Tracy Abbott told me it's a gossip group for Liston Heights parents. Isn't that awful?"

"Wow." Jamie's fork hovered over her Tupperware, and Isobel was sure she could see her hand shaking. "Have you seen it?"

"No."

Isobel gave her voice the hard edge she used when she goaded teenagers into the whole truth. "But is there something you're not telling me? You seemed flustered this morning when I asked about Facebook and flustered again now."

"It's just—," Jamie began, tears suddenly filling her brown eyes. She grabbed her napkin and covered her mouth. *Stalling,* Isobel thought, surprised by her own indictment. She waited. "I just get so nervous about parent attacks," Jamie continued. "I mean, after Peter."

She's lying. Isobel looked down at her soft lettuce and glistening mandarin oranges. "Well, I searched for the group," she said, "but I can't find it. I did some Googling, and apparently that means it's 'secret.'" She chuckled weakly, making air quotes around "secret." "I mean, so to speak."

"What happens if they don't like what they find in the investigation?" Jamie asked, seemingly recovered. "Like, what are they even looking for?"

"I'm not actually sure." Garlic and marinara steamed from Jamie's Tupperware. "What did Mary ask you?"

Jamie's nostrils flared with a quick intake of breath. "What do you mean?" she asked, off-balance again.

"I know Mary had meetings with everyone," Isobel said. "She told me that herself. What was it like?" She looked at Jamie as Lyle might, with skepticism.

Jamie chewed. Finally, she said, "We talked about your mentorship. I told her how much you've helped me. It can be really hard." Jamie's voice was nearly a whisper. "Teaching here, I mean."

"Did you share some of those difficulties with Mary?" Isobel's voice wasn't as warm as it would have been eight days ago. Still, Isobel thought, peering at her whimpering colleague, Jamie seemed naive, yes, but hardly calculating.

Jamie stared into her Tupperware. "I told her how grateful I am for your help," Jamie said.

JAMIE PRESTON

Jamie sniffed her underarm after her American Lit class that after-noon. Despite the frigid temperatures outside, she'd been sweating since lunch. She'd put most of her lasagna—it was hard to eat while Isobel talked about the investigation—back into her backpack. She shouldn't have been so surprised about news of the Facebook group getting out. One couldn't really expect discretion from nearly seven hundred people. Still, she'd been shocked by Isobel's questioning and flubbed the follow-up over lunch.

When she'd started the group that fall, Jamie had been amazed how quickly parents signed on and invited their friends. As a precaution—to keep the group smaller—she'd approved only those who friended Lisa Lions. She'd verified that they were indeed parents of students at the school.

But in October, when the group had reached four hundred mem-bers, she realized that she was providing a service: Clearly the parents needed a community. What was the harm? The group was secret; Lisa Lions wasn't friends with any teachers at the school or anyone Jamie knew in her real life. More people friended her, requested access; Jamie approved them, and the discussion became lively. She combed the posts, on the lookout in case—hoping?—a comment would appear about her own teaching. Around Thanksgiving, someone finally asked about her on the #WednesdayWonderings thread: **What do we know about that very young English teacher, Ms. Preston? Will this be a problem for letters of rec?**

Lisa Lions had responded right away. **No,** she'd written, fingers trembling, **Ms. Preston agrees to write letters for anyone who asks. She gets it. She graduated from LHHS herself.**

Jamie grabbed from her top desk drawer the stick of Secret, which she surreptitiously applied, spinning her chair away from the closed classroom door. Keeping deodorant at school had been one of Isobel's first tips. Before the bell on Jamie's first day with kids, she'd dropped off a bud vase of four daisies, placing it with a flourish on Jamie's clean desktop. She'd handed over a small gift bag containing the deodorant, as well as smiley-face stickers and a few flair pens in fun colors. A good-luck gift, she'd said, and they'd hugged.

Smelling once again like baby powder, Jamie thought of logging in to monitor the responses to Julia Abbott's bombshell post about Isobel's dad, but as she raised the lid of her laptop, Mary poked her head into the room.

"Everything okay?" Mary asked.

Why wouldn't it be? "Yes?" Jamie said.

"I peeked into your room over lunch and saw you eating with Isobel," Mary offered.

Jamie thought back to her anxious tears. "Will Isobel be all right?" Jamie blurted.

Mary's skin looked sallow beneath the fluorescent tube lights. "It's nice of you to be concerned." She walked toward a desk. "Of course, Isobel has done a lot for you. Can I sit for a minute? I need to ask you," said Mary, her long purple skirt skimming the gray carpeting, "have you heard of a Facebook group called Inside Liston?" She looked down at a lime green Post-it stuck to her left thumb. She read from it. " 'Inside Liston: A Behind-the-Scenes Look for Concerned Parents Who Need to Know'?"

"No?" Jamie reflexively gripped the side of her chair. "What is it?" She fought to keep her face neutral. She'd failed this morning, but the shock of the question had dulled.

"Apparently, it's a Facebook group with a bunch of Liston Heights parents on it. A gossip page." Mary blew a breath out of the corner of her mouth. "Just what we need, right? Someone who calls herself Lisa Lions moderates it. She provides the 'behind-the-scenes' information."

"What kind of information?" Jamie's voice echoed in her head. *Do I look guilty?* Jamie's mother always joked about her giveaway "hand caught in the cookie jar" expression.

"Wayne told me that whoever Lisa Lions is knew about Isobel's suspension the morning after it happened, like, before Judith even got here." Mary shifted, a crease deepening between her eyebrows.

"Like, someone who works here?" Jamie managed, an ache beginning behind her eyes. She brought a hand up to the top button on her shirtdress and rubbed it between her thumb and index finger.

"Maybe?" Mary rounded her shoulders over her Post-it, the bags under her eyes particularly puffy. "Anyway, I'm checking with everyone to see if they've heard of it. Wayne would really like to shut it down." She sighed. "Obviously."

"I haven't heard about it, but I'll keep my ears open." Jamie stood. She couldn't wait for Mary to leave.

"Thanks anyway," Mary said, and Jamie sank back into her chair, far more pleased with this performance than with her earlier show for Isobel.

Seconds later, a student knocked on her doorframe. Jamie bolted up. "Sorry," the girl said. She held up a black-and-white marbled composition notebook. "You're Ms. Preston, right?"

"Yes," she said. "Sorry. You startled me."

"I'm Tracy Abbott." She stuck a hand out, holding her notebook and pencil against her chest with her free hand. "You were my brother's teacher last trimester? Andrew?"

"That's right." Jamie felt her eyebrows lift toward her hairline as she remembered Mrs. Abbott's voice mails. "What can I do for you?"

"I'm on the Liston Lights," Tracy said, "and we do the Humans of LHHS Instagram? I think you follow it."

Despite herself, Jamie smiled. She'd been waiting a year and a half to be featured. She'd even imagined her photo. She'd be sitting at her desk, over her shoulder her bulletin board, the one on which she kept personal photos and a postcard with an inspirational reminder: *You can't start reading the next chapter of your life if you keep rereading the last one.*

"I do follow it," Jamie said. "I love it." She hoped she didn't sound too eager. She'd been unabashedly jealous when Peter Harrington had been on Humans of LHHS just three weeks into their first year. Of course, she realized, it helped that Peter's scruffy stubble and casual clothes appealed to the female Liston Lights reporters.

"Awesome. I'm assuming you're willing to be interviewed? It's my turn to run the account next week, and I decided my theme would be teachers without tenure. Do you have time for a couple of questions right now?"

Jamie glanced at the clock. She still had twenty-two minutes until the bell would ring for her next class. "Sure. How did you decide on that theme?" She leaned back in her chair as she hoped to pose in Tracy's photo. She pointed at the seat next to her, and Tracy opened her notebook on her lap as she sat.

"I heard there were layoffs coming," Tracy said. "I know the kids at school would hate to lose the young teachers they've loved, right? Maybe the Instagram can spotlight some of the young teachers' strengths? And my brother said you were really good."

Jamie felt buoyed. Kids fighting for her continued employment?

That would be fantastic—certainly convincing to Mary Delgado. "I'm flattered," Jamie said honestly.

"Okay, first," Tracy began, "why did you decide to accept a position at LHHS?"

Jamie thought back to Sue Montague's phone call. Her hands had been shaking so violently, it had taken two tries to hit the green answer button when she saw the school's number on caller ID. "I have firsthand experience of this school's excellence," Jamie said. "I graduated in twenty fourteen. It was an honor to be invited to work alongside the teachers who shaped my own worldview."

Jamie watched Tracy transcribe the answer. The girl bit her bottom lip as she scanned her list of questions. "Okay," she said. "And what do you think younger teachers bring to the LHHS experience? Do you feel like you connect better with the kids, being closer to their ages?"

Jamie did feel that way, actually. The teachers over thirty, with their station wagons and minivans—they seemed to lack the empathy that Jamie still felt for the students. But she couldn't say this to Tracy, obviously. "I do think there's an advantage to being young," Jamie said. "Of course, there's also an advantage to being more experienced." She laughed lightly, and Tracy leaned toward her bulletin board, squinting at the photos, including one of Jamie and her LHHS soccer teammates with their arms around one another.

"You played soccer?" Tracy asked. "Did you ever think of coaching?"

"Maybe someday," Jamie said, "when I've had a few more years to refine my teaching." Should she admit that the teaching job was hard for her? She tried to imagine the text of the Instagram profile, the tone Tracy would take. Hardworking, Jamie decided, was her angle.

Tracy stared at her notebook. Without looking up, she asked, "What do you see as the role of social media in high school life?"

"What do you mean?" Jamie flashed back to Mary's recent questions about Inside Liston.

"I mean, do you think the extent to which people post about school online—do you think that benefits or, like, hampers the learning that we do here?"

"I think Humans of LHHS is a community builder," Jamie said. "People are busy. It's a great way to quickly learn about other people at school you might not have met." That answer fit with her work-ethic theme, right? Jamie started to feel uneasy and glanced at the clock above Tracy's head. The interview had barely started.

"What about other online communities?" Tracy asked. "For instance, there's one my mom is in on Facebook." Jamie thought she could hear anger on the edges of the question. "I helped her with something there, and I happened to notice it has about seven hundred members. Have you heard of Inside Liston?"

Jamie bristled, panic stirring. She willed herself for the third time that day to feign ignorance. "I haven't," she said, her voice reasonably neutral.

"You're mentioned there as someone who, though young, would write decent letters of recommendation for college."

She studied the posts? "I hope LHHS kids understand that there are lots of colleges that can help them achieve their goals," Jamie said, grateful for the out. "It's not just about the Ivys. And I'd be happy to write in support of my students."

"Have you heard of any other young teachers talking about a Facebook group?" Tracy asked. "It seems like the moderator of the Inside Liston group—she doesn't use a real name—it seems like, from what she posts, like she works here."

Oh shit. Jamie blinked at her jade plant. "Interesting," she said. "I haven't." And then she laughed again, incongruously. How could she allow herself to get rattled by a fourteen-year-old? "Are you planning to write about the Facebook group in your Instagram post? Because I don't really know anything about it."

Tracy squinted at her, her lips closed and her expression quizzical. "I'm not sure," she said. "Like I mentioned, my main idea was to talk about what younger teachers have to offer. Social media seems to fit, right? Since you haven't heard of it, do you have any guesses about which other newer teachers might decide to moderate an online group like Inside Liston?"

"Maybe Miss LaMere in the science department? Are you going to interview her?" Jamie thought back to Paige LaMere's chilly response to Jamie's invitation to happy hour that past August.

Tracy made a note. "Just one more question." She pointed at the postcard on the bulletin board. "Aren't you kind of rereading your last chapter in a way? Your sign says, 'You can't start reading the next chapter if you keep rereading the last one.' I mean, you're working at the high school where you were so recently a student. Do you ever feel that you haven't, like, broken out of the bubble?"

Jamie rolled her desk chair farther away from Tracy. Peter's Humans of LHHS piece had included his love of bluegrass music and a recommendation for deep-dish from McGregors'. It seemed like Tracy had a different tone in mind for her post on Jamie. "I'm really happy in my job," Jamie said. "And this conversation hasn't been exactly what I expected. Could I see your profile before you post?"

"Sure." Tracy stood and pulled her phone out of her backpack. "Ready for your picture?"

WAYNE WALLACE

o you get a sense that Ms. Johnson prefers any one set of ideas over another?" Wayne glanced through the mini-blind slats at the snow-blanketed lacrosse field. He'd checked off thirty-two of his required thirty-five parent phone calls.

"Do *I* sense that she prefers ideas?" the father asked. "I've never been in the room during her class." Wayne could hear computer keys clicking in the background. Clearly, Mr. Stewart had other priorities.

Wayne felt saliva pooling in his cheek. He swallowed. "Does Daniel?"

"Daniel has never mentioned that his English teacher shows bias," the man said. "In fact, he doesn't seem to care one way or another about English."

Wayne wrote a zero with a slash through it. He was about to offer the dreaded "anything else?" when Mr. Stewart forged ahead. "Actually, it's incredibly frustrating. Daniel doesn't seem to be engaged in any academic subject. He gets B's. Whatever. I got B's and C's, and now I'm running my own company. It's not like I really care that much about grades."

"Yes," Wayne said, "so—"

Mr. Stewart cut him off. "But shouldn't he like *something* at that school?"

"It would be wonderful if Daniel could discover his academic passion at Liston Heights." Wayne sounded wooden. These calls reminded him that he'd gone into education because he liked kids, not parents.

"Maybe it *is* the teachers," Mr. Stewart said. "Maybe if they were more dynamic, Daniel would take off that ridiculous video-gaming headset. You're asking about Ms. Johnson?" he confirmed. "English?"

"Yep." Wayne slumped now, eyes on the grainy dregs of his Odwalla.

"Write this down," Mr. Stewart commanded. "I wish my child liked her more."

Wayne clicked into his e-mail as he ended the call. Isobel's message sat there in his in-box, a request to meet. **New ideas,** she'd said. **I've had a realization, and I know I need to compromise.**

He'd seen the message earlier in the morning and avoided it, thinking of his final four—now three—phone calls. He'd rather have all of the data, and time to think through every scenario, before he heard her case again. Plus, he couldn't dismiss her total lapse in judgment on Facebook, commenting on that video. The school's digital citizenship curriculum, a good chunk of it housed in the English department, dealt so specifically with situations just like this—kids accidentally texting one another, taking screenshots of Snapchats, "inside" jokes gone viral. How did it look for a trusted adult in the school to make such a juvenile mistake?

"Wayne?" He turned, jerking his head up to find Isobel in the doorway, lightly knocking.

Not now, he thought.

"Did you see my e-mail?" Isobel asked. "I wanted to stop by. I know about the Inside Liston Facebook page—you may have heard about my father? Anyway . . ." She grabbed at her fingers as she spoke, clearly nervous. "I've had some realizations, and I wanted to know if we could check in for a few minutes." She paused, her face suddenly white, her freckles more prominent beneath her green eyes.

"Now's not a great time, Isobel," Wayne said. He turned his body back toward his monitor. "I think we'll be ready to talk next week."

"But you said one week." Isobel's voice had gone higher. "One week for the investigation?"

Wayne didn't look at her. "The Channel Six thing set us back," he said.

"Oh."

He could feel her standing there, her disappointment filling the room. Still, he couldn't give her any reassurance. Amanda from HR would insist on protocol, and besides, he wasn't sure what he'd decide to do. "We'll talk next week," Wayne said. "I'll send an invite via e-mail." He waited a few seconds and then looked up as he heard her turn to go.

JULIA ABBOTT

Julia had said good-bye to the trainer on Friday morning and was cracking a shimmering can of Diet Dew when her phone buzzed. She grabbed it from the counter next to the refrigerator. A text from Robin Bergstrom.

Curious, Julia slid her thumb across the screen to unlock it. Sorry about Andrew's part, Robin had written. Hope all is well.

Andrew's part? What did that mean? Julia took a swig of soda and typed a response. What about Andrew's part?

She waited. The three reply dots materialized and then disappeared. Well? Robin, no matter how tenuous their current connection, couldn't drop in with a bomb like that and then disappear.

The dots returned. Sorry, Robin wrote. I assumed you'd know. Anika told me Andrew exchanged parts with Tryg Ogilvie. So Tryg is now Inspector. And then another text repeating, Hope you're well.

Julia clenched her teeth. *This is not happening.* She abandoned her Diet Dew on the kitchen counter and grabbed her down coat and handbag from their hook in the mudroom. *John Dittmer had better have answers.* She got in the car.

Five minutes later, Julia used her pilfered ID once again to gain access through the performing arts wing, as she had two weeks ago on cast-list day. She marched purposefully toward the theater office and rapped on the director's door. "Mr. Dittmer?" she called. It was nine thirty a.m. She had no idea what time the theater classes met, but surely someone was in there. After a few seconds, Alice Thompson answered.

"Oh!" said Alice. "Mrs. Abbott." The young woman looked concerned. "What can I do for you?"

"As if you don't know," Julia said.

"Um?" Alice squinted. "Well, I know you aren't working on Booster business for this show—"

Julia broke in. "I'm here," she said, her voice louder than she'd meant it to be. She tried to adjust. "I'm here"—*that was better*—"because I've just heard that Andrew has been stripped of his role."

"Stripped?" Alice repeated.

"Yes!" Julia raised her arms to shoulder height, a show of disbelief. "I heard via text from Robin Bergstrom—she *is* involved in Booster business—that Andrew is no longer the inspector. Is this the case?"

Alice turned back toward the office and half closed the door to create a barrier between herself and Julia. "Let me see if John is available."

Julia put her foot between the door and its frame, preventing Alice from shutting it. She could see John moving from his office into the common area.

"Oh good," Julia called out, peeking her head around. "Mr. Dittmer, it seems there's been a terrible mistake, and I need to speak with you immediately." She could see from her limited vantage point that John and Alice exchanged a look. The door opened wider.

"Mrs. Abbott," John all but sighed as she entered, "come in."

Julia sat emphatically at the small conference table in his office. She'd been here before, of course, to go over prop lists and logistics for carpools and parties. It smelled of cardboard and Fritos.

"Tell me," Julia said, peering up at the director as he slowly made his way to a chair of his own, "what could Andrew have done already that was so egregious?" She banged the table with her fist. "Why couldn't you just give him a chance?"

John folded his hands, maddeningly slowly. He stared at his thumbs. "Your son has a great deal of self-awareness. He also cares deeply about the success of the musical."

"Of course he does!" Julia blurted. "He worked all summer on his voice and his acting. He could hardly wait to audition." Her right arm flailed, pointing in the direction of the drama bulletin board in the hallway.

John blinked. "One of my favorite things about Andrew is his commitment to the program."

"So?" Julia's voice went up a few degrees in pitch. "Why in the world couldn't you let him have this opportunity?"

"I'm trying to tell you," John said. "He came to me himself. The switch with Tryg Ogilvie was Andrew's idea."

"That's ridiculous." Julia could hear Alice Thompson rummaging outside the door, listening, no doubt. "Andrew would never just give up like that. He must have felt pressure." She looked toward the ceiling, thinking. "Was the Young girl bullying him? Was it retaliation?"

"Mrs. Abbott, I've told you everything you need to know. Andrew came to *me*. I thought he was here to talk about extra coaching, and instead he suggested that we switch the roles. I was quite surprised."

Julia felt shot through with rage. "You're expecting me to believe," she said, her voice a little shaky, "that Andrew just gave away his role? Just calmly suggested that Tryg Ogilvie—a *ninth* grader—take on the part?"

John started to nod, but Julia pushed back from the table and stood up. "I'm sorry," she said. "I just can't accept this. I need to talk to Wayne Wallace." She shoved her chair back to allow herself room to exit. "Immediately." She pulled the door open and avoided Alice's stare as she left.

Julia headed toward the main office. As she walked, she willed her breathing to slow. The air was cleaner than in the cramped theater office, traces of the antiseptic floor solvent detectable on each breath in the empty hallways. *I need to seem calm and rational,* she told herself. Her sneakers squeaked on the linoleum. In the administrative wing, Julia could see through the narrow sheet of glass on Wayne's closed door that he was on the phone. She knocked anyway, waving at him, forcing a smile, and taking a step back.

Wayne startled, his reading glasses halfway down his nose. *Come on, Wayne,* Julia thought. *This is critical.* The principal held up a finger at her, indicating that she should wait. *Okay,* she mouthed.

She pulled her phone out of her jacket pocket and glanced at the screen. Nothing. She opened the texting app and punched Andrew into the TO: field. Anything you neglected to share about play rehearsal??? SEND. She watched for the three dots, but none appeared. Wayne's door opened in front of her.

"Wayne," Julia said, walking in, "so sorry to bother you without an appointment." She followed his gaze to the clock above his conference table.

"I have just a few minutes, Mrs. Abbott," he said.

Julia sat. "Fine." She put her cell phone facedown on the table next to her and launched in. "You're not going to believe this, but it seems that John Dittmer has taken Andrew's role in the musical away from him." She felt tears threatening. *Those definitely won't help.*

Wayne lowered his chin to his hand. "What?" he asked rather lazily.

"John Dittmer!" Julia said, her back rigid. "He took Andrew's role, the inspector part we discussed, and gave it to Tryg Ogilvie. Andrew is now a luggage handler." She emphasized each syllable in "luggage handler," breaking the latter word into three.

Wayne curled two fingers between his nose and his top lip.

"Are you hearing me? You and I discussed the role of inspector. Then Andrew was cast as the inspector. And now I've gotten a text from the stage manager's *mother*—not even from John Dittmer himself!— that Andrew is no longer in that role. He's a luggage handler." She sat back in her chair, winded.

"I didn't know about the switch," Wayne said.

"You didn't *know*?" Julia's phone buzzed, and she flipped it over.

A text from Andrew: Are you at school?

How would he know? She put her phone down.

Wayne studied her. "Once a project is in motion at Liston Heights High," he said, "I pretty much just let it run."

"I'm surprised that details like this, especially concerning *my* family, unfold without your oversight."

"John is a capable director. Now, I don't know the particulars of this situation, but I'm sure he has the best interest of the program in mind."

"I'm afraid that's not good enough." Her statement rang true, but she wasn't sure what to say next. She surveyed the room, her eyes landing on a box of custom water bottles in the corner labeled LISTON LIGHTS. Through her distress, she felt a touch of pride that Tracy would be bringing one home.

Just then Julia jumped as she heard loud knocking. Andrew's silhouette filled the plate glass window, his knuckles pressed against it. "Mom," she could hear him shout. "Mom!" Julia turned back toward Wayne, unsure. *How did Andrew even know I was here?*

Wayne stood and gestured at Andrew to come in.

"No," Julia said reflexively, and immediately knew it was the wrong impulse. Wayne waved Andrew into the office.

Andrew stood in the doorway, holding the handle. Sweat gathered on his brow.

"Mom, what are you doing here?" Andrew's eyes focused on her forehead, his mouth slightly open.

Julia turned back to Wayne, who stared at each of them alternately. An awkward pause expanded, and Julia could hear Andrew breathing. *Did he run here?*

"Andrew," said Wayne finally, "why don't you join us?" He pointed to the chair next to Julia. "We were just talking about your role in the spring musical. Has there been a change?"

Julia suddenly felt as if she were moving through molasses, her body turning slowly toward her son's as he followed Wayne's direction to sit.

"Yes." Andrew's voice echoed in the small office. He faced Wayne as he said, "I asked Mr. Dittmer for a change. I don't want to be the kid who got his part because of the costume shop." He practically yelled this last bit. Julia scooted her chair away.

Wayne looked back at Julia, waiting for her to respond. "Andrew," she began, although she, too, looked at the principal, "you have your role because you've paid your dues. It's your turn."

"No!" Andrew shouted. Julia's eyes widened, and she saw him pound his fists on his thighs in her peripheral vision.

She looked toward the open door and saw Sue Montague walk by, making wondering eye contact with Wayne, who raised a hand, signaling he had things handled. "Should I?" Julia said, and she stood up to close the door.

"That's fine," Wayne agreed. "So," he said, looking at Andrew and then again at the clock, "it seems like you decided what you wanted, and you asked Mr. Dittmer for it."

"Yes," Andrew said. "I want to be the luggage handler. I don't want to be known as the kid whose mother bought his part and then punched his friend."

Julia winced. Wayne didn't correct Andrew's characterization. She opened her mouth to do so herself, but Wayne started speaking before she could. "Then I think we don't have anything to talk about. You've gone about this in a very adult way," Wayne told Andrew. "You recognized a set of circumstances that didn't sit well with you, and you found a mature way to rectify them." He looked at Julia and smiled. *Smugly,* she thought. "So, now that we're on the same page, I think we're done here."

"Thank you." Andrew's words came out in a whisper, and Julia watched his arms go slack. He was relieved.

She, meanwhile, felt a hollowness opening in her chest, as if something were being scraped out. Tears pricked at the corners of her eyes. *No,* she thought, *not in front of Andrew.*

"You're right," she said to the room. "I think we're done." She slipped her cell phone off the edge of the table and stood. "I guess I'll see you at home," she said to her son. She felt the cool metal of the door handle against her skin and turned into the hallway.

ROBIN BERGSTROM

Robin had cleared her calendar of work deadlines to accommodate the final rush before the 5K. *This is more demanding than my day job,* she realized. An event for more than five hundred people on a frigid February morning? The appeal of the Booster Board faded as she got more and more bogged down in these details.

So many last-minute tasks cluttered her headspace: check with Annabelle to be sure the route would be closed; confirm the table rental for T-shirts, registration, and hot cocoa; verify that Vivian would pro-cure the custom finishers' medals—the list went on. And she couldn't dislodge a persistent worry that Julia would show up and somehow complicate—or ruin—things.

Robin hadn't meant to provoke her by mentioning Andrew's role. She thought Julia would have known about the change. But, on learning that she hadn't, she supposed she wasn't surprised. Wouldn't it be hard for a child to confide in a mother like Julia, someone who had such a rigid idea of success? Robin looked at the potted succulent on the corner of her bookshelf. It had been a part of a birthday gift from Julia last year, along with a bottle of jasmine perfume, the package wrapped flawlessly.

Her cell phone rang as Robin held it, the calendar app giving way to the caller ID screen indicating that Annabelle Young was on the line.

"Hey, Annabelle," Robin said. "I was just thinking of you. I'm working on the five-K, just double-checking things. Has Martin cleared the final route with the Liston Heights police?"

"We're all good there," Annabelle said. "Cross that one off your worry list." Robin felt immediately lighter. These women—with the exception of Sally Hollister, whose responsibilities seemed murky— redefined efficiency.

"I'll skip ahead to double-checking the tables," Robin said.

"But also . . ." Annabelle's tone held a new gravity.

Both women hesitated.

"What?" Robin finally asked.

"Do we have a plan for Julia? Don't you think she'll show?" Robin didn't want to admit that she'd been fantasizing about the same possibility.

"She'll probably come," Robin said sensibly. "She always does. But what can one person really do to ruin the whole event?"

"You think, even with Andrew taking over as luggage handler?" Annabelle laughed meanly then, and Robin joined in. It *was* sort of funny—the mother who cared most intensely about prestige had the kid who gave away his part.

"Probably especially in light of that." Robin pictured Julia, enviably slim in her spandex outfit, stretching before last year's 5K. She'd want to make it seem like this year was the same as any other, as if she hadn't spent a huge chunk of her husband's bonus on a bribe for a lead role only to have her kid self-sabotage.

"What will we do when she arrives?" Annabelle asked. "I don't trust myself not to strangle her."

"Don't do that," Robin giggled. "We've got a police presence— you'd certainly be caught. I'll talk to Sally," she said, thinking of Sally's short to-do list. "We'll put her on Julia patrol with the goal of keeping her far away from you at the T-shirt table. Deal?"

"I guess," said Annabelle. "I should probably take a Xanax in advance, just in case."

"Whatever you need to do," Robin said. "I'm going to go, okay? Call the maintenance guys? Oh, and have you talked to Vivian today about the medals?"

TRACY ABBOTT

"Why are you so mad at Mom?" Andrew asked after Tracy hurled her backpack into the rear of the RAV4 and slammed the passenger door.

"Did you know she hates Ms. Johnson?" Tracy asked. Her feet were still cold from skiing, and she pushed them up against the heat vents, not caring about the wet smell that emanated from her wool socks.

"I've heard some of it." Andrew kept his eyes on the road as they pulled out of the parking lot.

"She's in this Facebook group," Tracy said. "It's a gossip group for parents of Liston Heights kids." She hadn't told anyone about what she'd read there—what Julia had written about Ms. Johnson's dad—but some of the others already knew. In English class that afternoon, Dylan Parkington had raised his hand and asked Mrs. Youngstead if she was the teacher now "because Ms. Johnson's family are crooks, or whatever." The substitute, thank goodness, had ignored him and continued her lecture on nominative pronouns.

"What does the Facebook group have to do with Ms. Johnson?" Andrew asked.

Tracy wasn't sure if she wanted Andrew to know. He'd been so mad at their mom, slamming around the kitchen and asking to be excused after what seemed like thirty seconds of dinner. Things had just started getting better. "Do you like Mrs. Youngstead?" Tracy asked, stalling.

Andrew shrugged. "She lets us watch the movie in between reading scenes of *The Crucible*."

"I think she's boring," Tracy said, suddenly angrier, "and not very creative."

Andrew glanced at her. "Fine," he said, undeterred, "but what's the connection between Mom and Ms. Johnson and the Facebook page?"

Tracy reached up to touch the fabric-covered ceiling of the car, leaning her head back against her seat. She'd have to tell him. It wasn't as if it was a secret, and she was planning to write about the group for the Humans of LHHS series that would begin on Monday. "Mom researched Ms. Johnson's childhood and found out that her dad went to prison."

"What?"

"Yeah," Tracy continued, "and then she wrote an essay about it and put it on Facebook. She's a bully, it turns out." Tracy had been thinking about that sentence for more than a week, since she first helped her mother untag herself in the video. She thought about it every time she got someone to sign her petition and every time Kate Awakened wrote another comment. She'd gone back and added some things in Kate's voice: a defense of the assistant principal's shoes, for one, and a vote of approval for the change from "freshmen" to "first years," which someone named Sheila Warner had complained about. Saying it aloud—that her mother was a bully—felt both affirming and disappointing.

"Is that why you're doing that petition?" Andrew asked.

Tracy looked over at him. She hadn't known he knew about it. "It's not fair," Tracy said. "The treatment of her. She's a good teacher. It's not her fault that I don't want to have kids."

"What?" Andrew asked, confused.

"Nothing," Tracy said. "Do you want to sign the petition? I have, like, a hundred fifty signatures. I'm presenting it to Ms. Montague tomorrow."

"Sure." Andrew was quiet for a second as he turned into their neighborhood. "Actually, we could add a version on Change.org. I could send it to all of the juniors, too."

Tracy smiled. "Great idea. Thanks."

"You should do a booth at the five-K. Bring a bunch of clipboards," he said. And then, before Tracy could answer: "Did you know Mom was at school today?"

"Again?"

"Yeah. She thought Mr. Dittmer took away my part, but actually I just traded with Tryg Ogilvie. It was my idea." His words were quiet and determined. And although she was curious, Tracy didn't think she should ask for details. She'd seen Tryg's profile on Humans of LHHS a couple of weeks before, just after he shot the video. Ninth graders hardly ever made the feed, but then, Maeve Hollister had been in charge that week, and he'd been the only ninth grader to be cast in *Ellis Island*.

"So, do you think she'll go to the five-K this weekend?" Tracy moved on. "With everything? You still have to volunteer, right?"

Andrew bit his lip. "Oh, she'll go," he said. "She's been training with Ron. I know she thinks she can run faster than she did last year."

"She'll go even though everyone hates her?"

"Probably," Andrew said, and Tracy knew he was right. She'd go, even though everyone would look at her. She'd go probably *because* everyone would look at her.

"Can I ride with you to the race?" Tracy imagined pulling into the parking lot with her mother, as she had the past several years. This time, kids who hadn't realized her connection to the woman in the cast-list video would put it together. She'd lose her anonymity, which was so critical for survival as a first year.

Andrew reached up to the visor to press the garage door opener. "If you don't care about getting there early, I can take you," he said, "but we've got a rehearsal afterward. You'll have to ride home with Mom. Or run home, I guess."

Tracy peered through the family room window from the driveway. She could see her mother's silhouette as she walked into the kitchen. "Okay," Tracy said. "I guess I'll ride home with her. It'd be super awkward to have to tell her I wasn't going to." Andrew parked in the garage, and they both set their jaws determinedly before walking in.

ISOBEL JOHNSON

Friday movie night felt less festive than usual, nine days into Isobel's suspension. She agreed to *The Incredibles* despite the gun violence. She'd been hoping to hear from Wayne before the weekend, had fantasized about an immediate reinstatement. Instead, there had been silence, plus a pile of ninth-grade research papers delivered in an interoffice envelope by Lyle.

Next Friday would be two and a half weeks out of her classroom. By then the contingency lesson plans she'd written would be obsolete. Eleanor would supply Judith Youngstead with materials on Steinbeck for the ninth graders. American Lit would be onto *The Catcher in the Rye*, and the irony of missing *The Crucible* with her juniors felt like a gut punch. Melissa Young flitted into her consciousness then, Julia's elbow to her stomach an odd precursor to Isobel's own troubles.

"So, I'm looking at the calendar," Mark said as Isobel located the movie on iTunes, "and we're supposed to run the annual theater department five-K this weekend. Sunday. Is that right?"

Shit. She'd run the annual thespian 5K each of the past five years. She'd lectured Jamie about the importance of school spirit and seeing students outside the classroom. Plus, Isobel's own children had begun to see the event as a tradition, relishing their keepsake T-shirts and finishers' medals.

But the race drew members of the entire community—her students, their parents, other teachers, and administrators—they'd all be there. And they'd be talking about her suspension, the Channel 6 story, and the fact that her father was a felon. It seemed like a good year to skip.

"Maybe we skip this year?" she asked.

"Skip the five-K?" Callie cried, overhearing from her preferred spot on the chaise. "No! I practiced last weekend. I'm going to run the whole thing like we planned." She looked back at the screen as Isobel hit PLAY and Riley ran in from the bathroom.

Mark gave Isobel an apologetic look. "Maybe it would be good to make a show of confidence?" he suggested, quieter so the kids wouldn't hear. "You usually see a lot of friendly faces there. Kids high-fiving you and stuff?"

Isobel dropped her shoulders and shuffled to the kitchen. She didn't want to give Callie the idea that hiding from problems solved anything. Still, the thought of the 5K exhausted her, and she hadn't even considered the actual running.

"Mom!" shouted Riley from the couch. "We're not going to the five-K? I need the shirt!"

She felt Mark's hands on her waist as she poured herself a glass of wine. "I think we should probably just go," he said. "You're in shape for it anyway."

Isobel turned and hugged him, holding her glass behind his back. "Fine," she said, though she knew chances were high she'd regret it.

"You'll crush those assholes," Mark said, laughter in his voice, and Isobel tried to smile.

JAMIE PRESTON

Jamie scanned Lisa Lions's Facebook feed, a vodka soda in hand, legs folded beneath her on the couch. She'd thought of deleting the fake account, but worried it would look suspicious to shut the whole thing down the day after Mary, Isobel, and Tracy had mentioned it to her.

Her roommate hurried in, a miniskirt tight across her hips. "Is this too short?" she asked, a little breathless. As she spoke, she fastened a large hoop earring. Jamie considered the skirt a moment too long to conceal her actual opinion. "Shit," Leslie said. "I know, but I can't find anything Todd hasn't seen."

"You could try my black one—the one I wore to sushi that one time?"

"Thanks," Leslie said. And then suddenly: "Hey, did you want to come out with us tonight? Maybe at least a drink before dinner? It's Friday night." Jamie read pity in Leslie's eyes as she took in her sweatpants.

"No," Jamie said, "I'm distracted by work. Did I tell you I think my contract is going to get cut?"

"Cut?" Leslie sat down on the other end of the couch, her earring brushing her cheek, skirt riding up her outer thighs.

"Well, there's declining enrollment. Like, next year's ninth-grade class is smaller than this year's? Someone has to go to part-time."

"And it'll be you? Do you know for sure?" Leslie patted Jamie's knee, as if she were a child.

Jamie glanced at her screen and absently clicked on the shortcut to the Inside Liston page. "It's usually seniority," Jamie said, "unless some-one has some kind of disciplinary issue." She peeked up at Leslie. What would her roommate think of the Facebook tactics?

"Is someone having a disciplinary issue?" Leslie asked. Her legs twitched, and Jamie knew she was anxious to choose her outfit for the evening, to move beyond this show of caring.

"Leslie, how far would you go to keep your job?" Jamie asked, not ready to let her go yet. "We're young, right? If we don't act like we really want it, won't people just push us over?"

"I mean, I'd definitely fight for it." Leslie smiled then. "We have to pay rent, after all."

"Would you point out the reasons why you're maybe better suited for the job than people with more seniority?"

"Sure," Leslie said, standing. "I'm so sorry, Jamie, but can we talk about this later?" She started back toward the bedrooms. "Or tonight! Come for a drink!"

"Another time," Jamie muttered, and looked back at the group she'd concocted, the whole thing an effort to avoid Peter's fate. And here she was, embodying a false identity alone in her sweatpants on a Friday night with no guarantee of a full-time contract.

She read a new message at the top of the page showing a snapshot of a worksheet on the Trail of Tears. **What happened to Westward Ex-pansion?** the caption read. A new, but vocal, group member, Kate Awakened, had commented, **Maybe let's tone down the low-key racism**, which had sparked a flurry of defensive replies about the culture of the "American West." The second new post was from a parent whose name

Jamie didn't recognize. **Anyone care to speculate about which teachers will get laid off this year? Board says cuts, right? Who's getting the ax?**

Jamie breathlessly clicked the comments and scanned the names the parents suggested. She found her own rather quickly, only the second time she'd been mentioned in the group. Isn't Preston in English rather new? Besides that, she's bland. No spark. I bet it's her.

A couple of people had liked the comment, and Jamie felt like crying.

ISOBEL JOHNSON

"Mom, I'm nervous. Do I have to run the whole thing?" Callie whined from the backseat of the minivan as the Johnson family pulled into a parking space, twenty minutes ahead of the scheduled start time of the Theater Booster Club 5K.

"I'm running the whole thing, Mom!" Riley piped in.

"Suck-up," Callie muttered.

Mark squeezed Isobel's hand. "No one has to run if they don't want to."

In the rearview mirror, Isobel watched Callie glare at her brother. She felt queasiness rise in her throat. Was this really such a good idea, to face the families who knew about her suspension and about her father? And there was no guarantee she'd get her job back next week—this could be the last time she'd see these people, jogging along midpack in a stupid fund-raiser 5K.

"Let's put up a brave front," Mark had said that morning, and she'd agreed, in theory. She would have given the same advice to her students: Show up with a smile on your face. And now here they were. It wasn't as if she could tell the children she'd chickened out. *Get over yourself,*

Isobel thought, and reached for the door handle. "Let's do this, family!" she said aloud. "Riley, I'll run the whole thing with you if you'd like!"

"What about me?" Callie was saying as Isobel's feet hit the pavement and she adjusted her black running tights, making sure to pull her jacket firmly over her backside.

"Ready?" she asked the kids as their door slid open.

"Yeah, but, Mom," Callie said, "what about running with me?"

"If you're running, I'd love to do it with you." Isobel smiled. She slung an arm around her as they walked toward the registration table.

"Hey, Ms. Johnson!" Isobel caught a glimpse of Anika Bergstrom jogging, a lime green T-shirt pulled over her coat.

"Hi!" Isobel called. Anika pointed at the front of her T-shirt as she ran by, but Isobel missed the significance. "Here we go," Isobel whispered to Mark as they reached the table. Allen Song stood behind it.

"Ms. Johnson!" he said, grinning. "I'm so glad you're here. I want you to know I signed both petitions, the online one and the paper one. I don't even care if they're double counted. I'm not allowed to wear the T-shirt because of this." He pointed at his volunteer shirt and frowned. "When will you be back in class?"

Isobel smiled and glanced back at Mark, whose eyes said, *I told you this would be good.* "What petitions?" she asked. *Plural? And what T-shirts?*

"You don't know?" said Allen. "There are a couple. One was started by a ninth grader, Tracy something. And there's another one on Change.org. There are over two hundred signatures there." Isobel felt her chest expand, tears threatening beneath her delight. "I also want you to know"—Allen leaned toward her—"Ms. Johnson, my mom and I both told the bosses you're excellent."

Isobel smiled at his earnestness. "Thank you, Allen," she said. "I really appreciate that." He stood up straight again, looking proud.

"Is this your family?" The boy's eyes were suddenly wide, as Callie and Riley crowded in on either side of her. "Are you all running?"

"It's run-walk, right?" Isobel confirmed.

"Oh, absolutely," Allen said. "We're not even keeping times, although some people are gunning to win." He gestured toward the starting line, where a few students—Isobel noticed Maeve Hollister and Melissa Young—jumped up and down, warming up.

"Well, I certainly won't be giving chase." She pulled cash from her wallet. "So, can I have the faculty discount?"

"For sure," he said. "For four, then, it'll be sixty."

"Dollars?" asked Riley, shocked.

Allen laughed. "I know it's a lot." He tucked Isobel's twenties into the cashbox in front of him. "But it's for a good cause. Head over there for your T-shirts." Allen pointed at an adjacent table. "It looks like my mom and Mrs. Hollister will be helping you."

A fresh wave of anxiety flooded Isobel's stomach as she approached the parents, though Allen had assured her that his mom was on her side. Isobel felt Mark's firm hand on her lower back, guiding her toward the two mothers, who hadn't yet noticed her. She took a deep breath.

"Ms. Johnson." Vivian Song smiled. "I keep calling Principal Wallace. We need you back in the classroom." Isobel felt the tension in her shoulders ease. "I gave him an earful the first time we talked. Ridiculous, the whole thing."

"Thank you so much for your support," Isobel said. She knew without looking that Mark was beaming beside her.

"What sizes of T-shirts can we get you?" Vivian asked.

"Small!" piped up Riley, stepping in front. Isobel smiled down at the top of his head. As she looked up, she caught sight of a familiar blond ponytail behind Vivian. Julia Abbott. She strode determinedly toward the registration table, looking over the crowd.

Vivian turned her head to see what had caught Isobel's attention. "Oh my God," she said when she realized. "Sally, where's Annabelle? And didn't Robin come up with a plan for this? I can't believe she came."

The two women stopped fussing with the T-shirts and stood on their tiptoes, heads craning. Isobel looked, too, even though she hadn't seen Melissa Young's mother.

"There she is!" said Vivian suddenly, coming out from behind the table. "I'll go warn her. Sally, you keep going with the T-shirts."

"What's going on?" Callie pulled on Isobel's sleeve.

"Just some mom drama." Isobel couldn't help but feel grateful that the spectacle was someone else's. Perhaps Julia Abbott's notoriety overshadowed her own.

JULIA ABBOTT

When Tracy insisted on leaving early with Andrew for the 5K, Julia had almost bailed on the whole morning, despite her dedicated training. The past few years, Tracy had waited for her at the finish line, cheering her on. Now her daughter hadn't looked her in the eye since Thursday. Julia had tried to explain her rationale for publishing the information about Robert Miller. "Parents need to know who's teaching their children," she'd said, but Tracy had practically shouted at her about privacy and bullying.

Though she didn't say it aloud, Julia attributed Tracy's newfound volatility to Ms. Johnson. Before she got into that class, Tracy had not only been her easier child, but she'd actually been one of the most agreeable of all of the children Julia knew, eager to please and cooperative. Now she'd become angry, belligerent, and secretive. When Ms. Johnson asked her to "see multiple perspectives," Tracy tended toward the negative, articulating all kinds of exaggerated problems that hadn't bothered her before. And then there was Kate Awakened, whom Julia was almost certain was Tracy. She hadn't been able to rally herself to ask her. If she knew for sure, then other people might also: They'd know Julia's own daughter had trolled her on the Internet.

Julia looked for Tracy among the runners warming up for the race, but she couldn't pick her out. Maybe she was inside with Andrew, setting up the hot chocolate station. Julia approached the registration table, and Allen Song smiled blankly. "Just me," she said, handing over a twenty.

Allen pointed at the T-shirt table, which would provide the real challenge of the morning. *Maybe I don't need a T-shirt,* Julia mused, and then dismissed the thought. Of course she was getting a T-shirt. She'd paid her twenty dollars, and someday, long after they'd all forgotten about Tryg Ogilvie's video and Ms. Johnson's poor choices, they might actually want to remember *Ellis Island.* The T-shirt would be the reminder, and they'd laugh when one of them wore it—one of the three of them, anyway, since Henry had kept his usual Sunday morning squash game.

Sally Hollister stood behind the piles of shirts, hands on her hips, glowering at Julia. "I'd like a small," Julia said.

"They're running a little small this year. You might prefer a medium." Julia thought she could detect the beginnings of a sneer.

Julia glanced at Sally's lumpy middle and smiled placidly. "I'll take a small." She jogged the shirt back to her car, where she unfolded and inspected it—Lions' green with a yellow Statue of Liberty emblazoned right of center. *I would have switched those colors,* she thought, and tossed the shirt on the backseat. Then she headed for a spot near the starting line. She'd just pulled out her phone to scroll through Instagram photos when she heard a shriek from somewhere near the finish. She looked up and saw Robin Bergstrom and Vivian Song, both wearing blaze orange T-shirts over their winter jackets. *Not the color I'd have chosen,* Julia thought. They could have accomplished visibility without compromising everyone's skin tones. Annabelle Young approached them. "Here we go," Julia whispered. She turned back to her phone. The clock on the screen said nine fifty-one. The race began at ten. Surely she could avoid Annabelle for nine more minutes.

The next time Julia looked up, she found Tracy standing near the registration table, holding a clipboard and wearing a lime green T-shirt over her jacket. Had she signed up to volunteer? Tracy chatted with Isobel Johnson and what had to be the teacher's family. She studied Isobel and frowned. What was it about her that Tracy admired so much? Her chin-length hair poked out beneath a shapeless knit hat. Her fleece jacket fell loosely over generic black leggings. She didn't even seem particularly fit. Tracy reached down and put an arm around Isobel's son, her eyes still adoringly on her teacher.

Julia hung her heels over the curb, stretching her Achilles tendons. A toxic mix of sadness and anger began its run from her chest down her arms. *She's stealing my daughter from me,* Julia thought. Just then Tracy turned toward her and pointed. Julia felt herself flinch. She raised her right hand in a wave, her ubiquitous "This, too, shall pass" silver bangle clanking against her running watch. And then Tracy seemed to be walking toward her, and hope pierced through her misery. "Good luck!" she heard her daughter call. She looked back at her phone—nine fifty-four.

Tracy's smile evaporated as she approached. Julia read the block letters screen printed on Tracy's shirt—#FREEISOBEL—and she felt weak. The "I" in Isobel rose into a fist, primed for protest. "I just didn't want it to seem awkward," Tracy said, and then walked past Julia without saying anything else, the clipboard swinging in her hand. Julia turned after her, hurt all over again. Tracy hurried toward a table slightly apart from the starting line and dropped her clipboard in front of a girl wearing a matching shirt. As she moved on, Julia could read the sign hanging from the table. #FREEISOBEL, it read, in the same block letters as the ones emblazoned on her daughter's chest.

JAMIE PRESTON

Jamie slid into the back of the pack just moments before the race
started. She'd had second and third thoughts about showing up, but
decided she'd better, if only for the sake of appearing casual. She should
do what she'd done the previous year, before she'd gotten the e-mail
from Mary about declining enrollment, when she'd still felt like the
promising new teacher with a spark.

Jamie had parked her car on the street and planned to pick up her
T-shirt after she finished, when no one else would be near the registration tables. She wasn't sure why she felt she had to hide—it wasn't as if
anyone knew she was Lisa Lions. She also hadn't been suspended for
teaching radical curriculum, nor had she made that ill-advised comment on Channel 6. Isobel should have been the one who was embarrassed, and yet the night before she'd responded to Jamie's text that she
planned to bring her whole family to the fun run, as usual.

At the race, Jamie disappeared into the crowd. Without her sweater
sets and dresses, she looked even younger than normal. She felt anonymous in her black workout pants and skullcap, pulled low over her
brow. Only a single student had recognized her so far, and it had been

a double take. "Ms. Preston," the girl had said, "you look so different!" She felt different, too, less like an insider. The realization made her angry, and she shook her arms to dissipate the feeling. The whole purpose of the Facebook page was to elbow her way into the very parent world she'd now infiltrated, and yet she remained invisible and inconsequential. Maybe Monday's Humans of LHHS profile, the first of Tracy Abbott's "teachers without tenure" posts, would increase people's recognition. A girl lined up next to her, ready to race, a bright green T-shirt billowing over her turtleneck. Jamie cocked her head to read the lettering. #FreeIsobel, it said, and Jamie's anger verged on rage as she followed the "I" up into its fist.

Jamie searched the throng of runners for Isobel as one of the theater moms in a comically large orange T-shirt climbed a stepladder next to the starting line. It was hard to identify anyone in their winter attire, but she finally saw her, brown hair puffing out beneath a green hat. Isobel smiled down at Callie as Jamie looked on. How could she be here and smiling? Isobel was from some Podunk town and on the verge of getting fired, and yet somehow Jamie felt under attack while Isobel looked relaxed, silently defended by what Jamie could now discern was a large number of #FreeIsobel tees. She scooted up a bit in the crowd as the theater mom finished her announcements. She didn't want to weave around so many people at the beginning, and yet she needed several rows of distance between herself and Isobel.

ISOBEL JOHNSON

Robin Bergstrom held a bullhorn and stood to the right of the starting line on a stepladder. Feedback blared as she pressed the button to speak to the crowd. Isobel smiled at Callie. She felt suddenly relieved that her daughter was here with her, that her family had heard Vivian Song's compliments at the T-shirt table. Certainly, Callie had picked up pieces of her parents' discussions about Isobel's problems at work. Maybe the raves from Vivian would counteract any doubts Callie had about Isobel's competence. And then there were the many lime green T-shirts Isobel now saw in the crowd, matching the one Tracy Abbott had worn. Tracy said Susan, Isobel's earnest student in first hour, had designed the protesting-fist logo, which had almost made her cry. The kids cared more than she'd realized.

"What's wrong with the microphone?" Callie whispered.

"I'm sure she'll figure it out." Isobel squeezed her in a side hug.

As she pulled her arm back, she noticed Julia Abbott standing alone, the white cords from her earbuds trailing down over her black jacket. She crossed her arms over her chest and shivered. Fury replaced the warm feelings Isobel had been having for Callie. How dared this woman dig up information about her father and splash it on that Face-book page without any thought about Isobel's well-being?

Robin tried again with the bullhorn. "Welcome to the annual The-ater Booster Club five-K!" she said. There was some applause from the group. Isobel batted her mittens together in support. "We really appre-ciate you all coming out for this event," Robin continued. "Your entry fees will help us put on one of the best productions yet, *Ellis Island*." The theater kids, most of whom stood on the sidelines in orange volunteer T-shirts, whooped at this.

"Is it time?" Riley turned around, his eyes wide.

"She's going to tell us." Isobel pointed at Robin.

Robin continued. "The route is marked, and thanks to Annabelle and Martin Young, we have some Liston Heights police officers helping with traffic control." Robin pointed at Annabelle, who stood near the registration table. She waved at the crowd. When Isobel looked to see whether Julia Abbott would react to Annabelle's shout-out, she saw af-fixed to a table adjacent to the starting line a tagboard sign with the same clever #FreeIsobel logo. Susan stood behind the table, engulfed in a ski jacket under a matching T-shirt. Isobel pulled at Mark's sleeve and pointed.

"See?" he said, one arm encircling her waist.

"You'll see a clock at the finish line, so note your time if you want to." Robin was wrapping up. "Otherwise, have fun out there!"

The crowd clapped again, and Robin had descended two steps when something flashed on her face. "Oh!" she said, laughing into the bull-horn. "I almost forgot. On your mark." Riley bounced up and down in front of Isobel. "Get set!" Isobel caught sight of Julia, suddenly alert, shifting her weight from left to right, her ponytail swinging. "Go!"

The Johnson family started to move with the crowd. Isobel waved at Susan as she ran past the #FreeIsobel sign just as Riley shot ahead. "Mom," Callie said, "he's going too fast."

"He'll be back," Isobel told her.

"I'll go with him," Mark said, surging forward.

Isobel smiled down at Callie as the two jogged. "Fun, right?" Callie nodded, and Isobel felt buoyed by the students' visible support. When they reached the first mile marker, Callie asked for a walk break.

"Sure!" Isobel agreed. As they slowed, she patted Callie's back. "I'm glad you suggested a break." And it was true; it had been a long time since Isobel had run three miles in a row, though she'd been a regular runner in her early years of teaching. It was an efficient means of exercise for someone with no free time. Callie stretched her arms over her head. Runners plodded past them, including Jamie Preston.

"You made it!" Isobel called to Jamie as she ran by. "Good job!" Jamie gave a thumbs-up and kept moving. "How are you feeling?" Isobel asked Callie.

"Fine," Callie said. "I just wanted a rest. Where do you think Riley and Dad are?" The course had enough turns that they couldn't see far ahead.

"I bet we'll catch up," Isobel said.

On her left, Isobel saw Julia's blond ponytail swing past them, her legs kicking out to the side with each stride. Suddenly Isobel wanted to go again. "Should we start up?" she suggested to Callie. "Take it slow?" Callie shrugged, but Isobel pressed. "Let's just give it a try."

JULIA ABBOTT

Julia checked her Garmin and saw she'd run the first mile in just over nine minutes. *Not bad,* she thought, and increased the volume of her cardio playlist, a mix of Kelly Clarkson, Shakira, and Pink. She repeated her trainer's directive to keep her arms close to her body and her thumbs reaching her hips on their backswings. *Looking good,* she decided. If she could average nine-minute miles, even Ron the Trainer, as Henry always referred to him, would be impressed.

On her left, Julia noticed Isobel's frizzy bob and green cap. She was running with her daughter, and Julia could see a slight jiggle above the backs of Isobel's knees as she took each step. *Has Ms. Johnson's own daughter announced over dinner that she no longer wishes to have children? What kind of literature do they read together?*

Julia's eyes narrowed as Isobel crept a few feet in front of her. She felt the cold air on her cheeks and on the back of her neck. She glanced at her watch. Could she pick up the pace? At less than halfway through the race, it was risky. She watched Isobel move a few feet in front, and her palms felt suddenly itchy. Certainly she could keep up with Isobel Johnson, who didn't appear to adhere to any fitness regimen.

An uptick in pace begins with the arms, she told herself, parroting Ron once again. She pumped her elbows a little harder and brought herself even with Isobel, who ran ten feet to her left. She'd stay here, she thought, and glanced at her Garmin. Current pace: eight minutes and fifty-two seconds per mile.

Julia worked to regulate her breathing. As she thought about her belly, willing it to rise and fall per Ron's directions, she passed a few people. Her confidence surged. *Hold on,* she told herself. *Don't get too excited.* Every thirty seconds or so, Julia allowed herself a sidelong glance to check for Isobel. During one of these looks, she saw Annabelle Young wearing the volunteer shirt on the side of the road. "Straight on, runners!" she yelled, idiotically waving a Norwegian flag.

Julia rolled her eyes. She could just discern the second mile marker a couple of blocks up, opposite the Lutheran church where she'd sent the kids to preschool three mornings a week, back when they still appreciated her, and clung to her when the teachers insisted they come into the classroom. Julia began panting a bit, her breath coming harder. She reached into her pocket and turned up her playlist again. *You can do this. Only a mile to go.* She pictured Ron's red face at the end of her circuit training. "Get it!" he'd shout at her. She heard the words in her head and smiled. "Get it," she said aloud to herself on the next exhale.

"What?" A girl next to her swiveled her head.

"Sorry," said Julia. "Nothing."

The girl passed. But Julia was still even with Isobel, soldiering forward at an identical pace. She'd pass her in five minutes, Julia decided. Stay even for a half mile more and then go. The woman had poisoned her daughter against her, but she wouldn't beat her in a race Julia had prepared for. This was within her control.

ISOBEL JOHNSON

Every minute or so, when she looked over to encourage Callie, Isobel also checked for Julia, who continued to run about ten feet to her right. Her posture remained impossibly erect, arms swinging methodically at her sides, pointy nose toward the finish line.

"What's wrong, Mom?" Callie had asked after one of these status checks. Isobel realized she'd scrunched her nose and lowered her eyebrows, the same expression she'd employ if she found a hunk of moldy cheese in her refrigerator's deli drawer.

Isobel immediately relaxed her features. "Nothing," she said, and then, knowing it would make her daughter laugh: "I thought I smelled something."

"Wasn't me!" Callie giggled, and then pointed at Mark and Riley, who were walking less than fifty yards ahead. "Hey! There's Dad. You were right—we'd see them again."

"Slow and steady is a great option," Isobel said. Callie surged to reach them, and then walked. Isobel slowed, too, to greet her husband and son. She watched Julia run ahead, her knees lifting high—

ridiculously high, Isobel thought—and her ponytail swinging like a pendulum. "How's everybody feeling?" Isobel asked.

"Good. Just taking a break before our big finish." Mark winked and tipped his head toward Riley.

"That's great." Isobel reached a palm out, and Riley reciprocated her high five. "Hey," she said, looking over his head at Mark. "I'm feeling pretty good, and I was thinking of running the last mile. Could I . . . ?" The wind buffeted her cheeks, and yet she could feel the heat in them.

"Go ahead." Mark pointed down the road, urging her on. "Meet afterward by the T-shirt table?"

She nodded and looked up at Julia, who was now seventy or so yards away. "Yep." Isobel sped up. "I'll see you all at the finish. Proud of you!" she called back.

"Bye, Mom," Callie called. "Have fun!"

Isobel felt a new energy as she gained ground on Julia. Julia had left that horrible voice mail, and then questioned her motives and applauded her suspension. She might cost Isobel her job, but Isobel was determined she wouldn't lose to Julia in this race. And though her heart felt like it might burst with the effort, she drew even with her again.

When she looked over to verify, to make certain that she was indeed even, the two women locked eyes for a moment. Isobel drew in a sharp breath through her nose, a frisson of anger rippling through her as the wind stung her eyes. Suddenly her right foot caught on a crack in the asphalt and she stumbled. Although she quickly righted herself, adrenaline pulsed through her limbs. *I'm not going to lose this,* Isobel thought, and took a couple of quick steps to regain her pace.

Though Isobel's legs felt heavy, she urged her knees up. She found herself leaning slightly forward as she tried to increase her speed. She passed a few students wearing #FreeIsobel shirts, one of whom shouted, "Justice for Johnson!" She raised her right hand to acknowledge the encouragement, but she didn't look back. "I signed the petition!" another shouted, and Isobel quickened her feet.

The two women made the second-to-last turn of the race, and Isobel could see the faster runners strung out ahead of them. *Try to pass one person at a time.* Isobel's footfalls began sounding louder. She realized she'd acquired a slight wheeze on her inhales. *You only have a couple of minutes left,* she thought. *Push it.*

Isobel checked for Julia but didn't immediately find her. It was only when she looked over her shoulder that she saw her, chin up and mouth open. *She's hurting,* Isobel realized. The thought propelled her. Another surge here could demoralize Julia, but when she tried to turn her feet over faster, she came up empty. There was nothing to do but hold at her current pace. As it was, it had to be faster than she'd run in years.

The racers took the final turn, and Isobel could see the finish flag, about two blocks ahead, kids and parents standing on either side of the street, clapping. Isobel tried again to speed up, but the back of her throat burned with the cold air, and her thighs felt leaden. Julia's driving knees came back into Isobel's peripheral vision, the woman's arms pumping, her fingers balled into fists. *Come on!* Isobel squinted and sucked in the longest breath she could muster. *Go,* she willed, and miraculously, her body responded.

From the sidelines, she heard, "Go, Ms. J.! Wow!" She glanced left, and it was Tracy in her pom-pom hat and protest tee. It occurred to Isobel to wave, but she couldn't. Julia had pulled a few feet ahead. "No," Isobel said stubbornly. She gave it her last and best effort, closing her eyes for a beat as she sprinted. She didn't dare look over to see if Julia had matched her.

When she opened her eyes, she'd passed the finish line. She looked to her left. "You got me," Julia said then, not smiling, her hands on her hips as she walked.

Isobel blinked. Her chin tipped up, opening her airway. "Good job," she breathed, her congratulations automatic before Julia walked away toward the gym. Isobel stepped up on the curb and watched the other runners make the final turn. Jamie ran by, and then, after a minute or so, Mark and the kids appeared, jogging the last couple of blocks together.

JULIA ABBOTT

Julia found Tracy holding a cup of cocoa behind the #FreeIsobel table near the finish line.

"What is this?" Julia asked, deflated.

Tracy picked up the clipboard. "I'm collecting signatures to get Ms. Johnson back in the classroom." Tracy looked past Julia, seemingly searching the crowd for potential signatories.

Julia had hoped that some of Tracy's outrage would have dulled as she watched her favorite teacher take Julia down in the final moments of the race, but this clearly hadn't happened. Julia wished she could go back, wished she had accomplished a higher knee drive or pumped her arms with more vigor. She wished *she* had won.

"That was a fast finish," Tracy said after a long pause in which Julia flipped through the names of students next to their scrawled signatures on one of the clipboards. Andrew was there, as were most of the theater kids. "There are more signatures online," Tracy added. "Andrew worked on that version."

Julia stared at her Nike training shoes, wet with melting snow.

Silence stretched between them, and Julia held her ground as a couple of kids walked up.

Tracy handed over a clipboard and a pen. "Reinstate Ms. Johnson?" she asked.

"God yes," said the girl. "Mrs. Youngstead is so boring."

After they'd signed and left, Tracy turned to her mother. "Did you plan to race Ms. Johnson? What happened?"

Julia kept her eyes down. What had happened was that she succumbed to a rage-driven compulsion to beat Tracy's English teacher in an irrelevant fund-raiser 5K. But that didn't seem like the right answer for her fourteen-year-old. And besides, she'd failed.

"We kind of looked at each other at the second mile," Julia said, remembering the moment, "and then, as we got close to the finish, we both sped up."

"You ran a fast time," Tracy said.

But I lost. "Can we go to the car?" Julia pointed toward the door and began walking, not waiting for Tracy to answer.

Julia dug in her pocket for her key fob and hit the unlock button as they approached the car. It wasn't until she had pressed the ignition, pulled her down coat over her running clothes, and felt the warmer firing beneath the black leather seat that she realized how much tension she'd been carrying. She closed her eyes for a moment.

"Mom?" Tracy said, hesitant. "Are you okay?"

Julia tried to smile. "I think that just took a lot out of me." She imagined what she'd looked like as she sprinted down Liston Boulevard, even with Isobel Johnson. As she saw herself cross the finish line a millisecond behind, a zing of regret hit right at the base of her throat. What was the point of all that personal training if she couldn't even muster a final burst of speed? She'd tell Ron she needed to focus on power for next year.

She shifted the Mercedes into reverse and watched the in-dash camera as she eased back from her spot. "Whom did you run with?" Julia asked as she turned her car toward the exit. She hoped they could avoid the name "Johnson" at least until they reached home.

"Tatiana." Tracy scrolled through her phone. "Jessie. Some other people."

"All kids from your Nordic-skiing team?" Julia realized she wasn't sure where she'd put her own phone. She reached her hand toward her jacket pocket and patted it. Nothing.

"Yeah," Tracy said, not looking up. Julia switched her hands on the wheel and patted her other pocket. Empty.

"Damn it," she said. She reached beneath her coat and into her running-jacket pockets.

"What?" Tracy looked up.

"I can't find my phone."

Tracy opened the center console. "Not here," she said. "Didn't you just have it at the race?" Julia drove slowly through the lot toward the exit as she reached behind her, feeling the floor in front of the backseats.

"Can you see it back there?" Julia asked, her eyes on the blacktop in front of her. Tracy put an arm on the driver's seat and twisted around, head panning the length of the car.

Julia dipped her head for a moment, reaching into the well on the driver's-side door, feeling the bottom and sides of it. Just as she'd found the phone there, relief replacing her panic, she felt a thud and slammed on the brake.

"What the hell?" Julia snapped her head back toward the windshield, her eyes wide.

She heard a muffled yell from outside the car and, a half second later, a gasp from Tracy, who screamed as she pulled the passenger door open and ran around to the front, where someone was bent over in the crosswalk.

Julia blinked. More screams from outside, as a girl—the girl from the race, Julia realized, Isobel Johnson's daughter—ran toward the car.

"Mom!" screamed Tracy, gesturing at her through the windshield. "Mom! It's Ms. Johnson!"

ISOBEL JOHNSON

❧

Isobel's eyes blinked open. She lay on her side, her cheek against the concrete and her feet under the front bumper of a black SUV.

"Mom!" Callie screamed.

"Isobel?" Mark was pushing her shoulder back and forth, his face not two inches above hers. He stopped when they made eye contact.

"Okay," she said, and Mark leaned back, weight against his heels as he knelt. She tried to push herself to sitting. Too quickly. Her vision blurred as she moved, and she felt Mark's hands on her back, fingers reaching into her armpits.

"Go slowly," Mark said. She looked down at her leggings, one side scuffed where she'd hit the pavement. A film of anger spread through her as she realized how she'd ended up here on the crosswalk. She reached up and pushed against the black car with her mitten.

"God," she said. She shook her head. It thumped uncomfortably.

"Mom?" said Callie again.

Isobel reached out a hand to the voice and grabbed her daughter's fingers. "I'm okay." She willed her eyes up for a moment before she dropped her chin back to her chest.

"I'm calling an ambulance." Mark moved one hand to the center of her back as he reached for his phone.

"No," she said, suddenly furious. "Don't call."

"But—," Mark began.

"No," she said again, her voice low and rough. She put a hand on the ground, preparing to stand, ignoring the blurriness of her vision. She felt like screaming. She'd endured the voice mail, the horror of the suspension, and the revelation of her father's crimes. She'd fought for her job without knowing which families were in her corner and which were plotting against her. And now one of these horrible bitches had literally run her down in the parking lot.

"I'm okay," she said to Mark, grasping his shoulder with her free hand. She saw Tracy Abbott standing over them. Tracy's cheeks were pink, and tears pooled in her blue eyes.

Of course, Isobel thought. *I've been mowed down by Julia fucking Abbott.*

"Ms. Johnson?" Tracy's voice was choked.

Isobel shook her throbbing head. "It's not your fault," she said through gritted teeth.

"Isobel, we have to see a doctor," said Mark. "We need to check your head." He pointed at her right temple. She reached up and felt it under her hat. Already, a lump swelled there, pain radiating across her skull.

"In a few minutes," Isobel said. "Help me up." He hoisted her to standing, and Riley grabbed her around her waist. She kept one arm on Mark and wrapped the other around her son.

"Everything's fine," she told Riley as he let go. And then she saw Julia herself approaching, her eyes wide and fearful.

"I'm—," Julia began.

Isobel put a palm up to stop her speaking. She put one foot in front of the other to keep from swaying. "I don't want you to apologize." Julia shrank back, her mouth still open. Isobel, cold now that she'd finished running, took a deep breath, and a surge of fresh rage rushed in with it. She closed her eyes.

"Honey?" Mark said anxiously.

Isobel opened her eyes again, and things looked clearer. A small clump of people watched the interaction from behind Julia's car. "I'm fine," Isobel insisted. She took a step toward Julia, away from Mark. She felt surprisingly steady. "But"—Isobel looked straight at her—"I do want something from you."

A puff of Julia's breath hung visible in the winter air between them. Mark appeared again at her side, his arm back around her.

"Log in to Facebook," Isobel said. "I want to see the Inside Liston Facebook page."

Julia turned back toward her car, ostensibly to get her phone. Mark leaned in. "I think we should get you checked out," he said, hoarse.

"We can go to urgent care in a few minutes," Isobel said, "but first I need to see this."

Julia reached into her car, where the door still hung open. She grabbed the phone from her seat and walked back toward Isobel. Her mouth pinched as she navigated to the app. In a few seconds, she extended the phone.

Isobel looked down at it and blinked hard, willing her eyes to focus despite her dizziness. She leaned against Mark. "What does it say?" she asked him.

Mark squinted at the screen. He frowned. **Is the Liston Heights Teachers' Union lowering the quality of our kids' education?**

"As if," Isobel said. She pulled her fingers apart over the screen to enlarge the type. The words still ran together. She blinked hard to clear her vision. The next post, she could see, skewered the guidance office. Something about one of the college counselors being **inexcusably slow in uploading transcripts** and the **appalling inability of parents to screen all letters of recommendation.**

"For fuck's sake," Isobel muttered.

"Mom!" said Riley.

"Sorry." Isobel looked up and realized her family and the Abbotts were all standing in the middle of the crosswalk, the Mercedes SUV, its doors open, idling behind them. Other cars had begun backing up and turning around, heading for other exits from the lot. Somebody honked, an exasperated blast that made Isobel wince and reach for her head. "This could take a while," she said. She swiveled too fast toward her husband and stumbled. Mark's free hand went to her shoulder, righting her. "You and the kids could go get the van?" she asked.

"That doesn't seem like a good idea." He looked behind her at Julia.

Isobel smiled at Riley and Callie. "It's just going to be a few minutes," she said, her balance restored. And then to Julia: "I'd like to sit in your car, where it's warm." She turned to Tracy. "Help me." Tracy jolted forward and grabbed her teacher's elbow. Isobel put her free hand on the car for balance.

"You want to sit in the front?" Tracy asked.

"No, thanks," Isobel said, gripping the phone. "Why don't you and I get in the back? You can help me with this."

"Uh," said Julia, as she scuttled back to the driver's seat, "I'm just going to pull back around to a parking spot."

Isobel didn't answer. Tracy slid into the car after her teacher. Isobel had reached a post by the group's administrator, the so-called Lisa Lions.

"What does this say?" she asked, thrusting the phone at Tracy.

" 'Breaking,' " Tracy read. " 'Isobel Johnson reinstatement decision coming no later than next Friday.' "

Isobel squinted at the likes and comments, including one from Sheila Warner, which read, **The administration fails to acknowledge the harm caused by this out-of-control instructor. Let's demand action!** Someone called Kate Awakened had written, **If she's not back in the classroom, the students will likely riot.** Jake Tremaine's mom, Margaret, had replied, **Not my Jakey. He's happier with the sub.** *I bet he is,* thought Isobel, picturing Jake, perpetually confused. Isobel looked out and saw Jamie Preston approaching. She rolled the window down.

"I'm okay," she said.

"Kids are saying you got hit by a car." Jamie looked panicked.

"I did. This car." Isobel pointed at her seat. She didn't have the energy to make her explanation coherent. "But now I'm looking at Inside Liston," she continued. Jamie's eyes bulged, but Isobel rushed on. "You know, that Facebook group? I needed to see it, and Mrs. Abbott logged in. Can we talk later?"

Jamie backed away from the car, nodding as Isobel rolled up the window. Her back pressed against the leather seat as Julia pulled out of the lot toward another entrance. "I'm going to take some screenshots and e-mail them to myself," Isobel announced. She willed her eyes open despite the dizzying movement of the car. "Actually"—she shoved the phone toward Tracy—"could you do it?"

"Yeah." Isobel heard the iPhone shutter noise as Tracy took the first one. "All of the posts?" Tracy asked, her voice shaky.

"I'll tell you when." She reached for the phone back and blinked as she scrolled down. Lisa Lions posted two or three times per week, it seemed. It was all truly "inside" information—agenda items from faculty meetings, conclusions based on internal e-mails. "All of Lisa Lions's posts," Isobel said, and Tracy got to work. "Plus," Isobel added, not caring how uncomfortable Julia or even Tracy would be, "the post about my father, and a few others by parents."

Julia coughed as she pulled into a spot and shifted into park. "Okay?" she asked. "By the way—"

"Fine," Isobel said brusquely, interrupting. She had no interest in Julia Abbott's explanation.

"Who is Lisa Lions?" Isobel wondered as Tracy snapped pictures.

"I've been trying to figure that out, too," Tracy said. Julia's head snapped up toward the rearview mirror, but Isobel shifted her gaze away from her, up toward the ceiling of the car. *Who would know the deadline for the reinstatement decision?* Lyle knew, of course, but the idea of him informing on her via Facebook was laughable. Her temple pulsed. She raised a hand to touch the lump and flinched. Eleanor Woodsley would know, given her close contact with Mary Delgado. But with her impeccable reputation, what could she have to gain from Inside Liston? Eleanor hung her hat on being upstanding and completely, annoyingly appropriate. *No,* thought Isobel, *she's not Lisa Lions.*

"Can I see that?" Isobel reached for the phone. Tracy handed it to her silently. A Lisa Lions post from two weeks before was next in the feed. **Uptick in requests for Woodsley as senior English teacher because she so thoroughly teaches college essay writing.**

Isobel enlarged the post. February 13. This would have been posted just after the faculty meeting at which Eleanor had bragged about her requests. At the same meeting, Isobel had disclosed the voice mail. The only people present for that conversation were herself, Eleanor, and Jamie Preston. Isobel handed the phone back to Tracy and stared out the windshield at a cluster of snow-dusted trees in front of them. She let her eyes blur.

"Are you okay? Should I keep going?" Tracy asked.

"Just take a few more screenshots," Isobel said. "I need a bunch, especially by Lisa Lions."

"I've got, like, twenty examples," Tracy said, "from all of the posters." She paused. "Even my mom."

"I only posted the once," Julia blurted from the driver's seat.

"Shhh," Isobel interrupted. She closed her eyes. "Can you e-mail all of the images to me?" she asked Tracy. She leaned her head back against the leather headrest.

Tracy tapped busily. "They'll be in a few different messages to your school account."

Isobel's neck started to ache, and she rolled it gently. The car had warmed, and it smelled like sweat and wet wool.

Isobel tried to process what she'd discovered. She couldn't make sense of this, but she'd be stupid not to suspect that Jamie Preston had leaked information to this group.

She couldn't believe it.

"Anything I can do?" Julia asked. Isobel blinked her eyes open to see Julia peering at her again through the rearview mirror.

"Be quiet." Isobel surprised herself with her authority. She almost giggled, but she needed to think. She'd begun helping Jamie the moment the young woman arrived at LHHS. How could this be happening?

Tracy cleared her throat. "There's something else on the page," she said. "Look." She handed over the phone and pointed at a tab at the top labeled **Documents**. Tracy tapped it with her index finger. **Teacher Phone Numbers**, the first one said. Isobel clicked. A Google spreadsheet opened with Liston Heights teachers listed alphabetically by last name. Phone numbers appeared next to the names, and then cells labeled **Call**, which were sporadically filled. Isobel squinted at the list.

"Are they complaints?" asked Tracy.

Isobel didn't answer. She'd reached her own name, and sure enough, the voice mail she'd received was documented. **Content: Warned about anti-American sentiments and liberal agenda.**

Isobel swallowed. As it turned out, she hadn't been the only one to receive an unnerving voice mail. She reached the bottom of the list, and Eleanor Woodsley's line on the spreadsheet was blank. *Of course,* Isobel thought. Her eyes swam, but she forced herself to check Jamie Preston, too. Also blank.

"Um," said Julia from the front. "I'm getting nervous about your head. I read an article about looking at screens while concussed, and—"

Isobel put a finger up and kept her head down. "Shut up," she said, and then: "Sorry, Tracy."

She clicked out of the spreadsheet and looked back at the main page. She could hear Julia breathing heavily.

Although it seemed Isobel could scroll through several more sections in the group, she didn't think she needed to. "You sent the images?" she asked. Her head had gotten hot in the warmth of the car, and she gingerly removed her hat, stretching it over the lump on her right temple. Tracy nodded. "Thanks," Isobel said. She dropped the phone in her student's lap. "I'm finished."

Julia turned toward her, her face ashen and eyes glassy. She swallowed. "Are you sure there's nothing else I can do? A ride to the urgent care? Some kind of . . ." She paused, reaching for her purse, and Isobel felt certain she was about to offer her cash. Suddenly, Mark appeared next to the window. He tapped lightly with his knuckle.

"Absolutely not," Isobel said as she opened the back door. "But don't call me at home," she said. "Ever again." Julia's mouth snapped shut, and Isobel could read the guilt in her expression.

"I was . . . ," Julia tried, but her words died. "Tracy said motherhood was a waste," she managed, sounding desperate.

TRACY ABBOTT

After Ms. Johnson got out of the car, Tracy and Julia sat there for a minute, neither of them speaking. "Go," Tracy finally said.

"You're not getting back in the front?"

Tracy shook her head and looked out the window, where Ms. Johnson's husband helped her into the passenger seat of the minivan Tracy had seen so many times in the LHHS parking lot. She knew the decals on the back window by heart. "Kindness matters" was her favorite. She planned to order one just like it—she'd found the sticker on Amazon already—when she got her permit in the spring.

Julia pulled out of the parking lot and headed home. Though the drive would take only five minutes, each second stretched. Finally, when they'd made it off of Liston Boulevard, Tracy spoke. "You left Ms. Johnson a voice mail on her home number?"

Julia didn't say anything, which was the same as confirming it.

"It was because I said I didn't want to be a mother?" Tracy asked.

Julia depressed her turn signal and said nothing.

"Why aren't you answering?" Tracy asked. She could hear her tone rising.

"Because you don't understand," Julia said.

Tracy stared out the window again. She watched the houses in her neighborhood go by, their great room windows overlooking expansive front lawns. She'd go far away for college, Tracy thought suddenly. Maybe the West Coast.

"You don't admire me." Tracy looked up. Her mother stared at her through the rearview mirror as they pulled into their driveway. Her voice sounded thin, and the gray circles beneath her eyes were pronounced, even though Tracy knew she had applied concealer and mascara that morning.

Tracy looked through the windshield at the garage door lifting. She didn't actually admire her mother. Not particularly. Not only had she clocked Melissa Young, but she had written that callous post about Ms. Johnson on Facebook. And she'd apparently harassed her? At home? Tracy hoped Ms. Johnson would notice that she'd written *Kate Awakened* at the close of the e-mail she'd sent last, the one with the screenshots of her favorite comments in Ms. Johnson's defense. Julia pulled the car slowly into its stall. When it had stopped, Tracy got out and went inside without another word.

JULIA ABBOTT

s that my racer?" Henry asked, laughter in his voice, as Julia walked through the mudroom. The kitchen smelled like fresh coffee and toast.

Henry looked up from his newspaper. "Was it really hard?" he asked. "Tracy looked peaked. Said she was going to lie down."

Julia clasped her hands together over her stomach. Henry stood, alarmed. "Are you sick?" He reached an arm toward her. When he touched her back, his hand felt warm through the waterproof fabric of her running jacket.

"No." She'd tried to devise a way to avoid telling him about the accident, but she knew it was impossible. Tracy knew. Everyone would know. Doubtless, video footage from spectators was already posted on Inside Liston.

"What's going on?" Henry asked, sitting back down as Julia tucked her chair in beside him. "Did something happen?"

Julia closed her eyes. Henry grabbed her hand, nervous. "Yes," Julia said finally, opening her eyes slowly. "Something did happen, Henry, but before I tell you, I want you to know that it's all settled. I think everything's okay now." She wasn't exactly sure if this was true, but she hoped.

"Okay." Henry moved both his hands to his armrests, bracing himself. Julia hated that she recognized his posture. They'd been here before, him waiting for her explanation.

"There was an accident in the parking lot after the race." Julia had practiced this line during the silent ride home.

"Is the car damaged? Because we can fix that." If only it had been a fender bender, then Henry could go back to his coffee and the weekly transaction listings.

"There was no damage. But"—Julia drummed her fingers on the table and let out a tremulous breath—"I hit someone."

"Is there damage to the other car? I mean, that's a pain, but that's what insurance is for. Did you exchange details? I can make the call." Henry reached for his cell phone.

"That's not it," Julia said quickly, staring past him. "I hit a person." She paused. "Who was walking." It was her turn to brace herself. She knew he'd be livid.

Henry jutted his chin toward her and laid his hands flat on the table. "How? Is he okay? Did you call the police?"

"It was a teacher," Julia continued, "and, yes, she seems fine. Well, she went to urgent care, but she's walking and talking."

"Seems?" Henry asked. "Did you at least call an ambulance?"

"She insisted that we not do that." Julia began fiddling with the Tiffany bangle.

"What happened?" Henry said slowly. He looked away from his wife into the kitchen, where the red light of the coffeemaker glowed.

"I think I was reaching for my phone—it had fallen into the well on the driver's-side door—and I looked down for a moment. I was rolling toward the stop sign at the exit of the parking lot, not even five miles per hour, and I just"—she swallowed—"tapped her."

"You tapped her?" Henry repeated. "Who was this?"

"It was Isobel Johnson," Julia said, her head hanging.

"The English teacher? Of course," Henry said. He leaned back. Julia agreed the whole thing was massively unfortunate. She'd hit the woman who'd commented on the news story, Tracy's favorite teacher, who'd supposedly turned her against motherhood. People would think Julia had done this on purpose. "And did she fall?" Henry shouted. "Cuts and bruises? Head injury? What are we talking here, Julia?"

Julia's voice became a whisper and her tears immediately accumulated. "She fell on her side, I think. She seemed fine, although she had a lump on her temple." She pointed at the spot on her own head. "She sat in our car for a little while."

"In your car? Why?"

Julia studied the hydrangea in their yard. She'd hoped she would be able to skip this part, but now Henry had asked. "She wanted to see that secret Facebook group I'm a member of. The group called Inside Liston." She shook her head quickly, signaling him not to ask any questions just then. "There's been a lot in the group about Isobel Johnson because she was recently suspended. And I posted there about her father. Tracy saw it, and that's why she hasn't been speaking to me."

"What about her father? How is that relevant?"

"He's Robert Miller, that big financial criminal from the nineties. Remember him? Anyway, this teacher talks on and on about justice and, like, equity, and her own father stole millions from a charitable foundation. I thought people had the right to know." She twisted the bracelet. Henry watched her for a second and then stood and walked to the study.

"Where are you going?" Julia called from the table.

"I'm looking up the Johnsons' home number," he said. "Isn't there a school directory in here somewhere?"

"She said not to call her at home," Julia said. She dropped her head to the table, where it rested on her forearms. "Anymore."

"Anymore?" She might as well tell him the whole thing. He was already so discernibly disappointed. Henry came back carrying the spiral-bound directory. Julia hadn't realized he even knew of the book's existence. "Do they list the teachers in here? Why did you say 'anymore'?"

"They list them if they don't opt out. And I left Isobel Johnson a message a few weeks ago," Julia said, voice muffled, "on her home phone."

Henry grabbed his glasses and scanned the early pages, where the directory listed various committees and chairpersons. "Faculty," he said aloud when he found it. "Johnson. Is this a home number or a cell?"

"Home," Julia said.

Henry grabbed his phone from the table and started dialing.

"I told her she was anti-American." Henry look repulsed and waved her off. A few tears leaked from Julia's eyes, and she used one of her gloves to wipe them. They waited in silence, Henry listening to each ring. Finally, Julia could hear an answering machine, the same one she'd encountered weeks ago. "You've reached the Johnson residence," said a male voice. "Please leave us a message."

After the beep, Henry said, "Yes, this is Henry Abbott. Listen, Julia and I are both terribly sorry and concerned about what happened—about the accident—today in the high school parking lot. We'd love to know how you're doing, Isobel, and whether there's anything we can do. If you can—if you're willing—would you please call me? I'm leaving my cell." Henry recited the number and hung up. He sat back down with his wife.

"Julia," he said, sounding grave, "something has got to change."

Her whole body felt tired. "I know," she said. "Everything is always so messed up."

"What can we do?" Henry asked. "Don't you feel like maybe something's missing at this stage? Like, from your life? Are you happy?"

Julia sat back in her chair and pulled the elastic from her ponytail. She felt anger mix with her sadness and embarrassment. Her whole life had been about clearing obstacles for him, Andrew, and Tracy, and they had all benefited. And now Henry wondered if there was something missing, impeding her happiness? After he'd blissfully remained her focus for the past twenty years? The phrase she'd uttered to Tracy in the car came back to her now: *You don't admire me,* she thought.

"Well?" Henry prompted. She realized he was still staring at her.

"Maybe," she said finally. "Maybe I'm ready for something more."

ISOBEL JOHNSON

Isobel touched her bruised right temple as she and Lyle walked to Wayne Wallace's office on Monday morning. She'd called the principal the night before, Mark at her side, her voice shaking. "I'm sorry to bother you at home," she'd said, "but I have something important to share with you." Wayne had made a number of guttural sounds as Isobel delivered her rehearsed speech, and finally he suggested they meet before school.

"Will you invite Mary Delgado and Amanda from HR?" Isobel asked. "I'm bringing Lyle Greenwood."

"Yes," Wayne said, "I suppose that would be appropriate."

An hour later he'd called back. "You were hit by a car in the high school parking lot?" he said.

"Yes," Isobel replied, prepared, "and I'm happy to file any necessary paperwork after our meeting on Monday."

"But are you okay?" Wayne sounded worried.

Probably about the potential workers' comp claim, Isobel thought. "I'm fine, and I'd be happy to talk after our meeting."

Now Isobel gripped the handle of her laptop bag, its fabric rough against her skin. Once the doctor had determined she had a soft-tissue trauma and not a concussion, she and Mark had put the screenshots of the Inside Liston Facebook group into a PowerPoint so she could click through them for the administrators. She'd explain the timeline and, more important, who was behind the posts. She was ready.

"You've got this," Lyle said. "I really believe your suspension ends today." He'd agreed that the information from the group changed everything: The complaints, while perhaps genuine, were provoked and coordinated. Without Lisa Lions, the school would have heard from maybe one or two parents. And if it hadn't been Isobel, Lisa Lions would have targeted someone else.

When they got to the office, the three administrators were already seated at the conference table, looking toward the door. Amanda appeared sheepish, and Isobel realized she was furious, her cheeks flushing. They should have gotten to the bottom of the Inside Liston page as soon as they'd heard about it, but instead, it took her own head injury to make any progress on the investigation.

None of them said anything as she entered. Wayne finally cleared his throat and muttered, "Good morning."

Serves you right, Isobel thought, emboldened by their obvious discomfort. They weren't used to being the last to know about community sentiment.

Mary flipped open her laptop. "I'll take some notes," she said.

Isobel and Lyle sat across from them. "As you know," Isobel began, grabbing her computer, "I examined the Inside Liston Facebook group this weekend."

"I've been thinking since your call," Wayne interrupted. "How did you accomplish that?"

"I approached an amenable parent," Isobel said, confidently delivering the line she'd devised with Mark. She didn't want to explain the accident now; she wanted to focus on the site, on Jamie's involvement. She could incriminate Julia Abbott later, as Lyle had encouraged her to do, explain that she had admitted to leaving the voice mail and then unearthing the story about Isobel's father. "A pattern of harassment," Lyle had said.

Isobel smiled tightly. "Can I show you what I found?" Without waiting for a reply, she flipped the top of her MacBook. She'd made sure the slideshow was loaded on her screen, ready. She and Mark had enlarged each of her screenshots and put them in order, according to category. "Can you see okay?" Amanda scooted her chair closer to Wayne's so they were all more or less opposite Isobel. She'd decided to begin with the post about the teachers' union.

"This is one type of item," Isobel said as the three leaned forward. "Anti-union posts, presuming or wondering whether the teachers' federation makes students' experiences here worse." She paused, letting them read. Each of their faces appeared grim, eyes squinting. She'd started easy—these three might have the same covert wonderings about the teachers' union.

When they'd sat back, she clicked ahead. "I've included a few more posts with the same theme, some directly targeting Lyle Greenwood." She tipped her head toward him. "You'll notice that some of the posts are made by the group's administrator, the so-called Lisa Lions, and some are made by members of the group. Parents," she clarified, "all using their real names." *Except Kate Awakened,* she thought. But she planned to leave Tracy out of this meeting.

Wayne drew in a breath and let it out again. "What's the ratio of how many posts are initiated by Lisa Lions versus how many by parents?"

Isobel had anticipated the query. "I think about a third of the posts are by 'Lisa.'" She put air quotes around the name and clicked again. "Here's a second type of post. These complain about a school policy or decision, sometimes referencing a specific teacher." Tracy had captured a gripe about Wayne's handpicked leadership team, and Isobel included some of the caustic comment thread in the slide.

Wayne leaned closer. "They're attacking each other."

"Yep." Isobel nodded. She clicked ahead again. "And here's one about Sadie Eslinger's most recent AP European History exam."

Wayne reached up and massaged his hairline with two fingers. "Did Sadie consult the testing calendar?" he wondered.

The others looked at him blankly. As if that mattered. After a beat, Mary spoke. "Isn't that sort of beside the point here?" she asked. "A forum for antagonistic complaints hardly lifts the community." Isobel smiled at her, surprised. Speaking up for teachers in a meeting? It was a big step for Mary.

Isobel hesitated as she arrived at the slide with Julia's post about Robert Miller. "After I was suspended," she said—she'd rehearsed this part, too—"parents began questioning my qualifications. Some looked up my license, and others called my university to verify my degrees." Amanda's mouth dropped open. "Then Julia Abbott dug up a story from my past that I'm not proud of."

"To be clear," Lyle said, his voice soft, "it's a story from her father's past."

"Your father?" Wayne asked.

"He was a financial adviser, and he stole money from many of his clients." Isobel felt her skin dampen with sweat beneath her sweater. *Get this over with,* she thought. "This was in the nineties."

She paused, faltering, and Lyle delivered her next line. "Her father's imprisonment motivated Isobel to become a teacher in the first place, to highlight for teenagers that without empathy, people make terrible and dangerous choices."

Isobel half smiled at Lyle, silently thanking him for speaking up. "So," she said, once she was able to, "the comments on that report about my dad"—she clicked to an enlargement, skipping Kate Awakened's and Vivian Song's defenses of her—"were brutal."

Isobel gave them time to read words like "hypocrite" and "fraud," and then she advanced to the next slide. "Here's the last type of post," she said, relieved to have moved beyond her secret. "This subset is always made by Lisa Lions herself—or himself," she allowed, although she felt certain she knew who the culprit was. "It's insider information. Bits from e-mails like this one." She pointed at the screen, which showed a comment about the younger teachers updating their résumés due to declining enrollment. "Or this one"—she clicked—"announcing the deadline for determining my future at the school." She locked eyes with Wayne.

Amanda leaned in then. "But who could know?" she asked.

"That's what I wondered," said Isobel. She waited.

Mary squinted, obviously thinking. "Who knew about the conclusion of the suspension?" the department chair asked.

"The three of you. Lyle." Isobel paused. "I'm assuming someone told Judith Youngstead since she'd need to plan her time here. Mary, did you tell Eleanor Woodsley?"

Mary's eyebrows shot up. "I did tell her last week," she admitted, speaking quickly.

Isobel had figured as much. "And," Isobel said with an air of finality, "I told Jamie Preston." She looked at each of them—Wayne, Amanda, and Mary—deliberately, wanting them to understand the conclusion she was asking them to draw. When she'd revealed her suspicions about Jamie to Lyle, he'd snapped his fingers and said, "I've never liked her!" Isobel allowed him an "I told you so," especially since it wasn't about her own pedagogy.

"This one," Isobel said now, clicking, "made it hard to ignore Jamie's potential involvement." She showed the post about requests by seniors to be placed in Eleanor's classes. The bosses studied it.

Wayne looked at her, perplexed. "Why that one?" he asked.

"This was posted on the evening of the parent communication faculty meeting," Isobel said. "Jamie and I were partnered with Eleanor." Wayne nodded, remembering. "During that conversation," Isobel continued, "Eleanor reported that she had a high percentage of teacher requests for senior English, due to her excellent communication regarding college essays." She couldn't resist a sidelong glance at Mary here. Was Eleanor's assertion accurate? Isobel doubted she got quite as many requests as she'd indicated. Mary looked at the ceiling, considering. "Then three hours later," Isobel continued, "this post appears in the secret Facebook group. Seems like it's at least worth investigating." Wayne and Amanda exchanged a glance.

Isobel felt a swell of confidence, the attention off her and onto Jamie. Perhaps she could put this all behind her. She could restore her reputation in this community, in which reputation was arguably the most important thing. "Certainly this Facebook group will have to be shut down. In order to do that, we have to identify Lisa Lions. It seems we're well on our way there." She stared at Wayne. "Teachers aren't going to want to stay here if their lives are fodder for gossip sites."

Wayne sat back in his chair and rubbed his belly, the pink broadcloth stretched at the buttons. "Amanda and I," he said slowly, "and I guess you, too, Mary—we'll begin an investigation today. Did any of you see the Humans of LHHS post this morning featuring Jamie?"

"That's on Instagram?" Isobel asked.

"It's the Liston Lights' project. They switch off weeks. This week, Tracy Abbott is in charge. Her theme is teachers without tenure, and her profile is on Jamie Preston." Wayne pulled his phone out of his pocket, clicked a few times, and then handed it to Isobel. Jamie filled the screen, her brown hair framing her pale face, freckles distinct against her skin. Jamie's brown eyes were wide and worried, her hand raised halfway off her desk as if she was asking Tracy to wait to take the photo.

Doing whatever it takes to be rehired, read the caption below the less-than-flattering photograph. **It wasn't long ago that Jamie Preston walked these halls as a student. In fact, mementos from her glory days adorn the bulletin board behind Ms. Preston's desk along with a reminder to move on to the next chapters of our lives, rather than reveling in the past. Ironic, then, that Ms. Preston is back where she started, and without any assurance that she'll survive the layoffs that have been reported on the Inside Liston Facebook page, a "secret" group to which many of our parents belong.**

"Like she says, the group isn't public," Isobel said, not wanting to mention that Tracy had been the one to help her with the screenshots. Her student must have come to the same conclusions about Lisa Lions as she had. *Clever girl,* she thought. "But it's getting bigger. There are seven hundred fifty members. If that's one parent per family—and I did notice it's mostly, but not all, mothers—then almost half of our families are represented. Teachers can't be targeted in that kind of forum and also effectively do their jobs."

Lyle broke in. "I'd imagine, Amanda, that you'll start to see several complaints about a hostile work environment if parents publish mean-spirited exposés on teachers, like the one Julia Abbott published about Isobel. Not that the Humans of LHHS account is necessarily any better this morning. Don't you vet those, Wayne?"

"I do," Wayne said, "and I'll delete this one." His wide thumb moved over his screen, and he pocketed his phone.

Isobel closed her computer. "Wayne," she said, "I think you know that I take my work here incredibly seriously. I'm not sure you'll find a replacement for me with more passion." She stood, suddenly teary. "And I need this job. I have two children."

"Our investigation found that most students and families do value you." Wayne turned toward his desk and grabbed a thick file from its edge. Isobel looked wonderingly at Lyle, who shrugged. "In fact," Wayne said, "this is a petition—well, the paper version of the petition. In total there are more than four hundred signatures of kids asking us to reinstate you."

"Really?" Isobel asked. "Four hundred?" She felt more tears threatening. Even if their parents didn't, the kids understood her value. Four hundred was more than two years' worth of students.

"Can we end the investigation?" Lyle said, interrupting. "Based on what you just said, it seems that Isobel's likability is actually pretty high, perhaps above average." He gestured at the laptop, where they'd seen plenty of evidence of dissatisfaction directed at several of their colleagues. "And she's never had a negative performance review."

Amanda turned to Wayne as if Isobel weren't there. "There's the judgment issue on the Facebook comment about Julia Abbott."

Isobel's shoulders sank. "That was thoughtless, and I'm sorry. It never occurred to me that a post on my own private profile could make its way public. I'm not friends with any teachers or students on Facebook. But you're right. . . ." She wiped at her eyelids, determined not to cry in this meeting. "I should have been more careful. I regret the comment."

"Then again," Lyle said, "it's not as if Julia Abbott didn't retaliate in a pretty big way. She asserted that Isobel's qualifications are void because of a mistake her father made almost twenty-five years ago."

"I'd like to get back to work," Isobel said. "Immediately, if that's possible."

JAMIE PRESTON

⁓

Jamie had obsessively refreshed the Humans of LHHS feed that morning and been horrified by the photo Tracy Abbott had posted. The girl hadn't responded to her e-mail reminder that she'd like to review the post, and she'd been livid. But before she could go to Mary Delgado to complain, it had been deleted. Maybe Wayne Wallace actually supervised his Liston Lights.

Jamie had just taught John Proctor's gallows speech in act four of *The Crucible* for two class periods in a row when Isobel walked in at lunchtime.

"Did you want to eat together?" Jamie grabbed her wallet from her top desk drawer as she stood. "Did you get my text? How are you feeling?"

Isobel narrowed her eyes at the quotation Jamie had tacked to the bulletin board behind her desk. *You can't start reading the next chapter of your life if you keep rereading the last one.* Jamie had seen Tracy's mean-spirited interpretation of that on Instagram, of course, but hadn't yet taken it down.

"What *is* the next chapter of your life?" Isobel asked suddenly, tilting her head as she studied the words.

"What?" Jamie asked.

"Really," Isobel said, an edge in her voice that Jamie hadn't heard before, "what are you planning to do next?"

Jamie couldn't quite read her expression, but it wasn't friendly. She put her wallet back on the desk and sat down. "Are you okay?" she asked.

"I'm okay," Isobel said. "Are you?" Kids streamed past the open door on their way to the cafeteria or their next classes.

"What's going on?" Jamie asked.

Isobel squeezed her knuckles together. "When you saw me this weekend in Julia Abbott's car, I was looking at Inside Liston. Remember?" She peered at Jamie. "I'd asked you before if you'd heard about it."

Though it was difficult, Jamie lifted her head and met Isobel's gaze. "What did you find?"

Isobel raised her eyebrows. "You sure you don't know?"

"I don't." Jamie's voice sounded plaintive, and she blinked. *Don't admit anything,* she told herself.

"It's a horrible group for overly involved Liston Heights parents, and it's run by someone on the inside." A slightly antiseptic smell wafted from the desktop in front of Jamie, the remnants of a Clorox wipe she'd just used. Isobel's lip curled. "There are gossipy items about the union, the testing calendar, declining enrollment." She articulated the "t." "Julia Abbott and others challenged my credentials, and then Julia published that piece about my father, to whom I haven't spoken in fifteen years."

Jamie closed her mouth again and stared at Isobel. *Speak,* she told herself. "You think this has something to do with me?"

Isobel squinted, her face hard. The expression was so different from the encouraging, admiring glances her mentor had bestowed over the last year and a half. For some reason, Isobel had taken her under her wing, nurtured her "spark," which Jamie had always known was an illusion. "There were posts about my suspension," Isobel said. "Assignments from my class. Little nuggets"—she smiled sardonically and raised her thumb and forefinger, showing a small chunk—"from conversations you and I were part of."

"Wait," Jamie said. She straightened and raised a palm. "Are you saying you think I post on this group?"

"I think you're the administrator and creator," Isobel said. Jamie flashed back to the previous week, the many chances she'd had to delete the whole thing. How she wished she'd done it. It would have been easy, and then Isobel would never have seen. "Delete it," Isobel said as she walked toward the door.

"Wait, Isobel—"

"No," Isobel said. "We're done here. You nearly ruined my career."

JULIA ABBOTT

By dinnertime on Monday evening, the Abbotts hadn't heard from Isobel or Mark Johnson. "Was Ms. Johnson at school today?" Julia asked. She'd made Andrew's favorite, mac and cheese, again, desperate to get at least one of the children back on her side.

"I saw her in the hallway," Andrew said, his mouth full.

"Really?" Tracy asked, speaking her first word of the meal. "Because I'm getting really sick of Mrs. Youngstead."

"What's wrong with her?" Henry asked. Julia was grateful he tried to keep things going.

"Nothing." Tracy shrugged. "She's just obsessed with, like, pronouns, and I think she's in love with John Steinbeck."

"I'm pretty sure that guy's dead," Henry joked.

Tracy rolled her eyes, but Julia could see a smile flitting across her scowl.

They hadn't really talked again after Julia confessed the accident and Henry had told her, not for the first time, that she needed to change.

A drowsy sadness had overtaken her after he'd said that. She had retreated to their bed, alternately sleeping and reading snippets of books from her nightstand. She'd picked up *The Everything Guide for High School Set Design*, but put it down when she realized she'd probably never again be allowed to help on a build. She went back to sleep.

On Monday morning, she hadn't bothered to get up with the kids, as neither of them wanted to see her. Andrew remained mortified, she was sure, about her impromptu meeting with Wayne about his role. Tracy—well, Tracy preferred Isobel Johnson and had spent her free time organizing to save the woman's career while Julia had tried to torpedo it. She pulled the covers up to her neck and ignored the noises from the kitchen while she waited for them to leave.

That evening, however, Julia sat with her laptop in her usual spot at the kitchen counter, her Tiffany bracelet clicking against the wrist rest. She opened her e-mail and pressed COMPOSE. In the TO: field, she typed **IJohnson@lhhs.org**, and then took a long sip of prosecco. In the subject line, she wrote, **Many apologies.**

Most of the times she'd contacted a teacher, she had been sure she was in the right. Her e-mails conveyed imperiousness. In this one, she'd grovel.

Dear Isobel, she began. **I cannot tell you how much I regret my behavior in these last weeks. I know it's an above-and-beyond request, but would you consider meeting me to talk about how I could make things right? I'd like to hasten your reinstatement, if I can. As a start, I removed the post I wrote about your father on that Facebook page. I also unfriended Lisa Lions and left the group. As I'm sure you know, Tracy adores you. You may have noticed her comments in your defense under the name Kate Awakened. "Kate" is not currently speaking to me, which I guess I understand, but which also breaks my heart. Could I buy you a coffee? Really, I'd be so grateful. Please consider it.**

She reread what she'd written and typed her name to close. *Please,* she thought, and clicked SEND.

ISOBEL JOHNSON

Callie was a disaster when Isobel picked her up at the middle school on Monday afternoon. As soon as she saw Riley in the back of the van, she snapped. "Ugh!" she shouted. "Can we turn off your stupid music?"

"Hey!" Isobel recoiled at her tone.

"No one ever thinks about what I might want," Callie spit, grabbing the seat belt and fastening it roughly.

Riley and Isobel made eye contact in the rearview mirror, exchanging a wondering shrug. Once she'd pulled out of the school parking lot, Isobel tried to engage her daughter. "Did something happen today?" she asked.

"No!" Callie said. "What are you even talking about? Things happen every day."

"Okay," Isobel said, backing off.

By the time they'd gotten home, Callie had criticized Riley's hair and Isobel's shoes, in addition to accusing her mother of always "having to be better," as demonstrated in the previous day's 5K. When she stomped up to her room, Isobel was happy to let her go. Nothing improved during dinner—not even Mark could cajole their daughter out of her unpleasantness—and Callie staged a repeat of her indignant march upstairs the second she had finished chewing her last bite of roast chicken.

Before she loaded the dishwasher, Isobel refreshed her work e-mail on her phone. Bile stung her throat as a message from Julia Abbott appeared. She wasn't interested in Julia's "Many apologies." She and Mark had heard Henry Abbott's voice mail, and she'd forbidden Mark from calling back.

"We could at least let them cover the out-of-pocket medical expenses from the accident," Mark said reasonably. "That would make them feel better and also help us. We could knock out the deductible."

"No," Isobel said. Any contact with Julia Abbott was too much, and the idea of cashing a check from her was disgusting. "She's the worst kind of person," Isobel told Mark. "Never engage."

And yet curiosity led her to open Julia's e-mail. What would she apologize for, exactly? And how would she phrase it? Despite her reservations, Isobel clicked on the message. When she got to the line about Tracy not speaking to her mother, Isobel was surprised to notice a pang of empathy. She glanced at the ceiling toward Callie's room. *Don't engage,* she told herself. And yet, somewhere upstairs, Isobel's own daughter was sulking for who knew what reason and barely speaking to *her.* Isobel noted the first signs of adolescence and foresaw the battles she and Callie would fight, similar to those that most teenage daughters waged with their mothers. She'd read enough personal essays about that relationship to cover any scenario she and Callie would enact.

Julia had quit the Facebook page. She'd removed the horrible, holier-than-thou post about Isobel's father. Though she'd alienated many of her own friends in the aftermath of the cast-list incident, Julia still had knowledge of the Liston Heights parental elite. Maybe now that Isobel knew who was behind Inside Liston, Julia could help her figure out how to make other parents understand its danger.

Though astonished by her own rationalization, Isobel hit REPLY. Yes, she typed on her phone. **Should we meet at the Starbucks close to school? I think Liston Heights needs a culture makeover. It sounds like you could help.**

ISOBEL JOHNSON

They'd agreed on noon at Starbucks, a time when Isobel imagined that almost no one would be there. The other mothers, if they were out, would be having lunch. Isobel arrived five minutes early to give herself time to order a decaf latte and settle into a corner booth. By the time Julia arrived in her black leggings and long down coat, she felt less jumpy.

Mark had encouraged the meeting. "Get a check!" he'd said, and Isobel had swatted at him. But with her nerves fluttering and her stomach perhaps too upset for coffee, she was starting to agree with him. The Abbotts owed her. Julia arrived and waved at Isobel. When she'd ordered, she came to the table while she waited for her drink.

"Thanks for meeting with me." Julia sounded breathless. She folded her coat over the back of a chair and then accidentally dropped her phone—the thick rubber case bounced on the laminate flooring. She shook her head. "I'm nervous," she explained as she bent down to retrieve it.

"Me, too," Isobel said. "This is my first coffee with a parent." She smiled wanly, not showing teeth.

Julia pointed to a large table across the shop. "That's where the Booster Board normally sits. I haven't been to the meetings for this show because I'm suspended." She spilled these words quickly, and then, as if unsure what to say next, she turned abruptly toward the pickup counter. Isobel stared after her. She hadn't known there had been consequences— beyond the public shaming—for the Melissa Young incident.

Julia slid into her chair and shook her ponytail out of a green Liston pom-pom hat. "This is Tracy's," she said.

"Were you suspended for the Melissa Young thing?" Isobel asked. She realized that they'd both been banished that month. At least they'd have a place to start.

"Yes," Julia said earnestly, leaning in. "It was an accident! The Youngs threatened to press charges, and Wayne Wallace suspended me." She took a sip of her drink and flinched against its heat. "For a year!" she added before Isobel could respond.

"A year? I'm hoping my suspension lifts before the end of the week," Isobel said.

Julia looked at the tabletop and cleared her throat. "Tracy will be thrilled to have you back. She loves you, you know. You're her absolute favorite teacher."

"That's so nice to hear."

Julia looked as if she were about to cry. "She's not speaking to me," she said. "She thinks I'm a mean-spirited gossip."

Isobel raised her eyebrows. Of course, she herself had arrived at the same conclusion about Julia.

"Okay, so maybe I acted that way," Julia admitted, "but I have some ideas, and that's why I asked you here." Julia's intensity overtook the sadness Isobel had just witnessed. Julia had pulled out a spiral-bound planner and flipped to a page where she'd written a series of bullet points. "The Inside Liston Facebook group has got to go, obviously," Julia said. "I think we should replace it. I searched, and there isn't a group like the one I want to create—a community Facebook page, yes, but the focus is appreciation." Isobel almost laughed.

"No, it's cool," Julia insisted, noticing Isobel's reaction. She seemed so sure of herself that Isobel had to stifle another giggle. Julia went on to describe a page on which people could share news about Liston Heights teams and clubs. They'd also celebrate teacher accomplishments and birthdays.

"I think we can get Shane McGregor to donate free pizzas for your birthdays," Julia said. "The McGregors have run a popular pizza place in Liston Heights for fifty years." She stabbed the bullet point in her planner corresponding to this idea and then blinked at Isobel, waiting for her response. She was so fervent about the pizza that Isobel laughed outright.

"What?" Julia demanded, crestfallen.

Isobel felt immediately sorry. "It's a good idea," she said quickly. "You're just so serious about it that I laughed."

Julia sighed. "Everyone says I'm overinvested."

Isobel was surprised by her candor. "Are you this passionate about everything?"

"What's the point of doing anything if you're not doing it well?" Isobel understood the mind-set, but at the same time, it seemed like so much pressure, having to be excellent in every endeavor. When Isobel encountered students with this tendency, she tried to talk them out of it.

"Sometimes," she told Julia, just as she'd tell a teenager, "it's just the effort or the learning that's important. Sometimes, it's totally fine to get a B plus."

Julia wrinkled her nose. "I noticed you've given both of my children B pluses," she said. "Were you trying to teach them a similar life lesson?"

Isobel laughed again then, and Julia did, too.

"I'm really sorry," Julia said after the moment had passed. "I'm obviously sorry for hitting you with my car." Isobel couldn't help it; she laughed again. "Are you concussed?" Julia blurted.

"No," Isobel said, wondering at Julia's phrasing. The woman was hilarious. "Soft-tissue trauma."

"Thank God," Julia said. "And while I'm at it, I'm also sorry about that Facebook article about your father. It wasn't my business."

"Are you also sorry about leaving me that voice mail?" Isobel asked.

Julia cocked her head. "Only if you're sorry about that Channel Six comment."

A rush of shame squashed some of Isobel's mirth. "I'm really, *really* sorry about that," she said. "It was stupid and thoughtless, not to mention bad for my career." She had an inclination to reach out and touch Julia's hand, but stopped herself.

"I don't have a career," Julia said. Isobel couldn't quite discern the sentiment beneath the statement. She thought back on the well-constructed sentences in the article about Robert Miller. Julia had command of both the hyphen and the em dash. *She's a good writer,* Isobel thought, but didn't say it.

"You do have two beautiful and successful children," she said. Julia's face immediately brightened, and Isobel asked, "What are we going to do about Tracy not speaking to you?"

JULIA ABBOTT

ONE YEAR LATER

Julia and Henry sat in the center of the third row when Andrew stood in a straight line of actors across the stage for the curtain call of *Rent*. Julia grinned at Andrew's floppy hair and his green short-sleeved T-shirt layered over a white thermal. The costume shop had hardly been necessary this year, except for Angel's getup for "Today 4 U." Henry offered his usual whoop, deep and commanding. Andrew's smile expanded as the audience cheered. Julia choked back happy tears.

In the lobby afterward, Julia slid her arm around him and kissed his cheek.

"I'm so proud of you," Julia said, but Andrew's attention migrated to Sarah Smith. Julia ruffled his sweaty hair and dropped her arm.

"Thanks, Mom," he said.

Sarah thrust a clutch of carnations in Lions yellow and green toward him. "You were fantastic." She blushed and whispered something in his ear.

Henry grabbed Julia's hand, and they turned toward the door, though Julia couldn't resist a look back at Andrew. Her baby! He'd be headed to college in the fall, his eye on the theater club at the University of Minnesota–Duluth. As she imagined him moving out, someone bumped her shoulder.

"Oh," Julia said, startled. It was Sally Hollister.

"Julia," Sally said. "Excuse me."

Julia smiled, recovering. "Maeve was great. What a way to end her theater career at Liston Heights. And as Mimi, such a powerful role. I mean, really"—she felt the words tumbling out quickly—"pitch-perfect."

"Thanks," Sally said. "Andrew was wonderful. I could see his emotion in the Life Support scene. And"—she paused—"I think, honestly, Julia, our publicity was better than ever. I know it was a challenge, too, with the less-than-PC subject matter of the show."

Julia flushed. A compliment? From the old guard? She had quietly joined a Booster committee at the start of the winter season, after having stayed away for the full twelve months required by the suspension. Obviously, the executive committee was not the place, but publicity had had a vacancy. The group, mostly ninth-grade moms, had been grateful for her leadership. "Well, the kids lobbied for *Rent*." Julia shrugged. Andrew had been at the helm of the effort, telling her earnestly that the school musical should serve a dual purpose—entertainment *and* social commentary. Tracy had nodded solemnly behind him, and Julia knew that though Isobel herself might not be involved in this effort, she'd certainly influenced it.

"Are you joining us for drinks?" Sally asked. It was tradition to toast their children after opening night.

Suddenly, Annabelle Young appeared behind Sally and wrapped both arms around her shoulders and squeezed. "She was wonderful!" Annabelle sang. "Just sublime. Look at me. I'm still crying." Julia looked down. The maroon carpeting appeared unevenly worn in places. She made a mental note to add its replacement to the list of Booster priorities.

"You're sweet," Sally said. She turned away.

Julia looked back to Henry and grabbed his hand. "You ready?" she asked. "We got invited to the theater parents' thing," Julia said, looking back toward Annabelle, "but that might be a little much?"

"Let's visit the Tuolomee," Henry said. "It's almost done, and a new wine bar opened across the street. Martin Young even says he likes their selection."

She and Henry walked to the door as she pulled her gloves out of her purse. The cold air blew her ponytail up as she walked out into the darkness. "Just one drink," she said. "I've got a blog post to finalize for tomorrow morning. Plus, the Liston Heights Striders meet at nine thirty."

Henry steered her around a slow-walking clump of kids. "One viral post, and you're obsessed," he joked.

The entire family had been surprised when, the previous spring, Julia launched a website called Helicopter Repair Shop. "It's about my adventures," she'd told them over family dinner. "Well, misadventures," she clarified, "in helicopter parenting."

Tracy and Andrew had glanced at each other. "Wait," Tracy said. "Are you saying you're a helicopter parent?"

"I'm hoping," Julia said, "it's going to be a past-tense kind of thing. Like, I *was* a helicopter parent." Andrew smirked, looking exactly like Henry had as a young man.

Now Julia swatted Henry's jacket with her free hand. "I got about two hundred new subscribers from that HuffPo thing," she said. "You never know when—"

"I know," Henry said. "And you have a race coming up?"

"Next weekend." She nodded. "I think I can run a personal best."

JAMIE PRESTON

⁓

Jamie's cell phone dinged, and she leaned forward to grab it from the coffee table, her fading Liston Heights Lions sweatshirt folding over her black leggings.

Nightcap? the text read. It was from Jordan, the latest happy-hour guy. She looked down at herself, bits of Ruffles potato chips sprinkled on her clothes and a tiny dot of red wine soaked into the gray cotton near her belly button. The whole room smelled like her dinner, a frozen Salisbury steak, the charred bits of the sauce fused with the plastic tray it had come in.

Can't, she typed back. Working. Walk tomorrow? She reopened the copy of *Lord of the Flies* she'd been reading, an uncapped red flair pen acting as a bookmark.

On Friday night? Jordan wrote back.

Jamie chose a meh-faced emoji as a response, put her phone down, and leaned her head back against her couch.

She'd wondered when she accepted the position at Amory Prep, a charter school in another Minneapolis suburb, if the workload would decrease in proportion with her salary.

Alas, if anything, she felt more harried. Amory was only two years old, still adding a grade per year, working up to high school. Jamie's assignment was seventh- and eighth-grade English, and she was writing the curriculum herself. Peter Harrington had warned her that they were basically "building the plane in flight." Why did so many education people use that phrase?

Anyway, she didn't have much choice about Amory. Certainly she'd have been cut after Isobel's glorious return, and there were all those questions about the Facebook group. Jamie had taken the new position in April, ending Wayne and Mary's interest in getting to the bottom of things. Her parents, while unwilling to subsidize her rent, did agree that she could curtail her retirement contributions for a year or two.

Judging by how excited Peter seemed to hire her, Jamie got the sense that Amory didn't have too many applicants for the job. After all, there would be no colleagues in such a new school—Jamie was to be the entire English department—and no curriculum. Jamie found once she'd started that she had to devise all of the systems. Together, the teachers decided how to grade, how to discipline, when to have lunch. Oh, and there was no cafeteria. She had to brown-bag it and supervise kids eating at their desks in her classroom. One kid muttered, "Bitch," when she told her to throw away the uneaten crusts of her turkey sandwich.

"Should we have recess?" Jamie had asked Peter.

"What do you think?" Peter responded, same as always.

Once, just before winter break when she'd seen a striking picture of Isobel on the Humans of LHHS Instagram feed, her mentor looking down at an essay with light streaming in from the windows to her left, she'd texted her. Thinking of you, she'd written. Are you going to make it to vacation?

She hadn't gotten a response.

ISOBEL JOHNSON

On Monday afternoon, the spider plants on Isobel's windowsill looked extra healthy, the contrast between the green edges and the cream centers of the leaves crisp and clear. She sat at her desk after the last junior had left her classroom, fist-bumping her as he passed her desk.

She put her copy of *The Great Gatsby* down in front of her. The rips in the corners of the cover extended a bit toward Daisy's disembodied eyes, staring out over blurry carnival lights. Isobel smiled. Today had been the first day of discussion, the day she'd drawn Long Island on the board in green marker, dividing the Eggs.

Nick, first-person observer, unreliable narrator, Midwest. All of the teaching points bubbled to the surface of her consciousness, even after a year between readings. She loved this book, and she'd seen the enthusiasm in the faces of her students, too. She'd have them, she knew, just like always.

In December, she'd convinced Mary and Eleanor that the students should read *The Crucible* first, before Fitzgerald's classic. "Let's show them, more blatantly, desire gone wrong," she'd argued in a team meeting. "Let's show them what a powerful motivator lust really is."

Eleanor had flinched at "lust," which made Isobel smile. Mary waited a beat, glanced sidelong at Eleanor, and then said, "I agree with you, Isobel."

And so she'd gotten her way.

Isobel turned toward her bookshelf, where she'd placed the Excellence in Teaching certificate, signed by Wayne Wallace himself, she'd received last spring. Allen Song hadn't just acknowledged her in the *Ellis Island* playbill; he and Maeve Hollister, both active in collecting petition signatures, had nominated her for the Liston Heights Teacher of the Year award. At the luncheon, she'd clapped along with everyone else when a physics teacher who performed weekends at a comedy club downtown was chosen. But still, she was there.

Isobel slid her workout bag from beneath the desktop and rummaged through it, pushing aside her new heavy tights and jacket. (You're shopping at a real store? Caroline had gasped when Isobel had texted photos of the outfit. And it's not Old Navy?!) She wanted to be sure she'd remembered both of her shoes as well as a hat and mittens. The Liston Heights Striders adult running club was meeting in fifteen minutes. She'd seen the club advertised on Julia's Facebook group, Celebrate Liston: Behind-the-Scenes Information for Parents Who Care. The page had also featured her picture as a Teacher of the Year honoree.

Want to run a personal best at the annual Theater Booster Club 5K? the ad for the running club had asked.

She surprised herself by finding she did, in fact, want that. And a month after she'd achieved it, finishing once again in a dead heat with Julia, she was still in the club.

She strode out to the parking lot just in time to meet a group of twelve others, including one well-bundled woman she could identify only by her long blond ponytail.

"Julia," she said, walking up to her. "Hi."

"Ready?" Julia's voice was slightly muffled under a pink fleece neck warmer.

"I think so." Isobel stood next to her, feet apart and stretching. "Race this weekend," she said.

"Yep." Julia leaned over, gloved hands reaching for the asphalt. "I think I'll go faster than last month," she said, a hint of laughter in her tone.

"Me, too," said Isobel. "No doubt about it."

A loud and tiny PE teacher from East Liston Middle, whom Julia had hired to lead the workouts, piped up from the front of the group. "Okay! We're warming up for ten minutes, and then we're doing tempo-paced loops around the building to simulate the end of this weekend's five-K. Ready? Let's go!"

Isobel and Julia began the run in the middle of the pack, not speaking much on the warm-up. Between intervals, they whispered breathless "Good jobs," and both ran decidedly faster than prescribed on the last repeat, each trying to edge in front of the other.

ACKNOWLEDGMENTS

Thank you to my agent, Joanna MacKenzie. You're brilliant and caring, and I appreciate so much your impeccable eye and your sky-high standards. I look forward to working together on many more books. Thanks also to the team at Nelson Literary Agency that helped with every segment of this big, exciting project. I want to extend a particular thank-you to Angie Hodapp. Your editorial notes pushed me to reimagine so many critical aspects of this book.

Thank you to my editor, Kerry Donovan. From the moment we first spoke, I knew your vision for this story would lift it. It's better and bigger—more than I thought it could be—because of our work together, and I feel so lucky to be on your team. And thank you to the fantastic crew at Berkley: Diana Franco, Jessica Mangicaro, Dan Walsh, Craig Burke, Jeanne-Marie Hudson, and Claire Zion. And thank you to Anthony Ramondo for the cover, which dazzles me every time I see it.

Thank you to Mary Carroll Moore, who taught me how to structure a novel, and thanks to the Loft Literary Center for offering Mary's classes. Thank you to Chadd Johnson, my genius friend who fixed this story on no fewer than three separate occasions, including at least once while we were doing recess duty together in the middle school gym.

My writers' group is the best writers' group. Thank you to the Toucans: Nigar Alam, Maureen Fischer, and Stacy Swearingen. You keep me laughing and honest, and you require my absolute best while still being gentle. Our collaborations are invaluable. Thanks also to my online writers' groups, The Ink Tank and Every Damn Day Writers. You make me feel capable and reasonable, even on those days I'm neither.

I have the best friends, early readers, and stalwart cheerleaders. Thanks to those who tackled partial, messy, incoherent drafts of this novel and never once told me I was foolish to think I could finish it: Jordan Cushing, Lee Heffernan, Jessie Hennen, Emily Koski, Mary McAdaragh, KK Neimann (who also helped me dream up the whole viral video scene), Mary Scavotto, and Dan West. Thanks especially to my mom, Miriam Williams, who read every single iteration of this story even though there were about a thousand. And thanks to the friends who expressed their excitement and pride and urged me forward. These include Erin Dady, Susan Klobuchar, Adriana Matzke, and so many wonderful others.

As I've worked on this novel, I've thought so much about my excellent teachers and coaches at Visitation School in Mendota Heights, Minnesota. Thank you for encouraging me to be the very best version of myself. Thanks especially to Robert Shandorf, my sage English teacher for my junior and senior years. I'm not sure he would have liked this book, but I'm pretty sure I couldn't have written it if I hadn't been in his class. He loved *Gatsby* the very best.

Speaking of *Gatsby*, Isobel Johnson has clearly read Deborah Appleman's *Critical Encounters in Secondary English*, a seminal text for literature teachers everywhere. I read it, too, and it changed my practice. Thank you, Deborah. Isobel and I have also internalized the four dimensions of critical literacy as articulated by Mitzi Lewison, Amy Seely Flint, and Katie Van Sluys. These include "Interrogate Multiple Perspectives," which Isobel has quoted on the sign in her classroom. Thank you to these authors and a second thanks to Lee for teaching me about this framework.

Thank you to the many talented and dedicated teachers with whom I've worked in my twenty-year career. We all know teaching is a hard and sometimes ridiculous job, and if you're a teacher, you need your team. Thanks especially to Renee Corneille, Rachel Hatten, and Robin Ferguson for dealing with my daily dramas and assessing whether I needed to re-apply deodorant between classes.

Thank you to my students! You are now age nine to about thirty-three, and I've loved being with you! You've consistently inspired me and made me laugh, and I'd like it if you would all please send me your latest writing and updates.

I'd like to offer an insufficient but sincere thank-you to my parents, Miriam, Martha, and Paul; my siblings, Kevin, Loren, Devin, Mary, Rachel, Noah, and Ben; and my in-laws, Jane, Dobby, Sarah, and John. You've made my life a great adventure from birth to adulthood. I love you all, and I'm so lucky.

Thank you to Shef and Mac for being the world's best and most interesting kids. I adore you, and it's so much fun to be your mom. Thank you to Dan. I'm so grateful for our life together. Everyone knows I couldn't empty the dishwasher, let alone write a novel, without your support. Lucky for me, you're far better than the best I could do.

MINOR DRAMAS & OTHER CATASTROPHES

KATHLEEN WEST

QUESTIONS FOR DISCUSSION

1. Is Isobel a good teacher? How far should teachers go in the name of "making kids think"?

2. Julia desperately wants to be a good mother. Is she? What are her strengths and weaknesses as a parent?

3. Both Julia and Isobel want to be admired. Did you admire them? One more than the other?

4. Which character did you most relate to, and why?

5. Who benefits from competition among students in high schools? Are the teenagers in this story healthy and thriving?

6. Isobel and Julia clearly have an adversarial relationship. What does the ideal teacher-parent partnership look like in high school?

7. Kathleen West has been a classroom teacher for nearly twenty years, and she drew on this real-life experience to create Liston Heights High. Were there any school details, interactions, or relationships that surprised you?

8. Which of Julia's missteps is most egregious in your opinion?

9. What would you have done in Andrew's place?

10. Did Isobel deserve her suspension? Would you want your child to be in Isobel's class?

11. Why do you think Tracy is so drawn to Isobel? In what significant ways does she contrast with Tracy's mother, and what role is she filling in Tracy's life?

12. Why does Julia dislike Isobel so intensely? Does she feel threatened by Isobel, and if so, why?

13. What pressures does Jamie face? Did you sympathize at all with her plight?

14. What roles do Henry and Mark play in their wives' transformations in this story? Does each couple have a strong marriage?

Author photograph by Ann Marie Photography

Kathleen West is a veteran teacher of middle and high school. She graduated with a degree in English from Macalester College and holds a master's degree in literacy education from the University of Minnesota. She lives in Minneapolis with her family. *Minor Dramas & Other Catastrophes* is her first novel.